"I'll be fine."

Destiny could see that Logan was waiting for her to convince him. "I don't have any other choice. Paula's killer is out there somewhere and I intend to catch him. I can't do that if I fall apart."

"No, you can't," he agreed. "But if you need someone to talk to—or not talk to," he added with a smile that was beginning to weave its way under her skin even though she was doing her best to ignore it, "I'm available."

"You're a good guy, Logan Cavanaugh," she told him quietly just before she impulsively brushed her lips against his cheek.

Logan felt something within his gut tighten so quickly and so hard, for a second it was difficult for him to draw in a breath.

Every fiber of his being wanted to pull her into his arms and to kiss her back. The right way. And he had a strong feeling that he wouldn't get any resistance from her.

But that would be taking unfair advantage of her vulnerable state. Their time would come—he was fairly certain of that. But not tonight.

Dear Reader,

You are holding in your hands the latest book in the
CAVANAUGH JUSTICE series. Logan Cavanaugh is
another one of Sean Cavanaugh's (aka Cavelli) sons.
A free spirit who takes just about everything in stride,
Logan finds his laid-back attitude challenged when
he is temporarily paired with Destiny Richardson, his
father's chief assistant in the crime lab. She also just
happens to be the sister of what appears to be a serial
killer's latest victim.

The latter designation has yet to come to light since the
murders are all staged to appear like suicides—except
that Destiny is positive that her younger sister would
have never committed suicide, and she is prepared to
go to hell and back to prove it. Logan, the primary
investigative detective on what started out as an open-
and-shut case, has no choice but to follow Destiny in
order to keep her safe. But who is going to keep each of
them safe from one another?

I hope you enjoy this latest installment. As ever, I thank
you for reading and from the bottom of my heart I wish
you someone to love who loves you back.

Marie Ferrarella

CAVANAUGH'S SURRENDER

BY
MARIE FERRARELLA

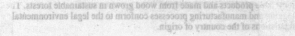

MILLS &
BOON

First published in Great Britain 2013
by Mills & Boon, an imprint of Harlequin (UK) Limited,
Eton House, 18-24 Paradise Road, Richmond, Surrey TW9 1SR

© Marie Rydzynski-Ferrarella 2012

ISBN: 978 0 263 90342 3
ebook ISBN: 978 1 472 00689 9

46-0113

Harlequin (UK) policy is to use papers that are natural, renewable and recyclable products and made from wood grown in sustainable forests. The logging and manufacturing processes conform to the legal environmental regulations of the country of origin.

Printed and bound in Spain
by Blackprint CPI, Barcelona

Marie Ferrarella, a *USA TODAY* bestselling and RITA® Award-winning author, has written more than two hundred books for Mills & Boon, some under the name Marie Nicole. Her romances are beloved by fans worldwide. Visit her website, www.marieferrarella.com

To
Sumay Li,
who is a joy
to know

Prologue

"Paula, I'm letting myself in with the key you gave me," Destiny Richardson called loudly as she stepped over the threshold into her younger sister's apartment. "It's Destiny, the sister you've been ignoring lately."

Again, she added silently.

She and Paula, her junior by a little more than three years, had finally gotten to a point in their relationship where they were getting along again. Where everything out of her mouth didn't get Paula's back up and mark the beginning of yet another prolonged argument that ended up with Paula not speaking to her for weeks at a time. That, mercifully, was now all behind them.

And then, for the past six weeks, it was as if Paula had stepped into a parallel universe. She was available only for a glimmer of time and then she'd disappear again. In between she'd return phone calls late and break lunch dates at the last minute.

Destiny had ridden it out for a couple of weeks, then finally asked her sister if this change in behavior was because of a man. Reluctantly—although she was glowing at the time—Paula had admitted that there *was* a new man in her life. But she wouldn't say any more, not even what his name was.

"Not yet, Des," she'd confided. "I don't want to jinx anything." Her eyes had all but danced as she'd added with a big grin, "He's just too good to be true."

Paula believed in the old adage that if something was too good to be true, it usually *was* too good to be true. But she'd bitten her tongue and said nothing, not wanting to jeopardize this new, improved relationship between her sister and her. It felt good to have Paula as a friend again, so she'd done her best to tread lightly and make no demands even though her gut had warned her that there was a problem.

She hated it when she was right in cases like this.

This morning, she'd gotten a text from Paula. It said simply: *He left me.* Thinking a few choice names directed at the man she'd never met, she'd called her sister almost immediately—and got no answer.

During the course of the day, she'd tried over and over again to reach Paula, using every single phone number associated with her sister. Home, work, cell, all with the same results. Paula wasn't picking up.

So, right after work, convinced that Paula was taking this breakup incredibly hard, she'd come to her sister's apartment and used the key Paula had given her for the very first time. She just wanted to make sure that her sister was all right.

She looked around now. Every single light in the up-scale, two-bedroom apartment was on.

"You better be home, kid," she called out, still addressing her words to the air. "Otherwise you're making the electric company very rich for no reason."

This was typical Paula, though. Her sister had a habit of turning on all the lights whenever she was depressed. She claimed it helped chase away the hopelessness she felt.

"Paula, where *are* you?" Destiny called, growing just a bit worried. Her mysterious "perfect" lover must have done a real number on her if Paula was too depressed even to answer her. "He's not worth it, you know," she said, making her way through the apartment. "Not worth being this upset over." She walked into Paula's bedroom. "If he could leave you just like that, you're better off without him. He doesn't sound very stable to me. He—"

For just half a second, Destiny froze in the doorway between the master bedroom and the lavishly remodeled bathroom.

Her heart stopped.

She'd found Paula.

"Oh, my God, Paula! Paula, what have you done?" she cried, racing into the bathroom.

The water in the bathtub had overflowed and spread out onto the tiled floor. The red tinge discolored everything. Her sister was immersed in the tub, and the water was red with her blood.

Paula's wrists were slashed.

Destiny Richardson had spent the past six years diligently working in the crime lab, at first part-time while she went to college and earned her degree in criminology, then, after graduation, full-time. From the very beginning, she had constantly gone the extra mile, putting in longer hours whenever she had a case.

In short order, she impressed Sean Cavanaugh, the man in charge of the crime lab's day shift. He promoted her to his chief assistant.

The first cardinal rule for a crime scene investigator was not to move or touch anything. But she wasn't a crime scene investigator tonight. She was Paula's sister, and she desperately wanted to save her.

But even as she grabbed her sister, ready to pull Paula out of the discolored water and perform CPR to try to save her, she knew it was too late. Paula's skin was abnormally cold and clammy.

And there was no heartbeat. Not even a faint flutter.

Paula was dead and had been for a number of hours.

"Oh, Paula, Paula, what did you do?" Destiny grieved, sinking down to the floor beside the bathtub. Water soaked into her clothing. She didn't care.

Because there was no one there and she had never felt so very alone in her life, Destiny allowed herself to break down for a moment.

Just for a moment.

She buried her face against the knees she'd brought up to her chest and sobbed as if her heart was breaking. Because it was.

Chapter 1

If police work wasn't for all intents and purposes the family business—doubly so now that he, along with the rest of his siblings and his father, had irrefutable proof that they comprised what amounted to the long-lost branch of the Cavanaugh family—Detective Logan Cavanaugh, known until recently as Logan Cavelli, would have been sorely tempted to give serious thought to another career choice.

Granted, Logan would have been the first to admit that he loved being a cop. Loved the idea that in some small way, he was fighting the good fight, righting wrongs and, along with his brothers and sisters, giving Aurora's everyday citizens that thin blue line that they knew was out there to protect them.

But there were times when the hours that went along with being a detective just about *killed* him. In the absolute sense, they were the same kind of hours that a doctor was expected to keep.

Doctors and police detectives were *always* expected to be on call—except that a doctor made a hell of a lot more money than he made, Logan thought darkly as he now drove—*alone*—to the address his lieutenant had handed to him when the man had torpedoed the very eventful evening he had planned for himself and his utterly luscious date.

One minute.

One lousy little minute. Sixty seconds and counting down, that's all he'd had left to his shift and then this evening with all its sensual promise would have become a reality.

He had already powered down his computer because Stacy, displaying a rare flair for punctuality, had just waltzed through the squad room door and had instantly made him the envy of every other breathing male in the vicinity.

Stacy, with the hips from heaven and the sinful mouth, who simply by walking across the floor could cause a eunuch to have lustful thoughts, was his date tonight. He was taking her out for dinner, dancing and a hot night of even hotter sex. The blond would-be model was his kind of woman. Gorgeous, passionate and totally uninterested in a permanent relationship.

Tonight had all the makings of an absolutely perfect evening.

But then his lieutenant had summoned him away from the doorway just as he was a hair's breadth away from being free and clear and making it into the hall.

No, that wasn't actually true, he thought in resignation, his hands tightening on the steering wheel until his knuckles were all but straining against his skin. Even if he had been in the middle of that passionate evening, enjoying all of Stacy's fabulously assembled attributes, his cell would have rung, calling him away from the ecstasy that shimmered before him, beckoning him onward because duty called.

When you're the next one up, you're the next one up. It was a simple, albeit hard, fact of life that went along with carrying a shield and a weapon.

So, instead of hot filet mignon, his dinner tonight would probably be the last couple of slices of the cold, leftover pizza in his refrigerator. And instead of a hot woman in his bed, he'd be sleeping alone tonight.

That was, if he got any sleep at all. A homicide detective with four years of experience under his belt, he'd learned that some cases unfurled slowly, inch by painful inch, while others ran you right into the ground from the moment you stepped into the crime scene arena and silently pledged to solve whatever needed solving.

Daylight had receded and the evening was making itself comfortable. He drove, looking for the right building, still wishing that he'd been engaged in a job that defined specific hours where the end of the day was the end of the day.

Wishing wouldn't make it so. Besides, Stacy, pouting prettily, had perked up at the promise of a rain check.

He laughed softly to himself, wondering if the woman thought that rain was actually involved in a rain check. He wouldn't put it past her. Luckily, it wasn't her brain that attracted him. After having to be on his toes all the time, it was nice to kick back sometimes and just let his brain rest.

Pulling up before the right apartment building, Logan saw that there were absolutely no empty spaces available along the long block. He debated driving to the parking structure on the next block, but he decided instead to double-park his vehicle in the fervent hope that his part in this wouldn't take all that long.

From the sketchy details he'd been given, it sounded pretty much like a cut-and-dried suicide—end of story. Once he verified that it was, maybe he could still even get hold of Stacy and at least get to enjoy the second half of the evening—that was, after all, the only thing that either one of them actually wanted from the other. Hot sex, enjoyable and a few minutes respite from the world they dealt with on a regular basis.

The thought made him smile as he got out of the car and locked it behind him.

The apartment in question was on the third floor. Once he got off the elevator, Logan found he didn't need to acquaint himself with the floor's layout or the way the apartment numbers were arranged to locate the one where his services were needed. The yellow tape and the stoic police officer standing guard did that for him.

Vaguely recognizing the weary-looking older officer, he nodded at the man. Their paths had probably crossed at one point or another, Logan thought.

"My dad here yet?"

It was actually meant as a rhetorical question. This was the tail end of the day shift, but his father, the head of the CSI day lab, was dedicated beyond belief. He was the one who had instilled his work ethic in him and his siblings long before they had discovered that they were related to the Cavanaughs.

Besides, there was all this yellow tape across the front of the entrance, a sure sign that his father and some of the team who worked for him were in there, carefully documenting and preserving everything with such precision it would have absolutely stunned the average mind.

The officer, Dale Hanlon, shook his head. "No, not yet."

Logan stopped, surprised as he turned to regard the officer. Unless there were multiple crime scenes happening at once—something that had yet to occur in Aurora—in the past year—his father had taken to being present with his team at each crime scene that they processed.

This wasn't making any sense to him. "Then who put up all this yellow tape?" he asked.

"I did."

The low, controlled female voice came from behind him. The vague thought that the voice was more suited to an intimate dinner than a crime scene crossed Logan's mind as he turned around again.

Logan found himself looking into the saddest blue eyes he'd ever seen.

They were also, quite possibly, the bluest eyes he'd ever seen, which was saying a great deal considering that the Cavanaughs were fairly littered with members who had blue eyes of all hues and shades.

The eyes were set in a striking, heart-shaped face that would have easily launched a thousand love songs, he couldn't help thinking. Sometimes, Logan decided, this job did have its perks.

"Are you part of the crime scene investigation unit?" Logan heard himself asking as he quickly assessed the slender, pale-looking blonde standing before him. "Or do you just have a thing for crime scene tape?" he quipped wryly, trying to lighten the moment. She seemed much too serious for someone so young. He knew this job, especially this part of the job, could really get to people if they didn't take any precautions and insulate themselves properly.

His flippant manner caught Destiny off guard for a second. Since the officer at the door hadn't tried to turn the man away, that had to mean that he was with the Aurora police force.

Terrific. Just her luck. They'd sent a brash, cocky detective who looked as if he was in love with the sound of his own voice and, most likely, with the image he saw in his bathroom mirror each morning. Dark-haired, green-eyed, he was as handsome as they came, and she was certain that he knew it.

She was familiar with the type, and right now it was the last thing she needed. She needed a professional detective, not a male model.

"I'm with the crime scene investigation unit," she told him, her voice low and remarkably stoic. She surprised herself.

It was all she could do to hold it together. Part of Destiny still didn't believe that any of this was actually happening. The other part felt as if she was slowly slipping into shock and would, at any moment, just completely lose it.

You can't. If you do, you won't be able to help Paula.

The moment the thought formed, it struck Destiny as ironic. After all, at this point *nothing* would help Paula. Nothing was going to bring her back.

Destiny struggled to keep her angry tears in check.

Logan nodded, taking the attractive woman's information at face value. "I guess this is just an open-and-shut case," he surmised. "A suicide," he added, telling her what the lieutenant had told him. Then, his mouth curving in a particularly captivating smile, he asked, "How is it that I've never seen you before?" He would have certainly remembered someone who looked like her. He had a feeling that if she smiled, she could light up a room. Even somber, there was something exceedingly attractive and compelling about her. "Are you new to the team?"

She didn't bother answering his last question. At another time and place, she might have been more than mildly interested in his attention. Destiny wasn't averse to having an occasional good time, as long as no promises were exchanged or expected. She was married to her work, and most of the men she'd encountered felt that they should come first in a woman's life, not second.

Right now, all her energy was focused on not breaking down and, more important than that, on finding who had done this to her sister.

"It's not a suicide," Destiny informed the detective firmly.

About to walk to where he could view the deceased's body, Logan turned instead and focused on the intense crime scene investigator. She sounded as if there was no room for argument.

"Why?" he asked, the detective in him pushing the playboy far into the background. "Did you find something that would indicate that the woman was murdered?"

"Not yet," Destiny answered between clenched teeth. "But I will."

Okay, he was officially confused, Logan thought. Was there some sort of an agenda he was missing? Exactly what did this woman mean by "not yet"? What did she know that he didn't? He didn't like playing catch-up.

"If there are no indications that it's *not* a suicide, what makes you think that it isn't?" he asked the shapely blonde.

"Because she *wouldn't* commit suicide," Destiny informed him heatedly.

Really curious now, Logan looked at the young woman who, he realized, had more going on, even without the aid of painted-on clothing, than Stacy ever did. She didn't reek of raw sex, but there was a subtle promise there that intrigued him. A lot.

Since the department paid him to solve cases, not ruminate on beautiful women who said baseless things, Logan forced himself to focus on the wild claim the crime scene investigator had just made and not the fact that the words had come out of nearly perfect lips.

"And you know this because…?"

A very tempting chin shot up like a silent challenge. "Because she's my sister."

It took him a second to absorb that. "You weren't called in, were you?" Logan guessed.

No, she hadn't been. She'd come here looking for answers and had wound up face-to-face with a dreadful question: Who killed Paula?

"I did the calling," she told him.

As if in a bad dream, once she knew that Paula was beyond resuscitating and she'd stopped crying, she'd pulled herself together and called her boss, even though protocol would have had her calling 911 first.

The sound of Sean Cavanaugh's voice had almost made her lose it again, but Destiny had managed to hold herself together enough to describe what she'd found when she'd walked into her sister's apartment. Sean in turn had set everything else in motion, promising to be there as soon as he possibly could. He told her not to leave.

As if she could.

With no knowledge of what had taken place between his father and the crime scene investigator, Logan had a different take on things.

"You can't be here," he told her, transforming from a devil-may-care man who enjoyed his share of the night-life to a homicide detective who was considered to be damn good at his job.

Logan saw the woman's slender shoulders stiffen as if she'd been jabbed with a hot poker. She reminded him of a soldier, galvanized in order to withstand whatever came her way.

The flash of anger in her eyes was almost mesmerizing to him.

"The hell I can't," she snapped. "She's my baby sister and the only family I have left. Had left," Destiny amended, trying hard not to allow the words to choke off her air supply. "Somebody killed her, and I intend to find out who."

Having brothers and sisters of his own, Logan could easily relate to the way she felt. But she still needed to go. "I get it, but leave it up to—"

"To who?" Destiny demanded. "To you? To the professionals?" She guessed at the word he was about to use. "I *am* one of the professionals."

That might be true, but there was another, bigger factor that she was apparently missing—or deliberately ignoring. "You're also personally involved—"

"You *bet* I am," Destiny snapped, her eyes flashing again, "and no rules and regulations are going to make me stand on the sidelines like some clueless civilian, waiting for someone to find something that would point to my sister's killer—especially when they're not even going to be looking."

"Now wait a minute—"

No, she wasn't going to "wait a minute." And she certainly wasn't going to allow him to snow her with rhetoric.

"A minute ago, you were all ready to write this off as a suicide. You were willing to go with what you saw— or *thought* you saw."

Only up to a point. Where did she get off, criticizing his work if she hadn't seen him in action? Gorgeous or not, she needed to be told a few things and put in her place.

"Not if the autopsy contradicts the idea of a suicide."

Autopsy.

The very word brought up a chilling scenario with it. Someone cutting up her little sister, reducing Paula to a mass of body organs examined, weighed, catalogued and then impersonally stuffed back into her body like wrinkled tissue paper that has served its purpose.

Suddenly, Destiny could hardly bear the wave of pain she felt.

Logan saw the horror that washed over the woman's fine-boned features before she apparently got herself under control again. Observing her, he had to admit he felt really sorry for the woman. He knew how he would have reacted if that was Bridget, or Kendra, or Kari in the next room.

No rules or orders would have kept him on the sidelines. If he couldn't have been part of the investigation outright, he would have found a way to conduct his own investigation covertly until he found answers that satisfied him.

Until he found the killer.

He felt a budding respect as he looked at the woman for the first time, not assessing her comely features but taking measure of the person who existed beneath. Thinking of what she was feeling and taking stock of what had to be crossing her mind right now.

Logan relented, backing off from his initial stand.

"Look, what if I promise to keep you filled in? Will that be enough for you?"

The moment the words emerged from his mouth, he knew they had come out wrong. He made it sound as if he was trying to dismiss her. He wasn't doing anything of the kind.

Destiny tossed her head, anger and sadness mingling with the very stubborn streak that had seen her through a less than typical childhood, one that would have conquered a lesser person. And she had been a child at the time.

"No, sorry, not good enough," she fired back.

"He's right, you know."

She didn't have to turn around and look to know who was behind her. But she turned around anyway. Turned around and looked up at the man she respected and secretly regarded as the father she hadn't had for all these many years, not since he'd walked out on her, Paula and their mother.

"I thought you'd be on my side," she said to Sean. She was more than a little disappointed to hear him taking the side of company policy.

"I am *always* on your side," Sean reminded her kindly. "But the rules are clear about working on a case that you're personally involved in."

She knew all the rules backward and forward. She also knew they weren't going to stop her from working this investigation.

"Sean, please," she implored hoarsely, her voice brimming with emotion. She laid a hand on Sean's arm in mute supplication.

"Of course," Sean continued loftily, as if she hadn't said anything, "you are a grown woman and I can't be expected to tie you up and throw you into some corner if you happen to do some poking around into the present case behind my back." He saw his son staring at him, undoubtedly surprised at this break with protocol. "Oh, like you and those brothers and sisters of yours never bent a single rule," he mocked.

"Not saying we didn't," Logan replied to his father, deliberately flying above this minefield. "But I've got to say that I'm really surprised that you're considering it."

"Not considering it," Sean corrected, putting down his fully loaded case that he meticulously organized at least once a week. "But well, what happens when I'm not looking, happens," he told his son innocently. "Now, if you'll excuse me, I believe the actual scene of the crime is in through there?" He pointed to the bedroom, looking to Destiny for confirmation.

Destiny only half nodded. "That's the way to the bathroom," she confirmed. "Whether or not that's the actual scene of the crime remains to be seen."

Sean gave her an encouraging smile. "An open mind is the best way to approach anything," he agreed.

With that, he walked ahead of his son and the young woman to process this particular crime scene.

Chapter 2

Following Sean Cavanaugh through the bedroom and into the bathroom where her sister's body was, Destiny could feel every single bone in her own body stiffening as the battle began all over again. Her protective instincts warred with the ones she had developed as a crime scene investigator.

The latter dictated adherence to the first cardinal rule of investigation: that nothing was to be touched, nothing was to be moved. It was of the utmost importance that the scene be preserved just as it was when the deceased died. This had to be done to piece together facts leading up to that person's final moments. And, with that, the identity of the killer, if there was one.

But Destiny's protective instincts were just as deeply rooted within her, if not more so. She was the older sister, the one who had always looked out for Paula.

Yeah, and how's that going for you? Destiny silently mocked herself.

Being the older sister hadn't been easy. Though she had never doubted her sister's love for her, Paula had fought her all the way, desperately wanting to assert her independence.

"I'm a big girl now, Destiny. You can't hover over me forever."

Destiny could feel the corners of her eyes beginning to sting again as she struggled for the umpteenth time to hold back her tears.

Yeah, well, you would have done better if I had hovered, Destiny couldn't help thinking now. There was no doubt in her mind that Paula would be alive right now if she *had* hovered.

If.

Her protective instincts had made her want to cover Paula up, to give her sister some small semblance of modesty and dignity by draping something over her— at least a towel. She didn't want to leave her where everyone coming into the beige-and-blue-tiled bathroom could see her like this, utterly naked and exposed.

As if sensing her turmoil, Sean told her, "I promise I'll make this as quick as I can, Destiny."

She was grateful to him for his kindness. Pressing her lips together, Destiny nodded, doing her best to smile her thanks and succeeding only marginally.

"Thank you," she said hoarsely.

Logan, who had entered behind his father and the victim's sister, squatted down now, his attention focused on the opened cell phone that apparently had slipped from the dead woman's hand just as life had ebbed away from her.

The cell phone was in the open position and it was still turned on. As he crouched closer to it, Logan could see that there was a text message on the screen. One last message just before death had found her.

Was it a last-minute regret and a plea for help? Or was this intended to be a virtual version of a suicide note?

Using his handkerchief to keep from getting his fingerprints on the phone or contaminating any prints besides the victim's on the device, Logan was about to pick it up when he stopped and looked over toward his father. "Did you already take a picture of this?"

"Tagged and photographed," Sean answered as he continued examining Destiny's sister.

Logan lifted the phone and looked at the screen. There were only three words in the text message: *He left me*.

"We need to find out who this number belongs to," Logan said, thinking out loud as he examined the cell number the message had been sent to.

"Not necessary," Destiny told him stoically.

Each word she uttered felt as if it scraped along an incredibly dry tongue. Her whole mouth felt like a desert in the midst of a seven-year drought. And she was having trouble getting air into her lungs. Part of her was numb, the other was almost on fire.

"She texted you?" Logan guessed, glancing toward her and reading her body language.

Right now, the woman appeared to be shut down

tighter than Fort Knox. Logan absently wondered what it would take to loosen her up, then dismissed the thought since right now, knowing that wasn't going to help him. Thinking of her as a woman was completely out of line. She was the victim's sister and his father's assistant, nothing else.

At least, not right now.

Logan caught himself hoping that there would be a later.

Destiny heard the detective's voice as if it had originated in an echo chamber. It sounded as if it was coming at her from a great distance.

She blinked, forcing herself to stay focused. If she let her mind wander, she wouldn't make it out of this room without coming apart. She'd already cried once. That was all she could afford to grieve. She had work to do.

"Yes, it's my number. I called her back almost immediately after she sent the message, but she didn't pick up." She pressed her lips together, taking a breath before continuing. Her voice sounded strained. "I'd been calling her all day without a response, so I got worried."

"Why?" Logan asked. "Was she unstable? Were you afraid that she was likely to harm herself?"

Destiny stared at him. What was he talking about? He didn't know Paula. He had no right to his assumptions. She took offense at the implication behind his questions.

"I got worried because I'm her *sister,*" she retorted angrily. "Because Paula normally keeps in touch. And she doesn't send short text messages." The three-word text was out of character for Paula. "She goes on and on, whether it's a phone call, a text or in person. My sister is—was," she corrected herself painfully, "not a person of a few words. She never said anything in three words that she could say in forty."

He thought of pointing out that distraught people, especially people about to commit suicide, didn't always conform to their normal behavior, but he had a feeling she wasn't in the mood to be contradicted.

Instead, he focused on another piece of the puzzle. "Who's this 'him' she's referring to?" he asked.

"I don't know."

Destiny took a deep breath, angry with herself for not having pushed when Paula had opted to keep the man's name a secret. If she'd badgered Paula enough, she *knew* Paula would have finally caved in. Why hadn't she pushed? Why had she just elected to respect her sister's boundaries? At the very least, this mystery man of Paula's could give them insight to her frame of mind the last time he saw her as he left.

If he'd left her, Destiny amended, ruling out nothing.

"You don't know?" Logan echoed, more than mildly surprised. "Then you two weren't close?" That was the only conclusion he could draw.

"No, we were," Destiny insisted. "Very close." They had been that way once and they had gotten that way again just in the past couple of years.

"Then why don't you know the name of the guy your sister was seeing?"

Because I'm an idiot.

"Paula was a little superstitious. She said she didn't

want to jinx the relationship by saying anything about it too soon."

God, that sounded so lame, so childish now that she said it out loud, Destiny thought, on the edge of exasperated despair. Why hadn't she pushed? Insisted? Maybe if she'd known more of the details, she could have somehow prevented this. Even though she didn't believe in her heart of hearts that her sister had done this, had committed suicide, a tiny part of her was afraid she had.

"All she'd tell me was that he was someone 'important.' And, that for now, he wanted to keep their relationship 'special' by keeping it out of the public eye. Apparently, I was part of the public eye," Destiny said with barely controlled frustration.

Most likely, the guy was married, Logan thought, and when he'd decided to go back to his wife, the victim had killed herself.

"And you don't think that this is a suicide?" Logan asked again. It was obvious from his tone that he felt that the evidence they'd reviewed so far clearly pointed in that direction.

"No," Destiny said with feeling. "If this 'important' bastard had left her, she wouldn't have killed herself. Paula was the type to have gone upside his head, to have raised a stink, not taken the breakup docilely, given up all hope and killed herself." She raised her chin defiantly as she added, "I know my sister. That's just not like her."

Did anyone really know anyone else? Logan wondered. Of late, since the big revelation that had jolted his family down to their roots, he'd faced that question more than once.

"That's what you *think*," Logan pointed out. And, as far as he was concerned, there was an entire world of difference between prejudiced perception and actual fact.

"No," Destiny said flatly. "That's what I *know*. My sister believed in revenge," she was quick to add, seeing the suspicious light coming into the detective's all-but-magnetic green eyes. "And by that, I mean she would have dolled herself up, found the first good-looking male she could and deliberately shown up somewhere where she knew that 'Mr. Special' would most likely be. Then she would have flaunted the fact that she was having an exceptionally good time with someone new and gorgeous. Paula was not the kind to just give up," she insisted. "She was stubborn that way."

How long was it going to take to get used to referring to Paula in the past tense? Destiny wondered, her heart aching in her chest.

"I take it stubbornness runs in the family?" Logan surmised, watching her. There was just a hint of an appreciative smile on his lips.

Her blue eyes narrowed into slits. "Damn straight it does."

"You might be right," Sean interjected as if there was no other conversation taking place. Having completed his preliminary examination of the dead woman, he straightened up.

"About which part?" Logan asked, just taking it for

granted that his father was talking to him and not to the sexy, headstrong woman before him.

Instead of answering his son immediately, Sean focused his attention on the person in the room who needed him the most.

"Was your sister right-handed?" he asked Destiny.

She shook her head. "No, Paula was left-handed. Why?" Had he found something to substantiate her gut feeling that her sister hadn't taken her own life? Without realizing it, Destiny began to pray.

"Just trying to get my facts straight," Sean said thoughtfully, never one to give away anything too soon. Pausing a moment longer, he then said, "I don't believe she killed herself."

Yes!

The relief that flooded through her limbs just about took Destiny's breath away. At least she wasn't going to have to fight everyone tooth and nail about this. If the head of the crime lab backed her up, the battle over that at least was over. Now the major one began: finding Paula's killer.

"Thank you," she said to Sean. The words came out on a nearly breathless sigh.

While he knew that his father wouldn't just say something like that to put his assistant at ease, Logan still wanted proof.

"What makes you say that?" he asked his father.

"When a person slashes their wrists, depending on whether they're right-handed or left-handed, the cut is deeper on the opposite wrist since they're using their good hand."

If the person followed regular procedure, Logan thought. Maybe this one hadn't. "She might have slashed her right wrist first," Logan suggested. "That would have made her right hand weaker when she was delivering the final cut."

"True," Sean allowed.

Concerned, Destiny immediately asked, "Then you're changing your mind?"

Again, rather than answering directly, Sean turned toward his son, opting for a demonstration. "If you were to slash your wrists, how would you go about it?" he asked.

Logan firmly believed that there wasn't anything in the world that would cause him to give up all hope and just apathetically end his life.

"I wouldn't," Logan said flatly.

"Good to know," his father murmured. "But if you did, if you put yourself in the place of someone who'd lost all hope and given up wanting to live," Sean proposed, "*how* would you slash your wrists?"

Logan honestly didn't know what his father was getting at. "The usual way," he answered with a careless shrug.

"Show me," Sean urged. Taking a pen out of his breast pocket, he handed it to Logan. "Pretend this is a knife. Show me how you'd go about 'slashing' your wrists if you were committing suicide."

With another, somewhat more pronounced shrug, Logan took the pen from his father and then, holding it in his right hand, traced a slightly slanted line from left to right across his left wrist. And then, changing hands, he took the pen into his left hand and reversed the process, "slashing" his right wrist from right to left with the imaginary knife. Both times the lines he created were slightly slanted, going from higher to lower.

"Okay, consider them slashed," Logan said, handing the pen back to his father. His curiosity had been piqued. "Now what?"

"Now you'd bleed out," Sean said matter-of-factly. "All right, keeping your methodical procedure in mind, I want you to take a look at Paula's wrists," he told both his son and his assistant. "What do you see?"

Each wrist had a long, deep cut going across it. "Slashes," Logan answered.

Destiny narrowed her eyes, distancing herself from the actual person in the bathtub and focusing only on the victim's wrists. She looked intently at the cuts that had caused her sister to die.

After scrutinizing the two cuts, she felt no more enlightened than she had been at the outset.

Shaking her head, she said, "I don't—"

"Look carefully," Sean repeated, cutting her off.

"I did," she protested.

And then she saw it, saw what Sean was trying to point out without actually physically doing it. Her eyes widened and she looked at him.

"The slashes are both going in the same direction!" But there was more than just that, she realized. "And they're both upside down."

Instead of slanting slightly at the top and then dipping down as it reached the opposite side, each cut seemed to go from the bottom to the top, left to right, on both wrists.

"This is too awkward," Destiny concluded, her excitement growing. And then she repeated what she had been maintaining all along. "Paula couldn't have done this to herself. Someone else had to have done it to her."

He could see his father trying to spare his assistant and make her feel better, but there were other matters to consider, Logan thought.

"There's no sign of a struggle," he pointed out, then continued, "There's no huge amount of water along the perimeter of the old-fashioned tub, leaving the actual tub low, as if there'd been a wild, last-minute struggle. There are no outstanding bruises visible on the victim's body, and her long, salon-applied nails all seem to be intact. They wouldn't have been if she was fighting for her life."

"There wouldn't be any struggle if the victim was drugged," Sean told his son, his voice as mild as if he were discussing the garden section of the Sunday paper. Turning, Sean pointed to the wine goblet he had already photographed and that now stood, bagged, on the bathroom floor exactly where he had found it. "A simple analysis can tell us about that."

Logan still didn't see that as proof. "A lot of suicides build up their courage with a drink first. Maybe the victim wanted to make sure that she wouldn't experience a last-minute surge of regret that might cause her to stop what she was doing." He looked at his father. "Despondence can do that to you."

"Maybe to you," Destiny fired back. "But not to

Paula. She did *not* kill herself. I'd stake my badge on it," she insisted.

"Besides," Sean interjected, "there are the cuts to her wrists. Our killer obviously slipped up there." Returning the items he'd taken out previously, as well as packing up the samples he'd taken into his case, Sean glanced at Destiny. "Are you absolutely sure your sister never mentioned this man's name? Dropped a hint, used initials? Something like that?"

To each suggestion, Destiny could only shake her head no. Each time she did so, she felt her frustration growing larger and larger.

"No."

The truth of it was that despite her initial concerns, she'd been really hopeful that Paula was finally looking to settle into a lasting relationship. And due to that, she hadn't wanted to cause any waves by hounding her sister for details.

"And you didn't press her?" Logan asked incredulously. What kind of a woman didn't ask for details? he couldn't help wondering. Was it because she was too wrapped up in her own love life? Was there some guy she was going to go running home to, to cry on his shoulder?

From out of nowhere, Logan felt just the slightest prick of jealousy. He shrugged it off, thinking he was just frustrated because he'd had to break his date with Stacy.

Destiny could only shrug impotently. "I figured she'd tell me when she was ready."

He couldn't help staring at her. Was she for real? If

this had been one of his sisters, the other two would have been all over her until she finally broke. The life expectancy of a secret in the household where he'd grown up had been about a day and a half—if the one with the secret was in a coma.

"Wow, a woman with no curiosity," he marveled, only half in jest. "I thought that was like, you know, an urban myth or something. Kind of like a unicorn," he tagged on.

If nothing else, the man was mixing his metaphors. He was also being colossally annoying.

"Unicorns don't wander around urban areas," she pointed out, irritated at the detective's flippant manner and not bothering to hide the fact, even if he was Sean's son. Maybe he was adopted, she thought. Her eyes narrowed as she pinned him with a glare. "Are you going to take this seriously or not?" she asked.

"I'm officially ruling this a murder," Sean announced, interrupting what appeared to be an argument in the making—he knew for a fact that Logan didn't like being challenged. "Don't worry. He'll take it seriously now," he assured his assistant with a note of finality in his voice.

She was overreacting. Her sister's murder—just finding Paula this way—was making her lose her perspective. If she continued down this road, then she really would wind up being thrown off the case.

And soon.

At the very least, she wasn't any good to anyone if she unraveled this way.

Destiny took in a deep, shaky breath, getting herself back under control. Her spine snapped into place, ramrod straight.

"Sorry," she said to Sean.

"You have nothing to be sorry about," Sean told her warmly. Placing a fatherly arm around her shoulders, he gently escorted Destiny from the room.

The sound of fresh activity was heard coming from the living room. The M.E.'s team had just arrived, pushing a gurney between them.

Nodding at the duo, Sean said, "The victim's in the bathtub. She's had a preliminary workup and is ready to go."

"It's a suicide, right?" one of the men asked, looking at the sheet attached to his clipboard. The latter was lying on top of the gurney.

"No, it's a homicide," Logan corrected, answering for his father.

He wasn't oblivious to the relieved smile that Destiny shot him. Though it lasted only half a second, he'd been right. Her smile did have the makings to light up a room.

Hearing what Logan said, one of the two men sighed and shook his head. "It's going to be another long night," he anticipated, addressing his words to no one in particular.

"C'mon, don't just stand there and make it any longer," the other man prodded.

Pushing the gurney before them, they entered the next room.

Once they were gone, Sean turned to Destiny. "I should be the one who's saying he's sorry," he said to her, continuing what he was saying before the two assistants from the M.E.'s office had entered the apartment. "And I am. I am *deeply* sorry for your loss," he emphasized. "And we *will* find the person responsible for this, Destiny," he said. "I give you my word."

Destiny blinked back her tears. It felt as if she'd been fighting them all along. Her supervisor wasn't making things any easier for her.

"I believe you," she murmured, her voice hardly above a whisper. Any louder and she knew she would risk breaking down entirely.

Again.

To the best of Logan's knowledge, it was the first time he'd ever heard his father make a promise that he wasn't a hundred percent certain ahead of time that he could back up.

This assistant had to mean a lot to him, he concluded, then couldn't help wondering why.

Chapter 3

"Were you two on the outs?" Logan asked Destiny as his father continued processing the rest of the small apartment.

Why did he keep coming back to that?

"No. She was my only family. We were close—as close as two people who lived two different, busy lives could be," she qualified, emphasizing the word *busy*. "We didn't get together as much as I would have liked, but that couldn't have been helped." Her eyes narrowed slightly as she regarded Logan, looking for some kind of an indication as to what was really on his mind. She began to suspect that he wasn't the typical vapid, shallow pretty boy. There was substance, a trait she'd always found far sexier than looks.

But right now, she was in a place where things like that didn't matter.

"Why are you asking?" she asked.

He answered her question with a question. "Is there any reason you can think of why she wouldn't have told you who she was seeing?"

Logan was still having a lot of trouble swallowing the scenario the woman's sister had given him. All three of his sisters not only knew everything there was to know about each other's boyfriends, or, in Bridget's case, her fiancé, they were also aware of their friends' current dates. He couldn't fathom a woman who was willingly oblivious to that sort of information—and actually content to remain that way.

Suppressing a sigh, she said, "Probably to avoid hearing me tell her to go slow and to be careful." She saw the question in the detective's eyes. Under another set of circumstances, they might have even been intriguing eyes. Right now, they were just annoyingly probing. "My sister doesn't—didn't," she corrected herself, hating the fact that she had to, "have the greatest track record when it came to picking men. They were all very good-looking on the outside. On the inside, not so much."

Holding her hand out, she waffled it to indicate just how much each of the previous men in her sister's life had deviated from the straight-and-narrow path. There hadn't been a decent one in the lot.

"So in other words, she didn't give you any details about who she was seeing because she didn't want you to be judgmental," Logan concluded succinctly.

She nodded, wishing with all her heart that she hadn't come down as hard on Paula over the last one as she had. Not that he didn't deserve every insulting adjective she had hurled at his memory. Slick, charming, with a Southern drawl, Bo Wilkins had managed to deplete half of Paula's bank account—granted, that didn't exactly amount to a king's ransom, but it was *still* Paula's money—before just vanishing off the face of the earth.

She'd begged Paula to let her know the next time she gave away her heart, because she'd said she intended to run a check on whomever the next Romeo was. If no prior arrests came up, then at least her sister would have a fighting chance of keeping the fillings in her teeth.

Paula hadn't found that funny, she recalled. And she deliberately hadn't said anything about meeting someone new—until she'd been pinned down.

That was when Paula had told her that she didn't want to say anything yet because she didn't want to jinx the relationship. And, if it became serious, *then* she would say something.

Given that, Destiny had seen no reason to push.

But apparently, it *had* been serious. Which meant that Paula had lied to her, Destiny realized with a sharp pang. It obviously had to have been serious if Paula had been despondent enough to text that message to her.

If she texted that message, a little voice in Destiny's head whispered.

Her eyes widened as the thought sank in.

What if Paula hadn't even been the one to text that message? What if her killer had? The same killer who had botched the appearance of a suicide by slashing her wrists upside down.

Trying not to get ahead of herself, she turned toward Sean. "We have to process her cell phone for any fingerprints on the keypad that aren't hers. The guy probably wore gloves, but maybe he got careless...."

Destiny's voice trailed off as she made eye contact with her supervisor. He wasn't saying anything, just letting her talk, but she could see by the expression on his face that he was already way ahead of her. He always seemed to be two steps ahead of everyone.

"You already thought of that," she said, nodding her head.

"We're on the same page," Sean told her kindly. "Same page that Logan's on," he said, nodding toward his son.

Feeling anxious and yet dull-witted at the same time, an area she had never inhabited before, Destiny turned toward the detective, curious why he wasn't saying anything.

The answer to that was simple. Because he wasn't standing there anymore.

"Cavanaugh?" she called, raising her voice.

"In here," Logan answered, his voice floating back to her from the back of the apartment.

Apparently a thought had occurred to him and he'd gone back into the bedroom to look at something, or *for* something.

Actually, the man had gone back to the bathroom, Destiny realized as she followed the sound of the detective's deep voice.

As she entered the bedroom, she had to shift to one side. The medical examiner's team had slipped Paula's body into that one-size-fits-all black body bag and was now wheeling her sister back out. Once outside the building, they'd put her into the coroner's van they'd driven over here.

Paula didn't like the color black, Destiny recalled with a pang. It was the only color missing from her meticulously arranged wardrobe.

"Black is the color of death, Destiny. I don't want it anywhere near me."

It is now, pumpkin. It is now, Destiny thought, feeling her heart twist inside of her.

Walking into the bathroom, painfully aware that her sister was no longer here—no longer anywhere—she found Logan standing before the medicine cabinet. The door was open and the detective was peering at the shelves. He was obviously taking inventory of what was inside. She didn't exactly care for the thoughtful frown she saw on his face.

Now what?

Bracing herself, thinking that she would have to defend her sister again, Destiny forced herself to ask, "What?"

Logan read the generic name imprinted on the container's label again. This put a crimp in the woman's theory. He held the container up so that she could see it, as well.

"This was just filled," he told her.

She had no idea what "this" was but had a feeling she wouldn't be happy once she heard the answer.

Even so, though she knew Logan had to do it, she resented this man's prying into her sister's life. And, by proxy, into her life. Resented the lack of understanding and compassion in his voice.

Granted, as a good detective, he was supposed to be impartial, but keeping this kind of a distance between himself and the victim didn't help him understand the kind of person her sister had been. Didn't make him fiercely want to solve this tragic crime because the world was that much the lesser for the loss of her.

Taking yet another breath, Destiny was satisfied that her voice wouldn't crack. Only then did she finally answer him. "Yes, so?"

Still holding the bottle up, he shook it. Hard. There was no sound to correspond with the movement, no pills being disturbed and forced to rattle around the small container.

"So it's empty," he pointed out needlessly. "According to the date it was filled, there should be approximately twenty-five pills in here. There aren't." He looked at her. "What do you want to bet that toxicology is going to find that those pills are in your sister's system? Her wrists didn't need to be slashed," he told her. "Your sister swallowed enough of these things to have killed a small horse."

"Or was forced to swallow," Destiny interjected. She wasn't going to let him just forget about what his father had pointed out. Evidence that pointed to her sister being murdered.

"There's no sign of a struggle, remember? Maybe, before the full effects of the pills kicked in, your sister actually *did* try to slash her wrists but she was so loopy from the pills that she did an awkward, botched job of it."

Taking the vial from him, Destiny turned the container around so she could read the label. When she did, the name of the drug was vaguely familiar. Her sister was taking prescription sleeping pills, one of the newer ones on the market.

"Ever since we were little, my sister has had trouble sleeping. When these came on the market—" she nodded at the empty container "—and she tried them, she was overjoyed. She'd finally found something that worked. But she never took more than the prescribed dosage," Destiny maintained firmly. "It wasn't because she was a saint," she added angrily, reading the skepticism in Logan's eyes. "She just didn't want to feel drugged in the morning. The idea of falling asleep behind the wheel while driving to work terrified her," she emphasized.

Logan took back the container, intending on giving it to his father to send to toxicology.

"Still, over time, people develop a tolerance for medications. Maybe she found that one pill wasn't enough for her anymore and she took two—and then more. Or maybe she just wanted to sleep forever because her boyfriend dumped her."

He was back to that again. What was he, Johnny One-note? she thought angrily. How many ways did she have to say this before it finally sank into the thick skull of his?

"No," Destiny insisted with feeling. "Paula wouldn't have done that. Someone killed my sister," she said, enunciating each word separately. "I don't know who it was, but I do know that Paula didn't do it herself—accidentally or otherwise," Destiny added in case he was going to suggest that next.

"All right," Logan relented.

His father's lead assistant wasn't about to come around to his side or even remotely entertain the idea that her sister had committed suicide. And since his father seemed to believe that someone else had delivered the slash marks to the young woman's wrists, for the time being he'd go along with the popular theory.

Besides, he really didn't enjoy upsetting her, considering that she was still dealing with the shock of finding her sister dead.

"We'll approach it that way for now." Leaving the bathroom, still holding the prescription container with his handkerchief wrapped around it, Logan handed it to his father.

"The pills are probably all in her stomach," he told him not as his father, but as the head of the crime scene lab.

"You're most likely right," Sean agreed. "Whoever killed her probably slipped the pills into her drink. That way there'd be no resistance to what he was going to do next." He lowered his voice so that only Logan could hear. "Poor thing never stood a chance."

Logan nodded vaguely. He wasn't doing anyone any good just standing here, he decided, and announced, "I'm going to canvass the floor, see if anyone heard or saw anything out of the ordinary."

"But you don't think so," Destiny surmised.

"I didn't say that," Logan maintained. He didn't like being second-guessed. For the most part, he liked to think that on the job he was unreadable. He prided himself on that.

Besides, he was always open to possibilities. This job consisted of equal parts skill *and* luck.

"Hey, you never know. Stranger things have happened. And not everyone works nine to five," he added cavalierly. "So maybe someone *did* hear something." Logan paused just next to his father as he began to head out the front door. "Maybe I'll see you this Sunday." It was as close as he allowed himself to get to making a commitment that involved his new family.

"Maybe," Sean echoed with a faint nod.

"Sunday?" Destiny repeated, her smattering of curiosity getting the better of her when it came to this handsome, arrogant would-be crime fighter. "What's this Sunday?"

Since he knew that this woman worked closely with his father—it had to be closely for his father to display this kind of regard for her, treating her as if she was another one of his daughters—he was surprised that she didn't know.

"The former chief of police, my new uncle," he added, amused by the whole concept of getting such a huge number of brand-new blood relatives at his age. "He likes to throw family get-togethers. Word has it that any of us can drop by his table to get a full breakfast any day of the week, but apparently he goes all out on Sundays.

"My father is settling into this new life and doing

his best to show up every Sunday to prove how serious he is about being assimilated by the Cavanaughs—and making up for lost time."

Destiny nodded. Though Sean Cavanaugh wasn't an overly talkative man, he had shared some of this with her already. She had to admit that she rather liked the fact that he confided to her about this new venue of his private life.

It also made her realize how much she missed having a family of her own, people to talk to and use as sounding boards. People who cared how she felt and if she was getting enough sleep or running herself into the ground. After her mother had died, there'd been only Paula. And now even she was gone. That left only her, and it was true what they said. One *is* the loneliest number.

"Must be nice having more family than you know what to do with," she commented, trying to sound offhanded.

He would have had to have been completely deaf to have missed the wistfulness in her voice. Although he wasn't given to being touchy-feely and was rather careless at times about other people's feelings, Logan upbraided himself now for not realizing that he was talking about family life to a woman who no longer had one.

He felt a genuine stab of guilt.

The next moment he heard himself trying to make amends. "Feel free to drop by on any morning or on Sunday," he added. "The man goes all out then," he repeated. When he saw her looking at him, obviously puzzled, he guessed at what was going through her mind. "Don't worry, the chief won't mind."

"But you just said that he had family gatherings," she pointed out. And right now, she was part of no one's family.

"To the chief, anyone who's part of the force is family."

Okay, so maybe the handsome detective wasn't just an empty vessel. He was being kind to her because she was alone. She got that. But she was no one's charity case. Allowing a spasmodic smile to reach her lips, then go, she thanked him.

"I'll keep that in mind."

Logan knew a brush-off when he heard one, and ordinarily he'd just let it ride. But this woman was obviously someone special to his father, and initially he had been rather coarsely oblivious with her.

"No, really," he emphasized. "I'm sure my father would like you to come, too. He seems to regard you as another daughter," he said, trying to add weight to his invitation. He waited for that to sink in before saying anything more. Overkill was just as bad as neglecting to say anything at all.

At the mention of his father, Destiny allowed herself a small smile. Glancing over her shoulder to make sure the man was still in the other room, she said, "Your father's a very nice man."

"Well, we agree on that," Logan told her.

And more than likely on very little else, Destiny added silently.

With a preoccupied nod, she began to leave the apartment. She'd let Sean do his work. If she felt there was anything to add, she still had the key to Paula's apartment in her pocket. She could come back at a later date, when there was no one to get in her way.

Her hand on the doorknob, Logan's question made her pause in midstep.

"You want someone to take you home?"

Was he treating her like a civilian? Or did he just assume that she'd locked down her hysteria and was just a tiny step away from having a complete meltdown?

Turning to face the younger Cavanaugh, she looked at him, not exactly certain just how to interpret what he'd just said.

"What?"

"Would you like an officer to take you home?" he asked her, tendering the offer with a smile. "I'd offer to take you home myself, but I seem to be a little tied up at the moment."

He was serious. Either he was being too kind—or too cynical and doubting her actual feelings. She wasn't sure which bothered her more.

"Why would you think that I'd need someone to take me home?" she asked.

Why did she take everything as a challenge to her authority? He was trying to be understanding. Obviously that was wasted on this woman. "Well, you did just have a big shock."

"I'm not going home," she told him. Not wanting to explain herself any more than she absolutely had to, Destiny walked out.

"Are you going to be all right?" Sean asked as she passed him.

Sean's concern, at least, she didn't have to wonder about. She knew it was genuine and smiled with gratitude.

"Yes," she told him, not wanting the man to worry about her. He had enough to deal with these days. He didn't need her to burden him. Besides, she wasn't about to share her pain with him or with anyone. That was hers and hers alone to deal with.

And the way to deal with it was to keep busy.

She wasn't going home right now, even though the hour grew late. Home was just a medium-size shell that she got to rattle around in, waiting for the beginning of her next workday.

And, since technically she wasn't supposed to be working this case on the city's dime, she had to do it on her own time. That meant going into the lab and the small cubbyhole that comprised her "office" during something other than her regular work hours.

As in now.

She took the elevator down to the ground floor. It went straight down without a stop. Getting off, she walked directly to the double outer doors and pushed them open. The night air was chilly and damp as it greeted her.

Destiny drew in a deep breath and then another, trying to make herself come around.

With renewed purpose and borrowed energy, she walked briskly from the entrance to the apartment building to the curb where she'd parked her car.

And then she stopped dead.

There was no way she was going anywhere. Some jerk had double-parked his car parallel to hers and was completely blocking her exit.

She was stuck.

Biting back a barrage of less than flattering words that leaped to her lips, Destiny peered into the offending vehicle, trying to see if she could ascertain what kind of village idiot belonged to the car.

That was when she saw the official markings. And the communications radio that was mounted beneath the dashboard.

A standard Crown Victoria, the white car was an unmarked police vehicle. And she had a really strong hunch she knew whom it belonged to.

Chapter 4

When he heard the elevator opening, Logan automatically looked in that direction. He was surprised to see Destiny getting off.

"Forget something?" he asked, raising his voice in order to be heard.

Canvassing the floor, he was clear down the hall from the elevator. So far, he'd had next to no luck getting anyone to answer, despite the hour.

The only door that had opened so far had been by a very grumpy older man in a stained T-shirt and rumpled trousers of an indeterminable color. Both items of clothing looked as if the man had slept in them for at least the past year.

The man also, when questioned, didn't seem to speak any English. Whatever language he did speak, Logan was entirely unfamiliar with it. He was fluent in Spanish and knew a handful of other languages well enough to at least identify what they were. The old man was muttering at him in what he could only guess was an offshoot of some Slavic language, definitely not Russian in origin.

Thanking the man, Logan went to the next door. And the next.

So far, no one else had answered, but he'd canvassed only a quarter of the floor before his father's chief assistant had stepped off the elevator again.

"No, I didn't forget anything," Destiny retorted, irritated because she wanted to be on her way already, "but I think you did."

Logan cocked his head and eyed her, the person who might or might not be behind the next door temporarily forgotten. He watched as she walked toward him, appreciating the subtle sway of her hips. She was one of those people who was totally unaware of just how stunning she was.

But it wasn't lost on him.

She didn't seem like the type to play games, especially not at a time like this, so whatever she was referring to had to be on the level. The problem was, he had absolutely no idea what that was.

"Come again?" he finally said.

"You double-park your car downstairs?" she asked pointedly.

"No. Yeah," he amended in the next breath, remembering.

His automatic response was "no" because as a rule, he never double-parked. Aside from it being against the rules, he liked his car, and that was a good way to get it nicked and dinged. But this evening he'd made an exception because there'd been no spots and he thought he'd be finished and out in no time. But he'd obviously miscalculated.

"That was your car I blocked?" he asked incredulously. Wow, what were the odds?

"That was—and still is—my car," she told him. Why wasn't he moving? "Could you come down please and move your car?" It really wasn't a request.

Logan could see that begging a couple of minutes' indulgence, until he was at least finished with this side of the floor, was just *not* going to fly in this case. So he dropped his hand away from the door he'd been knocking on, nodded and said, "Sure," just as the door in front of him opened.

This time, the responding tenant was definitely *not* a rumpled, grumpy old man. It was a barefoot blonde wearing the tightest cutoff denim shorts he'd ever seen. The white T-shirt she had on told him that she didn't believe in bras.

"Yes?" she asked in a small, soft voice. She looked from him to Destiny and then back again, making no secret of the fact that she preferred talking to men.

Holding up his badge and police ID, Logan flashed what one of his sisters referred to as his "bone melting" smile at the woman in apartment 3D.

"Detective Cavanaugh with the Aurora P.D., ma'am. I need to ask you a few questions, but first I have to tend to something else. I'll be right back, I promise," he said, sounding as sincere as a preacher on Sunday. He held up his index finger as if that somehow reinforced the fact that he wanted her to just hold on for a few minutes until he could get back to her.

"What's this about?" the woman asked, calling after him as he walked into the elevator right behind Destiny.

"I'll explain everything in five minutes," he called back, raising his voice as the elevator door slid closed, cutting him off from the blonde. "Sorry about the car," he told Destiny, turning his attention to her and never missing a beat. "I thought I wasn't going to be here long."

"I guess it's a night for surprises," Destiny quipped dryly, saying the words more to herself than to him.

But something in her voice managed to catch his attention. As the stainless-steel door opened and she stepped out, Logan caught her by the elbow before she could get too far.

Startled, she turned to look at him quizzically. Now what?

"Do you have anyone?" he asked her.

No, not anymore. The words seemed to echo in her head, draining her soul. Shaking it off, she stared at him.

"What?" she demanded.

"Do you have anyone to talk to?" he elaborated. "Someone to stay with or to have them come over and stay with you?"

Destiny raised her chin, the barricade she kept around herself growing a little higher. "Look, I'm not exactly sure what you're asking, but I don't need a baby-sitter."

That meant the answer was no, Logan thought. The woman had already said that her sister was her only living kin. With her gone, that left no one to call family. He had no idea what that was like. All of his life, from his very first memory, he'd always had siblings and cousins, and now that he knew he was a Cavanaugh, he had enough relatives to populate a small city.

Despite the fact that there were times he felt as if he would have traded his soul for some privacy, for an island of time alone with his thoughts and away from well-meaning relatives, he knew that if he had to endure that on a full-time, daily basis, it would have eaten away at him.

"I didn't say that you did," he told her, his voice low-key. "But if you want to wait around for a bit while I finish knocking on these doors to see if there's anyone willing to talk and tell me if they saw or heard something, maybe we could go out afterwards, catch a cup of coffee. Talk," he emphasized. The elevator stopped. A moment later, as if it first had to pause, the door to the lobby opened.

She walked out of the building's glass doors ahead of Logan. Her first thought was that he was hitting on her, but that cocky expression she'd noticed earlier on his face was absent. And to give him his due, he did sound sincere. Since he was Sean's son and she dearly loved the man, she gave Logan the benefit of the doubt. After all, since he *was* Sean's son, maybe a little compassion had rubbed off on him.

She realized, in a moment of weakness, that she appreciated the offer. But that still didn't mean that she wanted him hovering around her, possibly witnessing her break down.

"I'm not going to do anything stupid or drastic," she assured Logan.

Logan shrugged as if that had never crossed his mind. "I'm just in the mood for some decent coffee. By definition that means not the kind that comes in a paper cup," he told her.

She'd never been discerning about her coffee. As long as it was black and hot, that was all that she required.

"I'll be fine," she insisted, then softened a little as she added, "But thanks."

"No problem," he murmured. He caught himself wondering, just for a split second, what she was like without all that barbed wire around her.

She watched him get into his vehicle. A moment later, he turned his ignition key and the car came to life. With his eyes all but glued to the rearview mirror, he eased his car out slowly, going backward one inch at a time. Traffic was light at the moment, but that was subject to instant change, even at this hour of the evening.

Clearing her vehicle, he pulled up the handbrake. Logan allowed his engine to idle as he waited for her to get into her car and pull it out of its current parking spot.

"I'll take a rain check," Destiny impulsively called out through the open passenger side window just before she peeled out of the spot and seamlessly merged into the flow of cars.

She didn't stop until she came to the next light. It

was red, but the color barely registered with her brain in time.

She was too busy upbraiding herself.

A rain check? What the hell had possessed her to say that? Was it just to establish some kind of connection with another human being, subconsciously comforting herself with the knowledge that she didn't have to be alone if she didn't choose to be? That she could establish some kind of contact with another human being anytime she wanted to? And that if she was alone, it was because she *chose* to be that way.

Words, she was playing with words.

It didn't make the empty, gnawing feeling in the pit of her stomach go away.

She vacillated between being numb and being shattered.

"Oh, Paula," she murmured under her breath, blinking back hot tears. "What did you go and leave yourself open to?"

No matter what the answer to that was, if her sister had openly invited her killer into the apartment or the person had let himself in with a copy of her key, Paula was still dead.

She was still not coming back.

Paula had always been a delicate, small-boned little thing, and even if she hadn't been drugged, she wouldn't have been able to fight her attacker off if he had been any larger than a small field mouse.

"I tried to get you to take self-defense classes," Destiny angrily shouted into the emptiness, the feeling of helplessness snowballing into outrage and fury. "Why didn't you listen to me? Why the hell didn't you *ever* listen to anything I said to you?"

It seemed to her as if, up until these past two years, anytime she'd made a constructive suggestion, Paula would turn around and do the exact opposite.

And yet, she knew her sister had always loved her. Loved her as fiercely as she loved Paula.

A lot of good that did either of them now, Destiny thought sadly.

With a sigh, she stepped on the gas.

One Police Plaza looked mournful silhouetted against the dark, moonless sky. The building had a minimum of lights on, beneath which a handful of detectives were burning the midnight oil, trying to solve a case or just tying up the loose ends on one.

A slightly lesser complement of officers patrolled the streets now than during the daylight hours. She didn't know if that was a good thing or a bad thing.

Parking her vehicle near the building, Destiny got out and began to hurry up the ten stone steps.

What she was really doing, she knew, was trying to outrun the loneliness inside her. She was having little success at that.

The only way she would be able to get through this, Destiny told herself, was to find Paula's killer and make him pay.

"Damn it, Paula, you should have told me who you were dating."

Maybe the guy wasn't responsible for what had ultimately happened, but at least it would have been a start, someone to question so she could begin putting the disjointed pieces together.

The last phrase echoed in her head. *Begin putting the disjointed pieces together.*

Well, if she didn't have Paula's mystery man's name, she would have to start somewhere else to make this puzzle come together.

Destiny suddenly thought of the prescription bottle that Logan had found in the medicine cabinet. Now that she thought about it, the whole thing just didn't seem to ring true to her. It didn't seem like Paula.

Granted her sister did have a lot of trouble sleeping and she had taken the drug when it had first come out. But Paula was stubborn. She would have never allowed herself to be dependent on a drug. Most likely, she would have tried her best to use the prescription as little as possible.

Now that she thought about it, she remembered that Paula was adamantly against taking drugs of any kind. This even went so far as to include simple painkillers. She wouldn't take them even when she had one of her excruciating headaches.

She and Paula had argued over that more than once. But Paula wouldn't be budged. Her deep aversion came from the fact that her best friend in high school had had a drug problem. A week before her graduation, the girl, Rachel Wyman, had accidentally overdosed. She was dead before she ever reached the hospital.

Paula had been the one to find her.

Just like I was the one who found you, Destiny thought ruefully.

That was when Paula started getting involved in anti-drug campaigns, volunteering her time and considerable artistic talents to do whatever she could to try to save someone else from ending up the way that Rachel had.

So, feeling that way, what was Paula doing with a brand-new prescription for sleeping pills?

Making a decision, Destiny turned on her heel and hurried back to her car. Blessed with what amounted to total recall, she had the ability to remember anything that had crossed her line of vision.

Right now, as she concentrated, she remembered the name of the pharmacy that was written across the top of the bottle.

She also remembered the prescription number on the bottle, a long fourteen-digit number. What she hadn't noted at the time, because she'd been so focused on keeping herself together, was the prescribing doctor's name. She wanted to speak to him because, as a rule, her sister didn't go to doctors.

The pharmacist on duty expressed an initial reluctance to answer her questions about her sister's medication until Destiny flashed her badge and ID for him. Mentally, she crossed her fingers that the young pharmacist wasn't the belt-and-suspenders type. Because if he was, she had the sinking feeling that he would have felt compelled not just to take note of her ID but to call in and verify with her superior whether or not she was really supposed to be there, asking questions.

Destiny held her breath until the pharmacist finally lifted his rather thin, sloping shoulders, then dropped them again in what amounted to a disinterested shrug. With that, he went to the computer to access the prescription in question.

After several minutes had passed and the pharmacist still hadn't stopped searching, Destiny felt compelled to ask, "Is there anything wrong?"

"That depends on your point of view," he told her. His brow furrowed in frustration. "I can't seem to find that prescription number. Are you sure that you got the numbers down right?"

There were a great many things that she was uncertain about, but that didn't include her ability to recall things in crystal clarity. "Positive," she told the pharmacist.

The young man frowned, his thin lips all but disappearing. "What did you say the patient's name was again?"

"Paula Richardson," she repeated, then recited, "Her date of birth is oh-three, oh-six, nineteen eighty-six." Taking a breath to help steel herself off, she said, "She was found dead today."

Startled, the pharmacist immediately asked, "And you think that the prescription was responsible? I assure you, every chemical used is of the highest grade. It couldn't have been our—"

She held up her hand to stop him. When she spoke, it was in the small, soothing voice she'd once used to chase away Paula's nightmares.

"No one is accusing your pharmacy of anything. We're just trying to gather as much information as we can right now."

Temporarily placated, the pharmacist returned to his computer. Hitting the keyboard, he scrolled down several pages.

"Well, she's here in our records—we filled a standard antibiotic for her at the beginning of the year. Amoxicillin. For the flu," he said, still staring at the screen. He hit several keys that took him back and forth between a couple of screens. "Nope, no sleeping pills," he verified. "You're sure that was her name was on the bottle?"

"Yes, I'm sure." Her mouth curved for a second in a semblance of a smile, doing her best to silently reassure the man that no one at the pharmacy was in trouble. She had the information she needed. "Thanks for your help."

He seemed a little confused. "But I didn't find anything."

No, on the contrary, you did, Destiny thought. The pharmacist with the baby face had indirectly found that someone had gone to a great deal of trouble and had carefully staged her sister's death scene. The person had even gone to the trouble of replicating a prescription medication.

That meant that someone had *planned* to kill her sister. Had actually targeted Paula.

But why?

And to what end?

This didn't sound like the work of an obsessive serial killer, because there were too many details adhered to. Besides, as a rule of thumb, a serial killer didn't try to make a murder victim look like someone who committed suicide. Covertly or blatantly, serial killers were usually quite proud of their sick handiwork and enjoyed showing it off. Enjoyed basking in splashy headlines. At the same time, they usually were daring law enforcement agents to try to catch them.

This had been covered up, its sole purpose appearing to have been to kill Paula.

Again, *why?*

It was half an hour later and she was back mentally staring at that question. And back driving toward the police station.

With this new information, there were things she needed to check out, to look into. The precinct was the only place she knew of with the kind of wealth of information and access to that information that she needed.

The precinct parking lot looked almost emptier this time than it had just a little while ago. Blocking the effects, Destiny hurried up the stairs for a second time, eager to get started. Eager to get to her desk.

She needed to document what she'd discovered. In the morning, she'd get in touch with Cavanaugh—she assumed the good-looking detective would be the one to work her sister's case—and let him know that the prescription he'd found in the medicine cabinet and felt went a long way in supporting his suicide theory didn't belong to her sister.

It belonged, in one way or another, to the killer. The prescription number, when she'd finally prevailed upon the pharmacist to look through the pharmacy chain's archives, had once been the number on a bottle of cough medicine that had been prescribed for a child with bronchitis.

She couldn't help wondering if there was some obscure connection there. Tracking down the name on the actual prescription would be her first order of business, she decided.

Armed with coffee from the vending machine and her determination, Destiny got off the elevator when it came to a stop and opened in the basement. Trying to think only of making progress and not about her sister, she made her way down the winding corridor to her office.

It never occurred to her that she might fail in reaching her objective. Because, as the popular saying she believed with all her heart went, failure was not an option here. She wouldn't allow it to be.

Chapter 5

"So, Dad, how's it going?"

Walking into the newly redecorated, state-of-the-art criminology lab at the ungodly hour of 7:00 a.m. the next morning, Logan crossed to the middle of the room. His father stood over a table that was rivaled only by the enormous one in Andrew Cavanaugh's dining room.

The head of the crime lab was busy testing the contents of some substance Logan wasn't even going to try to identify.

Wearing his white lab coat, Sean glanced up to see his son approaching. Surprised, he looked over Logan's head at the clock on the wall behind him.

Well, this was unusual.

"You're in early," he commented. Logan was the one they used to have to dynamite out of bed to get him to school on time. As far as he knew, his son still loved sleeping in. *Early* was not a word Logan regarded with any semblance of approval. "Something to do with the case?"

Logan moved his shoulders in a vague shrug. "In a manner of speaking, I guess, but I wasn't asking you about the evidence just now."

Still working, Sean raised a quizzical eyebrow in response. "Oh?"

"No," Logan told him, "I was asking you 'personally' how it was going."

"Fine." There was a note of amused caution in Sean's voice. Then, because he did possess a measure of curiosity and Logan was behaving rather strangely, Sean pressed for details. "Are you asking about anything specifically—personally?" he tacked on, deliberately highlighting the word Logan had used.

Oh, the hell with it. He might as well just blurt it out, Logan decided. "Kenny said that you and Matt's mother are seeing each other," he said, referring to his sister, Kendra. "Regularly," he added in case his father was going to try to pretend not to know what he was talking about. "I just wanted to ask how that was going."

So, that was it. Sean had wondered how long it would take for word to spread. Apparently not very long at all. The Cavanaugh grapevine seemed to have an even faster connection than the Cavelli grapevine did.

"Sabrina Abilene and I are more than 'seeing' each other, Logan," he informed his son, doing his best to sound serious and keep the laughter at bay.

Logan sighed dramatically, leaned his hip against the long, sleek stainless-steel table that displayed a host of mysterious instruments and said to his father in a low, serious voice, "Well, young man, I think it's time that we had 'The Talk.'"

Sean laughed then, affectionately cuffing the back of his son's head the way he'd sometimes done when Logan and his brothers were younger and had been guilty of doing something stupid.

"That's enough out of you, or there'll be some serious consequences, Detective Cavanaugh. Go, make yourself useful." He pointed toward the door. "Do some detective work and earn that big, hefty salary the city's paying you."

"That only takes about two hours out of my day."

If he looked at his pay and divided it by the number of hours he put in overall, he was getting paid a pittance. But he wasn't in it for the money, or even because it was the family business. He believed in his work. Believed in making a difference. But that wasn't anything he wanted to advertise. It clashed with his devil-may-care image.

Nodding toward what his father was testing, he asked, "You find anything new?"

"Nothing we haven't already surmised. Paula Richardson had enough sleeping pills in her system to put a school of sharks to sleep. The slashed wrists were just overkill. Too bad. She looked like a lovely girl."

"A lovely girl somebody really wanted dead," Logan commented. "How's your chief assistant holding up?"

Sean smiled, noting how hard Logan was trying to appear as if he was completely detached in his view of the case and Destiny's connection to it. If Logan had really been detached, Sean mused, he wouldn't have felt the need to have that point driven home.

"On the surface, she's behaving very professionally. But I won't pretend that I'm not concerned about her, Logan. She's keeping everything bottled up inside, and that kind of thing can only be sustained for so long before the inner pressure gets to be too much. Keep an eye out on her for me, will you?"

Logan was surprised by the request. "Dad, I'm going to be working the case, remember?"

"Yeah, well, so will she, no matter what anyone says to the contrary." He smiled to himself. "She's stubborn enough to be one of us," he told his son. "By the way, she went by the pharmacy where the prescription was issued."

Logan was about to protest that he had kept the prescription container in his possession, dropping it off at the lab last night, but that obviously hadn't made a difference.

"And?"

"And it turns out that they never issued the prescription to our victim. They have a file on her and the number came out of their pharmacy, but years ago and not for sleeping pills but for some cough medicine for a little girl. Backs up Destiny's theory that her sister was murdered. By the way," he added mildly, "her desk is at the other end of the floor—in case you want to swing by sometime and, you know, exchange theories," he concluded euphemistically.

Logan merely shook his head. "You know, Dad, if I

didn't know better, I'd say you had something up your sleeve."

Sean innocently raised one hand into the air, demonstrating. "Just my arm, boy. Just my arm."

It was a well-known fact, especially around his family, that people in love tended to want to pair up everyone else in the firm belief that *everyone* should be as happy as they were.

Standing in the doorway, Logan took a good look at his father, seeing him in a completely different light since when he had first entered.

"Dad?"

Sean was already refocused on his task. His "Yes?" was more than a little distracted.

The thought of his father in a romantic relationship had never really crossed his mind before. He wasn't certain how to react, really. But he and his siblings had always been cautioned about leaping to conclusions, so he decided to ask first before trying to get used to the idea.

"You're not in love or anything, are you?"

"Define 'or anything,'" Sean countered, amused by the question. When his son seemed at a loss for words, Sean told him. "You'll be the second to know when and if I am," he promised.

"Who'll be the first?" Logan asked suspiciously. He fully expected his father to say "Sabrina."

But again, his father surprised him. "Me," Sean replied simply.

Logan left the lab, feeling more than a little bewildered even if he didn't show it. His world had been turned upside down. First they had discovered that his father had been accidentally switched at birth with another male infant and that he, and thus *they,* were actually part of the Cavanaugh family. If that wasn't enough, now it looked as if after years of being content to be their sole parent, his father was dating.

Seriously dating, from the sound of it.

At twenty-eight, Logan felt he was too old to be entertaining the idea of getting a stepmother. Wasn't that something children acquired?

You're not the one who matters here.

That was just plain weird, he thought. He could almost hear Bridget's voice in his head. Bridget, the one who always put him in his place.

The main thing to remember, he told himself, was that his father seemed happy, and heaven only knew his father *deserved* to be happy.

Arriving at the closed elevator door, he was about to press the button on the wall beside it when a light pooling along the floor down the hall caught his eye, and then his attention. He'd come in early to catch his father alone so that he could feel him out about the woman he was seeing—he'd run into Kendra and Matt on his way out of the precinct last night and they had mentioned the change in his father's evening schedule. Logan knew his father was always in early and always alone, which made it a good time to talk to him.

Was he wrong? Did his father have a kindred spirit amid the CSI unit?

Curious, Logan moved away from the elevator bank and made his way down the hallway.

He had a hunch the light was coming from Destiny's

office even before he actually got to the doorway and looked in. Given the current case the unit and he had just caught, her being here early didn't exactly come as a great shock to him.

But it did surprise him that Destiny appeared to be wearing the same clothes she'd had on yesterday.

"Didn't you go home last night?" he asked.

Completely absorbed by what she was doing, Destiny jumped at the sound of Logan's deep voice intruding into her world. She pressed her lips together just in time to suppress the yelp of surprise that automatically rose to her tongue.

Taking in a shaky breath as she tried to calm her nerves, Destiny turned her chair halfway toward the doorway to confirm what she already knew. That Logan was standing there.

She shrugged in vague dismissal. "I lost track of time."

There was something extremely attractive about the rumpled way she looked, he thought. He found himself wishing that they weren't involved professionally so he'd be free to get involved another way. "Then let me clue you in—it's tomorrow."

She frowned. Why was he even here at this hour? "Just what everyone needs, a talking desk calendar. Thank you, your work here is done," she said, hoping he would leave so she could concentrate.

"And so will you be if you don't go home and get some rest."

Her frown deepened. Was that a note of concern she heard in his voice?

No, she was just tired, that's all. And then she remembered his offer of coffee and to listen if she just wanted to talk. Maybe he really was being nice and she was being too hard on him because her temper had shortened by half. Lack of sleep tended to do that to her, to make her irritable and impatient.

"I'll rest when we catch the bastard who did this," she told him.

"Your sister wouldn't want you running yourself into the ground like this," he pointed out.

Now that was just empty talk. He didn't even know her sister—and now he never would, she thought with a pang before she could tamp down the pain. With effort, she firmly put her emotions under lock and key. Anything she couldn't use to help her catch Paula's killer would just need to wait.

"My sister didn't want me doing a lot of things," she pointed out briskly. "She wasn't the easiest person to get along with."

Logan had a feeling his father's chief assistant was using anger to keep herself from falling apart. Whatever worked. With a smile, he made an observation. "She probably said the same thing about you."

"Yeah, she did." Logan had expected her to admit as much. The half smile that accompanied the words, though, was a surprise.

It was the first time he'd seen her *really* smile. It was a nice smile and not one of those smirky, snarky smiles that had a person bracing for some sort of witty, biting put-down. Hers was a sunrise-type smile that brought warmth with it. Definitely lit up the recipient, he realized, charmed.

"You know, you're really not supposed to be working on this," he reminded her tactfully.

He was aware that his father wouldn't take her to task for this. He'd already demonstrated as much. But the homicide lieutenant who had put him on this case, he was a different story. He liked things by the book. So had he, Logan thought—when he was twelve. Now, solving cases was more of an improvisational theater at work. He made things up as he went along, and when it worked it was fantastic.

Destiny pointed to the square silver clock on the opposite wall. "I start work at nine. This is still before my workday." Her eyes narrowed as she looked at him and dug in. She really couldn't seem to concentrate with him here. It was as if he was eating up her oxygen and making the room very, very warm. "Anything else?"

He remembered what his father had just mentioned. "Yeah. Did you find anything else besides the fact that the prescription with her name on it didn't really belong to your sister?" he asked. Then, because his question had caught her off guard, he added, "I stopped to talk to my father this morning. He filled me in."

She just naturally assumed that meant that Logan had stopped by the lab to check on the progress being made on the case. Why else would he be here? She had to admit that the detective's thoroughness took her by surprise. Cavanaugh or not, she wouldn't have thought that Logan was that dedicated to his job. He hadn't given her that kind of an impression when she'd spoken with him yesterday.

For once it was nice to discover she was wrong.

"Yes, actually, I did find out something." And then she raised her eyes to his and qualified, "I think."

"That sleeping with your head on your desk will give you a pretty bad crick in your neck?" he guessed.

"Besides that," she told him. She turned her monitor so that he had a better view of the screen. "I think I found a pattern," she said excitedly.

Actually, there was no "think" about it. Destiny *knew* she had. The cases, all appearing to be singular in nature, were far too similar to one another for this to be some unhappy coincidence occurring again and again—especially since there had been five other cases in as many years.

"What kind of a pattern?" Logan asked, looking at her rather than at the screen.

"The kind of pattern that involves apparent "suicides" of attractive young women ranging between the ages of twenty-one and thirty-five who, according to the police files, killed themselves after breaking up with—or being dumped by—a mysterious boyfriend whom their family and friends not only didn't get to meet, but didn't even know by name." Finished, she looked at him again. "Sound familiar?"

Sounded identical, he thought, but he was never one to get ahead of himself on a case. "If they were called suicides, why were there police reports filed?" he asked.

That was a good point—and she had an equally good answer. She'd known the only way to sell this was to stay one step ahead of Logan. "Because in all the cases, someone in the family didn't think that it was suicide, that the so-called mysterious boyfriend did it." She stopped for a second, straightening and pulling her shoulders back so that a minor cracking noise was heard, like the salute of old-fashioned cap pistols going off one at a time.

"They're all open cases," she informed him, sitting back now. "In each case there was not enough evidence to lead them to a suspect." And then she frowned slightly as she leaned back in her chair and rocked. "I didn't think so in the beginning, but it looks like we might have a serial killer on our hands. Or at the very least, a killer with an agenda."

Logan studied the last screen she'd pulled up. The details there were very close to matching the ones that had come up last night. Very slowly, he nodded.

"It looks like you might have something there." And then he smiled at her. "Nice work, Richardson. I'll take it from here."

The nascent smile vanished. "No, you won't," she countered with feeling.

"Look, I don't want any of the credit, but you know you're not supposed to be involved in this. It's a conflict of interest."

The hell it was. "I don't have any 'interest' to conflict," she shot back. "All I want is to help find Paula's killer—and apparently the killer of a lot of other innocent women, as well," she added, pointing to the monitor. "I don't have anyone to 'pin' this on, so it's not like

I have an agenda or anything. The only agenda I have is to solve this."

He wasn't going to leave her office without agreeing to let her work the case. She didn't care if she had to bodily restrain him. The thought brought an unexpected flash of heat with it that she quickly dismissed.

"Look," she argued, "I've already been a help. I found out that the prescription wasn't filled under my sister's name despite what the label said and I found all these other so-called suicides that match Paula's killer's M.O. Who knows what else I can find out if I go on working this?" she pushed.

"You don't have to convince me," he told her.

It was the brass she would be going up against, not him. After talking to her, after seeing her at work, he wasn't about to be a stickler about rules and regulations. He fully sympathized with what she was going through right now. In his opinion, finding her sister like that was an absolute living nightmare. Solving the case might actually give her sweet dreams. At the very least, it would give her the night back.

Besides, the woman was damn easy on the eyes, and she did keep him up on his toes. It would definitely be simpler to join forces than have to fight her.

"Well, then my working the case is a go, because you're the only one I care about right now." When she saw the grin slip over his lips, she knew she hadn't worded her answer to him correctly. A bright pink hue took her cheeks prisoner. Just in time for him to see.

"Wait," she cried, determined to straighten this out. "That didn't come out right."

"Came out fine from where I'm standing," Logan told her. And then he sighed. He wasn't going to even pretend to stand in her way. He didn't belong with the establishment, only the rebels. "Okay, keep at it. I know my dad's not about to come down on you. He completely understands the idea of family loyalty—"

"Do you?" she heard herself asking, realizing that she wanted to hear a positive answer out of him.

He watched her for a long moment, green eyes meeting blue. And, for the briefest of seconds, soul touching soul. "Yeah," he heard himself saying quietly, "I do."

"Good," she said so softly he read the words on her lips more than heard them. "Then I'll just get back to work and touch base with you later."

"Later," he echoed as he walked away.

Part of him had an uneasy feeling that he was getting in over his head here, but there was nothing he could do about it.

The other part was damn well looking forward to it.

Chapter 6

"**D**amn it!" Lieutenant Bailey's disgruntled voice greeted Logan even before he crossed the threshold into the squad room.

This, Logan thought, did not sound good.

Usually it took a few hours before the day began to look as if it was going to hell. Having it begin in hell guaranteed a slow, unmerciful torture for him. When Lieutenant Bailey wasn't happy, *no one* in his squad was happy.

Walking in, Logan saw the reason why the lieutenant's voice had carried so well. The man was not in his office. Right now, he was standing near the doorway, talking on his cell. Or rather, the older, disgruntled-looking man was cursing into his phone.

"Problem, Lieutenant?" he asked mildly as the other

man abruptly disconnected the call that was apparently creating his less than jovial mood.

"Only if you call working with half a squad a problem. That was Wakefield, calling in sick. This is worse than when we had the blue flu," he grumbled, referring to an incident several years back. At that time, an inordinate number of the uniformed officers called in sick in protest over what they felt was a wrongful disciplinary action of one of their own. Now that he recalled, Brian Cavanaugh had looked into the matter, found the charges to be false and had all actions dropped.

"Nearly half of my men are out sick," the lieutenant bit off in frustration. "I just hope the crazies don't start coming out of the woodwork." He looked at Logan as if seeing him for the first time. "You close that suicide case that came in last night?"

"Funny thing about that, Lieutenant."

Bailey's dark eyes grew even darker as he glared at him over his hawklike, patrician nose. "You're not going to tell me that wasn't a suicide, are you?"

Logan ignored the warning note in the lieutenant's voice. He didn't believe in hiding information. The man needed to be kept in the loop, at least to some extent. "Well, yeah, actually I am," Logan told him, then quickly added, "But there's more," before Bailey could unleash his mercurial temper.

"More?" The lieutenant stared at him in disbelief. "What kind of 'more'?" he asked.

Logan knew what he was about to say wouldn't be welcome, but in this case, he found himself agreeing with Destiny. "It looks like this might be the work of a serial killer."

Bailey sank down in Sullivan's chair. "Aw, hell, no."

Taking a seat behind his own desk, Logan nodded. "I'm afraid so."

It took less than a minute for Bailey to rally. He was back in fighting form and ready to issue a challenge. "Who the hell says it's a serial killer?" he demanded angrily.

Logan was about to say that it was the victim's sister, but then decided it sounded better if he fell back on Destiny's title at the crime lab instead. If nothing else, it carried some weight.

"One of the CSIs. The head of the day shift's chief assistant," he said, deliberately not referring to him as his father. He and his siblings had all earned their present positions, and the less attention paid to the fact that their father was the head of the crime lab, the better for everyone all around. "She found five other open, suspicious 'suicide' cases that had far too many similarities to this case to just shrug off and pass over."

"And you looked these cases over and agreed?" Bailey pressed.

"I haven't had a chance yet," Logan told him truthfully. "But I was just about to do that." As he talked, Logan turned on his computer. It took the machine several seconds to respond and come to life.

"All right, you do that." Bailey sounded exasperated as he issued the order. Rising to his feet, he nodded at the desk he'd just vacated. "When's Sullivan supposed to be coming back?"

The wedding had taken place only last weekend. The lieutenant had been invited but hadn't attended. Unlike Brian Cavanaugh, he didn't believe in socializing with his men.

"Not for another week and a half," Logan answered.

The news was not well received. Bailey's frown intensified.

"Well, I can't give you anyone else from the squad. Half of them are out sick and the other half are up to their ears in unsolved cases. This month's stats are going straight to hell."

"The chief assistant offered to work with me on this one—if it's okay with you, Lieutenant," Logan added.

As a rule, he preferred to ask forgiveness rather than permission, but seeing as how this was right out in front of him and the lieutenant was bemoaning the lack of bodies to do the work, Logan decided that this might be the better approach.

Bailey sighed. It was a known fact that the man wasn't much on accepting outside help. He preferred the "glory," as he referred to it, to remain within the department. But in this case, he had no choice. They needed to close some of the cases. After a moment, he nodded.

"Desperate times require desperate measures, I guess. All right. Use whatever resources are offered," he said, and Logan had the distinct impression that the man was blatantly hinting that he could turn to the chief of D's if it proved necessary.

"Oh, and one more thing—I don't want this going out to the media until I give the okay. The last damn thing we need right now is for the public to start panicking and seeing a serial killer behind every building." Bailey's penetrating gaze met Logan's. "Understood?"

Translation, the lieutenant doesn't want to look as if he's not doing his job.

Logan had always thought that bringing the public in was a good thing. For every thousand crazies who called in with dead-end tips, they'd get one really good, valid one that enabled them to nab their perpetrators a lot quicker.

But this was the lieutenant's call. "Understood," Logan answered.

"Good."

The conversation over, the lieutenant marched back into his office, looking like the very personification of a disgruntled man who had far too much on his plate.

Logan waited until Bailey was out of earshot, then he picked up his telephone receiver and called the extension in Destiny's office. Detail oriented, he'd taken note of the number when he'd walked into her office.

The phone rang a total of four times. He was just about to hang up, thinking that she must have stepped away from her area, when he heard the phone pick up.

"Crime lab."

The voice sounded preoccupied, as if he'd interrupted her. "Destiny?"

There was a slight hesitation, as if she was surprised that anyone would recognize her voice. "Yes?"

"This is Cavanaugh. Logan," he added since there were so many of them. "Good news—"

"I know who you are," she cut in. "I recognized your

voice." What she hadn't liked was that not only did she recognize his voice, but her pulse had jumped when she heard it. Maybe she was just sleep deprived and not just reacting to his resonant and sexy voice. "What good news?" she asked, trying not to let herself anticipate anything and not quite succeeding. "Did you find who did this to Paula?"

"Not that good," he qualified.

"Then what is it?" she asked impatiently.

"My lieutenant just said that in light of the fact that my partner's on his honeymoon and half the detectives up here are out with the flu, he officially okayed the two of us working together for the time being."

She had learned to take most everything with a grain of salt and a great deal of caution. "Does your lieutenant know who I—"

"No, he doesn't, and I purposely didn't mention you by name, only by your title."

"By my title?" she questioned. She didn't think he was even aware of that.

"Yeah, you know, chief assistant to the crime lab's head of the day shift." That was quite a mouthful to get right. "Right now, that seemed to be good enough for the lieutenant. He said because we're so shorthanded up here, you and I should work together on this case— at least until Sully gets back."

"Sully?" she echoed. Who or what was a "Sully"?

"Yeah." And then he gave her his partner's full name. "Detective Eric Sullivan. He's on his honeymoon at the moment and isn't due to be back for another week and a half."

She'd take whatever she could get. "That gives us a little leeway," she commented.

"Yeah," he agreed. Who was she kidding? The woman wasn't nearly as laid-back about this as she was trying to portray. "Oh, and one more thing—"

There was always just "one more thing," she thought. She could feel her shoulders stiffening as she braced herself. "And that is?"

"The lieutenant wants this kept from the media for as long as possible. He said he doesn't want single women to be afraid to go out in the evening."

"The serial killer doesn't kill his victims in the street," she pointed out, adding grimly, "He apparently kills his victims after he gets tired of them and dumps them."

"I kept that little detail from him," Logan told her. "I've come to the conclusion that the less I share with the lieutenant, the more leeway I have to work on a case."

"As in bringing me in and not telling him my last name," she surmised.

He didn't think that she was going to have any particular problem with that. "It's what you wanted, wasn't it?"

"Absolutely," she told him with feeling. It was just that by *not* telling his lieutenant her name, she felt as if they were actually lying to the man. And that could come back and bite them. "Don't think that I'm not grateful—" she began.

He cut her off right there. "We'll get to that later," he promised her with a definite grin in his voice, instinctively knowing that was going to distract her and get under her skin. He had a feeling that messing with her and getting her annoyed with him would focus the woman on solving the case and not on her personal loss.

"Okay, so how do you want to do this?" she asked.

"Do what?"

"Work together," she underscored. She felt a warmth creeping up her cheeks when she realized that he might have thought she was making a reference to something personal. More than likely he was probably more accustomed to that sort of thing than to working with a woman professionally. "Do you want me to come upstairs to you, or do you want to come down to me?"

He disliked having to rely on another computer, preferring to work on his own. Logan glanced toward Sully's desk. That was as good a place as any. Actually, now that he looked around, there were a good many empty desks in the immediate area. This flu thing really *was* taking its toll.

"A lot of detectives are out sick," he told her again. "So there's plenty of space up here." The crime lab had always struck him as rather claustrophobic, not to mention subterranean. "Might do you good to work aboveground for a change."

"I'm not exactly a gopher," she told him, picking up on his inference. "I go out in daylight on occasion." She didn't attempt to hide the note of sarcasm in her voice.

"Actually, I was thinking more along the lines of a vampire, not a gopher." When she made no response, he added, "You know, a creature of the night, that sort of thing."

"I know what a vampire is," she told him shortly.

Was this his attempt at humor? Or was he flirting in some strange, abstract way? Either way, he needed to stop it. This was a serious case they were working on. There was no time to waste on distractions. Her sister and a lot of other women were dead. They had to find the killer before he found another victim.

She blew out a breath, told herself to calm down and focus, then said, "I'll be up in a few minutes."

"Looking forward to it," he told her.

In response he heard a loud "click" in his ear. She'd hung up. Logan smiled to himself. Mission accomplished. He'd gotten her annoyed, he congratulated himself, and right now, "annoyed" was a lot better than "sad," which was what he'd picked up on in her voice earlier. And while the woman had every right to be sad, the emotion tended to paralyze a person. Annoyance, or its first cousin "anger," on the other hand, tended to light a fire under a person, which at the moment would serve them both a lot better than her being sad.

"Any particular place you want me?" Destiny asked ten minutes later. She'd come up carrying a large cardboard box filled with files, notebooks and miscellaneous information.

The expression on his face when Cavanaugh looked up told her that she'd made a tactical mistake with her wording. Again. What was it about this man that kept her tangling her words? She was seriously going to have to watch that. "To sit?" she added with emphasis, then repeated the question more fully. "Where do you want me to sit?"

"You can take Sully's desk. I don't know when the others are liable to come back, and there's no point in you having to play musical desks every morning, looking to see which is still unoccupied."

She deposited the cardboard box right in the middle of the desk and began to take out the files. Several looked thicker than he thought they should be, given that they'd only started their investigation.

Finished, she placed what appeared to be a jump drive on top of the files. The neat way they were stacked was in complete contrast to the rest of the desk, which overflowed with papers and folders. In truth, it looked as if the other detective had just stepped away from his desk to make a quick run to the vending machine, not a trip to Hawaii for the better part of two weeks.

Sitting down in the chair, Destiny found herself momentarily flustered when she discovered that her feet wouldn't reach the floor.

"Is your partner a giant?" she asked. Who would want their chair to be this high?

"Close," Logan allowed. He thought for a second, then said, "He's six-six." He watched as Destiny felt around along the bottom perimeter of the chair, looking for the height adjuster. "It's on the right," he told her. "The thing that adjusts your chair's height," he prompted.

"Oh. Thanks."

Finding the adjuster, she pressed hard and suddenly found herself dropping down, seat and all, like a stone.

The action jarred her, and it took a couple of moments for Destiny to start to feel all her individual parts back in working order.

"Don't mention it." His grin grew wider still. And more inviting. He had to be some lady-killer when he got going, she couldn't help thinking. That smile of his could definitely melt a rock at close range. "Anything I can do to help."

She merely nodded in response, not trusting herself to speak.

"Oh, and speaking of help..." he interjected, his voice deliberately trailing away.

"Yes?" she asked guardedly.

"As soon as you're settled in, I want to ask you a few questions," he told her.

What was it about this man that had her reacting so defensively? And heating so quickly? "What kind of questions?" she asked.

"About your sister's social life."

Oh. He was talking about the case. That was all right, then. She relaxed a little—but not all that much. "I've already put together a file addressing that." She took it from the pile and placed it on his desk.

"Of course you did," Logan said more to himself than to her.

This woman didn't need his help to be detached, he thought. She needed his help in staying in contact with her human side. And while he was at it, he needed to get her to relax a little. He could *feel* her tension.

"I'm not much on reading," he finally told her after a beat. For now, he ignored the file she'd pushed toward him, preferring the personal touch. "Why don't you just tell me what you wrote, and I'll listen?"

"You're not much on reading," she repeated in disbelief.

If he noticed her reaction, he gave no indication. Instead, he merely shook his head in response. "Not really."

She stared at him. "You're serious?"

"Why?" he asked her innocently, doing an excellent job of hiding his amusement. It was his way of trying to get her to loosen up. In his experience, this was the only way to work a case without letting it get to you. Because if you allowed cases to get to you, it was only a matter of time before they became your undoing, and then you weren't good to anyone, least of all yourself. "Don't I look like I'm serious?"

What he looked like was a guy who didn't have a care in the world—except where his next romantic interlude was coming from.

She wondered if she could appeal to Sean and ask him if anyone else could work on the investigation with her. But then she remembered that technically, she wasn't really supposed to be working on this at all and the investigation belonged to this laid-back detective who seemed more interested in wordplay than in solving six homicides.

She pressed her lips together. Logan Cavanaugh *had* to be better than she thought he was. Otherwise, last name or not, he would be out on his butt. According to what she knew about Brian Cavanaugh, he was a good man who was always there for his men and he didn't suffer idiots. So this all just had to be an act on Logan's part.

Why?

With a sigh, Destiny resigned herself to the fact that it was either work with Logan or return to the bleachers and watch the investigation into her sister's death unfold from the sidelines.

There was absolutely no way she was about to do that. So, for better or worse, she was stuck with the man.

"My mistake," she murmured. "You look serious." And with that, she launched into a summary of what she had entered into the file he wasn't opening.

Chapter 7

There was one thing wrong with the summation that Destiny had given him regarding her sister's social life. For the most part, it involved the past. The present was covered only in generalities. There was no mention of actual names. Was that because there were too many— or because she didn't know any?

"Do you know the names of any of your sister's current friends?" he asked, cutting in when she paused for a breath.

Destiny flushed. "I used to."

God but she hated admitting that.

Once upon a time she and Paula had been closer than two shadows on the wall. But then things began to change. Maybe Paula had seen her as too much of a mother figure and not enough as a sister-confidante. That had come about because she'd been the one left in charge, despite the fact that she wasn't really *that* much older than Paula. It happened out of necessity. Because their father had just walked out on them one day, their mother was forced to take any work she could to pay the bills and hold body and soul together. Most of the time, that took two jobs. Their mother was hardly ever home, which put the burden of responsibility on Destiny's shoulders. Paula grew to resent having to listen to her sister. Rebellion followed.

All in all, though, Paula had turned out all right. She'd gone to college, gotten a degree and went on to make a good career for herself.

And they were finally getting closer again—until this had happened.

"Our careers took us in different directions," she told him. "We moved around in different circles. But we were getting in touch more often again," she said with emphasis.

That wasn't the part he was interested in. "What kind of circles did your sister move around in?" he asked.

Her sister was a fundraiser, working for a charitable foundation. That put her in touch with a broad spectrum of people. Interesting people, Destiny imagined.

"Mainly they had to do with her job."

"Remind me what that was again," he said.

She'd mentioned it in passing in her summary and for a couple of minutes there, he'd been so busy just *watching* Destiny speak that he had lost the thread of what she was saying. That was probably when she'd mentioned her sister's job title.

"She was a fundraiser for the Children's Hospital of

Aurora," Destiny told him again. Was he trying to trip her up? Bait her? Or what? "And she was very good at it. Even in these rough times, she knew just how to coax major corporations and wealthy CEOs into making sizable donations to the hospital."

She knew that because other people had told her. Paula had never been one to sing her own praises, and she didn't talk all that much about work whenever they did get together. Considering all that grief they'd gone through in the middle years, Paula had turned out well and she was proud of her.

Damn it, this shouldn't have happened to you, Paula.

Keeping an angry wave of tears at bay, she said, "The hospital is breaking ground on an oncology wing, thanks to her efforts."

Logan saw the way she was struggling to keep herself under control. To keep the grief at arm's length. He couldn't help but feel sorry for her. But he knew that saying so would be the last thing that she would want to hear. Instead, he said the only thing he knew would be welcome.

"Your sister sounds like she was a really good person."

His remark surprised her. She felt a little salvo of pleasure spread from her stomach and radiate outward. A small smile curved her mouth.

"She was," she acknowledged. "Just not an overly talkative one. At least, not to me." Which really hurt because there'd been a time when they had shared *everything.* "I got the feeling she didn't think I'd understand about the relationship she was hiding from me.

Even when things got better between us, Paula would say that I was too straitlaced."

"Maybe she didn't want to tell you because the guy might have been married." He studied her face to see her reaction to the suggestion.

Defensive of her sister, she began to deny the assumption.

"Paula wouldn't have—" But then Destiny abruptly stopped her own protest. "Well, maybe she did," she amended ruefully. She shook her head. "That would explain why she'd gotten so secretive."

Damn it, Paula, married or not, you should have come to me anyway. Maybe that would have saved your life.

Logan nodded. It was beginning to make more sense. At least they had an avenue to explore. "Considering that she met a lot of powerful men in her line of work, we need to get a list of the hospital's top donors."

That, she knew, would go over like the proverbial lead balloon with Paula's supervisor. "Looking for a killer in that group'll certainly put a crimp into the hospital obtaining any more charitable donations," Destiny prophesized.

"Not if we handle it diplomatically," he replied. He saw the skeptical expression that came over the woman's face. "What? You don't think I can be diplomatic?" He guessed at what she was thinking. "Well, you're wrong. I can be very diplomatic if the situation calls for it," he assured her.

Destiny couldn't picture the man sitting across from

her monitoring every word he uttered. He just didn't seem the type.

"If you say so," she murmured.

"I do." And with that, he rose to his feet. The next moment, Logan was heading toward the door. Destiny had no choice but to move fast if she wanted to catch up to him and not be left behind. "Decided to come along?" he asked innocently.

Destiny shot him a dirty look, but she kept quiet. She felt it was better that way. For both of them.

"Terrible, terrible thing," Marcia Ruben lamented, shaking her head. A crumpled, damp handkerchief was balled up in one of her hands and she dabbed at her eyes periodically as tears insisted on sliding down the highly polished cheeks. Paula's supervisor looked more than a little upset by the news of her death. Paula, she'd already stated twice, had been her very best mover and shaker.

"I don't know what I'm going to do without her. She will be greatly missed by everyone." She took another pass at her cheeks with her handkerchief. "She was the best fundraiser I ever had, and I've been here for a long time," she said with a touch of melancholy. Whether it was for the dead woman or the fact that she had been here for years was anyone's guess. "If there was any way to get another dime out of someone, Paula was the one to do it. Donations just doubled in the short time she worked at the hospital. Given a chance, I'm sure she would have eventually raised enough money to double the size of the hospital. She truly had a gift. It seemed like once Paula got rolling, no one could say no to her."

"Someone obviously had." Destiny wasn't aware that she had said the bitter comment out loud until she heard it herself.

Mrs. Ruben pressed her lips together sadly. "Yes, of course," the heavyset woman readily agreed. "But for the life of me, I cannot begin to imagine how someone could have done that to Paula. Or why."

After telling the woman that Paula was found dead, Destiny had deliberately added that it was staged to look like a suicide. She'd said it to see the expression on Mrs. Ruben's face. There was only horror and disbelief. Either the woman was a very good actress, or she was on the level. Destiny leaned toward the latter.

Pulling herself together, Mrs. Ruben looked from one to the other. "How is it I can help you?"

"We'd like to see a list of the people she approached for donations," Logan told her politely but without any fanfare.

Nonetheless, the woman's small brown eyes widened in stunned disbelief.

"You think that one of them had something to do with Paula's murder? That's impossible," she protested with feeling. "These are people who move around in upper-class circles, who give to the less fortunate—"

She sounded as if she was winding herself up for a long speech. Destiny was quick to head her off.

"We're just trying to follow up every possible avenue, Mrs. Ruben, in the hopes of stumbling onto something that might give us a clue to her killer's identity." She watched the woman's face closely as she added, "We believe that Paula knew her killer."

"How can you be sure?" Mrs. Ruben asked, bewildered.

"There was no sign of a struggle," Logan explained. "Nothing was tossed around. There were no scratches on the vic—on Paula. And no signs of any skin under her nails. She didn't get a chance to fight whoever did this to her. That's because this man caught her off guard."

The woman still appeared rather skeptical. "At the same time, I don't want to insult any of these donors."

"We won't tell them that the list came from you," Logan promised with a sensual smile that seemed to melt the older woman's heart, not to mention her knees.

"Think of it as doing something for Paula," Destiny urged, feeling as if she was moving in for the kill after Logan had softened the woman up.

Mrs. Ruben nodded vigorously. "Yes, of course. For Paula." She wiped away more tears as she turned toward the computer on her desk. "I believe I have the latest list right here. Ah, yes, here it is."

Pulling it up on her screen, the woman hit the print key on her keyboard. The grinding, somewhat labored sound of a machine coming to life was immediately heard from across the aisle. The old printer noisily spit out three pages of names, as well as the companies they were associated with and addresses to go with them.

Since she was the one standing closest to the printer, Destiny gathered together the pages and brought them over to Logan.

"Twenty-six names," she said, looking at Mrs. Ruben.

"Are these all the people she contacted in the last six months?"

"Yes." She bobbed her head up and down, her short, straight hair moving back and forth against her jawline. "Please, tread lightly with these people," she begged. "I don't want them taking offense and withdrawing their pledges." Her voice lowered after a moment's hesitation and the woman said, "I'm afraid they can be very thin-skinned."

"As far as they'll be concerned," Logan told her, "we'll just be asking them if they thought that Paula seemed preoccupied lately, or if she behaved as if something was wrong."

Mrs. Ruben sighed and shook her head. "They'll probably say no. I know that I never saw her looking happier than these last few weeks. She looked as if she was harboring sunbeams."

That, Destiny thought, was the perfect way to describe the Paula she knew and loved. As if she was keeping sunbeams inside of her.

Now it was up to her to find out who put those sunbeams out.

It seemed to Destiny over the course of the next five hours that she was hearing a mantra being repeated over and over again. Every person on the list whom they spoke to expressed shock and dismay at hearing that someone "so young and vital like Paula was murdered." No one could imagine someone doing something so cold-blooded and cruel.

The tall, thin, angular CEO of Practical Engineering, Jacob Deering, asked, "Do you have any suspects in mind?"

"None yet," Logan responded, fielding the question quickly because he was afraid that Destiny might be too honest in her answer.

None of the people they questioned were informed that she was the victim's sister, and he wanted to keep it that way. Nor had they been informed that he and the other investigator thought that Paula's lover might have been responsible for her death.

"Which is why we're going down the list of all the major contributors she dealt with," Logan continued. "Since she spent most of her time around people who could make a difference in building up the hospital's resources, we were hoping that Paula might have said something to you that would send us looking in the right direction for her killer."

The man shook his head. He appeared to be genuinely saddened by the news of her death. "I'm afraid I can't be of any help there. But what I can do is make sure her memory is kept alive by making a personal donation to the hospital in her memory," Deering told them, taking out his checkbook from the center drawer of his desk.

Logan saw the look in Destiny's eyes. She was wondering the same thing he was. Was this donation being made out of a sense of guilt, or was he being honest in wanting to honor Paula's memory?

It was impossible to tell.

Tearing off the check, the CEO of the engineering company who had been high on Paula's list held it out to them. "If you could see that the hospital gets this money—"

"I'm afraid we don't have the actual authority to—" Logan began to demur, but Destiny stepped in and accepted the check.

"We'll be sure to bring it to Mrs. Ruben, her immediate superior," she assured Deering. Then, looking at Logan, she deliberately added, "We did tell Mrs. Ruben that we were going to check in with her late this afternoon."

This was the first he'd heard of it—most likely because she'd just made it up. But for the time being, she was his partner, and that meant backing up her play no matter what. So he did.

"Right. I forgot." Logan kept the charade alive and waited until they were on their way out back to the elevator. "What the hell was that?" he asked once they were alone.

"Well, it's hard to pass up a donation," she told him with a careless shrug. And then her expression turned shrewd. "And this way, we have a sample of his handwriting—in case there's anything in her apartment to match it to." When he looked at her blankly, she spelled it out for him. "Like a love letter."

Logan snorted. Was that it? "Men don't write love letters these days," he pointed out.

"Men like you who don't want to put anything in writing don't write love letters," she readily agreed, getting on the elevator ahead of him. "But an old-fashioned man might."

Where had that come from? "What makes you think

we're looking for an old-fashioned man?" he asked as they rode down.

"I don't, but a lot of these men have held down their positions for a number of years, making them older, and there's no sense in ruling that out yet, is there?" The way she asked, the question was rhetorical. "If we don't know who we're looking for, we have to take all the different options into consideration."

He didn't see anything to argue with. "You have a point," he agreed.

"Yeah, well, I just wish I had an answer," Destiny said, more to herself than to him. The doors opened on the ground floor and she all but charged out. "C'mon," she tossed over her shoulder, "we've still got more names on this list."

For someone who'd slept on her desk last night, she seemed to have an incredible amount of energy, Logan thought darkly as he followed in her wake.

"How about a drink?" he suggested. They'd finally talked to their last donor—with no luck—and it was the tail end of a very long, long day. Evening was flirting with the darkening sky, and he was ready to put down his shield for the night.

But Destiny shook her head in response to his offer. "I don't drink," she told him. "I find that it clouds the mind."

"It also helps unclench your jaw," he told her pointedly.

She instantly squared her shoulders. "My jaw's not clenched," she retorted.

"You don't see it from my vantage point." He held his hands up, knowing she would take offense. "Look, you can't deny that if you were any stiffer, you could double as a landing field. Take a break. Relax. In the morning we'll review our notes and maybe get a fresh perspective on things," he told her. "But that's not going to happen if you don't go home and get some sleep."

Maybe because she'd been left in charge so early in her life, but she had never liked being told what to do, and she balked at it now.

"Don't worry, I'll get some sleep," she told him dismissively.

He wasn't placated. "On a surface that doesn't involve steel or wood," he told her pointedly. And then he smiled a smile that she was certain someone must have told him was boyish and charming—and while it was both those things, she also found it annoying. "I personally recommend dinner, a drink and a hot shower."

"Good, then you can eat, drink and wash," she told him.

"Don't make me get tough, Richardson," he warned. There was a glint in Logan's eyes that she couldn't quite read.

Destiny thought about ignoring him, but she had a feeling that he wasn't going to drop this until he saw her getting up and leaving the precinct.

Okay, if that was the way he wanted to play it, she could do that. She could leave. But she wasn't going to go home. She wanted to go back to her sister's apartment and see what she could find there now that she had something to look for—a love letter or a note, or some sort of communication that could give her more of a hint as to just who had killed her sister.

Or, at the very least, maybe she could discover the identity of the person her sister had been involved with before everything had fallen so ignobly apart.

"Okay. I'll go home," she agreed docilely.

This was too easy. Logan eyed her suspiciously. "Okay?" he echoed. "Just like that?"

"Just like that," she repeated innocently. She smiled at him, doing her best to seem guileless. "You're very persuasive."

He laughed, shaking his head. "And you must think I'm very dumb."

"No, on the contrary," she told him. "I think you're very smart and you make a lot of sense." She looked down at the outfit she'd had on now for close to forty-eight hours. "Besides, I *am* beginning to feel like I smell a little gamey in this outfit," she told him. "I could stand to take a hot shower, maybe eat a sandwich and then get some rest. I feel dead on my feet," she confessed with just the right note of sincerity to sell this.

Logan's expression was impassive as he appraised her. For just a moment, his mind had conjured up the image of her naked, with the hot water hitting her body. It took him a long moment to tear his mind away. When he did, he nodded at what she'd just said. "Nice to hear you being reasonable."

She shot him a wide smile. "Maybe you're just rubbing off on me."

"I'll walk you to your car," he told her once they'd reached the ground floor.

"Not necessary," Destiny protested, but only marginally since she knew he expected it. If she made too much of a big deal about his walking her to her car, he might suspect that she wasn't going home the way she'd told him.

"Humor me," he said.

"You're the primary on this," she responded, symbolically waving a white flag.

So he walked her to her car, and under his watchful eye she got in behind the steering wheel and turned her ignition key. The car was instantly ready to peel out. Instead, she slowly eased out of her parking spot.

Using her rearview mirror, she could still see Logan watching her as she pulled out of the parking lot.

Destiny didn't let go of the breath she was holding until she had gone more than a mile. Remaining vigilant, she saw no sign of his vehicle following hers.

She'd made good her escape.

Releasing a deep, cleansing breath, she turned her car toward Paula's apartment.

Chapter 8

The yellow police tape was still up. Just as she'd hoped, the police guard was gone.

Destiny tried not to focus on the tape as she ducked under it. Just seeing it there, before the door of the apartment where Paula had lived, created an eerie, oppressive sensation in the middle of her chest.

Using her key, Destiny let herself into the apartment, then eased the door closed behind her.

Only then did she reach for the light switch and turn it on. The moment she did, she jumped, startled. Her gun was in her hand in less than a heartbeat despite the fact that her heart was beating fast enough to break the sound barrier.

"Easy, it's just me," Logan said to her, his hands up as he took a couple of steps toward her. And then, he slowly dropped them to his sides, watching her with awe. "My God, that's the fastest I've ever seen anyone draw their weapon. You should enter some sort of competition. You'd win, hands down—no pun intended," he tacked on.

Destiny drew in a deep breath, trying to steady her nerves. For a split second, she'd thought she'd stumbled across her sister's killer.

"What the *hell* are you doing here?" she demanded, holstering her weapon. It took all she could do to keep her hands from shaking.

"Same thing as you," Logan answered mildly. Actually, that wasn't true. He was here to see what she'd look for, fairly certain that left on her own, she wasn't all that keen about sharing what she found.

"I could have shot you," she cried. Didn't he realize that? Why had he been there, in the dark like some kind of creature of the night?

"But you didn't," Logan countered. "I like to look on the bright side," he added.

"How did you know I'd come here?" she asked. There was no other way to interpret his standing there in the dark like that. He'd been lying in wait for her, confident that she was going to show up, even though she'd told him she was going home.

"Just a hunch." Because she was obviously waiting for more, he elaborated. "You had me going for a while—until you said that I was the primary."

"Well, you are," she said. It came out almost like an accusation.

"It was more the way you said it," he amended. Logan shook his head. "It came out much too docile for you."

"What are you, an expert on me now?" Destiny stared at him, completely mystified. "You've only known me for, what, a day?"

"Almost two," he corrected, as if that explained it all. "And sometimes, you just know things." He smiled at her with an air of satisfaction that immediately got under her skin. "I would have done the same in your shoes."

Her eyes narrowed as she tried to understand. Was he drawing parallels between them? Or was he just trying to get her to drop her guard?

Don't hold your breath, Cavanaugh.

"So exactly what are you saying? That I'm just like you?"

"Oh, God, I hope not." He said it with such feeling that just for a split second, she believed him. "What fun would that be?"

Was that how he viewed his job? This investigation? As fun? Was he *that* irreverent?

"I wasn't aware that we were supposed to be having fun," she said cynically.

"You create little pockets of it along the way," he told her, and she had the feeling that despite the easygoing smile on his lips, Logan was absolutely serious. "Otherwise, this job'll eat you alive."

For now, she let that go. "How did you get here ahead of me?" she asked. "I drove away with you still standing in the parking lot, watching me leave."

"I took a shortcut," he told her. "Besides, I have the car with the pretty little dancing lights and the siren I can turn on whenever I'm stuck in traffic."

"What would you have done if I hadn't come here?" she challenged.

"Oh, but you did, and I figured it was a pretty safe bet from where I was standing. So," he said, getting down to business, "what is it that we're going to be looking for?"

For a second, the private part, the part that had always been protective of Paula and their mother before that, wanted to defiantly dig in. But what was the point? Protecting Paula no longer really mattered. What mattered was not letting whoever had done this to her sister get away with it. And if that person was the serial killer the way she believed him to be, well, then finding him and making him pay for all this as well as keeping him from killing anyone else would at least in some minor way give some sort of meaning to Paula's death.

She shrugged her shoulders in answer to his question. "Something. Anything."

"Well, that's really pinning it down." He laughed shortly. "In other words, we'll 'know' it when we see it."

"Yes." And then, as he began to head toward Paula's bedroom to conduct a second, more thorough search through her closet and bureau drawers, Destiny recalled something. She addressed his back. "When we were kids, Paula used to keep a diary. I don't know if she still does—still did," Destiny corrected herself, still struggling with the fact that she had to use the past tense. "But it's worth looking for."

The first wave of crime scene investigators had taken the laptop they'd found—presumably Paula's—back to the precinct. The technician who had gone over it—

Brenda Cavanaugh—the chief of D's daughter-in-law—was exceptionally thorough.

"They didn't find anything besides her daily schedule on her computer," Logan told her.

That was no surprise. "They wouldn't have," Destiny told him, beginning her search in the kitchen. "In some ways, Paula was kind of old-fashioned. She liked the thought of writing personal things down using a pen and paper." Her mouth curved just a little as she remembered her sister's words. "Paula said she thought it was more 'romantic' that way."

Logan paused and glanced in her direction. "Sounds like she was a really unique person."

Destiny suppressed the heartfelt sigh that rose in her throat.

God, but she was going to miss Paula. Even though they hadn't gotten together all that much and Paula had her own set of friends, friends that she gathered she, Destiny, didn't have all that much in common with, she would miss the *idea* of Paula, the comforting feeling that Paula was somewhere in the world with her. Now she had to accept the cold, hard fact that she would never see Paula again no matter how much she wanted it or how hard she wished for it.

Her baby sister was gone, and she couldn't do anything about it.

But the next best thing would be finding Paula's killer and making him pay for this. It was all she had to cling to.

"Yeah, she was," Destiny agreed in a small, strained voice.

With that, she turned back to the kitchen and began opening all the drawers, checking all the shelves, including the refrigerator and the freezer. Paula wouldn't have put it somewhere obvious, not since Destiny had accidentally stumbled across it under her sister's mattress when she was changing the sheets years ago. Because Paula had become secretive and uncommunicative, she'd read a couple of pages—just enough to discover that David Chesnee had been Paula's first and that Paula had been disappointed because there were no shooting stars, no wild feelings of fulfillment.

That was as far as she'd gotten before Paula walked in and caught her. Absolutely livid, Paula didn't talk to her for a month.

With all her heart, she wished that Paula wasn't talking to her now. That it was just anger and not death that separated them.

Pressing her lips together, she blinked several times to keep back the tears. She had no time for tears.

Destiny moved about the kitchen methodically, carefully going through one section at a time. But the result was still the same. She was coming up empty. The diary—if it existed—wasn't wrapped in a plastic bag and tucked in the recesses of the refrigerator. It wasn't in a plastic case on the bottom of the freezer. And it definitely wasn't in any of the cabinets or the small pantry.

Stumped, Destiny was on the verge of admitting that her sister no longer kept something as old-fashioned as a diary when her foot hit the bottom of the refrigerator. The long, rectangular plastic section just beneath the refrigerator door came loose.

She looked down at it and frowned. She had the same problem with the one in her apartment. Having removed it to clean the coils in the front, she'd found that reattaching the section was far trickier than she had anticipated. It kept coming loose, bedeviling her. In Paula's case, Destiny doubted that she'd taken it off to clean the coils. Cleaning had never exactly been high on her sister's priority list. Most likely she—

Destiny stopped and stared at the loose section as if seeing it for the first time.

The next moment, she dropped to her knees in front of the refrigerator. Pushing the rectangular section out of the way, Destiny reached beneath the refrigerator as far as she could. Fingers outstretched, she felt around.

Which was just the way Logan found her, hunkered down, flat on the floor with her arm underneath the refrigerator. Not knowing what to think, only that she was lying on the floor, he rushed over to her. Logan quickly got down on the floor beside her.

"Richardson, you okay?" he asked, concerned.

She could have sworn that her fingertips had just barely brushed against something. Positive it had to be the diary, she focused on coaxing it out and was oblivious to whatever Cavanaugh was saying.

The next moment, a pair of strong hands pulled her back, away from the refrigerator. And then, just as if she was some weightless rag doll, she was off the floor and in his arms. How she'd gotten turned around, she wasn't sure. Just as she wasn't sure how he'd managed to get her up without tearing off the arm that had been snaked under the refrigerator. The only thing she *did* know was that there were less than two inches between them and she found herself looking into those magnetic green eyes of his.

Her stomach tightened into a knot. He was much too close.

There was concern written all over his face. "What happened?" he asked. Then, before she had a chance to utter a single word, Logan urgently demanded, "Are you all right?"

For just a split second, as her breath struggled to move back into her lungs, Destiny was utterly at a loss for words. Her mind had gone numb. But not her body. Her body felt as if a blanket of heat was wrapped all around her.

And then, with a determined surge of strength, she pulled herself together. The heat receded and her senses returned. Her mind was functioning again.

"Yeah, I'm fine, except that I think my right arm is longer than my left one now." The sarcastic tone faded as she told him, "I think I felt something." Turning, she pointed to the refrigerator. "It's under there. I'm sure of it."

"It's probably just dust—or the dead carcass of a rodent," he guessed.

She blocked the latter image from her mind. She'd seen more than her share of dead bodies—Paula's included—but a dead rat made her squeamish.

"No," she insisted, "this felt like something straight and flat—like the edge of one of those black-and-white copybooks. You know the kind I'm talking about." She looked at him expectantly, as if, for this one moment, he could access her thoughts.

A black-and-white copybook could have easily been turned into a diary, he thought. At any rate, since she seemed so positive, it was worth a look.

"Stand back," he told her. "If it's there, I'll get it out."

Destiny shook her head. "Your arm's too big to angle under the refrigerator," she told him. "You'll only get stuck."

He was way ahead of her there. "Wasn't planning to go under it," he said.

And then, very slowly, grasping the side of the refrigerator closest to him, he moved it as far as he could. Positioning himself on the other side of the appliance, he repeated the process. Logan went back and forth several times until he'd finally succeeded in "walking" the refrigerator away from the wall and out into the kitchen proper.

It was all the encouragement Destiny needed. Hopping onto the counter, Destiny slid her bottom along the slick tile. Perched on the edge, she looked down into the space he'd created.

She could see a corner of a black-and-white book. Triumph surged through her. "I was right. It's a copybook."

He looked around the refrigerator he'd just taken for a dance. "She really had trust issues, didn't she?" he marveled.

Now, there was an ironic observation, given that they were about to read her sister's most intimate, personal thoughts.

"Obviously justified," Destiny retorted defensively for the sister who could no longer defend herself.

Scrambling over to one side, Destiny lowered herself into the small space. There wasn't really much room between the appliance and the wall. She had just enough space to bend her knees. Sinking down as far as she could go, Destiny once more felt around.

Tapping into her patience—it was more difficult than she'd anticipated—Destiny finally managed to secure the book using just the edge of her fingertips. She moved it closer and closer to her until she could finally wrap her fingers around one corner.

She didn't like what she was feeling.

The book was wet, as if the refrigerator had just recently leaked on it—or it had been dropped into something wet before someone slipped it back beneath the refrigerator.

But if that was the case, why go through all that trouble if she was dead?

Unless she hadn't been dead at the time.

But then, if there was something in the diary someone else didn't want coming to light, why not just take the diary and destroy it?

It didn't make sense.

Still, there might be some clue they could get off one of the pages. With a less than triumphant sigh, she placed the rippled copybook on the counter next to her point of entry.

Seeing what he assumed was the diary, Logan marveled, "Son of a gun, you're right."

Trying to vault out of the enclosure, to her dismay

Destiny discovered that her upper-body strength was not as good as she would have liked. Two more attempts to propel herself out of the small space failed before she finally turned her eyes toward Logan.

Logan appeared to be entertained by her unsuccessful attempts to get out of the small, enclosed area. His smile was annoying and far sexier than she would have been willing to admit.

"Can I get you something?" he offered. "A ladder maybe?" The suggestion was followed by the sound of his laughter.

Ordinarily, Destiny might have enjoyed the deep, somewhat sensual rumbling sound. But right now, she just felt exasperated.

"Okay, a little help here." It was just short of a demand.

"Sure thing," he said obligingly. "All you had to do was just ask."

"Otherwise you'd just stand there for the rest of the night?" she asked.

He looked at her as if she'd gone simpleminded. "And get my head bitten off? Nope. I find that with women, to stay on the safe side, you have to wait until they make a request. *Then* you can come riding to the rescue."

"Let's get this clear. This is *not* riding to my rescue," she informed him.

"It's not?" Logan said innocently. "Then what is it?"

"This is just giving me a helping hand," she fired back through gritted teeth.

He gave the impression of weighing her words. Finally, Logan lifted his shoulders in a careless shrug and said, "Whatever you say."

He was still laughing at her, even though there wasn't a sound. Losing patience, she said, "Get me out of here, Cavanaugh!"

"Your wish is my command," he assured her.

The next moment, he put his hands on each side of her rib cage. With what seemed to be a minimum of effort, Logan easily lifted her out of the narrow space behind the refrigerator.

Bringing her up and over the counter, his hands slipped a fraction of an inch and he wound up holding her along the sides of her breasts.

If that wasn't bad enough, somehow, as he brought her over the top, she'd wound up being *much* too close to Logan. For all intents and purposes, she was almost intimately close.

In response, her heart had begun hammering again and then that damn breath of hers had all but disappeared for a second time. But this time, exertion had nothing to do with it.

Proximity did.

When Logan set her down, the counter was against her back and he was pretty much against her front—or so it felt to her.

The world seemed to suddenly freeze in time for a moment—except that there was no ice, just heat. Lots and lots of heat, and it flashed back and forth between them with an intensity that would have taken her breath away—had she had any to take.

What the hell was going on with her? The question

came on the heels of her reaction. Her *atypical* reaction. For a second—for just the briefest of seconds—she felt a very real, very strong temptation—to kiss Logan.

His lips were less than the breadth of an eyelash away from hers. All she had to do was rise up on her toes, tilt her face up to his and there they were.

The temptation was enormous.

Especially when she felt Logan's breath along her face. The ache inside of her, hot and strong, came out of nowhere.

Destiny tried to tell herself that it came out of the emptiness she was experiencing because of Paula's death, but that still didn't make it go away or even lessen its intensity by so much as a fraction.

The longing grew.

Her pulse began to race as the urge multiplied, growing by leaps and bounds until it all but threatened to swallow her up.

What would be the harm? her conscience whispered, turning on her. *What would be the harm, just this once, to give in?*

Chapter 9

Damn, but he was tempted. *Really, really* tempted.

If they weren't working together, if they weren't focused on trying to find who had killed her sister and possibly several other women, Logan would have felt freer to indulge his curiosity.

But he *was* walking a tightrope here.

It was up to him to make perfectly sure there were no missteps with this investigation so that if they actually found a viable suspect, the case wouldn't be tossed out of court on some irritating-as-hell technicality.

Like tainted evidence.

Would kissing a fellow investigator in an unplanned moment of extreme attraction and overwhelming weakness be considered the basis for undermining such an investigation? Logan would have been the first to admit that he wasn't really clear on the concept, but all the same, he didn't think so.

Or was it that he didn't *want* it to be so?

Oh, the hell with it, he thought with a surge of impatience as he symbolically threw up his hands in frustration.

The next moment those hands framed her face—odd how delicate she actually felt, considering that she came on like some indestructible gangbuster.

And then, anticipation coursing through his veins, Logan lowered his head and contact was made.

Extremely pleasant contact.

No, on second thought, Logan amended, the word *pleasant* had no place here. Mainly because the kiss wasn't *pleasant*. It was overwhelming, breath stealing, earthmoving and a whole host of other descriptions meant to convey something incredible, something *leagues* out of the ordinary. *Pleasant* was a word meant to describe an old-fashioned drawing room comedy or a semicold beer—rather than a preferable completely cold one. *Pleasant* was a joke that made you smile, not laugh out loud.

This kiss made him want to *shout*.

Logan could almost *feel* his blood rushing through his veins and definitely could feel his adrenaline increasing in tempo. As for his heart, it was hammering so hard, he was surprised it hadn't broken through his rib cage and fallen at her feet.

Without fully meaning to, he deepened the kiss, and lost himself in the revelry.

Oh, no, no, no!

What was she doing? Destiny silently demanded. Why was she kissing him back? She should be the one calling a halt to this, the one setting an example, not melting in his arms.

But the plain truth of it was, despite the fact that she knew all the reasons she shouldn't be doing this, she knew of only one reason why she should.

Because she wanted it to continue.

Wanted to just lose herself in this man with the lethal lips. Wanted, just for a moment, not to think about *anything*. Not death, not being alone.

Not even Paula.

For this sliver of a moment in time she wanted just to *feel*. To absorb hot sensations and not make excuses or place them into neatly labeled categories.

Was that so wrong?

Yes, when it interferes with getting your job done. When it interferes with getting Paula's killer.

She had a dozen arguments against what was happening. And only one for it. It made her feel human. More than that, it made her *feel* something, and she hadn't been in that particular place in her life for a very long while now. Long before she had discovered Paula's lifeless body in the tub.

The desire that sprang up within her was fierce, intense, and it took her by surprise as it barreled through her.

Stop! Destiny ordered herself. There was too much for her to do to dally like this, to allow this sort of thing to happen.

And yet…

Oh, and yet this was so delicious....

With effort steeped in the strict discipline that had seen her through so many difficult phases of her life, Destiny finally managed to pull her head back.

For a moment, they were both silent, looking at one another, trying to gauge the other's thoughts and finding that they couldn't.

Right now, Destiny secretly admitted that she was having trouble gauging her own thoughts, much less his. And more than anything, she really wished her damn pulse would stop racing like that. It made her dizzy and breathless.

But then, so did he, she realized.

Get a grip. This isn't the time or the place!

"I think we'd better take a look at this copybook before we bag and tag it," she heard herself say to Logan as she awkwardly dropped her hands to her sides. Her voice, sounding hoarse to begin with, cracked by the time she came to the end of her statement.

Her eyes on his, she held her breath. She hadn't the slightest idea if he would pick up her cue—or demand to know if she was trying to lead him on and play him for a fool for some reason.

It seemed like an eternity later before Logan finally nodded.

"Makes sense," he agreed.

Only then did she realize that Logan was still holding her by the shoulders. The next moment, he released her.

Once that last contact was broken, Destiny suddenly felt unsteady—and alone again.

Taking a breath, she nodded at the refrigerator, standing now like a lone sentry in the middle of the tiny kitchen.

"We'd better push that back where it was. Otherwise, it might look suspicious. We're not supposed to be here," she reminded him in case he didn't understand why she wanted the appliance moved back against the wall.

It was the added explanation that brought a grin to his lips. "You just figured that out now?" he asked glibly.

Destiny resisted getting sucked into another round of trading remarks, even though for some reason the thought seemed oddly comforting to her. Maybe because that made it business as usual, or at least what seemed to be passing as usual between them.

Right now, she thought, looking down at the copybook, they might be holding the key to everything in their hands. Mentally, she crossed her fingers.

But the second she opened the copybook, Destiny felt her heart sink.

Despite the fact that it was definitely written in Paula's hand, the pages between the covers were warped and the ink was all but washed out thanks to the leak from the refrigerator. Water had penetrated the thicker cover and had gotten through to most of the pages, making them semi or completely illegible, depending on what section she turned to.

Nonetheless, she placed the copybook on the counter and carefully turned each page, doing her best not to let them shred beneath her fingertips.

Disappointed, Logan shook his head as he looked at

the halos of blue ink that seemed to brand each page to a greater or lesser degree.

"You're not going to get anything out of that," he told her. "You're just wasting your time."

Determined to find one viable scrap of *something,* Destiny was not about to give up.

"My time to waste," she said defiantly. "You're free to go home at any time, you know. You don't have to stay here waiting for me to get finished."

"I'm primary," he reminded her. "That means I'm responsible for you while we're working the case." He didn't add that he'd been told to keep an eye on her during the investigation. It didn't take a genius to know she would take offense at that.

"Not if you didn't know I was here," she pointed out. And if he hadn't played a hunch and shown up at the apartment, he *wouldn't* have known she was here.

His smile was amused—and damn annoying—as he said, "But I do."

Destiny sighed. Arguing with this man was like willingly banging her head against a wall—and just about as satisfying. Deciding to ignore him, she went back to carefully scanning each and every page.

She'd almost gone through the whole thin book when she saw it. A section that hadn't absorbed water from the leaking refrigerator.

And there was writing on it.

Every inch of her became alert as she squinted at the dry pages. There were still words missing, words that probably had gotten a little wet and then faded away when the paper dried. But she could make out a name. Just barely.

Her eyes widened. "Drake Simmons."

Because watching her turn pages threatened to put him to sleep, Logan had begun a second survey throughout the kitchen, going through spice jars at random, looking beneath the sink. The sound of her hushed voice had him looking up.

"What did you say?"

Beckoning him over, she waited until he was beside her and then she pointed to the top of the page that had caught her attention. She ran the tip of her finger beneath a line. "It looks like she wrote down 'Drake Simmons.'"

For a second, he couldn't recall where he'd seen the name before. And then it came to him. That was the last name on the list of contributors that Mrs. Ruben had given them.

Glancing over Destiny's shoulder at the copybook on the counter, he could make out the name—now that she'd said it. But nothing else, either before the name or after it, was even remotely clear.

Logan raised his eyes to hers. His were far less exhilarated than hers.

"Is she just mentioning that she has an appointment to see him, or did she make this notation because they had a date?" he asked.

Destiny shook her head. "I can't make out anything that would tell us," she said haplessly.

"When she kept a diary, was it just to chronicle who

she had a crush on, or was it like a miniautobiography?" he asked her.

Destiny wished with all her heart it was the former but she had to be honest.

"More like the latter. Paula liked rereading sections of it to see where her head was at at a particular time. I got the impression that her diary wasn't just to record the way she felt about things—or any one person. It was the sum total of her day-to-day activities."

"Great," he muttered. Then, curious, he asked, "Did you keep a diary like your sister?"

She shook her head. "I was too busy—and much too tired at the end of the day to come up with the energy to write. Why?" she asked.

Logan lifted his shoulders in a careless shrug, turning into the personification of innocence right in front of her eyes.

"No reason," he assured her. "Just curious."

Her gut told her that there was more to it than that, but it was safer all around not to push the subject. Maybe if she didn't, it would fade away.

Just like the effects of his kiss.

Yeah, good luck with that, she mocked herself. Because right now, she could still feel his lips on hers, and it was doing one hell of a number on the rest of her.

Destiny made a mental note not to let it happen again.

Having gleaned every single shred of information possible from her sister's body, the medical examiner released Paula's remains to her the next day. The doctor, a grandfatherly type who looked as if he was more suited to donning a Santa Claus costume and gathering small children onto his knee than meticulously dissecting bodies and then sewing them together again, looked at Destiny with kindness in his eyes. He was accustomed to working with her looking over his shoulder and asking questions, not having her as the deceased's next of kin. It made for a very awkward, uncomfortable situation.

"I'm really very, very sorry for your loss, Destiny," Raymond Mathews said in a low, sympathetic voice, his Deep South upbringing weaving itself around every syllable. "Doesn't seem like nearly enough to say, but I am."

She did her best to smile as she nodded her head. "Thank you," she murmured.

This was such an unnatural position for her to be in. She was ordinarily on the clinical end of things, not the emotional end. She felt guilty and angry and incredibly sad as she viewed her sister's reconstructed body.

The stitching, she noted, was exceptionally neat and small. Dr. Matthews had taken extra care to try to call as little attention as possible to the fact that her sister had been autopsied, and she appreciated it. Appreciated, too, though she had no idea how to express it, that rather than continue the investigation on his own while she was busy, Logan seemed to have opted to accompany her down to the M.E.'s terrain to reclaim her sister.

Logan watched her now, for the moment fading into the shadows. He'd sensed, despite her claims to the contrary and insisting that she was "fine," that Destiny could really use someone to lean on.

He was also fairly certain that his father's chief assistant was far too stubborn to admit as much. His suspicions were validated when, after telling him that he didn't need to do this, he saw a flicker of gratitude in her sky-blue eyes.

Which was why he also "tagged along," a silent but strong presence, when she went to make final arrangements at the funeral home.

Edward Michaels, the director of Michaels & Sons, the funeral home that Sean had referred her to, appeared momentarily surprised when she said that she didn't want the typical three-day viewing period for her sister.

"I want the funeral to take place tomorrow, so just do what you have to do to get my sister ready," she told the man.

"Why are you in such a hurry?" Logan commented in a low voice, meant only for her ears.

"I'm not," she bit off impatiently, then reined in her temper.

This wasn't Logan's fault. It wasn't anyone's fault—except for whoever had done this to Paula. She had to remember to keep her anger focused in the right direction and not let it flare the way it had been these past few days. She couldn't allow her normally even temper to be all over the map like this.

She lifted her shoulders in an indifferent shrug, letting them drop again. "She's dead. I don't want people staring at her."

Destiny couldn't remember the last time she'd felt so drained. Maybe never. The moment the medical examiner had released Paula's body to be transported, she'd gotten on the phone and called every number Paula had listed in her cell phone. She informed each and every one of the more than one hundred people of Paula's death, listened to their words of shock and condolences, then quietly told each person on the other end of her phone where and when the funeral services would be held.

Exhausted, she'd gone directly to the funeral home from there. Her shadow had insisted on accompanying her despite her protests. She was secretly grateful he had. She wasn't all that sure she was up to driving back to the precinct again.

And then, out of the blue, she thought of something.

Logan saw the startled expression on her face and automatically turned around. He expected to see someone walking into the chapel-quiet room.

But there was no one in it but the two of them. The director was still there, but he was just about to slip out of the room.

"What's the matter?" Logan asked her.

"I just realized that I'm going to have to hold a reception for the people who attend the funeral, aren't I? They're going to want to eat afterward." She closed her eyes, as if searching for strength. She wasn't given to hosting even intimate get-togethers over dinner, much less something on such a large scale.

Logan smiled. He might not be able to help her deal with the pain, but here at least he could provide her with the kind of help she needed.

"Don't worry," he assured her. "I can handle the reception for you."

Destiny looked at him, slightly bewildered. What was he saying? That he'd direct all the attending mourners to the local fast-food/take-out restaurant for her?

"You?" she echoed, waiting for him to explain further.

"Well, not me directly," he qualified with a laugh. Boiling eggs was a challenge for him. But it was all about networking and knowing where to turn. "But I can get this covered for you," he promised.

This new, enlarged family of his was turning out to be very handy. All he had to do in this case was call Andrew Cavanaugh. He was fairly certain he didn't even have to give the man all the particulars of the situation. The man's abilities to pull meals together—be they for four people or four hundred—were all but legendary.

On top of that, according to what his father told him, the former chief of police thoroughly enjoyed doing it. He'd heard that there was none better when it came to having everything ready at the same time as well as *on* time.

"You're telling me you have access to a fairy godmother?" she quipped. To her, holding a last-minute reception—and pulling it off with some amount of success—was in the realm of magic.

Logan grinned at her. She was beginning to find that grin more and more unsettling—as well as annoyingly appealing.

"Almost."

"With their own cooking show?" she added, because

as far as she was concerned, it would take a professional to pull this off. Everyone she called to tell them about Paula had sincerely promised to be there. Her sister's friends and coworkers were that affected by the news of her death.

"Even better," Logan told her. He paused for dramatic effect, though for the life of him he wouldn't have been able to say why helping her out both amused and pleased him as much as it did. "This is my father's brother's specialty. From what I'm told, you just have to tell him approximately how many people to expect and he'll take it from there."

Though she still found it hard to accept such effortless generosity, it was a tremendous relief.

"I'm not sure," she confessed. "Two hundred, two hundred and fifty." And if they all brought someone with them, that would make the number all but unmanageable.

Who was she kidding? If she were doing this, feeding four people would be unmanageable to her.

But Logan appeared completely unshaken by the fluctuating response. Instead, he merely nodded and said, "Hence the word *approximate*. Don't worry, 'Uncle' Andrew can handle it. The man loves a challenge, and from what I've heard he's never had a single occasion where he's run out of food or had to turn someone away. He's close to a miracle worker," he added without any fanfare.

There was just one small problem. "But he doesn't know me."

"Maybe not, but he knows me and I know you—as

does my dad." His eyes held hers. He could see another protest coming. It was obvious that the woman didn't like to be beholden to anyone. "Let me do this one thing for you," he said softly.

Damn it, there went her pulse again. At the most inopportune time, she thought in unbridled annoyance. What *was* it about Logan Cavanaugh that messed so badly with her inner peace?

"Okay," she heard herself saying. "If you think he won't mind—"

"He won't."

"—I'd really appreciate it," she concluded.

He was on his cell phone, calling his father, before she'd uttered the last word.

Chapter 10

Destiny stood off to the side of the living room, looking around at all the people here and throughout the first floor and the backyard. Earlier, they'd filled the small church beyond its capacity.

She'd had no idea that Paula had touched so many people. Her sister had certainly come a long way from the angry, rebellious teenager who insisted on arguing with her over everything at every turn. Paula had obviously gotten it together far better than she had, Destiny thought with no small pride. God knew she didn't know this many people.

The people she'd called to notify about her sister's funeral service had obviously called other people, and the small church where the service was held had gone from full to standing room only.

There, again, Logan had surprised her by coming

through for her. Although both she and Paula had had religious instructions as children, they'd drifted away from attending Sunday services or being part of any church in Aurora. She knew Paula would have wanted someone officiating over her funeral, and the thought of leaving it up to the funeral director hadn't really been what she'd wanted to do.

"How about my uncle Adam?" Logan had asked her when she'd told him the problem.

"What about your uncle Adam?" she'd said. She hadn't even known Logan *had* an uncle Adam, but that was obviously no longer the question. Why was he volunteering the man?

As it turned out, Father Adam Cavelli belonged to Logan's first family—the relatives he and his siblings had grown up believing were his father's brothers and sisters. Father Adam was a priest at St. Jude, a small, fifty-year-old church located on the far side of Aurora. When the hospital mix-up between his father and the real Sean Cavelli had come to light, the priest had made it clear that he was still their uncle, still loved them just the same as he had when they had been "the bratty Cavellis, driving saints crazy," and nothing would change that. He'd told them that he would continue to be available to them anytime, day or night.

It was when Logan told her that his uncle could take care of her sister's funeral service that she'd stared at her new partner in utter, fascinated disbelief.

"My God, Logan, you Cavanaughs are like one-stop shopping. Police protection, legal counsel, dinner and last rites—it's all taken care of in one neat little package. Unbelievable!"

"You might not want to say 'dinner' and 'last rites' in the same breath if you're talking around Uncle Andrew," Logan had advised. "He might not find it amusing."

Flustered, she'd murmured, "Right." There was no way she wanted to take a chance on insulting Andrew Cavanaugh, even accidentally.

So, thanks to Logan's efforts and, she was certain, in no small way Sean's input, she had both the funeral services and the reception that immediately followed all taken care of. That left her with very little to do— except to grieve.

No, damn it, you don't have time to wallow and indulge yourself, she silently upbraided herself now.

Paula's killer might be somewhere in this crowd of people, paying their last respects. Observing the effects of what he'd done. Getting high on the grief. She couldn't afford to let herself come apart. She couldn't fail Paula now. This was all she could still give Paula— her killer's head on a platter.

Standing next to her, Logan could feel Destiny tensing, and he automatically looked around to see if there was anything wrong. It was a large area to scan. The former chief of police had thrown open his doors— literally—and people drifted in and out, making use of not just the house but the patio and the garden beyond that.

Nothing seemed to stand out to him.

"What's wrong?" he asked Destiny. "Other than the obvious."

She took a deep breath before answering him, still carefully surveying the immediate area. "Her killer might be here."

Logan had his doubts about that. "I really don't think that—"

Impatient, she cut him off. "Think about it. The killer was someone Paula'd had a relationship with. Everyone listed on her cell phone told me they'd be here, and they are. Not only that, but they brought other people who knew Paula. Whoever she was involved with *had* to be on that cell phone list. Which means he's got to be here. I can feel it," she insisted.

Logan reconsidered. He supposed her argument had merit. Looking around again, he found the numbers to be almost overwhelming. If the killer was here, it was a matter of hiding in plain sight.

"So what do you want to do?" he asked Destiny.

Catching killers was a combination of luck and skill, she'd come to decide. Mainly luck.

"Mingle. Talk. Hopefully pick up on something." Right now, there was nothing else they could do.

"In other words, interact with the guests." He didn't see that as being any different from what one would expect a family member in this circumstance to do at a funeral reception. "Okay," he agreed.

Something in Logan's voice caught her attention. He was volunteering to join her. That wasn't what she'd had in mind. "I didn't mean that you had to do this, too."

There was no way she was getting rid of him, Logan

thought. Granted, Destiny was putting up a tough exterior, but he had three sisters. He knew an act when he saw one. Destiny was both fragile and vulnerable inside. She needed him.

"Two sets of ears are better than one," he told her philosophically. "Besides, I'm the—"

"Primary," she concluded for him. "Yes, I know." There was no note of exasperation in her voice the way there had been the other times. "Okay, 'Primary,'" she agreed. "Let's see what we can discover."

What she discovered was that, at least on the surface, Paula apparently had no enemies. Everyone thought the world of her. And, despite the fact that there were several people Paula had considered to be *very* close friends, not one of them had a clue who her new lover had been. Unlike all the other times she was seeing someone, this time she'd become very secretive, and for the most part she seemed exceedingly happy.

Until the night she'd sent out her last text message to her close group of friends.

Destiny felt as if they were going around in circles. It was getting incredibly frustrating for her.

"Why don't you take a break?"

The suggestion came from a deep voice behind her. Turning, she found herself looking up into Andrew Cavanaugh's slightly lined, kindly face. His eyes reminded her of Logan's, she realized.

"A break?" she echoed, not really sure what the former police chief and present-day miracle worker was telling her.

Andrew smiled at her knowingly. "I've been a cop

long enough to know when someone's on the job. Take a break for the rest of the evening," he advised. "Don't worry, you'll find your sister's killer."

"How can you know that?"

"Because I also know 'abnormally stubborn' when I see it," he told her. "You have that look in your eyes. You'll find the killer," he repeated. "Just not today. Today is for your sister."

"So is finding her killer," Destiny countered.

Andrew laughed, shaking his head. "Like I said, stubborn. Make sure there's something left of you after you find the killer," he advised, looking at her pointedly. "Otherwise, he would have gotten two victims, not just one."

"He's right, you know," Logan told her as they watched the senior Cavanaugh retreat into the kitchen to tend to something else he was making.

Destiny sighed, then moved her shoulders in what seemed like a semishrug. "I know."

Logan wasn't fooled. He was beginning to tune in to her body language pretty well.

"That doesn't mean you're going to take his advice to heart, though, does it?"

Her first impulse was to deny his assumption, but it didn't seem quite right to lie to Logan after everything he'd done for her. For Paula. So she shook her head and told him the truth.

"Nope." With that, she began to walk away. She had people to talk to. Lots and lots of people.

Logan sighed and picked up his pace. If she was determined to do this, he wouldn't let her do it alone.

Along with her friends and coworkers at the non-profit hospital, a great many of the people whom Paula had gotten to contribute to the hospital over the years were at the reception, as well. And, it seemed to Destiny, they too felt saddened that Paula had been cut down decades before her time.

Even so, when she saw Drake Simmons, the CEO whose name she had managed to make out in the otherwise useless diary, talking to another one of the mourners, Destiny felt her pulse accelerate.

Approaching him, she forced herself to thank him for taking time out of his busy schedule to attend the service. After introducing her to Howard Palmer, his assistant, he went on to express his shock and dismay.

"Terrible thing." Drake Simmons repeated the words with such feeling Destiny was convinced that he was about to make some sort of a confession to her. Perhaps take her aside and tell her about his affair with Paula. But the man made no effort to speak to her alone, saying what he had to say in front of his assistant and Logan. "Part of me still can't believe that someone so young, so lovely and full of life is really dead."

Was it her imagination, or did his voice tremble just then?

The CEO looked at her for a moment, then confided sadly, "I just saw her recently."

How did you see her? Did you see her in the bathtub, her wrists slashed because you slashed them? Did you watch the life oozing out of her? Destiny did her best to look curious so as to urge the man on with his narrative.

"Oh?"

"Yes," he told her, his voice taking on a somber tone. "We met in my office. I wanted to give her my company's contribution personally. That children's hospital she worked for, she was their brightest star," he said with feeling. "I really don't know what they're going to do without her. Usually the people behind fundraisers turn out to be irritating, incessantly asking for more and more contributions until you wind up slamming the door in their faces—figuratively, of course."

"Of course," Destiny echoed, a smile pasted on her face.

"But Paula was different," he told her. "She made you *want* to give and give until it almost hurt." He laughed softly to himself, as if reliving some private little joke the two of them had shared. And then he cleared his throat, coming back around to the present. "I don't know about anyone else," he said, deliberately raising his voice as he looked around the immediate area, "but I'm sending a personal contribution to the hospital foundation she worked for in her memory. I hope everyone else does the same."

Destiny smiled broadly and nodded. "That's extremely nice of you, Mr. Simmons. I'm sure that Mrs. Ruben will be very grateful and will appreciate your generosity. Just as she appreciated Jacob Deering's contribution."

Simmons looked a little annoyed to be sharing the spotlight with someone else, but then a sadness seemed to overtake him as he said, "It's the very least I can do for Paula."

It was only because she hadn't wanted to turn her

sister's wake into a spectacle that Destiny refrained from verbally cornering Drake Simmons and firing questions at him until she got him to confess his affair.

More important than that, she didn't want to publicly drag Paula's name through the mud, and that would be what calling Simmons out about his affair would amount to.

The moment she was alone with Logan, she told him exactly what she was thinking. "That sounds like someone with a guilty conscience to me."

Logan tried to get her to temper her assessment by presenting another take on the scene. "Or like someone who's genuinely going to miss your sister and thought this might be a fitting tribute, donating to the hospital for whose cause she worked so diligently."

She looked at Logan sharply and frowned. "Why are you taking his side?" she asked. It was a struggle to keep her voice down.

"I'm not taking anyone's side," he countered mildly. "I'm trying to keep an open mind."

He sounded way too calm for her. Well, why shouldn't he be? she silently demanded. It wasn't *his* only sister who'd been killed.

"Don't keep it too open, or everything's going to come spilling out," she retorted.

He stared at her, trying to make sense out of what she'd just said. After a beat Logan decided that frustration and anger were shutting off the woman's ability to think clearly.

Taking her by the elbow, he directed her toward one

of the tables against the wall. Bottles of beer, alcohol and soft drinks were all there, waiting for thirsty guests.

"I think you need a drink," he told her, then specified, "Just one," in case she thought that he was attempting to get her drunk. "So you can stop being so uptight."

Her eyes narrowed and she tossed her head. "Maybe I want to be uptight," she fired back.

Logan calmly mixed vodka and orange juice together over an avalanche of ice, taking care to go heavy on the juice. After holding it up for his own examination, he was satisfied. Only then did he hand the tall, frosted screwdriver to Destiny.

"Nobody wants to be uptight," he assured her. He nodded at the glass he'd given her. "Now drink up. 'Doctor's' orders."

Doctor, her foot. He was no more of a doctor than she was. Doctor Feel Good, if anything, she thought grudgingly, taking a sip without thinking.

"Trying to get me drunk, Cavanaugh?" she challenged, raising her chin as if daring him to take a swing at her.

"No, what I'm trying to do," he replied evenly, "is to get you to relax a little. Right now, you look like you're going to snap in two any second. Either that, or do double duty as an ironing board."

"Always looking out for me." The words were said sarcastically, but he pretended not to take them in that manner.

"As long as you're working with me, yes," he answered, "I am."

Destiny looked at her new and very temporary partner over the rim of her frosty glass. The anger and the sadness within her melted into the background, as if something in his eyes had physically pushed them back.

She took a deep breath to steady her nerves. "Thanks," she murmured.

Had he not seen her lips moving, he would have sworn that he was just imagining that he heard the soft sound of her voice.

But he *had* seen them move, and he did "see" the word *thanks* on her lips. Maybe there was hope for the woman yet. That was good, because being without any hope was a horrible place to be. He couldn't begin to imagine what that had to be like. Waking up each morning without wanting to.

Without a reason to.

That had to be terrible.

Slipping his arm through hers, Logan urged, "C'mon, let's get back to 'mingling.' Lots more 'suspects' to talk to."

She got the feeling that he wasn't just teasing her, he meant it. And she was grateful to him for that.

"I don't know how to thank you," Destiny told Andrew with deep sincerity.

It was late. The reception had been over for more than an hour. The last of the mourners had left about forty-five minutes ago after once again expressing their deep sorrow over Paula's death. Drake Simmons and his personal assistant were among the last to go. Though she'd made it her mission to have their paths cross several more times throughout the day and evening, nothing new was said.

She was forced to place her impatience on hold. She had a debt to repay in some small way. She began by preparing an endless stack of dirty dishes for the dishwasher.

"You already have. Four times at last count. This makes five," Andrew told her warmly.

The next moment, he took the dish she was rinsing out of her hands. Instead of putting it into the open dishwasher, he placed it on the counter. The dishes didn't have his attention. She did.

"Go home, Destiny," he ordered. "Get some rest. You go back to fighting the good fight tomorrow." And then he turned to Logan, who had never been very far away throughout the entire day. "You might want to follow her in your car, make sure she goes home," Andrew advised after a beat.

During the course of the latter half of the reception, she'd gotten a few leads that she wanted to follow up. For her that meant getting into the precinct computer.

Logan obviously sensed that by the look on his face. Was she that transparent? she wondered.

The thought was less than pleasing. Not that she had any desire to be a woman of mystery. After all, this was her partner for now. But neither did she want to come across like a person whose thoughts were right out there for everyone to read.

"I'm going home," she assured the man who had done so much for her today and had asked for absolutely nothing in return.

She didn't like owing people, but it was, as one of Andrew's daughters—Teri, she thought—had assured her, the Cavanaugh way. Everyone just helped out everyone else without thought to compensation—or bribes.

"Of course you are," Andrew said in a tone that told her that he most certainly *did not* believe, not even for a moment, that left to her own devices Destiny would drive home and just go to bed.

It came under the heading of When Pigs Fly.

"And I know you're going home because Logan's going to follow you," Andrew concluded with a satisfied, albeit irritating, smile on his face.

"You don't have to follow me," she insisted five minutes later as she walked out of the warm house with Logan right beside her. There might be a chill in the air, but every single light seemed to be on in the Cavanaugh house, thereby generating a great deal of warmth.

Destiny's vehicle was parked close to the house. Andrew had made sure a spot directly by the front door was left for her. At the height of the reception, vehicles had littered the neighborhood for several blocks in all directions.

Now, of course, there were only a few scattered here and there, for the most part belonging to other people in the neighborhood. Everyone who had attended the reception was gone except for two of the former chief's daughters and one of his sons and their respective families.

The chief led a perfect life, she couldn't help thinking. The kind of life she would have longed to claim as her own—if her father hadn't taken that walk to buy a pack of cigarettes one fateful afternoon. Twenty years later, he still wasn't back.

"Oh, yes, I most certainly do have to follow you home," Logan told her. "I hear that when Andrew Cavanaugh makes a 'suggestion,' the person he's making it to had damn well better follow it to the letter if he or she knows what's good for them. I'm new to the family," he told her, humor curving his mouth. "I don't want to mess up. Especially not after he came through the way that he did."

Guilt. The man was wielding guilt. Great. It wasn't bad enough that she was already struggling with a megadose of it because Paula was dead and she felt that she should have been able to somehow protect her sister if only she'd taken more of an interest in her private life instead of waiting for her to share on her own. Now Logan would make her feel guilty for not doing what the former chief suggested.

"Fine, I'll go home," she said.

Logan never slowed his pace. "And I'll follow you there," he told her cheerfully.

She was going to have an escort whether she wanted one or not. For now, Destiny decided to stop fighting it.

Chapter 11

Logan remained directly behind her all the way home. There was no need to look up into her rearview mirror. She could almost *sense* that he was there.

Traffic was light. It took her less than twenty minutes to get home. After pulling up into her apartment complex, Destiny got out of her car, turned and waved at Logan. She fully expected him to wave back, make a U-turn and drive away.

But he didn't.

Instead, he found a parking space in guest parking, as it turned out not too far away from hers. Getting out, he crossed over to her.

As he approached her, with the darkness settled in all around her like an oppressive long cape, she suddenly felt vulnerable. But she had no intentions of letting him know that.

"This is a little over and above the call of duty, don't you think?" she asked when he came up to her.

"Not really. I'm sure this is what Andrew meant," he answered. Destiny noticed that once away from the gathering, Logan no longer used the "Uncle" salutation. "Besides, it's generally customary to walk a woman to her door." He nodded toward the ground-floor apartment only a few steps away.

"That's when she's your date," Destiny pointed out, adding, "I'm not your date."

"No," he agreed. "But for now, you're my responsibility."

His words stepped all over her independence. Destiny drew her shoulders back, as if preparing for a confrontation. "And just how do you figure that?"

Logan knew he had to tread lightly. She was in a bad place right now. He chose his words carefully. "Well, for better or for worse, we seemed to have been partnered up for this case, and partners are supposed to have each other's backs, especially when one partner isn't feeling one hundred percent."

Her eyes narrowed, her very stance challenging him. "Meaning me."

He inclined his head, silently agreeing with her. But when he spoke, he tempered Destiny's assumption. "For now."

Sarcasm was thick and heavy as she asked, "Would you like to tuck me into bed, too?"

"Well, then, that would have made you my date, wouldn't it?" he said, going back to her initial disclaimer. "And you're not, remember?" The smile on his lips took on a sensual quality. "Maybe some other time." And then Logan grew serious as he smoothed down one side of her collar that had managed to curl under.

It was a simple, gentle gesture, and yet for some reason it threatened to bring tears to her eyes. That just told her that she was exceedingly vulnerable beneath the prickly words and all her efforts to appear to the contrary.

"Are you going to be all right by yourself?" he asked.

What did he care? He had a huge family to return to if he wanted. He had the best of all possible worlds, and she couldn't help but envy him that.

"Or what?" she asked in a mocking tone. "You'll sit next to my bed and read me bedtime stories until I fall asleep?"

He laughed softly, amused by the image that conjured up in his mind. "If that's what it takes, sure, why not?" he asked gamely.

He said it so straight-faced that for just a second, she thought he was serious. Who knew, maybe he was. What he said melted her defensiveness. Moreover, it made her smile. He seemed to take everything in stride, no matter what she said.

"You Cavanaughs are something else again," she marveled quietly. "Even you newly minted ones."

"You didn't answer my question," he reminded her gently. When Destiny raised an eyebrow in silent query, he obliged her by restating the question. "Are you going to be all right?"

For a moment, she said nothing, wondering if he actually cared one way or another, or if he was asking just because he felt it was expected of him. She refused to entertain the thought that it might be door number three: that he *did* care if she was going to be all right.

And then she nodded. "I'll be fine." She could see that he was waiting for her to convince him. "I don't have any other choice. Paula's killer is out there somewhere, and I intend to catch him. I can't do that if I fall apart."

"No, you can't," he agreed. "But if you need someone to talk to—or not talk to," he added with a smile that was beginning to weave its way under her skin even though she was doing her best to ignore it, "I'm available."

She nodded. That he was. To any girl with a pulse, she reminded herself. And she had never been one for team sports. "Thanks. I'll keep that in mind. But I'll be all right."

"Yeah," he said as if he had absolutely no doubt about the outcome. "You will."

She picked up the note of sincerity in his voice. He didn't have to say that. Didn't even have to be here. But he was.

"You're a good guy, Logan Cavanaugh," she told him quietly just before she impulsively brushed her lips against his cheek.

Logan felt something within his gut tighten so quickly and so hard, for a second it was difficult for him to draw in a breath.

Every fiber of his being suddenly wanted to pull her into his arms and to kiss her back. The right way. And he had a strong feeling that he wouldn't have gotten any resistance from her.

But that would be taking unfair advantage of her vulnerable state, and he didn't want things to go down that way between them. Their time would come. He was fairly certain of that now, but not tonight.

Because tonight was about healing, and she needed to do that on her terms, not his.

"Good night, Richardson," he said quietly. "I'll see you in the morning."

"In the morning," she echoed softly.

The next moment, she walked into her apartment and then closed the door behind her.

Logan turned on his heel and walked away.

It was the hardest thing he'd ever done.

And possibly the most selfless.

"You don't know how long I've waited for someone to take me seriously," Allison West said to them the next day as she sat in her living room. A huge sigh of relief accompanied the older woman's words.

Determined not to allow any more time to pass, Destiny had suggested to her partner that they interview the families of the other so-called suicide victims she'd found entered into the database.

"Debra was bright, outgoing. There was no way she would have killed herself the way the police insisted. I *know* my daughter," she said with feeling, looking from Destiny to Logan and then back again.

That was just the way she felt about Paula, Destiny thought. "The investigating detective said they found a prescription for sleeping pills near your daughter's body—" she began.

But Mrs. West was shaking her head. "That prescription wasn't hers."

"It was her name on the bottle," Logan pointed out gently.

She swung around to look at him, anger in her eyes. "I don't care what it said, I'm telling you that it wasn't hers. Debra was a personal trainer with an extensive list of clients. She really believed in what she was doing. She exercised religiously, was almost fanatical about what she put into her body. She wouldn't even take so much as an aspirin," Mrs. West insisted. "I don't know how they did it, but those pills were planted. They were not my daughter's."

Destiny tried another approach. "Can you think of anyone who might have wanted to get rid of your daughter this much?"

Again the woman could only shake her head. "No, I can't. If I knew, I would have confronted them myself, *made* them confess, even if I had to shake it out of them with my bare hands."

Given that the woman was barely five feet tall and most likely weighed as much as a pile of wet towels, her words didn't amount to much of a threat. But it was a testimony to where her heart was and how much she believed her daughter's death had been staged.

"The police said that your daughter left a suicide note, saying she was upset because she and her boyfriend had just broken up. Do you have any idea what his name was?" Destiny asked.

"No." Mrs. West's small voice hitched. "Debra wanted to keep it a secret. She said she didn't want to jinx the relationship by talking about it too soon."

Destiny stared at her, startled that Mrs. West had used the exact same words that Paula had used.

She didn't want to jinx the relationship.

"She did tell me that she thought he was perfect," Mrs. West was saying. "And that when I found out who it was, I was going to be surprised." Her eyes darkened as she took hold of Logan's wrist, squeezing it as she made her appeal. "Debra didn't kill herself. She didn't write any suicide note. It was *typed,* for God's sake," the woman cried in frustration. "Who types a note, then climbs into a bathtub and slashes their wrists? For all her outgoing nature, Debra was a very modest person when it came to her body. She wouldn't have wanted anyone to find her like that. She didn't *do* this," Mrs. West insisted again, growing progressively more agitated. "I'd stake my life on it."

Feeling compassion as well as a bond with this woman because of what she was going through, Destiny patted Mrs. West's arm. "You don't have to stake your life on it, Mrs. West. We'll find whoever did this to your daughter."

Grasping Destiny's hand between both of her own, the woman looked directly into her eyes. "Promise?" she pressed.

Destiny didn't even hesitate. "You have my word on it."

"She believed you, you know," Logan said to her when they finally left the woman's apartment some twenty minutes later.

Destiny knew exactly how committed she'd made herself. "I know."

Logan studied her profile as he asked, "And what are you going to tell her if you can't make good on that promise?"

That scenario was never going to happen, she thought fiercely. "I have every intention of 'making good' on it," she told him simply.

There was no way she could make a promise like that in good faith, and she knew it. "Destiny—"

She stopped for a moment to look at him. She knew what he was thinking. Hell, she could all but read his mind.

"Don't give me odds, Cavanaugh. We're going to get the bastard. Nothing less is remotely acceptable."

There was a fine line between being a dedicated detective and an obsessed one. "You ever read *Moby Dick?*" Logan asked as he got into the vehicle on the driver's side.

She pretended to take his question seriously. "We're not after a whale, we're after a human being. And human beings make mistakes. He will, too, if he hasn't already," she said confidently. "Somewhere, somehow, all those women I turned up have something in common. We have to find what it is."

Right. Simple, he thought sarcastically. "So, to sum up, we're looking for one needle that was in six different haystacks at one point or another."

He noted that she never even cracked a smile. "Precisely."

They returned to the precinct to review some things before planning their next course of action.

Once there, Destiny got busy compiling a file on all six of the women who had initially been thought to have committed suicide while in the throes of despair after each had supposedly broken up with the love of her life.

While she was printing up screen after screen, Logan borrowed a bulletin board and brought it into the squad room. One of the wheels had an unfortunate squeak that was heard with each complete rotation. Moving it faster only made the squeaking sound continuous, like an amorous rodent calling to its mate.

The noise drew the lieutenant out of his office and into the main area. He eyed the offensive bulletin board. "What's this?" Bailey asked.

"Visual aids," Logan told him, keeping it simple. "Richardson thought it might help if we put the victims' pictures up in chronological order with a summary of what we know about them under each."

"You mean the nonserial-killer case," the lieutenant corrected pointedly.

Logan was not about to argue with the lieutenant at this stage of the investigation. He would have needed more evidence at his disposition for that. "That's the one."

"It might not be a serial killer," Destiny said, coming up behind them. Both men turned almost in unison and looked at her quizzically. "At least, not a serial killer in the traditional sense."

"You want to explain that?" Logan requested. Seeing as how she was the one who had originally called this a serial-killer case, this was a complete one-eighty on her part and he wanted to know, in as few words as humanly possible, why she'd changed her mind.

Between arrangements for her sister's funeral and dealing with her own grief, Destiny had still managed to squeeze in some work. She'd been busy reading everything she could find on each of the other so-called nonvictims, plus she also had the benefit of the interviews she and Logan had conducted. There were still some details that bothered her. Details that didn't add up in the traditional sense.

"For one thing, I don't get a sense that our killer is enjoying this. That he's following some ritual dictates that he's unable to ignore. Most serial killers stick to a pattern religiously, one they can't deviate from, only embellish on."

Destiny looked at the photographs of the other women on the bulletin board, deliberately avoiding the last one. Her sister.

"It's almost as if the killer's doing this out of some need for expediency, like he *has* to do it *now* and quickly. And he changes things," she pointed out. "He's not slavishly bound by steps he has to follow." She pointed to one photograph, then another, moving from one pretty face to another. "One victim types her suicide note, another doesn't leave one at all. And a third sends a text message, while a fourth posts a note on her Facebook page, telling the world goodbye because 'he doesn't love me anymore.' It's like he uses whatever he can get, whatever's handy for him."

"So exactly what is it that you're saying?" the lieutenant pressed.

Frustrated, Destiny dragged her hand through her hair as she slanted a glance toward her sister's picture. The one taken at Christmas, one of the last times they'd been together. "I don't know. Just that something doesn't feel right."

Her answer did not please Bailey in the slightest. "Feelings don't stand up in court, Richardson. We need evidence. You're a crime scene investigator. You should know that," he all but barked at her.

For a second, she closed her eyes, pulling herself together. "Yes, I know that."

"Then get me some evidence!" Bailey shouted before storming away. Less than a minute later, he slammed his office door as if to underscore his order.

"Why don't we get that personal trainer's list of clients?" Logan suggested, acting as if the lieutenant hadn't even been there. "We can see if Debra trained anyone your sister interacted with. If we can just find that one point in common that they had—"

"Other than they were all in their twenties, blonde, more than reasonably attractive and supposedly committed suicide when they were 'dumped'?" she posed dryly.

"Yes, other than that."

He let his voice trail off, allowing her to fill in the silence that followed any way she wanted to. At this point, they didn't know what they were after, only that if they stumbled across it, they'd know it—if they were lucky.

"Debra West's list of clients?" Becky, the receptionist with the toothy smile repeated. She looked at them blankly for a full five seconds before saying, "We don't have a Debra West working here."

"No, you don't," Destiny agreed patiently. *Because she's dead, you idiot.* "But you did," she went on in the same calm tone. "A year ago."

"Oh. A *year* ago," she repeated as if that was the key to the secrets of the universe. "I've only been working here two months," Becky told them. "I don't know where I'd have to go to access that kind of information." She seemed perfectly happy to let the conversation drop at this point.

Sensing that she was near the end of her patience, Logan moved Destiny aside and addressed the intelligence-challenged receptionist.

"Do you think you might be able to call over someone who could possibly know how to do that?" he asked, speaking to Becky in a calm, level voice, all the while smiling into her eyes.

Whatever he was doing, Destiny noted, it had the desired effect on the receptionist.

"Sure. That would be Brittany," Becky volunteered. She jumped up to her feet as if her lower limbs had gotten the message delivered belatedly. "I'll get her for you."

"I'd appreciate that," Logan told her.

"Maybe I should have let you do the talking to begin with," Destiny murmured under her breath as Becky disappeared into the rear of the building.

"Maybe," Logan agreed, amused.

Now that he thought of it, the receptionist *did* remind him of the kind of woman he usually dated. Young, fun-loving, but definitely not a candidate for a Rhodes Scholarship in this lifetime. And, up until a few days ago, he was fairly certain that was the type he preferred and for the most part required. Because there was no chance of a meaningful or lasting relationship growing out of those sorts of liaisons.

But after trading barbs and dealing with a woman who continuously kept him on his toes, Logan began to view women like the receptionist as less appealing despite all her impressive physical attributes.

The realization, coming to him out of the blue like this, was more than just a little unnerving. It threatened to upend his world.

Just what the hell was he thinking? And why was he thinking it now?

"Something wrong?" Destiny asked as they waited for the receptionist to return with this Brittany person in tow.

Rather than answer her question, he asked one of his own, sounding, she noticed, just a little defensive. "Why do you ask?"

She shrugged, about to drop the subject when something stopped her. There was this unusual expression on his face, as if he'd suddenly realized something. About Paula's case?

"You look like you just had an epiphany," she told him.

Epiphany.

Well, that was as good a word for it as any, Logan decided.

If that indeed was what he'd just had. It sounded a lot

better than saying he'd suddenly come to his senses—
because he didn't know just how sensible he was.

"Maybe I have," he murmured more to himself than
to her.

Destiny's eyes narrowed as she tried to make sense
of what he was saying. She'd just thrown the word out
there, never once expecting him to do anything except
bristle at the term. It was a twenty-dollar word, and he
was a fifteen-dollar cop.

Was he humoring her or laughing at her?

Had he actually had an epiphany?

And why did *any* of this actually even matter to her,
she silently demanded?

*Because Paula's death knocked you for a loop and
you're trying to anchor yourself to something. And that's
understandable. But you know damn well that it can't
be him.*

No, she silently agreed, it can't be. Because a man
like Logan didn't stay for long.

Chapter 12

Logan leaned back in his chair as far as it could go. He was bone weary. It was past his shift and the squad room was empty except for him and the woman pensively staring at the bulletin board with her back to him.

Even her back looked obsessed, he thought. Where did she get her energy?

Sullivan had returned from his honeymoon, but the detective had been temporarily partnered with someone else until Logan either brought the case to a satisfying conclusion—or signed off on it. He wasn't about to give up.

He and Destiny had been at this nonstop for close to three weeks now, searching for that one common thread that connected all these so-called nonsuicides together. So far, they kept striking out.

Logan glanced over toward the bulletin board. Six

years, six women, and all they'd come up with were paralyzing dead ends.

And while he liked to think that he was a damn good detective, Logan felt as if his efforts paled in comparison to the efforts of his father's chief assistant. Richardson was there when he arrived in the morning, she was there when he left at night, eternally going over the information they'd gathered and searching for new angles, for that elusive "something" that would finally and once and for all break the case wide-open for them.

In the meantime, Logan mused, the woman *had* to be wearing herself out.

"An airline attendant, a teacher, the owner of an upscale restaurant, a wedding planner, a trainer and a fundraiser," Destiny suddenly said out loud.

Logan wasn't sure if she was addressing him or the dead women whose photographs were pinned along the top of the bulletin board.

She was reviewing their high-profile careers and frowned as she glanced at him over her shoulder. "What are we missing?"

"Right now, my best guess would be our sanity," he quipped wearily.

"Besides that," she retorted, exasperated not with him but with herself. What wasn't she seeing?

Turning back to the bulletin board, she looked at each individual photograph. The faces had begun to haunt her dreams.

"What am *I* missing?" she said under her breath.

But he'd heard her. Again he thought that Richardson was coming dangerously close to wearing herself out without even realizing it. Something had to be done before that happened.

"You want to take a break?" he asked suddenly.

"You mean like for coffee?" She was beginning to fade, she realized. Coffee might be just the thing to keep her going for another hour or so. "Sure. You can bring me back a container if you're going to the machine." She was already on to her next thought and waved in the general direction of the desk she was using. "My purse is in the bottom drawer. Take what you need."

Logan laughed to himself. "A loaded statement if I ever heard one," he commented. Richardson had handed him an absolutely fantastic straight line, and he was doing his best to be good.

Preoccupied, Destiny had only half heard what he'd said. "What?" When he didn't answer, she looked at him again. He was still sitting down. Had he changed his mind about the coffee?

"I'm talking about a *real* break," he emphasized. "Like getting away from the office—and this case— entirely. Tomorrow's Saturday," he interjected in case she'd lost track again, the way she had last Saturday— Richardson had spent the weekend at the precinct with the dead women and her computer for company, working hard and getting nowhere for her efforts.

"So?"

"So I've got a wedding to attend. My sister Kendra's getting married," he told her before she could ask. "Want to be my 'plus one'?"

For a moment, she said nothing, then decided that he had to be pulling her leg. "Don't you have a girlfriend to take?" The man, according to everything she'd heard, *always* had a girlfriend—or two—somewhere in the picture.

His mouth curved in amusement. "As my sister Kari so succinctly says, I'm in between meaningless relationships. And I don't want to go alone," he said, appealing to her. "Come with me."

Destiny stared at him as his words sank in. Was he actually asking her out? "A pity date? For who?" She was definitely unclear on the concept. "You, because you're in between 'meaningless' relationships, or me, because I haven't been in a relationship since slightly after the dawn of time?" Or at least it felt that way. Put on the spot, she wouldn't have been able to say just *when* her last so-called relationship had ended. It had been *that* long ago.

"How about we split the difference?" he offered gamely. "Or, if it makes you feel any better, we can say that it's for me. Your pity, my date," he said, summing it up cheerfully.

Though the idea of going out with him on an unofficial date was intriguing—hell, it was downright tempting—she was still suspicious. "Why do you want me to come?"

"Because I think it'd do you good to get away from all this, clear your head, put things in perspective. A couple of days away from here will do you a world of good," he predicted. "And," he stressed, "because you can't keep talking to computer hardware indefinitely. Eventually, you're going to start thinking it's talking back, and then you'll *really* be in trouble."

Destiny laughed then. She didn't exactly know why, but what he'd said sounded so absurd that she had to laugh. It was the first time she'd laughed since before she'd found Paula's body.

And then, glancing one more time at the photographs that were lined up along the bulletin board so neatly, Destiny blew out a long, steadying breath.

"Maybe you're right," she allowed.

"It's been known to happen," Logan acknowledged, giving her a killer grin that she was fairly certain had melted more than its share of kneecaps. She felt her own turning slightly watery.

Her mouth curved in amusement. "Well, even a broken clock is right—"

He closed his eyes as he finished the old saying for her. "Twice a day. Yeah. I know." Opening them again, his eyes held hers for a moment. "Thanks."

She wished he'd stop looking at her like that. It made her feel completely at loose ends and unfocused. "So you're really serious about that invitation—to your sister's wedding?" As she said it, she had to admit that the idea started to appeal to her. Not that she was much of a party person, but a change of scenery for a few hours might not be completely out of order.

Logan nodded, trying his best to appear solemn rather than just dead tired. "Serious enough to come get you and drag you over to the church tomorrow whether you're ready or not."

"Then I guess I'd better be ready. What time?"

He thought for a second, trying to get the details right. "Ceremony's at eleven." He did a quick calculation backward. "I'll pick you up around a quarter after ten." And then he smiled, the expression on his face a self-deprecating one. "Kenny vividly described what she'd do to my anatomy if I show up late."

She'd met Kendra briefly at her sister's funeral. Even so, the woman had impressed her as a kindred spirit. "Is your uncle Adam officiating?" she asked.

The only way they could keep the priest from presiding over the ceremony would be to have the man kidnapped. Logan laughed. "Absolutely."

"And your uncle Andrew, is he taking care of the reception?" The latter was basically a rhetorical question.

"Who else?"

Destiny nodded. It was hard to imagine so many people being so close—but they obviously were. "A real family affair," she commented. And she truly envied him that. Especially now that she had no family of her own anymore.

Her voice, stripped of any emotion or intonation, gave him no clue as to what she was thinking—but he had a strong hunch.

"Yeah, it is."

She would have said that he was the rebellious type, not someone who conformed to the wishes of his family. And yet, here he was, sticking to the script. Just showed that you could never tell about a person.

"It doesn't get old for you?" she asked, curious.

"Hasn't been going on long enough to get old," he told her, "although, to be honest, I doubt if it ever will. They're there," he said, referring to his family members, "just enough to let you know you've got a support system if you need one, and not enough to be annoying or get under your skin."

Destiny regarded her temporary partner for a moment. He'd impressed her. "I didn't know you were that deep, Cavanaugh."

Logan shrugged off the compliment. "I didn't either." His computer already shut down for the night, Logan pushed his chair away from his desk and stood up. "I'm going to call it a night," he told her, then asked, "How about you?"

Destiny rotated her shoulders, working out a kink. "I think I'm going to stay a little while longer."

He would have bet money on that. "What a surprise," he commented dryly. Then, passing her on the way to the door, he said, "Remember, ten-fifteen, whether you're ready or not, I'm taking you to the wedding."

She thought of the clothes in her closet, and a twinge of panic momentarily telegraphed through her. "I don't have anything to wear."

He wasn't accepting excuses. "Naked might be an interesting change of pace."

"I'm serious," she called after him.

Stopping for a second, he turned around and grinned at her. "So am I." And then he relented. "I could ask Bridget to lend you one of her dresses." He did a quick assessment. "You look like you might be around the same size."

As far as she recalled, she and Bridget hadn't been anywhere near one another, so he couldn't be drawing on that to form a conclusion. "How would you know?"

He winked then and told her in a low voice, as if he

was sharing a secret, "I've got an eye for things like that."

She found herself dealing with his wink and the unexpected tidal wave it had created in the pit of her stomach. Maybe she *was* punchy.

"Don't bother your sister. I'll find something," she said dismissively.

"Don't worry. You'll look great in whatever you decide to wear."

Without thinking, Destiny pressed her hand to her stomach.

His parting words hung in the air long after he had walked out of not just the squad room but the precinct, as well.

The man knew how to make an exit, Destiny thought ruefully.

This was a bad idea.

A really *bad* idea.

The words echoed in her head the next morning as Destiny looked at her reflection in the full-length mirror on her closet door.

What was she doing, going to this wedding? She wasn't good at small talk, and she definitely wasn't in a festive mood. These people had been nice to her, and she didn't want to put a damper on the wedding by bringing anyone down.

She'd just tell Cavanaugh when he came to pick her up that she'd changed her mind. *He'll understand,* she assured herself. After all, it wasn't as if he was going to tie her down to the roof of his car and drive away.

He didn't need her as a date. The second he walked in alone into the reception, he'd have women flocking to him. Most likely, it would become a feeding frenzy.

The thought didn't ease her conscience the way she thought it would. Instead, it irritated it.

Another sign that she needed some rest. Making up her mind to stay home, she started taking off the dress that Paula had given her last Christmas. The one she'd had no occasion to wear—until now.

Or not.

There was a militant row of tiny pearl buttons from the base of her neckline to her waist on the Wedgwood-blue dress whose straight skirt stopped a few inches short of her knees. She began working them loose and had only managed to get six of them undone when she heard the doorbell.

Damn it, Cavanaugh was early. She should have known that he would be.

Biting off a few choice words, Destiny hurried to the door.

"I changed my mind," she announced as she swung it open.

Logan's deep green eyes appreciatively went from her face to an even more arresting area of her anatomy. The smile that curved his mouth would have gotten him arrested in several third-world nations.

"You've come up with something else for us to do?" he asked, his voice resonating with sensuality as well as sounding incredibly suggestive.

"No, I—" And then she remembered that she'd been unbuttoning the top of her dress, affording him a view he didn't get to see during regular hours. "You could look away," she pointed out, fumbling with the tiny buttons as she pushed them back through the loops as quickly as possible.

"I could," he agreed. "But then I'd really be missing something," he pointed out. His eyes lowered just enough to revisit the tempting, albeit disappearing view.

"Nothing you haven't seen a hundred times before, I'm sure," she said stiffly, fervently wishing that she could tamp down the flush she felt beginning to creep up her cheeks.

But she couldn't.

Nobody blushed anymore, she upbraided herself. What was wrong with her?

"Not this particular view," Logan assured her.

For a second, she was almost tempted to believe he meant it. But that would make her even more naive than she already was.

"Okay, I'm not unreasonable. We either go to the wedding, or we stay here and find another way to amuse ourselves," he said.

Her eyes narrowed. He was bluffing. "You wouldn't miss your sister's wedding."

Rather than concede that she was right, he pretended to shrug carelessly. "I have other sisters, there'll be other weddings."

Her eyes widened. "You don't mean that," she said, calling his bluff.

"What I mean," he told her seriously, "is that one way or another, I'm not leaving you alone today. How we spend the day is up to you." He looked at her pointedly.

The flash of heat came out of nowhere, telling her that if she was going to be around him, she needed at least a few other people around, as well.

Otherwise...

"All right." She surrendered. "We'll go to the wedding."

Pleased, he nodded. "Good choice. You've made my sister Kendra very happy. By the way—" he indicated her neckline with his eyes "—you missed a button."

Caught off guard, Destiny looked down at the neckline that had been plunging just a bit more than she'd intended a minute ago. "I did?"

"I could do it for you," he volunteered.

Over her dead body—then they'd never get out of the apartment.

"I see it, I see it," she said, verbally swatting him back.

Logan laughed softly to himself under his breath as he took her arm and escorted her out the door.

Some twelve hours later, they were back in front of the same door.

It might have been only half a day later, but it felt as if days, not hours, had passed by since this morning. Or maybe even a lifetime, she amended silently, smiling to herself.

It had been quite a day, at least to her.

Rather than keep to herself and sit quietly on the sidelines the way she had intended, almost immediately Destiny had found herself drawn into one conversation after another. Her opinion had been sought out on a variety of subjects, most of which had nothing to do with work.

Not only was her opinion sought out, but her likeness, as well. Despite her protest, she got pulled into more than a few family photos. It seemed to her that every few minutes, another camera went off and someone else framed a photograph and pulled her into it.

They were a pushy, boisterous bunch of people, and she enjoyed their company even more the second time around than the first. But then, this was a wedding, not a funeral.

"I think your family now has more pictures of me than my mother ever had in her family album."

The faded-green album she was thinking of had actually been rather sparse for what it purported to be. Its contents spanned not just her early life but the life of her mother and her mother's mother, as well. Three generations and there were less than twenty pages of photographs in total.

She shrugged carelessly as her words came back to her. "My family wasn't much on taking pictures."

That was *not* the problem with his family, especially not his immediate family.

Standing on her doorstep, Logan laughed. "Kari has over twenty albums or so," he told her. "It's almost an obsession with her."

His mind turned to more intimate things as he watched Destiny. Even in this light, he could see her face was ever so slightly flushed. The woman had a slight buzz on. He would have figured she'd need more drinks than the number she'd had to blush. Showed that you just never knew.

"So, I take it you had a good time," he guessed. Even as he made the assessment, he found himself fighting a very strong temptation a second later.

Destiny turned her face up to his and smiled.

She knew she was feeling the effects of a few glasses of champagne and that margarita—or was it two?—that she'd had a little while ago.

Better tread lightly here.

But despite her warning, she had to admit that she did like this fluttery, uninhibited feeling. And she *definitely* liked the fact that everything felt as if it was smiling inside of her.

"Yes," she told him. "I had a *very* nice time." Her eyes smiled into his. "Thanks for dragging me."

"My pleasure," he told her. It was getting harder and harder not to close his arms around her. "Anytime you want to be dragged somewhere, just let me know. I'm your guy."

I'm your guy.

Wow.

The three-word sentence stood out in blaring neon lights, completely cornering her attention.

Not that the words were true, of course. He wasn't "her guy." Why would he want to be? There were so many more exciting women for him to choose. But wouldn't it be nice if just for a moment, she could pretend that he meant it. And if…

If.

The single word that could make everything else possible, she mused.

God, now she was babbling even in her head, Destiny thought, trying to get hold of herself.

He was looking at her. Looking *into* her.

"I'm not used to partying," she heard herself saying as her throat grew progressively drier.

Amused, Logan pushed back a wisp of her hair that kept falling into her eyes. His fingertips lightly brushed against her skin.

"Really?" he teased. "You could have fooled me."

"I doubt that anything could really fool you," she murmured.

He didn't know about that. It seemed that all this time he'd been fooling himself, claiming that empty, shallow relationships were all he wanted.

That didn't seem to be enough anymore.

Not nearly enough.

The night breeze was just warm enough as it wrapped itself around them. The area was still, its inhabitants either asleep or away.

Everything seemed to be focused on the two of them.

On her.

Destiny's face was still turned up to his. A soft invitation he couldn't make himself refuse even though he knew he should.

The next moment, his lips were against hers.

And all hell broke loose.

Chapter 13

Logan wasn't sure just what he was thinking when he leaned over and kissed her. Most likely, he *wasn't* thinking.

Somewhere in the back of his mind, he had to have told himself that this would just be a simple, uncomplicated kiss. But in the depths of his soul, he had to have known better.

There was nothing simple about sharing a kiss with Destiny.

He'd already learned that the first time around. No reason to expect that the second time would be any less exhilarating.

If anything, it was more so.

Because the moment he kissed her, Logan wanted more. An entire galaxy more. He wanted to *be* with her. He wanted to *experience* her and lose himself in whatever followed.

It was as if he'd lived for years in a cave and had, just now, walked out into the bright sunlight. It might take some adjusting, but it definitely did not even begin to flirt, even remotely, with anything that was even *close* to regret.

Maybe, if Destiny hadn't kissed him back, he would have been able to harness this wild energy pulsing through him. Might have been able to get himself under control and stop after a few moments had gone by.

But she *did* kiss him back.

Hard.

And just like that, all bets were off, all the scaffolding that was carefully holding up his reconstructed walls now cracked and broke apart.

Logan's hands ran up and down along her body, increasing her body temperature until Destiny was certain she was standing in the center of a lit fireplace instead of on her doorstep.

"Hold it," she urgently breathed against his mouth as he continued to kiss her and make her head spin.

The words penetrated half a beat later, and with grave effort Logan drew back from his partner. Was she having second thoughts? Or had he misread her signals? Was he guilty of pushing too hard?

"If we keep this up out here," she told him, her words coming out in breathy spurts as she turned toward the door and did her best to stick her key into the lock, "we're going to get arrested."

So he *hadn't* misread the signs. Logan grinned. "I've

got my handcuffs in the car," he volunteered. "I could handcuff you."

He found himself talking to an empty space. Destiny had unlocked the door to her apartment and left it open for him.

"Are you coming in?"

When he didn't immediately answer, Destiny reached out, grabbed his arm and pulled him inside, impulsively taking the decision out of his hands.

"I guess I am."

His words would have been followed with a laugh, but by then, the door had slammed shut and her lips were locked onto his again. It was all he could do to keep breathing. She had a way of stealing the air right out of his lungs.

Logan could feel his body heating as an urgency surged through him.

Eager to make love to every inch of this woman, he started to undress her—or tried to. He'd forgotten about the pearl buttons running along the front of her dress. There had to be a thousand buttons in the way.

A fail-safe obstacle to allow her a last chance to reassess the situation?

"Who designed this dress?" he asked in frustration. "Nuns in some cloistered convent in the Swiss Alps?"

Destiny's heart was already beating in her throat, threatening to leap out of her body entirely. She'd never felt like this before, never experienced this level of desire before. It was all she could do to keep her whole body, including her fingertips, from trembling. This was by far the prettiest dress she owned, but in hindsight, she shouldn't have worn it.

Too late now.

"It'll go faster if we work together," she told him, her words emerging in tiny bursts of sound. "You start at the top and work your way down. I'll come in from the bottom and work my way up."

He was already doing his part, his long, slender fingers more than equal to the delicate task. "Sounds like a plan to me," he murmured, his lips and his breath grazing the side of her neck and sending shock waves through her body with every small, sexy kiss he pressed against her flesh.

The touch of his fingers against the sensitive length of the skin along her breasts generated one hell of a response within her. Yearning had multiplied in geometric proportions, and it was all she could do to keep from ripping her dress off.

But she didn't want to destroy it. She wanted to preserve it, because in a very short while, the dress—and her memories—would be all she would have left of an evening that promised to go far beyond anything she could have possibly imagined.

Their fingers brushed against one another as they both reached the very last pearl button that needed to be freed.

Destiny dropped her arms to her sides as she let him do the honors.

And when he did, slipping the back of the halter over her head, the soft blue dress floated to the floor, leaving her dressed only in his warm gaze, a pair of high

heels and a scrap of white lace that had to be the ultimate minimum in undergarments.

That he didn't bother being gentle with. In a second,
the undergarment was history.

The next moment, naked, Destiny was wrapped
around his torso, her mouth all but hermetically sealed
to his as a second wave of fire ignited between them.

He was kissing her, stroking her, touching her until
she was utterly mindless. None of her surroundings
registered.

They could have been in her living room, her kitchen,
or on her bathroom floor for all she knew. The only
things she was aware of were the all-consuming craving within her and the fact that he wasn't sating it. He
was feeding it, making it grow.

And she was aware, too, of the fact that somehow,
though she didn't remember if she was responsible or
he was, his clothes had vanished from his body. What
was beneath was tanned and toned and hard.

Doing her best to draw air into her lungs in small
fits and starts, Destiny began at first hesitantly, then
progressively with more confidence, to run her hands
along his utterly tempting body.

Touching, teasing, stimulating.

With each pass, the thrill increased for her until it
was all but unmanageable.

She wanted him with every fiber of her being, her
very core moist and yearning for that final burst of
fulfillment.

But even as she raised her hips to him in a silent,

sensual invitation, she discovered that Logan was intent on prolonging her experience.

Instead of driving himself into her, he took her a little at a time, making love to her body with his hands, his lips, his tongue. Creating small, lethal climaxes for her.

Even as he brought his mouth down on the hollow of her elbow, she felt a strange, wondrous miniexplosion within the center of her very core.

Her eyes flying open as her breath caught in her throat, she looked at Logan. Just what was he doing to her?

But even as she sought to ask, he'd moved on to another part of her body. And it was the same thing all over again. He was re-creating the explosions. She felt them along the slope of her throat, the swell of her breasts—first one, then the other—and then he began to move lower.

The area around her navel quivered uncontrollably with anticipation as he left a soft, hot, moist trail of intertwining kisses, working his way slowly, methodically down to his primary target.

When he coaxed her legs apart, she was certain that Logan was preparing to enter.

And he was.

But not the way she'd thought.

His breath just barely brushed along the most sensitive part of her, causing ripples of desire to seize her.

To prepare her.

Nothing could have prepared her. Not for this. Not for the sensation that followed as he lightly, subtly flirted along the outline of her femininity with just the tip of his tongue, teasing her until she thought she was going to scream.

And then he finally thrust his tongue into her.

She scrambled up eagerly to meet the explosion, her hips arched and raised as she grasped what turned out to be the sheet from her bed with both hands. She was yanking, pulling, trying to keep herself anchored to earth even as she rushed to absorb the incredible sensations that were rocking her body.

Bringing her to the edge of ecstasy and then pushing her into its swirling cauldron.

Every single part of her felt as if it was lit up and rejoicing.

And then, exhausted, spent, her body collapsed back against the mattress.

Dazed, trying vainly to somehow seal in all the delicious sensations still humming through her body, Destiny became aware that Logan was moving seductively up along her body, his body's hard ridges rubbing against her softer contours.

Arousing her all over again.

As if what had just transpired had been only an appetizer, foreshadowing the main course.

She'd thought herself completely drained, but she was wrong. From somewhere deep inside of her, a second wave of energy materialized, eagerly rushing up to meet what was about to come.

Gathering Destiny into his arms, Logan looked into the dazed wonder in her eyes for a moment, savoring it before he sealed his lips to hers.

He'd done this—made love to a woman—so many

times before that he had actually lost count. And yet, somehow, though he couldn't quite explain why even to himself, this felt different.

Was different.

The look of dazed wonder mixed with absolute pleasure in her blue eyes didn't feed his ego, didn't give him the usual sense of satisfaction that he'd done his job by pleasing his partner. Instead, the look in her eyes stirred him, excited him.

It made him want her in a way he couldn't remember wanting anyone else.

Ever.

His heart pounding hard against his rib cage, Logan pulled her closer than a breath to him.

And then he entered her.

Not with a driving force but with a measured gentleness that grew and steadily increased until the rhythm seized them both. They moved in unison to a timeless melody that grew more powerful and demanding until the final crescendo resounded and the ultimate fallout drenched them both, echoing through their bodies simultaneously, as if they truly were one.

The starbursts receded.

Logan didn't loosen his grasp, didn't draw back as the final coda faded softly into the whispers of the night. Instead, he continued to hold her, continued to savor what had just happened between them and found himself more than a little reluctant to let that sensation go, forcing him to return to earth and to reality.

He could *actually* feel her heart hammering against his. Hammering so hard that with very little effort at all, he could see the two hearts—hers and his—merging into one.

The thought lingered on his mind.

The fact that it did startled him. Since when was he given to something so sentimental? Something so, for lack of a better word, *sappy?*

What the hell was happening to him?

Having rolled off her and gathered her into his arms, Logan looked down into the face of the woman who had coaxed forward this person within him that he didn't recognize.

He wasn't certain whether to be worried that he had momentarily had some sort of a hallucination, or whether to just plain run for the hills because what had just gone on was decidedly different from anything he had ever experienced before. It had in effect exposed him to his own vulnerability, and that *couldn't* be good.

"I guess," he murmured, the words settling against the top of her head, "that you're never too old to be surprised."

Was he saying that she'd surprised him? That he hadn't thought she would be any good at this and discovering that she was had knocked him for a loop? Or was there some kind of other, hidden meaning behind Logan's words?

She was having trouble thinking clearly. All she knew was that her insides still vibrated like a tuning fork struck hard against a concrete surface.

"I surprised you?" she finally asked, needing to know. Bracing herself for his answer.

"No, *I* surprised me," he told her honestly.

He really hadn't thought that he would respond to her this way. That making love with her so completely, he'd find himself not satisfied but actually craving more.

Craving her even as his body was still warm from their first go-round.

Destiny shifted, her body brushing up against his as she looked up at him.

"I don't understand," she confessed.

Neither do I, really.

But that wasn't an answer to give her. He was supposed to be the one with all the answers. Or at least that was the way he felt.

"I'll explain it later," he promised, tilting her face up to his with the tip of his finger against her chin. Logan proceeded to lightly graze her lips with his own.

The excitement struck like lightning in a cornfield, instantly setting him on fire.

"With pictures," he added, his breath growing shorter again.

"Pictures?" she repeated, feeling her pulse once again threatening to break right through the sound barrier.

How was it that he could make her so crazy so fast? Half a second ago, she'd been too exhausted to even breathe properly. How, then, could she possibly be ready to go at it again with him?

But she was ready. Oh, so ready, as anticipation hummed in her veins.

"What kind of pictures?" She pushed the words out with difficulty, all of her focused on the explosions gathering within her throbbing body.

Excitement swiftly moved through her, filling every nook with sunshine.

"Pretty ones," he told her with effort.

Or, at least he *thought* he told her.

He definitely couldn't swear to it because his mind was, even now, retreating, losing the ability to form even simple complete thoughts.

All that was there now was desire, once again growing to gigantic proportions and promising to be even more unwieldy the second time around.

Which was more than all right with him.

It was the very last semicoherent thought Logan had for a long, long time.

Chapter 14

Destiny was fairly sure that what had happened between Logan and her that evening after his sister's wedding was a one-shot deal.

Well, technically, it was a three-shot deal, she'd corrected herself, because they'd made love a total of three times by the time Sunday-morning light had crept into her bedroom.

She had a feeling that Logan pretty much felt the same way.

Given that, it was rather difficult to estimate which of them was more surprised when Sunday began to take on the same qualities of the night before.

They were making love less than five minutes after they woke up.

Destiny wasn't even sure just how it started, only how it ultimately wound up. She'd even, for a few seconds before she'd become aware that Logan was awake, started to think about the case.

Or rather, she'd realized that something in the back of her mind was bothering her about the case. Something elusive nagging at her that she felt she should have caught by now.

But before she could fully concentrate on trying to summon it to the foreground and begin to explore exactly *what* was bothering her, her body was otherwise engaged, sending her mind back into the netherworld.

"You know," Logan told her a little while later as he collapsed beside her on the bed and another exquisite marathon lovemaking session between them had taken its place in history, "we just might be setting some kind of record here."

It took her a moment to pull enough air into her lungs to be able to answer him. "Well, I know that this is certainly *my* personal best."

The moment the words were out, Destiny realized she'd shared too much information. On the one hand, it seemed rather silly to feel awkward about what she'd just told him. After all the man had now seen her naked for the better part of three-quarters of a day.

But on the other hand, a month ago she had not even *known* him well enough to say hello to him when she passed him in the hall. Other than the fact that he was Sean's son, Logan had been a stranger to her.

He certainly isn't a stranger now, is he?

No, he wasn't. But, other than being her temporary partner for this case, she really didn't know *what* Logan was.

Logan had propped himself up on his elbow and was looking down at her face. The smile on his lips went straight to the place responsible for taking memories and pressing them between the pages of time, to remember and treasure for as long as possible.

"I certainly have no complaints on my end," he assured her softly.

Destiny could feel desire stirring within her. Again.

Okay, this was just impossible. How could she have turned into this insatiable, love-hungry creature after all these years of doing without and getting along just fine? she silently demanded. Until yesterday, she'd been completely convinced that she didn't need this kind of reaffirmation, that sex was something she could easily do without, thank you very much.

Now, given a choice of lovemaking or breathing, she would have gravitated toward the former without a second thought.

He was making her want him just by *looking* at her, for heaven's sake. Just by smiling at her. Not to mention that feeling his breath on her skin was making everything quicken inside her.

She needed to get up, to start moving, to distance herself from this man who had such power over her, Destiny told herself.

Otherwise, she was just going to jump his bones again. It was only a matter of time.

"I'm going to make us breakfast," she announced, sitting up. "You hungry?"

"Yes," he answered, his eyes on hers, his voice so low it seemed to softly ripple along her skin.

He wasn't talking about food, Destiny thought, her stomach muscles quivering. She thought about rallying, about resisting.

And then she stopped thinking altogether.

"Oh, the hell with it," she cried, surrendering.

Logan yanked her back down onto the bed. "My thoughts exactly," he agreed just before he brought his mouth down on hers.

And just like that, they set each other's worlds on fire again.

Destiny congratulated herself on getting better at giving back as good as she'd gotten, taking things that Logan had done to rock her world and using them to do the same to his. A sense of euphoria wove itself through her.

As the final climax seized her, it was all Destiny could do not to yell out Logan's name. But the sensation, rather than bursting apart and then fading, insisted on building, taking her up even farther than she'd already gone with him those other times.

Exhausted, drained and contented beyond words, she focused on the hard task of just breathing.

Cocooned in the vanishing embrace of ecstasy, she had absolutely no idea why this extraneous thought had come out of nowhere and engaged her brain.

If, propelled by a need to know, she had attempted to explore its origins, she might have said that her own lovemaking experience had made her more sympathetic to her sister, to what Paula must have felt when she suddenly found herself abandoned by the man she had planned to be with for the rest of her life, and *that* was why her mind kept returning to the case.

"Cell phone!" Destiny cried suddenly just as the euphoria faded.

Spent, Logan turned his head and looked at her quizzically. "Well, that's a new one. I don't think anyone has ever yelled that out when they've climaxed."

Her brain, still in a haze, was going three different directions at once, and his comment only confused her. "What?"

"You just yelled out 'cell phone,'" he told her. "Is that your new nickname for me, or were you just thinking of calling someone while we were…?"

Embarrassed, she covered her face with her hands. "No. Oh, God, no," she cried.

And then it began coming together for her. She could slowly make sense of everything, especially the blurry, elusive thought that had nagged at her.

Destiny bolted upright in the bed, the light blue top sheet pooling about her waist. For the moment, she was completely oblivious to the fact that she was naked from the waist up.

She grabbed Logan's wrist as she talked, as if to pull him into her thought process.

"We've cross-referenced all the people the six dead women worked with, all the people they socialized with, the churches they went to, and none of it has turned up a link."

He could see that she was going somewhere with

this. "Keep talking," he encouraged, waiting for the bottom line.

That was just the problem. She knew if she let herself, she'd start rambling, pulling in sidebars. Destiny forced herself to focus.

"Okay, if you have a lover who wants to remain out of the spotlight, in order to humor him you wouldn't have his name anywhere that someone else could discover it, like on a list of clients." The last was a direct reference to Debra West's list of people she worked with as a trainer.

"Makes sense," he agreed, still waiting for Destiny to get to her "eureka" moment.

"But you do want to be able to get in contact with him whenever you want to talk to him or see him, right?" She didn't wait for Logan to agree. "So, what would be the harm in having his number programmed into your cell phone?" she posed.

Her question gave birth to another question in his mind. "Is that what you did?"

She hadn't seen that one coming. For a moment, to save her pride, Destiny was going to say something flippant, or just say "yes" and move on with her point, but that would be lying and she didn't want to lie to him. Besides, lies had a way of tripping you up.

So she shrugged and told him the truth. "I've never had a lover I wanted to reach at a moment's notice." That still conveyed the wrong message, and she knew it. That sounded as if she'd had lovers before, but those men in her past, they had just been casual relationships.

She didn't want Logan thinking something that wasn't true. "I've never actually had a serious lover before."

That surprised him. He looked at her for a long moment before finally asking, "So that makes me your first?"

"In a manner of speaking, yes." She wasn't a virgin. She figured he was experienced enough to realize that. But, if there was such a thing, in the past few years she'd become practically a virgin—until last night.

Wait—what was he saying? She looked at him, her surprise and confusion registering plainly on her face. "Are you saying that you're my lover, or just that we made love?" She needed to get that straight. It might not make a difference to him, but it made all the difference in the world to her.

"Yes," he answered, deliberately leaving it ambiguous for now. And then, before she could ask anything further, the detective in him stepped to the foreground. "But I think you have something there with the cell phone."

She knew she did. It only made sense. She knew Paula. Paula would have wanted to be able to reach the man she was involved with whenever she could.

Thinking out loud, Destiny said, "What we need is to get the records of all the dead women's cell phone calls for, let's say the last three months before they were killed, and what we *really* need is someone who can come up with a program that will cross-reference all the calls our victims made to see if there's a phone number that shows up on all six phones."

From where she stood, that sounded like an incredibly daunting task that, undertaken manually, would make a person cross-eyed and send them running to an optometrist within a matter of a day. But it didn't need to be done manually.

"You have access to anyone like that?" he asked.

Destiny grinned, surprised that he didn't know the answer to that. "Your cousin Dax's wife, Brenda. She can make a computer roll over, sit up and beg in less than sixty seconds."

He'd heard his father mention the name a couple of times, but to be honest, he hadn't been paying all that much attention. He hadn't realized that the woman was a computer wizard *or* a relative, although the latter was by marriage.

"We don't need it to beg," he told her. "We just need it to come up with a common phone number."

"That, too," she promised. Excited, she said, "I think we're finally getting somewhere."

Logan liked the way her eyes danced when she was excited. He surprised her by pulling her back down onto the bed and then beneath him.

"I'm counting on it," he told her, his voice a deep, sexy whisper.

There went her heart again, skipping beats and pounding madly in between.

And in that heart, she knew that as lovely as this interlude with Logan was, it was only temporary. Maybe even just for the weekend, no matter how beguilingly he talked.

Which meant that she needed to savor every second of it before it no longer was.

"It's Sunday," she told him, her body heating as he pressed a kiss to the side of her neck. "I can call her later."

"Good idea," he agreed, getting back to the earnest, all-consuming endeavor of making love with her for as long as he had a breath left within him.

The way he saw it, it was a noble ambition and one hell of a way to go.

It took Brenda less than twelve hours after she was presented with the challenge to come up with a program that could take all six lists of cell phone numbers called and cross-reference them against one another.

And in exactly twelve hours and thirty-nine minutes, Logan and Destiny had their linking phone number.

"Do you know who it belongs to?" Logan asked the chief of detective's daughter-in-law.

Brenda grinned. "Is the pope Catholic? The number belongs to Drake Simmons. It's apparently his private number." Then, in case they didn't know, Brenda added, "He's a big-shot CEO with—"

Destiny cut her short. "Yes, we know," she said between gritted teeth. And to think that he'd had the nerve to look so mournful at Paula's funeral. "He spoke to me at her funeral and told me to call on him at any time if there was any way that he could help us find Paula's killer."

"Apparently, it looks like he's in a good position to point him out to you," Brenda surmised.

Nodding, disgusted, Destiny was in a hurry to get going. "Thanks, Brenda, you're the best."

Brenda flashed her a grin. "Of course I am. Now, if you'll excuse me, I've got a stack of emergencies all waiting to be first." She was already turning her attention to the next case as Destiny and Logan walked out.

"Let's go get the bastard," Destiny said, seething.

"Let's see just how he's connected to all the other women before we go paying Mr. Simmons a visit," Logan advised.

He wanted to be able to make this stick, and he knew she did, too, but she was letting her emotions get the better of her. Not that he could really blame her. If it had been one of his sisters who had been murdered, he knew he would have gone off half-cocked himself. Which was why detectives had partners.

"I don't want to 'talk' to him," Destiny retorted angrily as she walked toward the elevator. "I want to beat him to a pulp."

"Talking first," he emphasized. "And then we'll see about the beating part."

She knew he didn't mean it. Most likely, he knew she didn't either. That she was just blowing off steam, just talking. But for the first time in her life, the thought of physically beating someone did not leave her repulsed. Drake Simmons had killed her baby sister, and she wanted to make him pay for it. She wanted to hurt him.

Being civil to this man who'd made such a show of wanting to help bring Paula's killer to justice, all the while knowing that he was the one responsible for killing her, would not be easy.

As if sensing the turmoil within her, Logan looked at her just before they got on the elevator. "You going to be all right?" he asked.

No, I'm not going to be all right. I may never be all

right. Paula's dead, and that preening Cheshire Cat killed her.

But that, she knew, wasn't what Logan wanted to hear, and if she told him that he'd find a way to stop her from coming with him.

So instead, she said, "Once we nail this son of a bitch and he's in jail, I'll be just peachy."

There was sarcasm if he'd ever heard it, he thought. And he had a feeling that he had his work cut out for him.

Once they knew that Simmons was the "mysterious lover" whom each of the six women were involved with before their untimely deaths, finding the exact connection proved to be easy.

Five years ago, Adele Atkins, the flight attendant, had been on duty on a trans-Atlantic flight that Simmons had taken. Their affair started the moment the plane landed.

Four years ago, Barbara Watson had been his son's junior high school math teacher, and they'd met on back-to-school night. Apparently, what he'd met at back-to-school night he'd taken back to his love nest. That lasted six months before it abruptly ended. Her "suicide" followed in less than a week after the affair was over.

Jennifer Bedlow was next. She was the wedding planner three years ago who handled his daughter Margaret's wedding and was in turn *handled* by Simmons for what appeared to be four months before that, too, ended, only to be shortly followed by her death three days later.

Two years ago Eloise Jorgansen was the hands-on

owner of what was, for nine months, Simmons's favorite restaurant. And then he just stopped going there.

A year ago Debra West had taken Simmons on as her "special" client, training him in private whenever he called, day or night. For that she was paid twice her going rate before she, too, joined the suicide brigade.

And last but definitely not least, Paula had met and apparently fallen for Simmons while asking him to have his company contribute a sizable sum to the Children's Hospital of Aurora.

At first glance, Simmons had very aboveboard reasons for his initial interaction with all these women. It was only when the interactions became intensified and exclusive that things began to look questionable.

And she had just the questions she wanted to ask him once they brought Simmons in.

I'll get him, Paula, she silently promised as she got into the department vehicle beside Logan, who was driving. *He's going to pay for what he did to you, I swear.*

The polite greeting and tight smile Drake Simmons offered when Logan and Destiny were brought into his office quickly faded when the nature of their visit became clear.

Stunned, he could only repeat what he'd just been told. "You're accusing me of killing Paula? Are you out of your minds?" Simmons thundered in a voice that made his underlings quake. "She was a wonderful woman. I would have *never* hurt Paula."

"This went beyond hurt," Destiny bit off, tired of the virtual hide-and-seek game they were playing. "You had an affair with my sister, and when you got tired of her, the way you got tired of all the other women before her, you found that she wasn't going to go quietly. That made her a liability to you and that perfect little world you lived in, so you killed her."

Obviously, Simmons had had enough. "Get out, both of you," he ordered. Then, glaring at Destiny, he added, "You are insane."

"And you are under arrest," she fired back. She glanced in Logan's direction, fully expecting him to back her up. "Put the cuffs on him, Cavanaugh."

Her eyes on Simmons, she was positive she had the right man. His prints were found in Paula's apartment, and she was fairly confident if they showed his photograph to the pharmacist where the sleeping pills had been obtained, the man would ID Simmons as the person who paid for that medication.

"You have the right to remain silent," she recited. "If you give up that right, what you say can and will be held—"

"All right, all right," Simmons cried, pulling away before Logan could secure the handcuffs on his wrists. "I had an affair with your sister," he admitted angrily, "but that's not a crime."

"Killing her is," Destiny snapped.

"I didn't kill her!" Simmons shouted desperately.

Her face was expressionless as she looked at the CEO. "Convince me." It was an order.

Simmons no longer projected cool confidence. Instead, he looked like a man who'd been cornered—and was terrified.

"Tell me what time she was killed." There was a frantic edge to his voice. "And I'll tell you where I was."

When Logan gave the CEO an approximate time of

death, Simmons hesitated for a few seconds, trying to recall his whereabouts that day.

"Wait a minute," he cried. "Let me just call in my assistant—"

"So he can lie for you?" Logan asked knowingly. He wouldn't have been the first high-powered man who'd convinced an underling to take the fall for him.

"No, so he can bring me my schedule. He makes all of my appointments. Howard knows my schedule better than I do."

"And this schedule," Destiny wanted to know, "does it go back five years?"

Simmons paled beneath his very expensive tan. "Why?"

"Because it seems that all the dead women have your private cell phone number programmed into their cell phones."

Pressing the button that connected him to his assistant, Simmons requested that Howard bring the schedule in quickly.

"Make sure you bring in my schedule for the last five years," he emphasized nervously just before releasing the button on the intercom and turning toward Logan and Destiny.

"I know how this looks," he said in a voice that was no longer arrogant but subdued and possibly just a little fearful. "But I didn't kill any of those women. I'm not a monster."

"We'll see" was all Destiny trusted herself to say for now.

Chapter 15

Still handcuffed, Drake Simmons was brought in, then booked and fingerprinted, all while angrily protesting his innocence and demanding to see his lawyer.

"When last seen, your assistant, Howard, was trying to locate your lawyer for you," Logan told the man evenly. "Meanwhile, rather than sending you off to a holding cell in our jail, we've arranged for you to wait in one of our interrogation rooms."

Logan knew it would be just a short matter of time before the CEO's lawyer would post bail for the man. Though he couldn't legally question him, there was always a chance that Simmons, in his anger, would let something unintentionally slip, so it was better to have the man close by than in lockup.

Logan looked at the policeman who'd escorted Simmons down to booking and back. "Put Mr. Simmons in interrogation room three and see that he stays there," he instructed.

Just as Simmons was taken away, Sean Cavanaugh walked into the squad room.

"Dad," Logan said, surprised to see his father. He could count on the fingers of one hand the number of times he'd seen the man out of the lab at the precinct. "What are you doing above the first floor?"

"I came to see if my chief assistant needed some moral support." He looked over toward the desk where Destiny was sitting. "Word has it that you made an arrest on the case."

Getting to her feet, Destiny quickly made her way over to her boss.

"We did," she confirmed. There was no pride in her voice, no indication that the battle was finally over.

Sean had always been able to read people. It was one of the reasons he'd gone into the line of work that he had.

"I sense a 'but' in the air. How airtight is your case?" he asked, looking from his son to Destiny. "What kind of evidence do you have?"

"Circumstantial," Destiny was forced to admit, but she quickly assured the older man, "But there's a ton of it. Simmons's fingerprints are at her apartment, and there are dozens of cell phone calls between them in the week before she died, not to mention too many to count over a period of eight weeks."

Sean shook his head very slowly. "That just proves that they knew each other, not that he killed her," he pointed out quietly.

She didn't want to hear any negative arguments. "He did it, Sean. He's responsible for Paula's murder. I can *feel* it," Destiny insisted.

Sean was nothing if not sympathetic. Although he placed a great deal of emphasis on black-and-white evidence, he also believed that at times, investigators had to go with their gut feeling.

"Then go for it," he urged. "And you—" he turned toward Logan "—help her." It was a direct order, not from a father to his son but from the head of the crime lab to a detective.

"That's what I've been doing, Dad," Logan replied. He wasn't defensive in his answer. There was no need to be. His father knew him well enough to know he didn't lie.

Sean nodded, as if he knew that but had just wanted to hear it said out loud—predominantly for Destiny's benefit.

Simmons's lawyer as well as his assistant arrived less than half an hour later. The delay had been unavoidable because it had taken Simmons's assistant, Howard, that long to find the sections from the CEO's schedule that had mysteriously gone missing.

The printout copies were now safely in Logan's hands, and the pages showed that Simmons had been clear across town, at another hotel room with his latest love interest at the time of Paula's death.

The man was disgusting, Destiny thought as she looked over the pages that provided Simmons with an alibi. He'd no sooner cut her sister loose than he'd hopped into bed with someone else.

Howard took the opportunity to preen before the police department duo. It was obvious that he was enjoying rubbing their noses in his boss's innocence.

"So Mr. Simmons couldn't have been in that woman's apartment, drugging her and slashing her wrists before putting her into the bathtub," Howard crowed as he haughtily looked down his nose at Destiny and Logan. "You're just going to have to pin this on somebody else."

It had almost gone sailing over her head.

Said so quickly by the little man, his words had almost not registered.

But then they did.

And when they did, they wound up hitting her like the proverbial ton of bricks.

Stunned, Destiny exchanged glances with Logan to see if he'd picked up on it, as well. Judging by his delayed reaction, the all-important phrase had taken the long way around getting to her partner, as well.

"Would you mind repeating what you just said?" Logan requested politely.

"You people deaf as well as blind?" Howard demanded nastily. "I *said* Mr. Simmons can't be blamed if that two-bit floozy pumped herself full of drugs and then slashed her wrists. He has important work to do. He's not her guardian angel, you know."

"Nobody would accuse him of being that, that's for sure," Destiny couldn't help saying with more than a little contempt in her voice. "But then, someone might just turn the tables and accuse *you* of killing Paula," she said, suddenly getting into the man's face.

"Me?" Paling, his eyes growing wider and wider, Howard croaked out a protest. "You're crazy, you know that? Absolutely freakin' crazy!"

"Oh, I don't know. That little detail about the drugs found in Paula's system, that was left out of the media story. As a matter of fact, from what I'd read in the other files, that salient point was left out of the articles about *all* the dead women. How is it that you were aware of that information, Mr. Palmer?" Destiny asked pointedly.

A little uneasy, Howard shrugged his sloping shoulders. "I dunno. I must have read it somewhere."

"You're not paying attention, Howard," Destiny told him. She could barely contain her excitement. They might have lost Simmons as a suspect, but Howard was shaping up rather nicely to fill that vacant slot. "That little fact was kept from any and all media. It's our ace in the hole, the let's-see-who-knows-more-than-they're-telling card. No one knew about the drugs in the women's systems except for the investigating detectives and the medical examiner—and the man who killed her." Her eyes narrowed as she leaned in over the table. "Which right now would seem to be you."

"No," he insisted, his voice going up an octave. "You're making a mistake."

"From where I'm standing, you're the one who made the mistake, Howard," she stated.

"You're just trying to pin this on someone!" he accused, then pulled himself up to his full five-foot-five height. "And I've had enough of these accusations. I'm going home."

But as he began to walk toward the door, Logan rose to his feet and all six foot three of him blocked the other man's path.

"I'm afraid I can't let you do that, Howard. It looks like you're going to have to be the guest of the city for a while." His eyes held the other man's. "With any luck, for a very long while."

Real panic seemed to set in as Simmons's personal assistant wobbled on his feet.

"You can't put me in lockup. There's nothing but lowlifes there." Breathing hard, he declared, "You're bluffing. You're just looking to pin these murders on someone," he repeated indignantly.

"Actually, yes, we are," Destiny agreed, then clarified, "The *right* someone, and you now seem to be even a better candidate than your boss. So tell me, how did this play out?" she asked, her voice growing harsh. "He has the good time and when he's done, you get to clean up after him? Does he *pay* you enough for that kind of thing?" she demanded.

Howard Palmer did nothing but whimper.

Splaying her hands on the scarred surface, Destiny leaned over the table, her face inches away from Palmer's. "You realize that this way, he gets to have an alibi and your fingers, so to speak, are all over the crime. He's dumping this all on you, Howard. Without your testimony, he gets to walk and you get the execution chamber. You're the fall guy, Howard." Still inches away from him, Destiny whispered urgently, "Don't let him do this to you."

But Palmer shook his head so hard, some of the sweat from his forehead flew off and managed to make contact with her face.

"You've got this all wrong," he cried. "All wrong. Mr. Simmons never asked me to do anything except offer his ex-girlfriends money, something to tide them over until their lives got back on track. He was never anything less than a gentleman."

Was that what passed for a gentleman these days? Well, not in her book, not by a long shot.

"Right, he's a regular prince," she spat out. "So, what are you saying here, Howard?" Destiny asked the man sharply. "You read between the lines and did what you *thought* Simmons wanted you to do?"

The man blew out a shaky breath as he stared up at the ceiling. He seemed to be hoping that a black hole would open up and swallow him.

Finally he said in a small, still voice, "I did what had to be done."

Logan could see that the second the words were uttered, they'd waved a red flag in front of Destiny. He indicated to her to let him continue asking the questions. They needed a confession, and they needed someone calm to go after it. Right now, that wasn't her.

"And exactly what had to be done, Howard?" Logan pressed.

"The threat had to be eliminated," Howard said, a desperate, pleading edge back in his voice.

"What threat?" Destiny asked. This wasn't making any sense. Her sister had never been a threat to anyone.

"Why, to Mr. Simmons's good name, of course," the assistant insisted, as if that was elementary and as plain as day. "If one of those whores decided to sell her story to one of those tabloid rags, his career chances would be over."

Destiny and Logan exchanged looks. Simmons had climbed up as high in his company as a man could go. "I'm afraid you lost us, Howard," Logan told him, then asked, "What career chances?"

Fidgeting, Howard sighed impatiently, as if trying to suffer through dealing with imbeciles. "It hasn't been made public yet, but Mr. Simmons has been planning for years on running for senator. If word got out about his insatiable sexual appetite—"

"Most likely he'd fit right in with the Washington crowd," Logan concluded cynically.

But Howard disagreed. "Mr. Simmons needed a spotless record. He might not have realized that, but I did," he said importantly. "He has a wife, a family. If his affairs came to light, he might not get elected."

It was beginning to come together. Destiny felt outraged as well as sick to her stomach.

"So you're telling us that you killed all those women just to protect Simmons's good name?" Destiny asked incredulously.

"Someone had to," Howard insisted with passion.

"And Simmons never asked you to do any of this? Not even indirectly?" Logan asked.

"Mr. Simmons, I'm ashamed to admit, was usually

already involved with someone else and not thinking about any woman who had come before." Howard pressed his lips together. "Mr. Simmons doesn't walk away from one woman without having his sights set on another one."

"A game plan, how very organized of him," Destiny bit off sarcastically. She rose from her chair. "Well, I think we've got enough on him to make this stick."

Logan was already on his feet. "I totally agree," he responded.

Howard looked from one interrogator to the other and then back again, his head all but spinning. "Make what stick?" he asked nervously, his voice rising and cracking on the last word.

"Oh, you're a smart man, Howard," Destiny told him in a syrupy voice. "I think you can figure it out." And with that, she walked out of the room with Logan right behind her.

Howard began to yell after them, but she made no effort to listen, or to turn around and walk back in. As far as she was concerned, her work here was done. She'd lived up to her promises, both her silent one to her sister and to the verbal one she'd given Mrs. West about bringing the woman's daughter's killer to justice.

"Take him down to booking," Logan told the detective they'd left posted outside the interrogation room.

The detective looked more than happy to comply.

Destiny sighed as she leaned back in the passenger seat. After making sure that everything was in order and all the right reports were filed, she and Logan were finally calling it a night and leaving the precinct.

It had been a long, long day, and she was more than tired. But happy. Very, very happy. And then it hit her. Right between the eyes.

It was over.

She'd found the man who had killed not just her sister, but also five other women. There was no need for her to hang around the squad room any longer.

And that was when the full implication of that hit her, as well. She could go back to the crime lab. Her work was done.

And so were they.

Out of sight, out of mind, right? And if she needed any proof of that, all she had to do was look at the life expectancy of any one of Logan's affairs. It gave new meaning to the words *short-term*.

It was probably over already. He might just drop her off at her door and not come in. Or, if he did, it would be just "one last time" and then they—she—would be history.

She'd been way too quiet, Logan thought. Not that the woman had ever been exactly a chatterbox, but this was eerily silent, even for her.

"You know," he said, glancing at Destiny as they came to a red light and stopped, "for a woman who just nailed the guy responsible for killing her sister, not to mention five other women, you sure don't look very happy."

"Oh, I'm very happy," she protested.

He shifted his foot off the brake and back onto the

accelerator. "If that's very happy, remind me to run for the hills when you're being very sad."

Right, as if he was going to stay one more second than he had to. "Don't worry, you won't be around to see that."

"Why?" he pressed. "Where am I going to be? You know something I don't?" Had there been some sort of a shake-up in the department he hadn't heard about? He had a habit of ignoring memos and email communications, which at times made him the last to know about precinct matters.

"I'll be going back down to the crime lab."

"Okay." He drew the word out, waiting for more, for some sort of enlightenment.

Annoyed, she blew out a breath. "And you'll be up here."

Still no enlightenment. "So? You're talking about four floors, not scaling the Himalayas or going halfway around the world."

"It might as well be that."

Okay, he needed to call her on this since she obviously wasn't going to volunteer anything remotely close to plain talk unless he deliberately *asked* her to.

"I've got three sisters, Richardson. I know all about sideways thinking and stuff coming out of mouths that make absolutely no sense to the male mind. I've always been good at putting the pieces together and solving puzzles, but I've got to admit you have me completely stumped. Just what the hell are you talking about?"

She stared straight ahead into the darkness as he

approached her apartment complex. "You don't have to pretend."

"Pretend what? That I'm confused?" he guessed when she didn't say anything. "This isn't pretending. I am *really* confused. What are you talking about?" Logan asked again.

She looked at him. "You don't know what I'm talking about," she said sarcastically.

Finally, at least they'd established that. "Hell, I haven't got a *clue* what you're talking about."

Now he was getting her angry. Did he think she was simpleminded? "I'm talking about moving on."

Pulling up into a space in guest parking, he turned off the ignition and looked at her, stunned. Where had this come from? He'd thought they were doing well. Progressing, even. And now she hit him with this. "You want to move on?"

Oh, God, *why* was he doing this to her? Torturing her this way? They both knew what she was like. "No, *you* want to move on."

He stared at her as if she'd lost her mind. And then a trickle of relief began to flow through him. "Well, if I do, I haven't told me yet, so let's just keep that a secret."

"This isn't funny, Logan," Destiny insisted, glaring at him.

"*Finally*. Something we can agree on."

For just a second, she was speechless. Was he saying that...?

No, this was Logan Cavanaugh, a man who'd refused to have any ties outside his family. For some reason, he was playing mind games with her. Well, no more beating around the bush. She intended to resolve this head-on. She couldn't take nurturing false hopes.

"You're telling me that you don't want to move on."

He never blinked as he repeated, "I'm telling you that I don't want to move on."

So maybe she had a little more time with him, but that didn't change what was eventually coming, and she knew it. They *both* knew it.

"Yet," she said.

"Ever," he countered.

No, no, she couldn't let herself get sucked in. She couldn't allow herself to believe that he was talking about something permanent.

And yet…

Her voice was far less confident and a little shaky as she began, "So you're telling me—"

He didn't want to go another round of trading barbs or having her toss accusations at him. He couldn't blame Destiny for being skeptical. He figured she knew all about his reputation. Hell, everyone knew all about his reputation.

But this had nothing to do with his reputation and everything to do with his new view on what life should *really* be about. About having the same person beside you, the same person to love and share things with, good *and* bad.

"That I love you and I intend to stick around until you toss me out," he said, concluding what he knew she hadn't been about to say.

Every inch of her was tingling now. It began to dawn

on her that he just might be serious. "And if I don't toss you out?"

His smile was almost radiant. "Then I become a permanent fixture in your life."

Everything inside of her was holding its breath, wanting so desperately to believe what he was saying. At the same time, she was afraid to believe it.

"How permanent?" she asked, her voice a low whisper.

"Permanent-permanent." He brushed his fingertips along her face, exciting both of them. "Bonding cement permanent. World-without-end permanent." The urge to kiss her was tremendous, but this had to be put to bed first. "Convinced yet?"

Her mouth was cotton dry. "Not yet. I'm still working on stunned."

"You work on 'stunned,'" he told her, moving aside the hair against her neck and then touching his lips to her skin. "I'll work on you."

Her eyes fluttered shut as delicious sensations sprang up, fully grown and raring to go. "You know I can't think when you do that."

She felt him laugh against her skin. Who would have thought that could excite her, as well? But it did. Very much.

"That's the whole idea," he told her, pressing another kiss to her neck. Sending shimmies of desire through her. "You've done entirely too much thinking. Time to bring your senses into play."

It was hard to think. Harder to talk, but she had to

tell him this. "Well, before my senses start playing, I just want to tell you that I love you, too."

"I know."

She drew back to look at him. How could he know when she'd just really found out herself? The moment he'd said he loved her, something strong and kindred had leaped to the foreground within her.

"You know?"

He nodded and there was that sexy smile again, completely turning her to mush inside. "Your eyes gave you away."

She laughed softly, finally beginning to relax, to feel that it was going to be all right. "I didn't realize you were a student of eyes."

He raised one shoulder in a careless shrug. "Eyes, lips, nose, vital body parts—I'm a student of everything there is to study and know about you. Now, if you don't mind," he went on, his eyes teasing her, "I've fallen behind in my homework and I need to catch up."

There it was again, that thrill of anticipation. "Far be it for me to keep you from your homework."

He laughed then and she hugged the sound to her. Getting out of the car, he rounded the trunk—or half the trunk.

They met in the middle.

"That's my girl."

"Yes," she told him, entwining her arms around his neck, "I am."

It was the start of a record-breaking kiss.

Logan had intended to ask her to marry him, but he

realized that she might not be ready to hear that just yet. That was all right. It would keep. He could be patient.

But not too patient, he thought as the kiss intensified.

Maybe he'd ask her in the morning.

It sounded good to him.

* * * * *

Casually Tab leaned against the fence beside Aiden. "It almost sounds like you're asking me to help."

"Does it, now?"

"You bet it does. It's almost like we're investigating. Both of us. Together." She covered her smug grin by draining the last of her coffee. "I seem to recall something you said about not wanting my help because it was too... What was it you said? It was too dangerous for a delicate flower like me."

"I'm real sure I never called you a flower."

"I added that part," she said. "You know what you said."

He shoved away from the fence and stood tall before her. "If you're done with your I-told-you-so, I'd like to put things into motion."

"And you want me to help you investigate." She looked up through her eyelashes.

"I reckon I do."

MONTANA MIDWIFE

BY
CASSIE MILES

MILLS & BOON

First published in Great Britain 2013
by Mills & Boon, an imprint of Harlequin (UK) Limited,
Eton House, 18-24 Paradise Road, Richmond, Surrey TW9 1SR

© Kay Bergstrom 2012

ISBN: 978 0 263 90342 3
ebook ISBN: 978 1 472 00690 5

46-0113

Harlequin (UK) policy is to use papers that are natural, renewable and
recyclable products and made from wood grown in sustainable forests. The
logging and manufacturing processes conform to the legal environmental
regulations of the country of origin.

Printed and bound in Spain
by Blackprint CPI, Barcelona

Though born in Chicago and raised in LA, *USA TODAY* bestselling author **Cassie Miles** has lived in Colorado long enough to be considered a semi-native. The first home she owned was a log cabin in the mountains overlooking Elk Creek, with a thirty-mile commute to her work at the Denver Post.

After raising two daughters and cooking tons of macaroni and cheese for her family, Cassie is trying to be more adventurous in her culinary efforts. Ceviche, anyone? She's discovered that almost anything tastes better with wine. When she's not plotting Mills & Boon® Intrigue books, Cassie likes to hang out at the Denver Botanical Gardens near her high-rise home.

In memory of Rosemary Heiser.
She will be missed.

Chapter One

On a high ridge overlooking the Little Big Horn River, Tab Willows sat up straight in the saddle and lifted her arm above her head. Finally, she had a signal for her cell phone. There was no way she could find Misty and her boyfriend unless they gave her better directions to their location. This horse didn't come equipped with GPS.

She hit the redial.

Misty Gabriel answered immediately. "Tab, where are you? I need you."

Panic trembled in her voice, which was understandable for a woman in labor with her first baby. For some unexplainable reason, Misty and Clinton had decided to go off-roading and had gotten their vehicle stuck in a creek bed that was damp with melt from a recent snow. The early November weather wasn't bad right now, but night was coming. With the darkness came an icy chill.

Tab hadn't been working with Misty as a regular client in her midwife practice, but she felt an obligation and a connection to this young woman she used to babysit, even though, as adults, they didn't appear to have much in common. Misty was the spoiled seventeen-year-old daughter of a wealthy ranching family. Bubbly and blonde, she giggled with every other breath. In contrast, Tab seldom laughed out loud. Her overall appearance—dusky-colored skin and straight black hair worn in a single braid down to her waist—favored her mother's Crow heritage. Her blue eyes came from her dad.

"I'm looking down at the area you described," Tab said, "but I don't see your Jeep. Give me directions."

"Like what?" She giggled nervously. "It's not like there are street signs or anything."

Focus, Misty. "Any unusual rock formations?"

"Oh, yeah. On the other side of the river and up a slope, there's a big cave we used to play in when we were kids."

"Half-Moon Cave."

That landmark told Tab the approximate whereabouts. When Misty had first called, she'd said there were no passable roads, which was why Tab was on horseback. She wished she'd taken her van; there was a decent route that ran fairly close to Misty's location.

"Half-Moon Cave, that's right." Her giggle broke into a sob. "You've got to hurry. Clinton hit his head."

Of course, he did. This situation just got worse and worse. "Is he conscious?"

"Kind of. He was trying to push the Jeep out of the mud and he slipped and conked his forehead on the bumper."

On horseback, there was no way to evacuate a man with a concussion and a woman in labor. "Let's talk about you. How far apart are your pains?"

"I don't know. It just hurts."

"And how many months along are you?"

"Eight-ish. The doctor said I could have the baby any time now."

In the best-case scenario, Misty was experiencing Braxton Hicks contractions that wouldn't lead to childbirth. Or she could be going into early labor. "I want you to stay calm. Take slow, steady breaths, okay?"

"Whatever you say, Tab."

"One thing I don't understand," she said. "Why didn't you call your brother to come for you?"

Her brother, Aiden Gabriel, provided a private rescue-helicopter service for the local hospitals, the sheriff and national park rescue teams. Because he also worked on the family ranch, he wasn't always available, but Tab knew that Aiden would drop everything to rescue his baby sister.

"Aiden is a big old jerk," Misty said. "And he doesn't like Clinton."

An opinion Tab could easily comprehend. Clinton had taken his very pregnant girlfriend on an off-road adventure, gotten them stuck and then knocked himself unconscious. Clearly, he wasn't the sharpest arrow in the quiver. "Brace yourself, Misty. I'm calling your brother. You need his help."

"Maybe not. I think I see somebody coming."

"Stay where you are," Tab said sharply. "I can't find you if you go wandering off."

"Okay. See you later, elevator."

"Real soon, harvest moon."

Tab smiled as she remembered the rhyming games she and Misty played ten years ago. Tab had been sixteen. Her life had been split between living with her dad in Billings and with her grandma, Maria Spotted Bear, on the Crow reservation. When her dad had been hired to do contracting work at the Gabriel ranch near Henley, she'd tagged along and had gotten recruited as a live-in babysitter for seven-year-old Misty.

That summer had been a rough time for the Gabriel family. Misty's dad had been killed in a car accident. Tab felt like she could understand Misty's grief because she'd lost her mom and knew what it was like to have a parent die too young. She and Misty had bonded but their friendship wasn't the main thing that happened that summer. That summer, Tab had fallen in love for the first time.

Looking down at her cell phone, she remembered the tall,

lean, handsome Aiden Gabriel with his thick brown hair and his dreamy gray eyes. He'd been twenty-one when he came home from college and shouldered the responsibilities of a ranch owner, helping his mom to cope when her husband died. Though Tab never told anyone, she'd dreamed of Aiden every night, imagining his kiss and what it would feel like to be held in his strong arms. Once, he'd given her a necklace with a shiny four-leaf clover pendant, which she'd worn for years before tucking it away in her jewelry box.

Tab hadn't spoken to Aiden since moving back to this area, but she'd seen him recently at a meeting in Crow Agency where the topic was the ongoing law enforcement problems on the reservation. After noticing that he was still the best-looking cowboy she'd ever seen, she'd grabbed one of his business cards and recorded his number on her phone to use in case of birthing emergencies. This circumstance qualified. She hit the speed dial.

On the third ring, he answered, "This is Aiden Gabriel."

"Hi, it's Tab." A pause stretched between them. He didn't remember her. And wasn't that a knife to the gut? She clarified, "Tab Willows. I saw you at that law enforcement meeting in Crow Agency and took your card."

"Tabitha." He was one of the few people who used her full name. "You haven't been around for a while. I heard you were at nursing school in Missoula."

"That's right." Hearing his voice cast her backward in time to when she was a lovesick teenager wishing on a star that he'd notice her. She swallowed hard. "I'm a midwife."

"We have some catching up to do."

Tongue-tied, she mumbled, "Guess so."

"It's been a long time, but I'll never forget that pretty, young girl with long black hair who used to race my fastest horse across the fields bareback."

He'd thought she was pretty? If he'd told her when she was

sixteen, she would have exploded in a wild burst of angst and joy. Even now, his compliment made it hard for her to breathe. "Misty needs your help."

"What happened?"

"She called me because she's having labor pains. She and her boyfriend got their Jeep stuck in a creek bed, and she needs to be evacuated."

"Are you with her?"

"On my way," Tab said. "But I can't bring her in because I'm on horseback. Misty said they were near Half-Moon Cave."

"I know where it is," he said. "Tabitha, I hope you remember what was discussed at that meeting. If you're riding alone, you should be prepared for trouble."

In her work, she often traveled alone, heading to remote locations to work with women in labor. And she didn't take unnecessary chances. A rifle scabbard was tucked under her saddlebags. "I'm armed."

"See you there."

With her cell phone tucked into the pocket of her brown denim jacket, she flicked the reins and nudged her heel into the flank of Shua, her grandma's blue-black mare with the white blaze on her forehead. With minimal direction, the horse descended from the ridge and galloped across a wide valley dotted with patches of old snow.

As she directed Shua uphill through a stand of pine trees, she wondered how she could arrange to ride back to the hospital in the helicopter with Aiden. Unfortunately, she couldn't abandon her horse, even though Shua could probably find her own way back to the corral outside her grandma's house. The chopper ride would have to wait for another day.

If she took Misty as a client, she'd have plenty of opportunity to see Aiden. Not that she needed an excuse. Her midwife work made it important to know the emergency providers.

She had every reason to call him and set a coffee date or invite him to her grandma's house and bake him a pie. Did he still like apple? Would he still think she was pretty?

A blast of gunfire echoed through the canyons and across the fields. Three shots.

Shua reared back. Tab's memories and daydreams shattered. There was trouble ahead.

If her reckoning was correct, Half-Moon Cave was just over the next rise. She urged her horse to go faster. From the hilltop, she looked down at a field near the canyon walls and saw the open-top Jeep with the rear tires buried up to the hubcaps in the mud. Taking her rifle from the scabbard, Tab held it to her shoulder and peered through the scope for a better look at the vehicle. There was a man sprawled in the backseat; she couldn't tell if he'd been shot. Misty was nowhere in sight.

This couldn't be good. Tab cocked her rifle and fired into the air. Her gunfire would warn off attackers and let Misty know that help was on the way.

Two more shots answered hers.

Rifle in hand, Tab rode fast. Her long braid bounced against her back, and the wind streamed across her cheeks. Her protective instincts came to the fore as she remembered the vulnerable child she babysat so long ago.

Approaching the Jeep, she shouted, "Misty?"

Loud sobbing came from a tangle of willows and cottonwoods that bordered the river. Still on horseback, Tab approached. If any real marksmanship was required, she'd need to dismount and brace herself. Right now, she wanted the option of fast maneuvering on Shua.

"Misty, are you all right?"

"I'm over here."

In a small clearing, Tab saw the body of a man who had

been shot in the chest. His jacket hung open. His eyes stared blankly at the darkening sky. He wasn't moving.

Kneeling on the ground beside him was Misty. She held her bloody hands in front of her as though afraid to touch anything. A rifle lay on the ground.

Misty turned her tear-streaked face toward her. "I didn't kill him. I swear I didn't."

THOUGH AIDEN WAS ALWAYS on call for emergencies, it usually took a while for him to get started because he had to drive to the air field in Henley to pick up his six-passenger helicopter, a Bell Long Ranger. Today, he needed only to walk from the barn to the helipad near his cabin at the Gabriel family ranch. Earlier today, he'd given piloting lessons to a couple of the ranch hands. With winter coming, there wasn't as much work for the cowboys to do, and Aiden could use some part-time help with his newly established rescue business.

Less than fifteen minutes after Tabitha's call, he was in the cockpit. He fastened his seat belt, depressed the starter, checked the fuel-pressure gauge, opened the throttle and pointed the nose toward the southeast. If he'd been following roads, the drive to Half-Moon Cave near the Little Big Horn River would have taken nearly an hour. Swooping through the sky cut his arrival time to approximately twenty minutes. Top speed was necessary. From what Tabitha had told him, Misty might be giving birth at any moment.

He hadn't been pleased when his baby sister turned up pregnant. Misty was fourteen years younger than he was, not much more than a child herself. Aiden still had a hard time thinking of her as a mother, but the idea of having a nephew had grown on him.

As his mom constantly pointed out, it was time for a new generation in the Gabriel family. Mom would have preferred a marriage before the baby, but she'd take what she could get, especially since it didn't look like Aiden would be heading toward the altar any time soon. His long-distance relationship had fizzled last month when they'd argued about where to spend Christmas. Aiden had point-blank refused to make the trip to Los Angeles to hang tinsel on palm trees, and his lady had no interest in coming to the ranch. The breakup had been inevitable. They'd grown apart.

Using his headset, he put through a call to Tabitha's cell phone. When she answered, he clarified his directions. "I think I'm getting close. I'm following the course of the river."

"We're on the east side. Near a dried-up creek. Please hurry, Aiden."

He heard the note of urgency in her voice. "What's wrong? Is it the baby?"

"Misty is fine." She paused. "There's been a shooting."

"Are you safe?"

"I think the shooter took off, but I can't be sure."

"I'll be there in a few minutes," he said. "Tell me when you hear me getting close."

"I think we're okay," she said. "We took cover by the river."

He leaned forward as though his will could force the chopper to fly faster. The landscape below was a rugged sea of dry field grass and clumps of sage brush. "Did you see the gunman?"

"I can barely hear you, Aiden."

"Stay on the line." Like a 911 operator, he needed to maintain contact so he'd be aware of the situation. "What can you tell me?"

"Not much. Misty will have to do the explaining."

A shooter had come after his sister? His grip tensed on the cyclic stick as he swerved to the left. He never expected anything like this, never thought violence would reach out and touch his family. "Was anyone shot?"

"Yes," she said tersely. "It's not Misty or her boyfriend. Somebody else."

"Is he seriously wounded?"

"I really can't hear you," Tabitha said.

"Don't hang up. Keep the line open."

He should have expected something like this. Law enforcement had become a serious problem in the area, especially on the Crow reservation. Tribal lands spread across nearly two and a half million acres with only a handful of officers and a couple of agents from the Bureau of Indian Affairs to keep order. And the situation in Henley wasn't much better. Budget cuts had sliced the police and sheriff's department to the bare bone.

At the meeting in Crow Agency, the tribal police told them to be on the lookout for two girls from Henley who were last seen on the rez before they went missing. Nobody mentioned the possibility of a serial killer, but the threat was implied. Both of the missing girls were blondes like Misty.

"Aiden, I can hear your chopper."

On the opposite side of the river, he saw the sandstone cliffs and rock formations. "I'm near Half-Moon Cave."

"Do you see us? Do you see the Jeep?"

He spotted Clinton's open-top vehicle stuck in the creek bed. Beside it was a black horse. Relief flooded through him when he saw Misty in her bright pink jacket step out from the cover of the trees and wave with both arms. She was safe. For now.

Chapter Two

Aiden stood over the body of a man who wasn't much older than his sister. The fresh blood on his shirt made a vivid splash of crimson against the dry prairie grass in the clearing. The wind sighed through the bare branches of trees, and the rushing of the river played a quiet dirge. The family and friends of this young man would mourn his passing. Out of respect for them and for the victim, Aiden spread a tarp from the helicopter over the body.

He stood and took a step back.

His sister had a talent for getting into trouble, but this went beyond her usual. When he turned, he saw Misty was standing by the Jeep with her boyfriend. This time, she'd gotten herself involved in a murder. There would be consequences.

Before landing, he'd done an aerial sweep of the area and had seen nothing that appeared threatening. In the afternoon sunlight, his vision extended for miles in every direction. He hadn't spotted the shooter fleeing or hiding among the rocks and brush. There were no signs of a getaway vehicle, which didn't surprise Aiden. Almost an hour had passed since the first phone call from Tabitha; that was plenty of time for a shooter to put distance between himself and the scene of the crime.

If there was a shooter…

As he moved to the edge of the clearing, Tabitha joined

him. "I'm glad you covered him," she said. "I wasn't sure if that would disturb evidence."

"We aren't exactly dealing with a crack team of CSI investigators." He'd done enough work with local law enforcement to know the drill. "The police will be more concerned with obvious stuff. That's Misty's rifle on the ground. Do you know how it got here?"

"You need to ask her."

"There's a smear of blood on the stock."

"When I arrived," Tabitha said, "Misty was kneeling beside the body. I think she was trying to help. She had blood on her hands."

"Do you think she did it?" He asked the question of the sky and the hills and the river. "Do you think she killed that young man?"

"I don't know."

Though he wasn't sure what he'd do, Aiden had to know the truth. "Misty isn't a murderer."

"No, she's not."

For the first time since he'd landed, he looked directly at Tabitha. Her blue-eyed gaze was disconcerting, partly because the color was unexpected and partly because she was a lot prettier than he remembered with high cheekbones and a strong, stubborn chin. Her long black braid glistened in the fading sunlight. Though he should have been focused on his sister and the murdered man, this beautiful woman distracted him. His fingers itched to unfasten her braid and caress her silky hair.

"There is a plus side," she said. "Emergency medical evacuation isn't necessary. Not for Misty, anyway."

He watched her full lips as she spoke. "Does that mean she isn't in labor?"

"I haven't done a full exam, obviously. But her mysterious labor pains seem to have disappeared, and she's a month away from her due date. I advised her to check with her doctor in case there are complications. She might need to be on bed rest."

"I like that idea." With an effort, he reined in his inappropriate thoughts about Tabitha's long legs and slender waist. "It'd be nice to keep Misty close to home before the baby comes."

"I'm more concerned about Clinton." Her crisp, professional tone helped create a distance between them. "I patched up his head wound, but he's had a concussion and needs to be under observation."

"I understand." But he didn't agree. He could have cited five or six times when he'd been knocked unconscious and had survived just fine. "I'm mighty glad you got here when you did. This situation could have been worse. Not that there's anything worse than murder."

Even if his sister was the killer? Surely, there was an explanation. Self-defense?

"We should call the sheriff," Tabitha said.

"But this is reservation land. That means we call the Crow police chief, Joseph Lefthand. I've worked with him before. He's good at his job."

"I agree. Joseph is a good, dedicated lawman."

He took out his cell phone. "I'll call him."

"Wait," she said. "The tribal police don't have the resources to process forensic evidence, and I want to make sure the investigation is done right. This isn't a straightforward murder."

"It's not that complicated." He didn't need to go into detail about how his aerial sweep failed to show evidence of a killer on the run, or how Misty's rifle was on the ground beside the body. "We're looking at an obvious case of self-defense."

"That's not what Misty says."

"Do you believe her, Tabitha?"

"I do. Your sister might be irresponsible, but she's not a liar." She arched an eyebrow. "Please call me Tab. The only other person who uses my full name is my grandma, and that's only when she's mad at me."

Her slight smile made him want to see a full-fledged grin and to hear her laughter. "I remember your grandma. Maria Spotted Bear." He looked past the Jeep to where a black mare was grazing. "Is that her horse?"

"Shua," Tab said. "Don't ask me why a black horse is named with the Crow word for blue. Grandma has her reasons."

"Is she well?"

"According to her, she's in great health. But she's been diagnosed with a touch of congenital heart failure. A couple of months ago, she fainted and broke her wrist. One of the reasons I moved back here was to take care of her."

"Sorry to hear that she's ailing."

Tab shrugged. A simple gesture, but he found it charming. "How's Sylvia?"

"Mom is strong as an ox. It's hard to believe she's almost sixty."

A silence stretched between them. Much had happened in the ten years they'd been out of contact. Though he'd never been a real chatty sort of guy, he had an urge to tell her everything about his life, his hopes and his dreams. With so much to say, he didn't know where to start.

Tab took the first step. "Let's talk to your sister, and then we can decide who to call."

Together, they returned to the Jeep where Misty leaned against the front bumper with her arms cradling her belly. Clinton stood beside her. He'd slapped his cowboy hat onto his head, almost covering the gauze bandage that Tab had applied.

"I know what you're thinking," Clinton said. "I should have protected my girl. But I was out cold."

"And you didn't see anything," Aiden said.

"No, sir."

He turned to his sister. "I'm guessing that you were attacked. Maybe this guy—"

"David Welling." There was a hitch in her voice. "His name is David Welling."

"Okay, David Welling came at you, maybe he—"

"I can't believe he's dead."

"Calm down, sweetie. Take a nice, slow, deep breath." He waited until she'd composed herself before he continued, "It's not your fault. You had to shoot David in self-defense."

"I didn't shoot anybody." She shook her head, and her curly blond hair whipped across her face. "I never would shoot anybody."

Aiden exchanged a glance with Tab. She'd warned him that his sister's story was complicated. "Take your time, Misty. Tell me exactly what happened."

"I was waiting for Tab. I heard a noise over by the river, and I got my rifle out of the back of the Jeep. I was scared that somebody might come after us. Poor Clinton was unconscious, and I couldn't let anybody hurt him."

"Whoa," Clinton said. "I'm not helpless. I could've got to my feet and taken care of you."

Aiden held up his hand, signaling Clinton to stop. "I'm listening to Misty, now."

She continued, "As soon as I got a little bit closer—"

"Did you take the rifle with you?"

"I left it right here." She pointed to the front bumper. "I figured that if I needed it, I could run back and grab it real quick."

"But I thought you were trying to protect Clinton?"

She tapped her foot. "Do you want to hear this, or not, Aiden?"

Understanding her motivations was like asking a chicken why it pecked in the dirt. "Go on."

"I recognized David. I dated him before he graduated high school and moved away from Henley."

As far as Aiden could tell, she'd dated most of the male population of Henley High, which made it even more astounding that she'd ended up with a pea brain like Clinton. "Is this David Welling any relation to Bert Welling who runs a gas station in Henley?"

"Bert is his uncle," Misty said. "David used to pump gas for Bert before he moved to Billings with his dad. Anyway, when I saw him standing there in the clearing, I said hi. And he said I shouldn't be here, and I told him that we were stuck, and he said I needed to get away from here, to get the hell away from here."

Her eyes welled up with tears. "Then I heard the shots. David grabbed his chest and fell down. And there was blood. Oh my God, there was a lot of blood."

"Did you see who shot him?"

"I hit the dirt. I thought they were shooting at me. I covered my head and I thought about my baby. I couldn't let anything bad happen to my baby, I just couldn't."

Her hands flew up to cover her face as heavy sobs shook her shoulders. For once, Clinton did the right thing, stepping forward to comfort her and hold her against his chest. His protective attitude made Aiden wonder if there was something Misty had left out of her story.

Clinton might have been the shooter. Misty could be claiming responsibility to keep her boyfriend from being a suspect. But that didn't make sense. A self-defense plea worked just as well for Clinton as for Misty. Aiden doubted that either one of them would be charged with murder…except for one hitch. The victim appeared to be unarmed.

As Misty's sobs abated, Aiden asked, "Why was your rifle in the clearing?"

"I ran back to get it, but the gun wasn't where I left it."

"Where was it?"

"Right about here." She pointed to a clump of sagebrush that was about twenty yards from the clearing. "I could tell it had been fired."

"Are you saying that the killer used your rifle?"

"I don't know."

"Did you see him?" he asked.

"He must have run off."

Or maybe he turned invisible. Aiden was getting more and more frustrated with her story. "How long between when you heard the shot and ran back to get the rifle?"

"I don't know."

"Think, Misty."

Tears streaked down her cheeks. "Don't be so mean to me."

"I can help," Tab said. "When I heard the first shot, I was on the other side of those hills. It took five or six minutes before I got to the crest and could see the Jeep. Clinton was unconscious in the backseat. I fired a warning shot in the air to scare off anybody who might be hanging around."

"I shot back," Misty said. "I didn't aim at anything. I was just shooting in the air. Twice."

Aiden fitted the pieces together. According to his sister, a mysterious shooter had killed David Welling using her rifle, and then disappeared within five minutes. He gauged the distance from where she found the rifle to the trees and shrubs that bordered the river. Though it was possible that the killer could make that dash, it was unlikely. Why use Misty's rifle? Why choose this particular moment to kill David Welling? And what was Welling doing out here in the first place?

After patting his sister on the arm and offering reassurances that he hoped weren't empty, Aiden pulled Tab to one side. His senses registered the clean fragrance of her shampoo and the warmth that emanated from her body, but he kept his mind trained on the problem at hand.

"You're right," he said to Tab. "This investigation is beyond the resources of the tribal police. But we still need to contact Joseph Lefthand."

"I'm not sure of the procedure," she said.

He explained. First, they needed to notify tribal police of a crime committed on their land. In most cases, the Crow were happy to pass on the problem and cede jurisdiction through an agent of the federal government, namely someone from the Bureau of Indian Affairs. Then the county sheriff would take over.

"I hope the sheriff can get started with his investigation before dark." She looked toward the sun sinking in the west. "There might be footprints from the gunman. Or evidence of his vehicle."

"If Misty's story is accurate," he said, "ballistics will show that the bullets came from her rifle."

"There might be fingerprints."

"In addition to Misty's prints." She'd already said that she fired the gun and would, therefore, have gunshot residue on her clothes.

He wished that his sister had come up with a more convincing story—something about how David Welling attacked her, and she was forced to defend herself. The idea of a murderer who could appear out of nowhere and vanish in the blink of an eye was improbable. It sounded like a lie. And lying made Misty look as if she had something to hide.

If this investigation went wrong, it was entirely possible that his sister would be delivering her baby in jail.

Chapter Three

While Aiden and Clinton messed around with the Jeep, trying to dig out the rear tires, Tab took a striped wool blanket from her saddlebags and handed it to Misty. "Spread this on the ground. Choose a spot that's out of the wind."

"Why?"

"You might as well get comfortable. It's going to take a while for the authorities to get here."

Definitely an understatement. When Aiden had put through calls to the tribal police, the BIA and the sheriff, she'd heard the growing frustration in his voice. Everybody promised to respond just as soon as they could, which meant they had other business to clean off their plates.

Though Tab thought that murder should take precedence, she was accustomed to bureaucracy. There was nothing to do but wait. She dug through her saddlebag, ignoring the medical equipment, and found a square plastic container packed with more practical supplies.

"All this waiting around sucks," Misty said. She turned her gaze toward the clearing where the body lay covered by a tarp. "But I won't leave. I owe it to David to talk to the sheriff. I'm the only witness."

And the most obvious suspect. In spite of the giggles and the frequent flipping of her blond hair, Misty wasn't a fool. The girl had to realize how implausible her story about the vanishing gunman sounded. She had to know that she could be charged with murder.

Tab followed her to a spot beside a low flat rock and helped her lay the blanket over the dried prairie grass. "Tell me about David."

"We only went out on one date. There wasn't any kissing or anything." Misty gave her a conspiratorial grin. "Can I tell you a secret? You have to promise not to let Aiden know."

As Tab felt herself being drawn more deeply into the situation, her defenses rose. The smart move would be to back off. She was a midwife, not a policewoman. A murder investigation wasn't her problem. But her heart wouldn't let her abandon Misty. "Does your secret have anything to do with David Welling's death?"

"No way," Misty said.

"Then I won't tell anybody else. I promise. Wild horses won't drag it out of me."

"In sophomore year at Henley High, me and Lisa and Heather made a bet. Whoever was the first to date every guy in the junior and senior class was the winner."

"Why juniors and seniors? You were sophomores."

"The boys our age were dorks, and most of them didn't have their driver's licenses. That's why we went for the older guys. Our bet wasn't as wild as it sounds. There were only seventy-six guys total in both classes."

Their bet sounded like a sure way to get into trouble. Tab imagined these three little heartbreakers sowing havoc at Henley High. "What counted as a date?"

"The guy had to invite you. It could be a study date or a ski trip or going to a party. Or they had to buy you something, like if you went out in a group and they paid for your burger."

"What happened with you and David?"

"He was fixing a flat tire for me at his uncle's gas station—"

"Wait a minute. How old were you?"

"Not old enough to have my license, if that's what you're getting at."

"You stole the car?"

"Borrowed it from Aiden. He was too busy running the ranch and learning how to pilot his chopper to be worried about me." She rolled her eyes. "Geez, Tab. I started driving around on the ranch as soon as I was big enough to see over the steering wheel. You know how it is."

"I do." Tab had attended high school in Billings—a city where regulations were enforced. Though Henley was less than fifty miles away, she knew that different rules applied. "So, you and David were at the gas station. Then what?"

"We got to talking. I barely knew him. He was really shy and quiet, didn't play football or basketball. But he had a real cute smile."

"And you started flirting."

"He bought me an orange soda." She giggled. "He asked me out, too. But I turned him down."

"Why?"

"When he bought the soda, I could cross him off my list. And he was nice, you know. I didn't want to lead him on."

Tab was glad to hear that Misty had a conscience, after all. "Who won the bet?"

"Nobody. We all found boyfriends, and we didn't want to be with anybody else. It's funny, you know. I probably never would have gone out with Clinton if it hadn't been for that bet. And now, he's my baby's daddy."

"And you're happy about that?"

"You bet I am." Misty positioned herself on the blanket with her legs tucked under. With her pregnant belly, she looked like a blond Buddha. "This is a nice, thick blanket. Why did you bring it along?"

"When you first called and said you were in labor, I thought I might be delivering your baby out here."

"Oh. My. God. That is so totally not sanitary."

Tab didn't bother with a long, thoughtful explanation about how childbirth was a natural process not an illness that required hospitalization. Midwifery was her lifework, and she didn't feel a need to justify her profession. Some people got it. Others didn't.

"My ancestors have been having babies without hospitals for a very long time. So have yours."

"I guess you're right. The Gabriels have been ranching in this area since the early 1900s. I don't guess there were many hospitals back then."

An accurate assumption, but Tab was fairly certain that Misty's great-grandmother had the best care that money could buy. The Gabriels had a history of wealth and power that held true to the present day. Their cattle ranch provided employment for many people in the area. The family reputation might work in Misty's favor when it came to murder charges, but Tab suspected that there were those who resented the Gabriel clan and would take perverse pleasure in seeing Misty behind bars.

"I want to talk to you about stress," Tab said.

"Okay."

"When you're pregnant," Tab said, "it's not good for you to be under a lot of stress. That means it's not good for your baby, either."

"What can I do? Is there some kind of herb I can take?"

Many natural remedies were used to encourage labor, but Misty wasn't at that point. "You're already taking prenatal vitamins, right? And probably extra iron."

Misty bobbed her head. "And I'm drinking herbal teas, mostly chamomile. I like doing organic stuff. I made Clinton take a class on natural childbirth that they were teaching at the hospital in Henley."

"Good for you." Tab squatted at the edge of the blanket and opened the plastic container she'd brought from her saddlebags. "Those breathing techniques are also useful for dealing with stress. Concentrate on inhaling and exhaling. Do you ever meditate?"

"You mean like yoga? Nope, that's not my thing."

"What helps you slow down and relax?" Tab assumed from Misty's confused expression that slowing down wasn't part of her agenda. "How about music? Do you listen to music?"

"All the time." She dug into her jacket pocket and pulled out a tiny player attached to ear buds. "Mostly country and western. Is that unstressful?"

"Better than heavy metal," Tab said. "When you feel yourself getting tight inside, just plug in your music, close your eyes and tune out all the other distractions."

From the plastic container, she unpacked a simple picnic of crackers, cheese, jerky, an apple and a six-pack of bottled water. Misty pounced on the jerky. "You're a mind reader, Tab. I was starving."

Working with pregnant women taught her that she couldn't go wrong with healthy snacks. "Dig in before the guys figure out that there's food over here."

Aiden's effort to get the Jeep unstuck had deteriorated to walking about the vehicle, scratching his head and scowling. Clinton was doing much the same. Very likely, they'd come to the conclusion that when the sheriff got here, they could hook up a winch.

Sitting back on her heels, Tab watched as Misty devoured a chunk of jerky, took a huge swig from the water bottle and gave a loud burp followed by a giggle. "Sorry," Misty said. "That was gross."

"A little bit."

"My body keeps doing this weird stuff. I have to pee all the time."

"Can you feel the baby kicking?"

"I can." A happy smile brightened her face. "That part is really cool."

Tab was reminded of the seven-year-old she used to baby-sit. That summer had been rough on the girl. Not only had she lost her father, but her mother had been so devastated that she could barely drag herself out of bed. And Aiden had been preoccupied with the day-to-day operations at the ranch. Throughout, Misty maintained a relentlessly cheerful attitude to hide her pain and vulnerability.

"I wish I could stay here and wait with you," Tab said, "but I need to leave soon."

Misty nodded as she screwed the top back onto the water bottle. When she looked up, her eyes were troubled. "Can I ask you something?"

"Anything."

"Am I going to jail?"

Tab couldn't promise a good outcome. Even if Misty was completely innocent, there were no guarantees. "I don't know."

An hour later, the sun dipped low in the western sky. None of the law enforcement people had yet arrived on the scene, but Tab couldn't wait any longer. Nightfall came early in November, and she didn't want to ride home in the dark. It wasn't far to her grandma's house, probably only seven or eight miles, but there wasn't a clearly marked trail between here and there, and she didn't want to take a chance on getting lost.

After she gave Misty a hug, Tab made her way through

the sage and dried prairie grass to where Shua was nibbling at a shrub. Aiden strode toward her. "Leaving so soon?"

"Not that it hasn't been fun," she said. "The sheriff can contact me later for a statement."

"I'm glad you're heading out while there's still enough light to see where you're going. You haven't lived around here for a couple of years. Things change."

As far as she could see, the change was minimal. The local landmarks—rolling hills, ridges and the river—were much the same as when she was a kid. On the opposite side of the Little Big Horn, she saw the sandstone cliff and the familiar arch above Half-Moon Cave. The land was eternal; the people were different.

She glanced over her shoulder at Misty's little nest on the striped wool blanket. Though Clinton had his arm around her, Misty's shoulders slumped, and her head drooped. "I'm worried about her," Tab said. "If there's anything I can do to help, call me."

"Sure."

His hand rested on Shua's neck, and he stroked along the line of the horse's mane. The gesture was completely natural, like the absentminded way you might pet a cat that jumped on your lap. This casual attitude around livestock said a lot about Aiden.

Unlike most of the men she'd dated in Billings and Missoula, he'd grown up on a ranch and was 100 percent cowboy. Right now, he was wearing a baseball cap instead of a Stetson, but he still looked the part with his long, lean body, his scuffed boots and his well-worn jeans. His hands were calloused. His wrists were strong. And his gray eyes had that cool awareness that came from hours of staring across the wide prairies, watching over several hundred head of cattle.

Had he changed? She wasn't sure.

Though she wasn't sixteen anymore, she was still a little

bit blinded by her crush on him. When she looked at him, her pulse rate quickened. She had to swallow hard before she trusted herself to speak without stammering.

"I'm serious about having Misty call me," she said. "She needs a friend."

"You got that right. The girls she used to pal around with in high school are off at college, joining sororities and having all kinds of fun." A frown tugged at the corner of his mouth. "I wanted that for her. Misty's a smart kid."

"You make it sound like her life is over."

"She wanted to be a lawyer, talked about it all the time. She was planning to take on injustice and set the world straight. She'd sent off her application to a couple of universities, and she'd gotten accepted."

"A lawyer, huh? That's terrific."

"Now, she's going to be stuck on the ranch."

Tab didn't like his attitude and all that it implied. "She doesn't have to give up her dreams. Having a baby isn't the end of the world for Misty."

His gaze met hers, and she braced herself for a bullheaded argument about how womenfolk are supposed to stay home and tend the young. Instead, Aiden said, "You're right."

"You're damn right that I'm right." She'd gotten herself all puffed up for no reason. "Right?"

"I'm not fighting you, Tab."

"Well, good."

"Misty needs to hear that she's still got opportunities. She can still go to college and to law school." His expression warmed. "It'd be good for her to spend time with you."

Being close to Misty meant also being near him, which might be the very definition of a win-win situation. She cleared her throat and reached for her saddle. "I should mount up."

"Not yet."

When he lightly touched her shoulder, she spun around to face him. He was standing so close that she could see the prisms and facets in his eyes. "What is it, Aiden?"

"If you'll wait a bit before you get up on your horse, I'd like to walk with you."

"Suit yourself."

Taking the reins, she stepped in front of Shua and made a clicking noise. The horse ambled along behind her as she and Aiden strolled along a path that followed the winding course of the river.

"To tell you the truth," he said, "I'd like to escort you all the way back to your grandma's place and make sure you get home safely."

"I can handle myself."

"Can you? If Misty's story is true, the shooter might still be in the area."

She looked up at him. "That hadn't occurred to me."

"It's unlikely he's still around, but it's something to keep in mind. At that meeting in Crow Agency, nobody actually said we might be facing a serial killer. But it's possible."

She remembered the serious tone of the meeting and the warning to be on the lookout. "I thought the meeting was about two missing girls from Henley who were last seen on the rez."

"There's more to the story," Aiden said. "A couple of months ago, at the end of the summer, the sheriff in Billings found the body of a tourist who had been camping. She was raped and murdered. Since then, three other girls have disappeared. All the victims are blonde, like Misty."

Tab touched her long, black braid. "I guess that means I'm safe."

"You can't make that kind of assumption with a crazy person. His M.O. might change in a flash."

Fear nibbled at the edge of her mind. "I'll keep my rifle handy. And I won't dawdle."

"Call me when you get home."

Her cell phone wasn't much protection. Not only was the reception spotty but nobody would reach her in time if she called for help. "He used Misty's rifle. Does that mean he doesn't have his own gun?"

"I don't know," Aiden said.

"Have you been working with the police? You seem to know a lot about the murdered tourist and the girls from Billings."

"I volunteer my chopper to look for missing persons, keeping an eye on things from the sky. I like to go up as often as possible."

"You enjoy flying?"

"From the first time I rode in a chopper, I loved it—swooping through the skies, leaving gravity behind and soaring free." The tension in his face relaxed as he looked heavenward and grinned. "It's the freedom. No restraints. No regrets."

"And no responsibilities," she said.

"That, too."

Aiden had been forced to take on a lot after his father died. He'd had to leave college and take care of the ranch. No wonder he wanted Misty to have a wider scope of opportunity. "I've never been in a helicopter."

"A virgin," he said.

In more ways than one, but he didn't have to know about that part of her life. "You make it sound exciting."

"It's a different perspective," he said. "I know a lot about this territory. And that's one of the reasons I wanted to walk along with you. We might run into something along this path."

"Something?"

"Somebody," he said.

She heard a rustling in the brush beside the river and turned to look. "What is it?"

"You'll see."

A skinny man with a wild gray beard crept out from behind a tree. Over his shoulders, he wore a buffalo robe. He held a ski pole in each hand, using them as walking sticks.

"Visitors," he shouted. "Welcome, pretty lady."

Tab stood and stared. Her jaw dropped, and she felt her eyes pop wide like a cartoon version of herself. What the hell?

Chapter Four

Aiden relished the look of shock on Tab's face. It wasn't easy to ruffle her feathers, but he'd succeeded. She recovered her poise quickly. Her gaping mouth snapped shut, and her full lips smoothed into a slightly upturned line that wasn't exactly a smile. Under her breath, she muttered, "Good thing you warned me about this little *something*. I might have shot him."

No fear. Her first thought was to grab her rifle and stand ready to protect herself. He liked that attitude. This lady wasn't about to scream or take off running, not her. Not Tab.

Thinking of her as Tab instead of Tabitha was becoming easier. The longer name—Tabitha—rolled off his tongue with an almost musical resonance. Tab was one crisp, practical syllable. It suited her. The way he figured, a woman named Tab could stand up for herself while a Tabitha would be the type to flutter her eyelashes and swoon.

"Who is he?" she asked.

"His name is Wally, but everybody calls him Buffalo Man."

"Certainly not because of his size," she said. "He couldn't weigh more than one twenty-five including the fur cape and ski poles. What's he doing here?"

"He camps along the river. I spotted his tent when I did my visual sweep in the chopper."

Feet together, the scrawny gray-haired man hopped toward

them, mimicking the technique of a downhill skier. Gradually, he was coming closer.

"He could be the shooter," Tab said.

"I don't reckon so. His campsite is another mile or so downriver. He was there when I flew over." Besides, Aiden had become fairly well acquainted with the old man. "He's not a murderer. A thief? Maybe. But not a killer."

Wally claimed to be part Crow, but nobody on the rez claimed him back. A drifter, he'd been in this area for three or four years. When he occasionally showed up at the Gabriel ranch looking for work, Aiden would find him something to do with the stipulation that Buffalo Man take a long soak in a hot tub and shave his whiskers. In a lucid moment, Wally had confided that he'd lost his job, his wife and his house, but he wasn't sad or self-pitying. He'd chosen to go back to nature.

Usually, he wasn't so talkative, and today he said nothing as he approached. When he was about five feet from them, Aiden caught the whiff of a powerful stench—the smell of old campfires and dirt. He held up a hand. "That's close enough, Wally."

Buffalo Man bared his yellow teeth in a grin. "That's a pretty horse."

"Thank you," Tab said. "Do you live out here?"

"It's my right. I'm Indian, like you." He cocked his head to one side. "You're Maria Spotted Bear's granddaughter."

"How do you know that?"

"I know things. Lots of things."

"You'd better not be spying on my grandma," she said. "I wouldn't like that."

He dug the tips of his ski poles into the earth and planted his fists on his skinny hips. "I am not a Peeping Tom. I have my dignity. You can ask Aiden. Go on, ask him."

"Wally does work for me at the ranch. He's a good handyman."

"Handy Wally, that's my moniker."

Aiden watched Tab's expression as her suspicion faded. It was her nature to be friendly. Her tribe had a tradition of welcoming strangers and sharing whatever they had. She took a step toward Wally and held out her hand as she offered a Crow greeting. "*Ka-hay.* My name is Tab Willows."

He vigorously shook her hand. "Pleased to meet you, Tab."

"It must get lonely out here. If you're hungry or want company, come to my grandma's house."

"I don't take charity."

"I wasn't offering," Tab said. "We'll make a trade. My grandma can use the skills of a handyman."

His yellow smile split his wizened face. Peering through his tangled mop of hair, his eyes were alert and intelligent. "I would be honored to visit the home of Maria Spotted Bear."

Though Wally had never shared his prior occupation, Aiden believed he was an educated man. His use of language was usually correct, he had a decent vocabulary and he was smart enough to know how to survive in the wild. His antisocial weirdness came from a lack of interaction with other people. He chose to be a hermit. But that didn't mean he was nuts.

"I have a couple of questions for you," Aiden said. "No doubt you noticed the commotion this afternoon."

"Gunfire. I heard it. And I saw Tab riding across the hills, coming from the east. And the chopper." He looked up at the fading light of the afternoon. "I saw your chopper. You must have seen me, too. I waved."

Aiden nodded. "What about people? Did you see or hear any people on the ground?"

Abruptly, Wally hunkered down on the ground. His voice lowered to a whisper. "After the gunfire, I thought I should take a look and see if anybody needed my help. Voices carry a long way out here."

"Could you hear what anyone was saying?"

Wally pointed to Tab. "You. I heard you talking."

"What about earlier than that. Before Tab, did you hear voices?"

He shook his head. "I was too far away. When I got close, I heard your baby sister."

"Misty," said both Aiden and Tab.

"She laughs a lot." Wally gave a creaky chuckle of his own. "A pretty sound. Her laughter sounds like splashing water. Not like the other girls who come out here with their boyfriends. They squeal and shout and make a terrible ruckus with their parties."

Half-Moon Cave had always been a favorite gathering spot for high school parties and make-out sessions. The opening of the cave was a wide arch, similar to a band shell, and the interior provided shelter from the wind and rain. Aiden guessed that if they crossed the river and went to the cave, they'd find the remains of campfires and plenty of rusted beer cans.

"The sheriff is going to be here soon," Aiden said. "He's going to want to talk to you about what you saw or heard."

"No, sir. This is reservation land. I don't have to talk to the sheriff."

"Joseph Lefthand will be here, as well," Tab said. "It's important to help them. There's been a murder."

"I know." Wally popped up. "I got close enough to see the dead man, and then I turned around. None of my business."

"Did you know the man who was killed?" Aiden asked.

"I might have seen him before. Once or twice. I see a lot of things. People don't much notice me." He looked directly at Tab. "Not that I go out of my way to spy on people. I mind my own business."

Aiden stepped closer to Wally and looked him straight in the eye, compelling his attention. "Bad things have been happening on or near the rez. Young girls from Henley and Billings are going missing. At least one of them was murdered. Have you seen or heard anything that could lead to the killer?"

"The man who was killed was here with a girl. She had hair like a golden waterfall."

"If you saw her photo, could you identify her?"

Wally stroked his beard and considered. "It was after dark, and I didn't really see her face. She was wearing a baby-blue sweatshirt."

That item of clothing could help identify David Welling's companion. "Did you hear them talking?"

"He said her name." Wally tugged harder on his beard. "Ellen or Elizabeth. It was something like that."

David might have a connection with one of the missing women. And David had been murdered. If Wally stepped forward as a witness, it could put him in danger. He shouldn't be camping out here by himself.

Aiden patted him on the shoulder of his buffalo robe. "Until this is over, you might want to come and stay at the ranch. My mom has some work for you. She's going to be putting up Christmas decorations."

"I'll come after the weather gets colder," Wally said. "Right now, it's nice and warm. The river is low and slow. I go swimming in it every day. Keeps me young."

Aiden hoped Wally's outdoor skills would also keep him alive. He hated to think of anything bad happening to the eccentric old man.

AFTER TAB RETURNED TO HER grandma's house, she took care of Shua and fed the horse in the barn beside the corral. By the time she transferred her medical supplies from the saddlebags into the back of her van, the dusk had turned into dark—a still, calm night. The deep solitude soothed her. Not that she would forget the murder, the threat of a serial killer and the potential of jail time for pregnant Misty. Tab was involved, truly involved, and she was committed to doing whatever she could to help.

But not right this minute. For now, she needed to clear her mind. She inhaled. The cold night air swept into her lungs and refreshed her mind and her spirit.

A few months ago, when she moved back here, she'd been worried that she'd be bored to death. Though the Crow half of her DNA connected her to this land and the traditions of her tribe, she'd spent most of her life in cities like Billings and Missoula where there were things to do and places to go. Not that her social life had ever been a whirlwind of parties and dates. Instead, she'd kept herself busy with her schooling and with work. After graduating from nursing school in Missoula, she'd been part of a midwife clinic that also offered prenatal and postnatal care. She'd learned so much from the other midwives.

Now, she worked alone. She was the expert.

Outside her grandma's house, she looked up at the moon and the millions of stars that spread their silvery light across the hills and distant cliffs. A couple hundred yards away, she saw the lights from other homes where the Martins and the Tall Grass families lived. The only sound was the rustling of wind across the prairies and the winged swoop of raptor birds hunting in the night.

Light shone through the windows in her grandma's kitchen where Maria Spotted Bear was probably preparing dinner and not wearing her wrist brace. Though the cast had been removed, Tab wanted Grandma Maria to protect her injured wrist until she was full strength. Twice a day, they performed therapeutic exercises. Every night, her grandma wrapped her wrist in herbal poultices. The same combination of Western

medicine and Crow healing practices applied to the pills
Grandma took for her heart condition.

As soon as Tab came through the front door, she heard
Grandma singing in the kitchen. The stereotype of the stoic
tribal elder didn't hold true for her grandma who always
seemed surrounded by music and happy chatter.

Entering the kitchen, Tab saw her grandma remove a tray
of cornbread from the oven. The wrist brace was nowhere
in sight.

"Don't worry," Grandma said as she set the cornbread in
the center of the kitchen table. "I can lift this. It's not too
heavy."

"Smells good." Tab wasn't in the mood to argue. She
hugged the rounded shoulders of the small woman whose
long white hair was fastened at her nape with an ornately
beaded barrette. "Do you know the one they call Buffalo
Man?"

"A crazy old badger. He lives down by the river."

"Just to warn you, I kind of invited him to drop by anytime for dinner."

"That's my Tabitha." Her grandma chuckled. "From the
time you were a little girl, you were always bringing home
strays."

"His real name is Wally, and he's willing to work for his
supper as a handyman. Having him drop by might be useful. The barn roof needs patching."

"How did this new friendship happen?" Grandma sat at
the kitchen table. "You left the house to deliver a baby, and
you picked up an old man in a buffalo robe."

"Long story."

"The stew can simmer for a while."

Not holding back, Tab told the whole story of Misty and
the murder, the possible serial killer connection, the chopper and Aiden. When she mentioned his name, she heard a

breathless change in her voice. She pictured the tall, lean cowboy, and a rush of excitement went through her. In an attempt to hide that reaction, she turned her back on Grandma and opened the refrigerator door to take out a pitcher of cold water.

"Aiden Gabriel," her grandma said. "He's a handsome man."

"Is he?" Her tone pitched to a higher octave. "I didn't notice. I was more concerned about his sister."

"You don't fool me. When you were a girl and spent the summer at the Gabriel ranch, you liked him, liked him very much." She sang a little song about sailing away with the man of her dreams. "Didn't you ask me for a totem to cause a man to fall in love with you?"

Tab didn't deny it. "I was a silly teenager then."

"And now, you're both grown up. Could be good timing. From what I hear, Aiden broke up with his long-time girlfriend. She lives in California and doesn't care about ranch life."

Tab poured cold spring water into a Mason jar and took a sip. People who lived on the rez seemed isolated, and yet the gossip grapevine relayed information more quickly than cell phone texting. "How do you know so much about Aiden's love life?"

"His mother and I see each other often. I bring her baked goods, and Sylvia gives me beef. She's happy about the blessing of a new baby."

"It doesn't bother her that Misty is so young and so unmarried?"

"If anyone understands about unexpected pregnancy, it's Sylvia Gabriel." Grandma leaned back in her chair and folded her hands on her lap, a signal that she was about to tell a story. "Sylvia nearly died in childbirth. She had a difficult labor, ending in Caesarian section and a serious loss of blood. But after she had Aiden, she wanted more children. She and her husband tried everything. I know this because she came to me and asked how to increase her fertility."

Maria Spotted Bear not only had a reputation as an excellent baker but also for healing and cures. Tab had learned young how to locate, harvest and prepare many herbs for teas and salves. "Red clover, squaw berry and yams. Those are all good to promote fertility."

"Nothing worked and she gave up—satisfied to have a healthy son and a good marriage. Fourteen years later, when Sylvia was thirty-seven years old, she had Misty. A happy surprise."

Her cell phone buzzed. The screen showed Aiden was the caller. As soon as she saw his name, she remembered that she'd promised to call him when she reached her grandma's house.

"I'm home," she said when she picked up. "We're just about to sit down for dinner."

"I'm glad, but that's not why I was calling."

"Oh." She wasn't sure whether to be pleased that he trusted her to take care of herself, or to feel bad that he wasn't checking up on her.

"Misty asked if you could come over to the ranch tonight, maybe in an hour or so. Is that convenient?"

His tone was cool and distant, more appropriate for a business transaction than a personal request. "Aiden, what's going on?"

"They found another body. She's from Henley, and her name is Ellen."

That was the name Wally mentioned. He'd said that Ellen was with David Welling. "A blonde?"

"Yes."

She heard other voices in the background. They were arguing. "What else?"

"The victim was wearing a gold, engraved wristwatch. It belongs to my sister."

The link to another murder was bad for Misty. Her story about the mystery gunman who grabbed her rifle and disappeared sounded even more flimsy. Tab didn't know how she could help other than to offer moral support. Sometimes, that was enough. "I'll be there."

Chapter Five

Chapter Five

If Tab had gotten her way, she would have tucked her grandma into bed for a solid eight hours of sleep before she left. But Grandma really wanted to come along. She argued that Sylvia Gabriel was a very good friend of the family, and friends take care of friends. What Grandma didn't say was that these murders were more exciting than anything that had happened since the fire at the casino in Crow Agency.

Sitting in the passenger seat of Tab's van, she fiddled with the wrist brace Tab had insisted that she wear. "The tribe should have jurisdiction. The dead girl was found on the rez."

Tab was tired of running through the logistical reasons why Joseph Lefthand couldn't handle a complicated investigation. She jumped to the bottom line, which was something her grandma—who took part in tribal council—would understand. "It would be expensive. The tribe would have to hire a special coroner to do the autopsies."

"Are they going to cut that poor girl open?"

Tab shot her a skeptical glance. With her long white braids, patterned wool jacket, long skirt and moccasins, Maria Spotted Bear was just a few head feathers short of playing a tribal elder at the annual reenactment of Custer's Last Stand. Not an entirely true image. Grandma kept up with the times.

"Don't pretend that you don't know about autopsies," Tab

said. "You've got television on satellite dish. You've watched police shows."

"And hospital shows to keep up with what you're doing." Slyly, she asked, "Are those shows truthful?"

"Yeah, sure," Tab muttered sarcastically. "Every doctor is gorgeous, and every case is fascinating."

"You see what I mean? I've heard about detectives, but I don't know what they do."

Tab shrugged. "Neither do I. Not exactly."

"I can tell you one thing. To find a killer, you don't need fancy equipment or autopsies. You need to be smart." Grandma tapped the side of her head. "A real detective should have the instincts of a hunter."

"Do you think Joseph Lefthand has those instincts?"

"Better him than Sheriff Steve."

Tab had met both men at the meeting in Crow Agency. Both seemed decent and hard-working. Both were deeply concerned about the young women who had gone missing. Tab wondered if she ought to be more worried since she and Grandma lived alone without any security other than the rifles they kept in the front closet.

Her van jostled along the back roads between her grandma's house and the Gabriel ranch. Though Tab hadn't driven the route in years, she remembered the way. When she spent the summer at the ranch, she'd traveled back and forth many times. Later, on other visits to her grandma, she'd make a point of stopping by to see Misty…and maybe to catch a glimpse of Aiden.

"When was the last time you came to the ranch?" her grandma asked.

"It must have been two years ago. Misty was in high school." She'd been surprised by Misty's physical maturity. The little girl she'd once known had become a woman, but she'd still run to greet Tab and give her a massive hug. She hadn't seen Aiden on that trip.

Her grandma nodded. "After you moved to Missoula for nursing school, you barely had time for me on your visits."

When Tab came to her grandma's house, there was usually a specific reason, like taking care of home repairs or making sure her grandma got a checkup with the local doctor. Though Maria Spotted Bear was self-sufficient and didn't need constant watching over, both Tab and her dad made a point of checking in with Grandma, just to be sure she was okay.

As her van rounded the last curve leading to the Gabriel ranch, Tab saw lights shining from every window of the two-story, cedar-sided ranch house with the peaked roof. Several vehicles parked outside the three-car garage to the left of the house. To the right was a barn with a corrugated metal roof. She knew that Aiden lived in a separate cabin behind the barn. Did he keep his helicopter back there?

She parked her van at the end of a row of cars. From the back, she took a satchel containing a sweet potato pie and the cornbread her grandma had made for their dinner. Maria Spotted Bear never went visiting empty-handed, even though it seemed somewhat inappropriate to bring pie to a murder investigation.

Approaching the house, Tab glanced at the far left upstairs window under the eaves. That had been her bedroom during the summer she'd lived here. She remembered a long-ago night when she couldn't sleep and had perched on the sill, looking out at the long, straight driveway. She'd spotted Aiden, striding toward the house with his border collie trotting along beside him. For some reason—she'd never known why—he wasn't wearing a shirt, just his jeans, boots and hat. For a moment, he'd paused. His shoulders rose and fell as though he was sighing. He'd taken off his beat-up Stetson and tilted his head to gaze at the moon. The silvery light bathed him in an ethereal glow—an image that branded itself indelibly in her mind.

Her grandma climbed the three steps to the veranda ahead of her and rapped on the door. A stocky woman in a denim vest opened the door.

"Maria Spotted Bear," the woman said in an authoritative alto voice. "Is this an official visit? Are you representing the tribal council?"

"I'm here as Sylvia's friend," her grandma said. "This is my granddaughter, Tab Willows. Tab, this is Laura Westerfall. She's with the BIA."

Briskly, Laura shook Tab's hand. "You're the midwife. I've been meaning to pay you a visit."

"Pleased to meet you." Tab was actually more suspicious than pleased. Agents from the Bureau of Indian Affairs often caused trouble for the tribe.

"You're a trained nurse, right? And you worked with a women's clinic in Missoula."

"Have you been checking up on me?" Tab asked.

"Yes, I have. If you're planning to stay in this area, I might have a proposition for you. Recently, some grant money has come available for rural medical care, and I'd like to focus on women's health."

"On the reservation?" Tab found it hard to believe there would be any significant financial aid for the relatively small Crow population. Any money at all surprised her.

"I'm thinking of a wider area."

"So am I." The women in this wide-open country—on and off the rez—had a long way to go to reach a hospital. Many were too poor to afford decent medical care. Even the services of a midwife stretched their budgets. "Are you saying the BIA could help?"

Laura combed her fingers through her short brown hair

and smiled as she held out her business card. "Give me a call. We need to talk about a women's clinic."

In spite of the current problems, Tab's spirits lifted as she imagined being able to help those who had so few resources. A grant from the BIA might be a dream come true.

Grandma interrupted her thoughts, taking the satchel with the pie and cornbread from her hands. "Where are your manners, girl? I came here to comfort Sylvia."

"In the kitchen," Laura said.

"I'll take care of her," Grandma promised. "You two should go into the living room. The boys sound like they're arguing, getting ready to lock horns."

Through an archway to the left was a paneled living room with heavy leather furniture and rugged coffee tables. In front of the moss rock fireplace, Sheriff Steve Fielding stood toe to toe with Aiden. Since the sheriff wasn't much taller than Tab, Aiden towered over him and the two deputies he'd brought with him.

Aiden's voice was a low, dangerous growl. "I see no valid reason to take my sister into custody."

"If that's the only way you'll let me talk to her, I've got no damn choice." The sheriff waved his men into action. "Deputies, I want you to arrest—"

"Hold on." Laura inserted herself into their argument. "What's the problem, gentlemen?"

Aiden spoke first. "I wanted Sheriff Fielding to handle this investigation because I believed he was better equipped to pursue the trail of evidence in a thorough manner. Maybe I was wrong. Maybe all he wants is a quick arrest."

"You're the one who's wrong," Fielding said. "I came here to talk to Misty. Just to talk. I need some answers."

"You already took her statement."

"That cockamamie story about a mysterious shooter?"

"I won't have you harassing my sister. She's been through enough today."

Though Tab agreed that Misty shouldn't be subjected to more stress, she realized that Aiden was behaving in an unreasonable manner. And his overprotective attitude made it look like he had something to hide. "I have a compromise. What if the sheriff questions Misty while Aiden is present?"

The sheriff pointed his long, sunburned nose at her and squinted like someone who needed glasses. "You're Tab Willows, right? I need to take your statement."

"I'm happy to cooperate," she said.

"But that's not why you came here." His squint became even more pronounced. "You live with Maria Spotted Bear. Are you here to speak for your tribe?"

The politics were getting annoying. Just because Tab was half Crow, it didn't automatically make her a representative of her people. She was miles out of touch with local issues. Most of her life had been spent in Billings and Missoula. Not on the rez.

"I'm here as a concerned person," she said. "Young women are being murdered and their bodies dumped on the rez. I want to see the killer brought to justice."

"That's the voice of common sense," Laura said, backing her up. "Listen to her."

"You have no standing here, Agent Westerfall." The sheriff hitched up his belt. "You arranged for Joseph Lefthand to cede jurisdiction. This is my purview."

"Don't forget that I'm a federal agent, Sheriff. I'm not here to give orders, but I see no reason why we can't do as Tab suggested."

"Here's your reason," the sheriff said. "I can't get the truth from Misty while she's hiding behind her big brother."

Before Aiden exploded again with righteous anger, Tab grasped his forearm and squeezed hard, compelling his attention. He wasn't helping anything by being pigheaded. She stared into his eyes. "I'll be with Misty while she's talking to the sheriff. Is that all right with both of you?"

"It's done." Laura gestured toward the hall. "Sheriff Fielding will wait down here in the office. Tab will bring Misty to talk with him immediately."

Everybody moved quickly, anxious not to destroy the fragile moment of truce. Tab found herself being escorted up the staircase by Aiden. This time, he was holding her arm above the elbow in a tight grip. His outrage manifested in a bodily heat that sizzled in the air around him.

Under his breath, he said, "I'll be damned if I let the sheriff connect Misty to these murders. He's delusional."

"Calm down." She fought to keep from being drawn into the vortex of his anger. "We have only a few minutes. Fill me in."

"The first victim was raped," he whispered.

"And the girl they just found?"

"We won't know until after the autopsy. They're transporting the body to Billings." His jaw clenched. "Usually, the sheriff would call on me for transport in the chopper. Now he's treating me like a suspect. It's crazy. These are sex crimes. How could Misty be involved?"

On the landing at the top of the staircase, she gazed into Aiden's gray eyes, searching for the truth. "The sheriff must have a reason."

"He talked to Wally who went into detail about the wild parties he's seen up and down the river."

"Did he tell the sheriff that he saw David with a blonde girl named Ellen?"

Aiden nodded. "If Wally can be trusted, David knew the victim, but so did a lot of other people. She's a local girl. The sheriff thinks these disappearances might be a bullying thing gone wrong. When the second victim was found wearing Misty's wristwatch, he figured she was part of the gang."

Aiden had said that the sheriff wanted a quick solution, and she thought he might be right. Supposing these murders were the actions of a gang tied Welling's death to those of the missing girls. It made for a tidy solution.

She asked, "Why would he think Misty was involved?"

"She has a reputation for being wild." Aiden shook his head and looked away. "Whenever there's trouble, she seems to be the ringleader."

Tab attempted to put a positive spin on his words. "She's a leader. Headstrong. Determined."

"Great qualities if you're doing something good. And if not…" He drew in a breath and exhaled slowly. "It's not her fault. I haven't done a good job raising her."

"You're not her parent."

"Gabriel Ranch and everything that happens here is my responsibility."

He spoke with calm conviction as though his words were indisputable. When Aiden's father died, he took on that mantle. The buck stopped with him. He was the protector, the caretaker and the final authority, even though his mother had taken over the day-to-day chores and the running of the ranch.

Seeing Aiden with his head bowed made her realize that he wasn't the perfect, ideal man she'd cherished in her memories. He was real. He suffered just like any other man. Beneath his strength was a thick layer of sadness. He'd given up everything for his family. Somehow, that made him even more attractive to her. She wanted to comfort him and tell him that everything was going to be all right.

"Let me handle the sheriff," she said. "If Misty is under too much stress, I'll call an end to the questioning."

He looked doubtful. "What if—"

"Stop," she said quietly. "There's only one thing that needs to happen. Misty has to tell the truth."

"That's what scares me."

His fear touched her.

Though it seemed impossible, Misty could be involved in these dark, terrible crimes. Tab didn't want to believe it was possible.

Chapter Six

In the downstairs office at the ranch, the decor showed a more feminine touch than the rest of the house. Sylvia spent most of her time behind the polished-oak desk, surrounded by antique wooden filing cabinets. A jar of jelly beans sat at the corner of the desk beside a bowl of fresh yellow roses. The computer screen saver showed a Degas painting of ballet dancers.

Sheriff Fielding perched on the edge of the desk facing Tab and Misty who were at opposite ends of a blue love seat. From what Aiden had told her, Tab knew that the sheriff considered Misty to be a prime suspect. But she saw hesitation and doubt in his eyes.

With a flannel robe belted above her pregnant belly, Misty couldn't have looked less like the ringleader of a murderous gang. Under the pink velour robe, she wore striped yellow pajamas. Her freshly washed hair piled on top of her head with wispy blond curls escaping to frame her face. Her eyes were red-rimmed as though she'd been crying.

The sheriff cleared his throat. "Misty, it's very important for you to be honest with me and tell me everything, even if you think it might get somebody else in trouble. This isn't like high school. People are getting killed."

"I know," Misty said. "I saw David die."

"Do you know Ellen Jessop?" the sheriff asked.

"Is she...is she dead?"

"I'm asking the questions, young lady." His voice took on an authoritative edge. "Were you and Ellen friends?"

"We were both cheerleaders, but she's a year older than me. Oh God, this is awful. The last time I saw her, we argued."

"About what?"

Fidgeting on the sofa, she plucked apart a tissue she clutched in her hand. "I don't want to say."

Tab reached over and placed her hand on Misty's arm. "You need to cooperate. Tell us about Ellen."

"We were never really good friends. She used to date Clinton, and she hated that he was the father of my baby. She said that the only reason Clinton was with me instead of her was because my family is rich."

Tab watched as the sheriff nodded. Had he heard this story before? In a small town like Henley, word traveled fast.

Misty continued, "Ellen's family was going through hard times. After she graduated high school, they couldn't afford to send her to college, and she had to work at the Feed and Seed store in Henley."

"When was the last time you saw her?" Tab asked gently.

"About a month ago. She was coming out of the drugstore, and I was going in. She asked me what time it was because she was late for work." Misty giggled, and then frowned. "She said work was something I'd never had to think about, and she made it sound like I didn't have a care in the world. But I do."

The sheriff cleared his throat. "What did you say to her?"

"Everybody thinks my life is a breeze, but it's not." Her small fist clenched. "I'm having a baby. That's going to be hard, really hard. Why don't other people understand? All they see is money. They think being rich makes everything right."

"It helps," the sheriff said.

Misty lifted her chin. "I'd burn every dollar if I could have my daddy back. That's what I really want. People are all that matters. I miss my daddy. Every day, I miss him."

"I'm sorry for your loss," the sheriff said.

His perfunctory tone made Tab think that his former empathy was fading fast. In this part of the world, people assumed that Misty Gabriel was a pretty, rich girl without a care. Tab knew better—she remembered the seven-year-old who tried to make everyone happy with the sound of her laughter while she cried herself to sleep every night.

The sheriff leaned forward. "Let's get back to what happened when you saw Ellen for the last time."

"I told her the time, and she made a snotty comment about my solid gold wristwatch. It made me mad. I took off the watch and threw it at her. Then I walked away."

"Did you try to get your watch back?" the sheriff asked.

"I wanted to. Aiden gave it to me on my sweet sixteen, and he had it engraved with my name and birth date. I meant to call Ellen, but I never did."

Her explanation sounded plausible—childish but believable. And yet, Tab sensed that Misty was holding something back. There was more to the story of the wristwatch. "Is there anything else you want to say?"

Misty refused to meet her gaze. Instead, she giggled and placed her hands on her belly. "The baby is kicking, really hard. I think it's a girl, a dancer."

Was she being deliberately evasive? Sheriff Fielding seemed to think so. His attitude toward Misty turned more hostile. "Tell me about the party at Heather Gardener's house last weekend."

"I didn't go. Parties aren't much fun when you're pregnant and you can't drink and you dance like an elephant."

After another giggle, she asked, "Who told you I went to that party?"

Though the sheriff said nothing, Misty's eyes narrowed as she stared at him. "I know who it was," she said. "Your deputy's daughter. Christina? It was her, wasn't it? She told you I went to the party. But she's mistaken. I wasn't there."

"What about Clinton? Did he go by himself?"

"I don't know." With an effort, she pushed herself to her feet. "Are we done here?"

"Not yet," the sheriff said.

Tab fully expected Misty to win this standoff. Sheriff Fielding might have the law on his side, but Misty was a stubborn, pregnant woman with the power of rampaging hormones. Hoping to mediate, Tab stood. "Sheriff, it might be time for us to take a break. You still need to take my statement."

"I have more questions for Misty."

"No," Misty said as tears spurted from her eyes. "There isn't anything else to say. I just can't—"

From outside the house, gunfire exploded. Tab heard loud whoops and several shots as though two or more guns were being fired. In an instant, the atmosphere inside the house shifted from simmering hostility to a fierce, boiling anger. She heard people running, shouting, gathering their weapons and preparing to defend their property.

Whether the sheriff liked it or not, this interview was over.

AT THE SOUND OF SHOTS being fired, Aiden dashed from the kitchen where he'd been having sweet potato pie and tea with his mom and Maria Spotted Bear. In the front entryway, he saw both deputies peering through the window by the front door with their handguns drawn. They signaled for him to stay back.

Like hell, he would. In his house, Aiden gave the orders.

The ranch foreman, Blake Henry, pushed the front door open. "They're gone. The gunfire came from a pickup truck. They threw something and took off, heading south."

"Did you get a license plate?" a deputy asked.

"I barely had time to see the truck," Blake drawled. "If you drive like fury, you might catch them."

The sheriff stalked down the hallway from the office. "You heard him. Go."

Aiden knew the deputies didn't have a chance of catching up with a speeding truck. It was only about seven miles to an intersection where the paved county road led to Henley in less than ten miles. Though the sheriff already had his cell phone out, he didn't have enough manpower to set up an effective traffic net in a matter of minutes.

A crowd spilled into the front entryway. His mom and Maria Spotted Bear came from the kitchen. Two other ranch hands entered through the front door. Misty and Tab followed the sheriff down the hall. There wasn't time for Aiden to discuss his plan with the whole group. He knew what was needed, and he intended to do it. Pivoting on his heel, he bolted through the front door.

Anger pounded through his veins as he ran across the yard and past the barn. His home and family had been endangered. Shots were fired at his house, and he'd be damned if he let anyone get away with that kind of threat.

Behind his cabin, his chopper stood ready and waiting. As he flung open the door to the cockpit, he heard a shout.

"Wait for me."

"Tab?" What the hell was she doing here?

"Don't waste time talking. I'm coming with you."

There wasn't time to argue. He helped her into the cockpit where she dove into the copilot seat and fastened her belt. He hit the starter, throttled back and took off. Over the roar of the rotors, he heard Tab yelling as they swooped across the darkened landscape.

A quick glance told him that she wasn't screaming in fear. The lights from the instrument panel reflected the excitement in her big, beautiful blue eyes. Her mouth opened wide in the biggest grin he'd ever seen on her face.

"Headset," he said as he pointed to the equipment. "Put it on."

After a bit of fumbling, she got the headset on and activated so they could talk to each other.

"This is great," she said. "I know we have something else to be thinking about, but this is just so much fun."

"Why did you come after me?"

She leaned toward the windshield and peered into the night. "I had a pretty good idea about what you were doing, and I wanted to help."

"To help," he said. "How?"

"I'm a second pair of eyes. We're looking for a truck, right?"

Instead of discussing her plan, she'd acted on instinct, which was exactly what he'd done. He shouldn't be mad at her for that, but he sure as hell didn't need her help. Taking care of problems was what he did. He maneuvered the chopper until the graded gravel road leading to the house was beneath them, and then he turned on the wide-angle searchlight.

"How did you keep up with me?" he asked. "I was running."

"You're wearing stiff-soled boots," she pointed out. "I'm in sneakers. Plus, I'm pretty speedy."

"Is that so?" Her smile was adorable, but he refused to be charmed. As far as he was concerned, she'd stuck her pretty little nose into his family business. Misty might need the kind of comfort that Tab could offer, but he worked alone.

"The derivation of *Tabitha* is gazelle," she said. "And *Aiden* is fire."

Why did she know the meaning of his name? There was something going on here that he didn't understand. "Fire, huh?"

"It suits you. You're a fiery type."

"And you're fast."

"On my feet, I'm fast. In other ways, you can call me molasses." She pointed through the window. "There's the deputy's car with the lights flashing."

The truck was nowhere in sight, and they were almost to the county road. Aiden concentrated on piloting the chopper. They were flying low at high speed. For anyone else, this would have been a dangerous move. At night, the low-hanging power lines and high branches of trees were nearly invisible. But this was his territory. He knew when to zig and when to zag. "I think I'll go left toward Henley."

"Good plan," she said. "If we don't see them by the time we get to town, we can double back."

He aimed the searchlight on the road and surged forward. A mile down the road to Henley, he spotted the truck.

"There they are," Tab said. "Now what do we do?"

"If I were alone, I'd drop down and buzz the truck until they drove off the road. But I don't want to draw their fire with you sitting in the copilot's seat."

"Well, then. It's a good thing I came along."

Not if the truck got away while he was playing it safe. He didn't want these guys to get all the way into town where they could crawl into a hole and hide. "We're going to set up an ambush."

His plan was to get ahead of the truck and set the chopper down in the middle of the road. The truck would have to hit the brakes. When they stopped, he'd shoot out their tires. There wasn't time to explain all that to Tab.

"When I touch down," he said, "you jump out and run. Take cover. Understand?"

"Got it."

He zoomed ahead and set the chopper down in the middle of the road. In the distance, he could see the headlights of the truck approaching. Reaching behind his seat, he grabbed his rifle.

From the corner of his eye, he saw Tab throw off her seat belt and climb out. She hit the ground running, just like he'd told her. There wasn't a lot of cover nearby, but she found a couple of granite rocks and ducked behind them. He followed her.

Beside her, he went up on one knee and took aim.

The truck came to a stop.

Before Aiden could fire, both doors on the cab swung open and a couple of guys jumped out. Their hands were raised over their heads.

"Don't shoot." Both men were yelling. "We surrender. Don't shoot."

Aiden's trigger finger itched. He would have liked to blast the tires and put a couple of holes in the doors of the truck just to teach these guys a lesson. But he didn't want to give them a reason to press charges against him for destroying their property.

"Tab, you stay put." He stood with his rifle still held at the ready. "This might be a trap."

"Could be somebody else in the back of the truck," she said. "Be careful."

Walking toward them, he yelled, "On your knees. Hands locked behind your head."

Quickly, they followed his order. As he approached, he could see the fear in their eyes. They were young, not much older than Misty. One of them wore a beat-up Denver Broncos cap and an oversize jersey with the number fifteen celebrating Tebow, the former quarterback who pulled off a couple of miracle wins. The other appeared to be part Crow.

After he checked the bed of the truck and was satisfied that nobody else was hiding amid the junk that had accumulated there, he took a position in front of the young men. Aiden didn't lower his rifle.

"Where are your guns?" he demanded.

"In the truck," said the Bronco fan. "We didn't mean any harm. We fired into the air to get your attention."

"Nobody threatens my home." Aiden was dead serious. "If you have a problem, you come to me. Like a man."

"Yes, sir."

"Give me your names."

"I'm Woody Silas." He wore the Bronco cap. "And this here is Chuck Longbeak."

Aiden heard Tab come up behind him. "Longbeak," she said. "I know your sister."

His dark eyes pleaded. "You can't tell my sister. She'll tell my mom."

"Your mom will know," Tab said. "You boys are about to get yourselves arrested. The deputies are already on their way."

"We didn't do nothing wrong," Woody said. He was almost crying. If this was an act, it was a good one. "We just flung something in your driveway and fired into the air."

"You broke plenty of laws," Aiden said. "You fled a police officer. You were speeding. You did malicious mischief. If I really pushed, that mischief charge might get upgraded to assault with a deadly weapon."

"Nobody got hurt," Woody yelped.

"What did you throw into my driveway?"

The two young men exchanged a nervous glance. This time it was Chuck Longbeak who did the talking. "We wrapped up a note inside a hunting magazine so it would have some heft. Woody threw it. He's got a good arm. He was a quarterback."

"What did the note say?" Tab asked.

Chuck buttoned his lip. He was acting like this was nothing but a harmless prank, and Aiden was running short on patience. "Answer the lady."

"David Welling was my friend," Chuck said. "He got me a job with his uncle at the gas station. I liked David. He shouldn't be dead."

"His death," Tab said, "saddens us all. David should have had many more years."

Chuck turned his head to glare at Aiden. "It's your sister's fault. He loved her. And she shot him."

He spoke with the kind of assurance that came from knowing what had happened, almost as though he'd been there at the time of the shooting. "How do you know? Were you there?"

"No." Chuck shook his head. They both looked guilty as hell. Something else was going on with them.

"But you know the area. You know where David got shot." Aiden paused. "I'm going to ask you again. Think hard and tell me the truth. Were you there?"

"Not this time."

His answer implied that there had been other times. "It wasn't sheer dumb luck that David ended up in a place where my sister was. He must have been following her."

Woody spoke up, "We don't know nothing about that."

"I think you do," Aiden pressed. "I think you were all spying on Misty, keeping an eye on her. How many times did you drive by the ranch, looking for her?"

"Maybe once or twice," Chuck admitted.

"Shut up," Woody growled. "We don't have to tell him that. He's not a cop."

"I'm going to let you in on a little secret, kid. I'm a man

with a gun. That means I ask the questions and you give the answers."

Chuck lifted his chin. "I only know one thing for sure. David loved Misty, and she broke his heart."

"What did the note say?"

Chuck mumbled, "It's your fault, Misty. You killed him. His death is on your hands."

Aiden heard the deputy's sirens getting closer. He'd be glad to turn these two over to the law, not that he thought any of the charges would stick. Woody and Chuck represented the tip of the iceberg. Lots of townspeople would be quick to blame Misty, whether or not she was guilty.

Chapter Seven

From the copilot seat, Tab looked down at the road. The chopper hovered high enough that the wind from the rotors didn't churn up the dirt and dead leaves on the ground. She watched the deputies slap the cuffs on Chuck and Woody. While one of them kept an eye on the boys, the other gathered the guns from Woody's truck, moved their vehicle to the side of the road and slapped a police sticker on the door.

Beside her, Aiden said nothing. She had the impression that he was annoyed with her but didn't know why. The more she got to know him, the harder he was to understand. Life had been a lot simpler when she'd simply admired him from afar. Ten years ago, she'd thought he was perfect. Now? Not so much.

Reality had no place in idealized love. What did the poets call it? Unrequited love—a gut-churning passion, an obsession that was totally one-sided, like the feelings David must have had for Misty. From what Tab knew, poor David Welling didn't really know the object of his affection. He hadn't spent enough time with Misty to be irritated by her giggle or to see her when she didn't look her best.

People did crazy things in the throes of unrequited love. When Tab had her teenage crush, she'd pined away her entire summer at the Gabriel ranch without dating, not that there had been a lot of guys asking. Only two, and she had turned both down. She'd been saving her heart for the man of her dreams, the twenty-one-year-old Aiden who barely knew she existed in spite of the way she continually arranged to accidentally on purpose run into him. When he mentioned that green was his favorite color, she'd worn her one green T-shirt for three days in a row. Plus green eyeshadow. And green ribbons in her hair. *Crazy.*

What kinds of things had David done?

The possibilities made her shudder.

One thing seemed certain. His unrequited love for Misty made his murder less random. He was watching her. The fact that he'd turned up in the middle of nowhere to help Misty when the Jeep got stuck wasn't a coincidence.

Tab glanced at Aiden and spoke into the microphone on her headset. "Do you think David was following Misty and Clinton?"

"I do," he said tersely.

"Because he was in love."

"Or stalking her."

Below, she saw the deputies load the two lawbreakers into the back of their car and drive toward Henley. The boys would spend the night in the local jail, which would give them time to think. Would they change their minds about Misty? She doubted it.

As the chopper swept into motion, she spoke again, hoping to melt the glacier that had formed between her and Aiden. "I guess the whole town knows about David's murder."

"And they've already decided that Misty is guilty."

"A hasty conclusion."

"People are like that. They want answers."

"But there hasn't been an investigation. The sheriff hasn't even taken my statement, and I'm the closest thing he has to an eye witness."

"There's evidence," he reminded her. "Unfortunate evidence. Ballistics will show that Misty's rifle fired the shot that killed David. Her fingerprints are on the gun, and she admitted firing it. That might be all the proof the sheriff needs to arrest her."

That was the most talking he'd done since she got into the chopper with him. "Evidence might be fact. But it isn't necessarily the truth."

"My sister isn't a killer."

"I know." He had absolutely no call to make that statement; she hadn't once accused Misty. Still, she supposed he was under stress and she ought to cut him some slack. "Don't worry. We'll find the truth. Even if we have to do our own investigation, we'll find the killer."

"That's not going to happen, Tab. We aren't going to run around playing detective."

She wasn't sure if he was rejecting the idea of investigating or rejecting her personally. "You don't seem too pleased with the way Sheriff Fielding is handling things."

"I'm not."

"And I'm not suggesting that we get in the sheriff's way. But I don't see any reason why we shouldn't do some poking around on our own."

"I like you." He turned his head to look directly at her. "I'd like to get to know you better…but not like this. Protecting my family isn't your problem."

He was beginning to tick her off. "Because you don't think I can handle it?"

"I didn't say that."

"You know, Aiden, you're the one who called me and asked me to come to the ranch."

"Because Misty needed you."

"And you don't."

"Correct."

Waves of arrogance radiated from him. "I just want to help. Don't be so quick to turn your back."

Contradictory feelings braided into a knot that tightened in her belly. She ought to be elated because he wanted to spend time with her, but he was pushing her away at the same time.

"You're angry," he said.

"Confused."

"I don't want to put you in danger. There's a serial killer out there."

"Right," she said. "And I want to help catch him. You don't always have to do everything by yourself."

Though he nodded, she didn't really think he got her point. Why couldn't he understand? Nobody was meant to go it alone, not even a man like Aiden who had taken on big responsibilities when his father died. There was no shame in accepting help.

"I'm going to make you smile again," he said. "Get ready."

"You're trying to change the subject."

"Maybe."

He slowed the forward speed until they were standing still, poised on a current of air. Aiden adjusted the gears, and the chopper made a rapid ascent as though they were riding an invisible elevator. The land below them faded away. Higher and higher, they lifted into the night sky, and then they stopped.

With the flick of a couple of switches, he turned off the running lights and the lights in the cockpit. Suspended in the velvet darkness, she experienced a strange, almost magical sensation. The stars closed around her and she became part of the sky. She could feel the altitude. The only reminder of reality was the synchronized rumble of the rotors. Looking down, she saw dots of light from ranch houses and a warmer glow from the streets of Henley, miles from where they were.

"Do you like it?" he asked.

Though she hadn't been aware of holding her breath, she

exhaled in a whoosh. "I feel like the wind, a feather on the wind."

"You're not a helicopter virgin anymore."

"I understand why you love flying. It's so free."

"Up here, I can leave the worries behind. But only for a couple of minutes." He turned on the lights and set a course for home. "Usually when I'm up in the chopper, I'm on my way to a disaster. A rescue. A search. A medical emergency."

She closed her eyes, not wanting to come down to earth. Her memory bank made a permanent record of these magical moments with Aiden. "Thank you."

"Am I forgiven?"

"Not entirely," she said, "but mostly. And do you forgive me for coming with you without permission?"

"You bet," he said. "I'm wondering if you told anybody else your plan before you took off running after me."

"I told Grandma, and she was pleased." Come to think of it, her reaction was kind of odd. "She said something about how I was meant to be with you, whatever that means."

To her surprise, he chuckled. "This might be a good time to warn you about your grandma and my mom. I was with them in the kitchen while the sheriff was talking to you and Misty. And the two of them were plotting."

"About what?"

"Matchmaking," he said.

"Between you and me?" Though she'd been making that same match ever since she saw him, Tab didn't like being manipulated. "Why do you think so?"

"They kept winking and nudging each other. Then my mom announced that you didn't have a boyfriend and wasn't that convenient because I don't have a girlfriend, either."

"Subtle," Tab muttered.

"When I said I liked the sweet potato pie, your grandma told me that you made it."

"Why would she say that?"

"To let me know that you're a great cook."

Tab groaned. Of course, her grandma would push the anatomically incorrect old wives' tale about the way to a man's heart being through his stomach. "Does that turn you on? Thinking that I know my way around a kitchen?"

"Do you?"

"As a matter of fact, I'm fully capable of making a pie, but I didn't make that one. There wasn't time after I got back to Grandma's, took care of Shua and drove to your ranch."

"Busy day."

Running through the short list of what she'd done in one day made her aware of the time. Her wristwatch showed it was after ten o'clock. She should have been tired, but she wasn't. A restless energy coursed through her. No doubt, she was still feeling the effect of the adrenaline rush that came from flying and from being this close to Aiden.

As they approached the ranch, he turned on the searchlight and scanned the landing area behind the barn. Looking down on his cabin, she noticed a deck that was half the size of the house, a good place for a barbecue. "When did you build the cabin?"

"A couple of summers ago. I wanted to put some space between me and the main house. My mom and Blake—he's the foreman—are handling most of the ranch business. If I'm not around, they don't come running to me."

Apparently, he needed to physically move to avoid taking over. "And the separate cabin gives you some privacy."

"Mom and Blake are the ones who need space of their own. They still sleep in separate bedrooms, but they've been a couple for quite a while."

"Does that bother you?"

"Hell, no. I want my mom to be happy. Her life didn't end when my father died. It took her a long time to crawl out of her depression. When she did, Blake was there, waiting to give her a hand."

The chopper touched down, and the rotors stilled. Without that noise, the night seemed uncomfortably quiet. Tab wasn't sure where to go from here. "It's late," she said.

"You and your grandma should stay at the ranch tonight. We've got plenty of room."

Suspiciously, she asked, "Did you think of that invitation all by yourself? Or is it something your mom and my grandma suggested?"

"Both," he said. "About the matchmaking…"

"What about it?"

"I'm not opposed."

When she emerged from the chopper and set her feet on hard ground, her legs were shaky. After flying, the earth felt too solid and heavy. She circled the tail and stood beside Aiden. "When you say you aren't opposed, I'm not sure what that means. Are you asking me on a date?"

"I'm asking you to spend the night."

She avoided looking at him. His offer to stay the night hadn't been meant in a romantic way, and she didn't want to react like a moron. "Normally, I wouldn't impose, but this is a long day for Grandma. She needs her sleep."

"And so do you."

His low, sexy voice caressed her senses. Quickly, she said, "And I'm concerned about Misty. All this stress while she's pregnant isn't good for her."

"Look at me, Tab."

With great reluctance, she lifted her gaze. With the moonlight shining on his face, he reminded her of that iconic image of the perfect man she'd seen on that night so long ago when he was walking his dog. "Whatever happened to Reilly?"

"My border collie? Oh, man, I loved that dog." His mouth

relaxed into a smile. "I miss good old Reilly. He died last year and I buried him up on the hill. Why do you ask?"

She really couldn't say. Standing this close to him had turned her into a tongue-tied sixteen-year-old with a heart-rending crush. "I don't know."

With the back of his hand, he smoothed a wisp of hair off her cheek. "We've been through a lot together, Tab. But I hardly know you."

Her chin tilted upward. The intense focus of his gray eyes warmed her. A trembling heat rippled through her body. "What do you want to know?"

His hand nestled on the nape of her neck under her braid, and he held her in place. When he leaned closer, she knew he was about to kiss her, and the anticipation was almost more than she could stand. Her knees turned to jelly. For years, she'd dreamed of this moment.

His lips touched hers. The light pressure intoxicated her. *This is it.* This moment was something she'd waited for and imagined and cherished. She wanted more, and she couldn't hold back. Her level of excitement surged off the charts, and her heart raced madly. If she'd been hooked to a monitor, the machine would have exploded. She pressed her mouth harder against his. Their gentle kiss became fierce and passionate.

Her arm flung around his neck. Her body molded to his. She wanted to feel him in every fiber of her being. His arm snuggled around her waist and yanked her so tightly against him that her breasts crushed against his hard-muscled chest.

This kiss was as wonderful as she had imagined. Better, it was better because it was real and not the fantasy of a love-sick girl. In his arms, she was a woman.

Gasping, she ended the kiss and tucked her head into the crook of his neck. When her eyes closed, a tear squeezed through her lashes and slipped down her cheek.

"I'll stay the night," she whispered.

Tonight and tomorrow and the next day, she wanted to stay with him, even if it meant she might get hurt. Some risks were worth the pain.

Chapter Eight

As they walked toward the house, Aiden's mind was a thousand miles away. His instincts told him to fling Tab over his shoulder, carry her back to his cabin and make love to her real slow. The rational side of his mind reined him back. Too soon, it was too soon. He probably shouldn't have kissed her in the first place, but he was glad he did. For a woman who acted so professional, she sure as hell had a wild side and a sexy energy that bowled him over. That wasn't a friendly little kiss. It was foreplay.

"Aiden," she said, "are you listening?"

"I drifted off for a moment." He shook off his fantasies and dismissed the image of her lying in her bed with her long black hair spread across the pillows. "You were saying?"

"When Misty was talking to the sheriff about her wristwatch, she was holding something back."

"She was lying?"

"Not lying, but not telling everything. It had something to do with a party."

With an effort, he tamped down his desire. "I gave her that pretty gold watch, and I thought it meant something to her. I'm surprised she lost it."

"She didn't misplace it," Tab said. "She argued with the girl who was murdered, Ellen Jessop, and ended up throwing the watch at her."

Pitching a tantrum sounded exactly like something Misty would do. Not only did she have a temper but she often acted in haste without considering the consequences. "Did she ask for the watch back?"

"Not according to her."

Approaching the wide porch that stretched across the front of the house, he noticed that the sheriff's vehicle was still there. "I'm guessing that the sheriff talked to her while we were gone. She's got to tell the truth, but I hope that being honest won't get her deeper in trouble."

"It won't," Tab said emphatically. "She's innocent."

"I'll talk to her." He glanced up at Misty's second-floor bedroom window at the far right end of the house. The lights were still on. "Looks like she's still awake. I'll catch her before she goes to sleep."

"I have a question," she said. "Does Clinton stay here with Misty?"

"No." Aiden had laid down the law on this topic. "Unless they get married, Clinton doesn't live here."

"Well, aren't you the old-fashioned one."

"I don't have a problem with Clinton visiting and even spending the night, but there's a commitment that comes with having a baby, and they both need to step up, make plans and act like grown-ups."

"Does he have a job?"

"My mom hired him." He didn't like that arrangement, but the economy was tough, and Clinton hadn't been able to find other employment. "But he doesn't stay in the bunkhouse. He lives in Henley with his parents. The Browns are good folks, and they agree with me."

"But how does Misty feel about the arrangement?"

Most of his sister's feelings and attitudes were incomprehensible to him. She'd laugh when she ought to cry. She could handle a big trauma but would blow up over breaking a heel on her shoe. "I think she gets it. There's a reason she hasn't married Clinton, and it's not because he hasn't asked. He did the honorable thing and came to me for permission."

"Another old-time tradition," she said. "Is the Gabriel ranch in some kind of time warp?"

"Would that be such a bad thing?"

"Not for you," she said. "For someone like me, it's a different story. I'm half Crow and half white. I'm pretty sure I wouldn't fare well in the Old West."

"A beautiful woman like you always has an advantage."

"Thanks, but—" with a flick of her slender wrist, she brushed his compliment aside "—there's a lot more expected from a modern woman than being pretty. What's it going to take for me to drag you into this century?"

"Go ahead." He grinned. "You can try to change my mind."

"Challenge accepted."

They stepped onto the porch, and he made a point of opening the door for her. There was nothing wrong with his supposedly old-fashioned view of life. His father, his grandfather and his great-grandfather had raised cattle on this land, built a small empire and made a good life for their families. Not a damn thing wrong with that.

In the front room, the sheriff paced with his cell phone to his ear, still irritated and hostile. Misty occupied a big leather chair near the fireplace with her feet in fuzzy slippers up on an ottoman. His mom and Blake were opposite her on the love seat.

His mom rose and came toward them. She took Tab's hands and smiled. "Maria was exhausted. I told her to go to bed."

"I appreciate that, Sylvia. Grandma needs her sleep."

"Come here." Sylvia pulled her into a warm hug. "There

hasn't been time for us to say a proper hello. I'm so glad to see you."

"Same here."

Over his mom's shoulder, Tab gave him a wink. He wondered how long it would take for his mom to start fitting her for a wedding gown. For a woman so dead set on matchmaking, his mom was doing a good job of holding Blake at bay. Tab had included him in her hugging, and they resembled the beginnings of one big happy family.

He couldn't join in, not yet. Aiden had a job to do. He needed to mend fences with Sheriff Fielding who had just ended his phone call. Like it or not, the sheriff was his best source of information.

Aiden cleared his throat. "Your deputies did a fine job in arresting those two. They were thorough."

"Did you expect anything less?"

"You know how much I respect you and your men." And that was the genuine truth. More than once, the idea of becoming a lawman had crossed his mind. "We've worked together on rescues and searches. I've never turned my back when you've asked for help, and I hope we can continue with that kind of cooperation."

The sheriff nodded slowly. "Apology accepted."

Aiden hadn't actually humbled himself enough to ask for forgiveness. *Real men never say they're sorry.* He winced a little bit as he realized that was probably another example of his old-fashioned thinking. But it worked. He and the sheriff were back on the same page and he was free to ask, "What was in that note the boys threw at the house?"

"They wrote it in crayon on a piece of notebook paper," Sheriff Fielding said with obvious disgust. "Real childish. Real stupid."

Misty piped up, "I saw the note. My name was scribbled, all mean and nasty, and it said David's death was on my head."

He glanced toward his sister. Usually, she liked being the center of attention, but not like this. Her eyelids drooped. Her skin was pale. "Are you okay?"

"I'm tired."

While Tab and his mother rushed to Misty's side, Aiden lowered his voice to speak to the sheriff. "Is this the kind of nonsense you expect from Chuck and Woody?"

"They've both got juvenile records. Nothing serious."

"They claimed that they were just shooting in the air, but I want some serious charges so they understand that gunfire of any kind isn't acceptable."

"I agree," the sheriff said. "That prank could have turned dangerous."

The sheriff had been looking for a gang, and now he had the start of one with Woody and Chuck. Aiden wanted more information, but he didn't expect the sheriff to be forthcoming in front of the other people in the room, especially Misty. He nodded toward the kitchen. "Sheriff, you look like you could use some coffee."

"If I have caffeine at this hour, I'll never get to sleep."

"A beer?"

"I wouldn't say no to a cup of tea."

His mom caught the reference to beverages and was already moving toward them. Aiden gestured for her to step back. "I'll make the tea. You take care of Misty."

In the kitchen, he set the teakettle on the burner and sat at the table opposite the sheriff. "Earlier tonight, you said that you suspected the murders might be the work of a gang. Are there any other guys that Chuck and Woody hang out with?"

"All these kids pal around together. Like Wally the Buffalo Man said, they get together for parties and make a ruckus.

They can get away with a lot as long as they don't cause a disturbance in town."

"So they go to the rez."

"I guess they do. Two and a half million acres of land that's mostly unsupervised is real tempting."

"Is there anyone who stands out?" Aiden asked. "A leader of the pack."

"I've been keeping my eye on a guy who's only been in town for six months or so. He's older than these kids, probably twenty-six or twenty-seven, and a ski bum type. They call him Aspen Jim. His last name is Sherman."

"Where does he work?"

"At the feed store. He must have known the girl who got murdered. She worked there, too."

The teakettle gave a whistle, and Aiden put together a couple of mugs with tea bags and sugar. His natural inclination was to ask direct questions and expect answers, but he was still on thin ice with the sheriff and needed to be cautious. "I hope you don't mind if I ask about your investigation."

"Let's just keep in mind that this is my investigation. *Mine*, not yours." The sheriff raised his mug and took a sip of the hot tea. "And there are some things I can't tell you. After all, your sister is a suspect."

"I understand."

Aiden was counting on the years of goodwill his family had established with the people in these parts. The Gabriel ranch was a big employer, his mom attended church regularly, and Aiden had the reputation of being fair and honest. To keep Misty out of jail, he might need to call in a whole lot of favors.

"Tell you what," the sheriff said, "you go ahead and ask your questions. If I need to hold back, I'll tell you."

"Fair enough." He gave a nod. "When do you think you'll get those autopsy reports back from Billings?"

"A couple of days," he said. "They put a rush on it. If we've got a serial killer dumping bodies on the rez, we need to know."

Joseph Lefthand had strongly suggested that possibility at the meeting in Crow Agency. He'd warned people in law enforcement to be on the lookout. "What can you tell me about Ellen Jessop's murder?"

"Her body was found in a gully not far from where Spring Creek Road takes a jog. I wouldn't mind if you happened to fly over with your chopper. You might be able to see something that the guys on the ground missed."

Aiden nodded. "If I see anything, I'll report to you."

"Ellen's death might not be related to David's, but it's hard not to put the two together. Not that Wally is a reliable witness, but he said that he saw David with Ellen."

"What can you tell me about the other murdered girl?"

"Raped." The sheriff winced as he sipped his tea. "Bruising showed she'd been beaten, and the cause of death was manual strangulation. She'd been restrained. When they found the body, her wrists were still tied together."

"What kind of knots?"

"Nothing special," the sheriff said, "figure eight knots and bowlines. Sailors use those knots, but so do cowboys."

"No DNA or fingerprints?"

"Nothing." The sheriff finished off his tea and pushed back his chair to stand. "I'm about done here. Before I go, I'd like to take Tab's statement."

"She'll be relieved to give it to you."

"I remember her from way back. She was a skinny little thing, but when she looked at you with those blue eyes, she'd make you stop and stare. She's grown into a pretty woman."

"I won't disagree," Aiden said. She was most definitely a pretty woman, and she kissed like there was no tomorrow.

"Smart, too. We could use a professional midwife in these parts. I sure hope she decides to stick around."

Aiden intended to do everything in his power to convince her to stay. This was the place she belonged, the place she would learn to call home.

BRIGHT AND EARLY THE next morning, Tab took her coffee mug onto the porch and perched on the railing facing her grandma who had settled into a rocking chair. A relaxed smile stretched across Grandma's lined and weathered face. She reminded Tab of Yoda or the Native American version of Buddha—an icon of wisdom, strength and happiness.

If she told her grandma about the kiss last night, she wondered what Maria Spotted Bear would advise her to do. Should she play hard to get? Should she flirt? Or should she shamelessly throw herself at him? Seeing Aiden this morning could be complicated.

"It's a beautiful day," Tab said. Not a cloud in sight, the newly risen sun illuminated the big blue Montana sky. Flying in daylight would be a new experience, one she was anxious to try.

"Not too cold," Grandma said as she sipped from her own steaming mug. "It's a good November."

Tab savored the rich, fragrant coffee. Since her grandma preferred tea, she seldom indulged the coffee habit she'd developed in Missoula when working late nights with women in labor. "Are you ready to head for home?"

"Not so fast. Let me drink my coffee."

"Really? You're not having tea?"

"Sylvia adds a pinch of wild chicory root for me. It's good for digestion. I brought her a supply for when I visit."

"I never realized that you and Sylvia were so close."

"For many years," Grandma said, "even before you were born."

"Tell me." Tab settled back to listen. Her grandma's stories were always interesting and often had some kind of message. She considered it her duty to educate Tab, not only in the ways of the tribe but in the ways of life.

"When they were young mothers, Sylvia and your mom used to spend much time together. They worked on projects together, beading and knitting. My beautiful Emma was as dark and intense as the moon while Sylvia was blonde and bright. They both liked artful things. When Sylvia came into Billings to see *The Nutcracker* ballet, she stayed at your house."

Tab vaguely remembered going to the ballet when she was a little girl. Dancing wasn't her thing, but she loved getting all dressed up for the big performance.

"When Emma died," Grandma continued, "Sylvia was a comfort to me. And I returned the solace when she lost her husband. Why do you think I allowed you to spend that summer babysitting Misty instead of staying at my house?"

"To help Sylvia?"

"And to teach you a lesson. You never had brothers or sisters. Being with Misty showed you how to take care of another person who needed your help."

Since Tab ended up in a helping profession, she figured that the lesson had been well learned. "It might have been a turning point for me."

"Misty still needs our help," her grandma said. "I want to stay here at the ranch until I know she's safe."

Tab understood the sentiment, but staying here wasn't practical. "They might never catch the murderer."

"They will," her grandma said in a tone of certainty that ended all discussion.

"What about Shua?"

"I already called the neighbors. Sam Tall Grass will take care of the horse and tend to the house. He's done it before."

Tab couldn't object on the basis of her business. All she needed was her cell phone to stay in contact with her clients, and she usually went to them instead of the other way around. The real problem with staying at the ranch was Aiden.

After last night's kiss, she couldn't pretend that he meant nothing to her. But she didn't want to rush into a relationship that was very likely to blow up in her face. "I'm not sure if we should stay."

Aiden came around the corner of the barn. Striding toward the house, he waved. Even at this distance, she could tell that he was grinning, and she couldn't help smiling back.

"A piece of advice," her grandma said.

"Yes?"

"Follow your heart."

Thanks, Yoda. But her heart wasn't crystal clear. She wanted to take a chance with him, but she was afraid. An old-fashioned cowboy who didn't want her involved in his investigating wouldn't be happy with a woman who thought for herself, took care of herself and made her own decisions.

The closer he got, the faster her heart beat. She moved to the edge of the porch. The soles of her feet were itching to run, either to dive into his arms or to charge past him and keep on going. Reaching up, she grasped the porch railing, anchoring herself. She'd stay. Just for today, she would stay.

Chapter Nine

"Good morning, Aiden."

Gazing down at him from the porch, Tab combined her memories with the current version of Aiden Gabriel and decided that, in the past, he might have been a little too pretty. Maturity suited him. He was one of those men who would get more chiseled and sexy as he aged, the lucky duck.

"Same to you." After a wink at her, he touched the brim of his hat and nodded to her grandmother. "Good morning, Maria Spotted Bear."

"I had a good sleep," Grandma announced.

"I always like to have you visit. When you're here, my mom opens up like a sunflower."

"I'm glad." She treated Aiden to one of her Buddha smiles. "Tab and I will stay here until I'm sure that Misty is safe."

Tab sucked in her cheeks to keep her embarrassment from showing. Who plopped themselves down on somebody else's porch and announced that they were moving in? Apparently, her grandma did. "That's a huge imposition. We really can't—"

"Your family is always welcome at the Gabriel ranch."

"Are you sure?"

"A hundred percent."

If she hadn't known the real history of Grandma and the Gabriel family, she would have been perplexed by Aiden's invitation. She was glad Grandma had told her about the deep, close relationship between her and Sylvia. Tragedies had brought them together. Friendship sealed their connection. The next logical step, she supposed, was the matchmaking.

With a glance at Aiden, she wondered about his remembrances of her mother. He'd been a teenager when she passed away, old enough to form an opinion. He might be able to reveal a different aspect of the past.

"Go now." Her grandma shooed them away. "You two young people should walk in the sunlight of a new day."

"Yes, ma'am." Aiden took Tab's hand and led her down the porch steps. As he escorted her along the sidewalk that led away from the front door, he asked, "Do you know what she means? Walking in the new sunlight?"

"It sounds cryptic and wise, doesn't it? Like something that might be said at a Sun Dance ritual. I'm pretty sure it doesn't mean anything more than Grandma wants to sit alone on the porch and relax."

"Have you ever seen a Sun Dance?"

"Once." The ceremony was no longer practiced on a regular basis. Few outsiders were invited to attend.

"I've heard it can be brutal."

His comment touched a nerve. "Don't you mean savage? As in those savages on the rez are doing their weird dances?"

"I didn't mean that at all."

"What have you heard?"

"Young men in the tribe are pierced at the breastbone and attached by a leather thong to a tall pole. Sometimes, they get hoisted off their feet. It's a rite of manhood."

With his thumbs hitched in his pockets and his dusty boots shuffling in a casual saunter, Aiden was every inch the cowboy. She couldn't expect him to understand the ways of her people. It was her heritage, and she barely understood. Hoping to dismiss the topic, she said, "Great weather, huh?"

"What does the Sun Dance mean to you?"

A fair question. Maybe he was sincerely interested, but years of prejudice had taught her to keep her guard up. She didn't want him to think of her as an exotic Crow princess, which she definitely was not. Her inclination was to shut down, but if she ever expected to have a *real* connection with the *real* Aiden, the flesh-and-blood man who walked beside her, she needed to open up.

"The Sun Dance isn't about macho or magic," she said. "The suffering of the young men is a form of prayer, like a sweat lodge or a vision quest. Their silent endurance brings blessings to their families. And, I assure you, their lives are never in danger. In the day-long ritual, we give thanks to the earth and ask for wisdom. Even as a kid, I was moved by the powerful sense of community."

"I appreciate the explanation."

"And it's not more brutal than rodeo bull riding."

At the end of the sidewalk, he leaned against a split-rail fence and turned his face up to catch the light. "Growing up, it must have been strange for you, moving back and forth between Billings and the rez. Did you feel like you belonged in the tribal community?"

"I could never choose between my home with my dad and my mother's people. I'm not totally one or the other." She took a sip from the coffee mug she'd carried with her. "When I was a kid on the rez, I got teased for my blue eyes. In Billings, people gave me a hard time about being Crow. Now, I enjoy having a foot in each world."

"Could be an asset in your midwife work."

"Exactly," she said. "Right now, I have only six clients, and they're evenly divided between the rez and the people of Henley."

"You can make that seven clients," he said. "Misty wants you to deliver her baby."

"Did you talk to her last night?"

He nodded. "And you were right about her holding back something from the sheriff. The truth is that Misty didn't go to that party, but Clinton did. Misty sent him with the express purpose of getting the wristwatch back from Ellen Jessop."

Sending Clinton to the party didn't seem unreasonable, but she feared there was more to the story. "I'm guessing that Clinton argued with Ellen."

"Right," he said. "With Ellen ending up murdered, it looks bad for Clinton. I sure as hell don't want to think he had anything to do with her death, but he seems to be on the spot when people get killed. First, Ellen. Then, David."

"David?"

"Clinton is the most likely person to have picked up Misty's rifle and killed David."

"But he didn't," she said. "When I rode over the hill, Clinton was unconscious, sprawled in the back of the Jeep. I saw him. I'm his alibi."

"Was there enough time between when you heard the shots and when you rode over the hill for him to climb into the back of the Jeep?"

"Five or six minutes," she said quickly. Misty's story about the disappearing shooter made her very conscious of the time lapse. "Why would Clinton pretend to be unconscious?"

"You said it yourself. The concussion gave him an alibi."

After taking another sip, she stared down into her mug and swirled the remains of her coffee. Aiden had drawn a fairly logical conclusion, except for one thing. If Clinton had fired the shots that killed David Welling, Misty would have seen what happened. "Do you think Misty is lying to protect him?"

"If she is, she's not going to admit it. No matter how many times I ask, she keeps sticking to her story about the mysterious gunman."

"Maybe we should talk to Clinton," she suggested. "Not that I expect him to confess."

"Not at all." Aiden's hostility toward his sister's boyfriend showed in his body language. His eyebrows tensed in a scowl, and he folded his arms across his lean torso.

"He can't be that bad," she said. "Misty loves him."

"She also loves three-legged dogs, skunks and anybody with a sad story. My sister is a lousy judge of character."

"Still," she said, "it wouldn't hurt to talk to Clinton."

"He's not likely to open up to me. But you might get him to answer a couple of questions." He warmed to the idea. "You could start by asking him about the party and what happened when he tried to get the watch. Then, you'd ease the conversation around to what really happened when David Welling was killed."

"I could do that." She liked the direction Aiden was headed. Casually, she leaned against the fence beside him. "It almost sounds like you're asking me to help."

"Does it now?"

"You bet it does. It's almost like we're investigating. Both of us. Together." She covered her smug grin by draining the last of her coffee. "I seem to recall something you said about not wanting my help because it was too... What was it you said? It was too dangerous for a delicate flower like me."

"I'm real damn sure I never called you a flower."

"I added that part," she said. "You know what you said."

He shoved away from the fence and stood tall before her. "If you're done with your I-told-you-so, I'd like to put things into motion. Clinton is in the horse barn."

"And you want me to talk to him." She looked up through her eyelashes. "You want me to help you investigate."

"I reckon I do."

"Consider it done." She handed him her coffee mug. "I'll see you back at the house."

LOCATING CLINTON wasn't difficult. All Tab had to do was follow the smell. As the lowest employee on the totem pole, he had the most boring assignment—mucking out the stalls in the horse barn. He was more than happy to abandon his shaving fork and follow her outside to the corral where the horses were at the troughs.

Tab used the most obvious excuse to get their conversation started. "I wanted to see how you were doing after your head injury. Looks like somebody changed the dressing."

"My mom," he said as he pulled off his rubber gloves and flexed his fingers. "Just like you, she wanted me to go to the doctor."

"But you didn't go."

"I'm fine." When she reached toward the bandages, he jerked his head back and settled his baseball cap more firmly on the top of his head. "Really, I'm okay."

"How did you sleep?"

"Good."

She tugged his arm and pulled him closer to the corral gate. "Step over here into the sunlight and let me look at your eyes. I want to see if your pupils are dilated."

Reluctantly, he stared at her. Up close and quiet, he was more appealing than when he was strutting around, trying to impress Misty. Not a bad-looking kid, but he was young, so very young to be taking on the responsibilities of fatherhood.

"You need to be careful with a concussion," she said. "Have you noticed double vision or dizziness?"

He shook his head.

"Ringing in your ears? Persistent headache? Are you having any trouble focusing or remembering?"

"No, no and no."

"If any of those things crop up, I advise you to see a doctor. You're fortunate not to have any serious problem, at least not a physical problem." She studied him with a calm, measured stare. "In other ways, you're very unlucky."

"What's that supposed to mean?"

"You've got a talent for being in the wrong place at the wrong time." She remembered Aiden's accusation. *First, Ellen. Then, David.* "What happened when you went to the party and talked to Ellen Jessop?"

"Misty wanted me to get her gold watch. She said she'd pay Ellen to get it back, but I knew that wouldn't work. Ellen's family might have lost all their money, but she's still got her pride."

"How well did you know Ellen?"

"We had a couple of dates. She was pretty and blonde, tall with long legs. But, damn, she had a temper. She'd get so angry that I thought she'd bite my head off. And jealous."

And now she was dead, horribly murdered. He didn't seem too concerned about her death. "Did you like her?"

He eyed her suspiciously. "I've got nothing else to say."

As a midwife, Tab was accustomed to working with obstinate young people who were confused and scared. When it was time for the baby to be born, the fathers were usually more freaked out than the mothers. She'd learned how to talk them down.

"I want to help you, Clinton. Believe me when I say that I know what you're going through. You're trying to take care of Misty, but there's nobody for you to lean on."

His mouth pinched in a tight knot. "Especially not Aiden."

"I understand." She knew better than to get sidetracked by a discussion of Aiden. "Here's the deal, Clinton. Misty wants me to be her midwife, and that means you need to trust me. We have to work together. Okay?"

"I guess."

"I want the whole story about what's been going on with you and Misty and these terrible crimes," she said. "You can start by telling me about what happened between you and Ellen."

"She acted like she owned every minute of my time. We only went out two times and I never slept with her, but she got mad when I talked to other girls."

"Did she blame Misty for your breakup?"

"That's right." He nodded. "Misty and me didn't get together until three or four months after I ended things with Ellen, but somehow she thought Misty stole me away from her."

Once his barriers were down, Clinton had a lot to say. He couldn't stop his mouth from running as he described typical teenage incidents of two girls fighting over one guy. Though his story was mostly a boost for his own ego, he seemed truly perplexed about these two women.

Though he had a motive for disliking Ellen, the love triangle didn't seem like enough for murder. In an attempt to rein him in, she said, "What about the party?"

"I tried to talk nice to her, but she got louder and louder. She said mean things about Misty, and it made me so mad that I made a grab for the watch. Ellen drew back her hand, slapped me hard and threw her beer in my face."

"Did you threaten her?"

"No, ma'am. My mom and dad taught me never to hit a woman. I turned around and walked away. Last time I saw her. Now, she's dead." His mouth got tight again. "Was it the serial killer?"

Though the sheriff had avoided labeling the murders as a serial killing, Tab knew the gossip train would race toward the most sensational theory. One dead girl was an event. Two pointed to a serial killer. "I don't know."

"That's what people in town are saying."

"Those folks aren't always right. Did you hear about Woody and Chuck?"

"Misty called me and told me what they did last night. Damn, it makes me mad. How could they think that Misty was a murderer?"

"Some people think you're the one who shot David Welling." Offering him an easy out, she continued, "In self-defense."

"Even if I'd been awake and I saw him threaten Misty, I wouldn't need a gun to take him." He raised both fists. "I'd use these."

"You didn't like David."

"He was always sniffing around, acting like Misty was his secret lover. Well, she wasn't. She's my girl."

His anger sounded like the ravings of a seventeen-year-old, but Tab sensed something deeper and perhaps more sinister. "What are you hiding, Clinton?"

"Nothing."

"You can trust me," she encouraged him. "Is it something about David?"

"Some things are private." He glared. "Everybody thinks I'm stupid, but all of you smart people, including Sheriff Fielding, keep looking in the wrong direction for the killer."

"Fine," she said. "Tell me the right direction."

"Misty told you the God's honest truth. Somebody used her gun to shoot David, and then they ran off. All you've got to do is find their car."

"If there was a mystery shooter…"

"That's the only way it could have happened." He paced away from her and came back again. "We were smack dab in the middle of nowhere. How did David get there? He must have had some kind of transportation."

"Of course."

"Where did it go? What happened to David's car?" He poked a finger at her to make his point. "I'll tell you what happened, the only thing that could have happened. The mystery shooter used David's car to make his getaway."

"Find the car, and we find the killer."

His logic had a simple elegance that didn't fit with his scruffy appearance. David needed transportation to get to the riverbed where he confronted Misty, but his car was gone. Therefore, somebody drove it away. If that were true, Misty's story about the disappearing killer had some credence.

There was more to him than met the eye. For the first time, Tab thought he might just be worthy of Misty.

Chapter Ten

Aiden still didn't like the idea of Tab being involved in investigating, but he was impressed with how much information she'd gotten from Clinton. When she asked if she could hitch a ride into Henley with him, he hadn't refused. His plan was to talk to Bert Welling at the gas station and find out what kind of vehicle David had been driving. He didn't expect his conversation with David's uncle to be easy, especially since half the town believed that Misty was the killer. But Aiden had known Bert for years and had given him a lot of business. That ought to count for something.

Driving down the road they'd flown over last night, he noticed that Woody's truck was still parked on the shoulder. "I wonder if those two boys are still in jail."

"I hope the sheriff doesn't let them off easy," Tab said. "They need to know that pranks using guns won't be tolerated."

"A hard lesson. Guns are part of life around here."

"And Montana gun laws are practically nonexistent," she said. "That makes me wonder why Misty's mystery shooter wasn't armed. Why did he need to use Misty's rifle."

"It was an opportunity. He saw the gun and figured he could frame my sister." Once Aiden accepted Misty's story, it made all kinds of sense. "The mystery shooter and David must have come there together, probably following Misty."

"Because David had a crush," she said.

"I hope that's all it was." He didn't like to think about Misty being targeted for a darker reason. "After the murder, the shooter used the vehicle for his getaway."

"Find the car, and we find the killer," she said.

"It's not that simple," he said. "Like the mystery shooter, this vehicle is invisible…and silent. Neither you nor Misty heard an engine starting up."

"The rush of the river could have covered the engine noise."

"When I flew over, I didn't see a vehicle."

"He made a quick escape," she said. "There had to be a car for David to get to the site, and it was pretty clever of Clinton to focus on that. It wouldn't hurt for you to tell him he was helpful. Whether you like it or not, he's going to be a permanent part of your family."

"It'll take more than a single flash of intelligence for me to change my mind about him."

"You have an opportunity to mend fences. Don't build a wall instead." Unexpectedly, she chuckled. "I can't believe I said that. I'm starting to sound like Grandma Yoda."

Her laughter drew him closer. It had been a while since he'd had a pretty woman riding in the passenger seat of his truck. When he was still in his long-distance relationship, he hadn't gone out with anyone else, and it wasn't only because he was being faithful. None of the local women interested him. Not until Tab arrived.

Today, she wore her hair pulled back in a low ponytail fastened with an orange-and-blue beaded barrette. She looked fresh and young. The unbraided length of her blue-black hair shimmered in the sunlight, and he longed to tangle his fingers in the silky strands.

"When we get to town," she said, "you can drop me off at

the café on the corner of Main and Grant. That's where I'm meeting with my client."

"At the café?"

"She's a waitress, nine months pregnant. She called this morning and said the baby wasn't kicking as much, maybe only once or twice an hour. Sometimes, that's a sign that the mom is about to go into labor."

Aiden had participated in the delivery of cows, horses and other livestock, but it was hard for him to imagine a human woman giving birth. "I know who you're talking about. Her name is Connie, right? If she thinks she's going to have the baby, why did she go to work?"

"I told her to stay home, but she wanted to pick up the morning shift. She said her tips have been phenomenal since she started showing."

He nodded. "I've been slipping an extra couple of bucks under the plate when she's my waitress. And I've been feeling like I ought to help her carry something."

"Anyway, this is just a quick checkup. I'll pop in and say hi. Then I'll catch up with you at the gas station."

Aiden hesitated before replying. He wanted to draw the line about how involved she should be. Though he had no particular reason to suspect Bert, he didn't want Tab associated with his investigating. "I'd rather have you wait for me at the café."

"Why?"

"I'll meet you there for coffee. I've got a taste for one of their sweet rolls."

"I don't believe that. You just had breakfast," she said. "Why are you trying to keep me away from the gas station?"

"For your own safety." He could have made up a lie, but he knew she'd see through him. "I don't want any focus on you. We could be dealing with a serial killer, somebody who brutalizes and rapes his victims."

"Are you talking about Bert Welling? The man who runs the tidiest gas station in the state?"

"I don't know where the danger is coming from. That's the problem."

"Is it?" Her tone was frosty. "It seems to me that all you're doing is asking questions, which is exactly what I did with Clinton. I can help. That's why Grandma wants us to stay at your house. To help. To find the real killer so Misty won't be accused."

They drove past the scattered houses at the outskirts of town. The bad economy had taken a toll in this area. Some of these homes were boarded up and abandoned. Families were leaving Henley and moving to Billings where they'd have a better chance of finding steady work. Aiden feared that the small-town way of life he'd always cherished was coming to an end.

His world was changing before his eyes. He shouldn't be looking for a serial killer. Those kinds of crimes belonged in the big city, not in his sleepy little town. It used to be that Gabriel ranch commanded so much respect that nobody would dare to drive by and shoot off their guns, much less to accuse Misty of murder. *Changes.* Everything was turning upside down, and the worst part was how these changes struck close to home. His baby sister was about to become a single mother. His churchgoing mom seemed content to sleep with Blake and not marry him.

His idea of shielding Tab from the dangers of an investigation might be part of a bygone era when the menfolk did the protecting and the womenfolk stayed home and baked pies. Tab sure as hell didn't fit that mold. If she had, he probably wouldn't have found her so appealing.

"Fine," he said. "Meet me at the gas station when you're done."

"I intend to." The chill in her voice turned crisp and professional. "And I'm coming along this afternoon when you take off in the chopper."

That suited him just fine. In the chopper with him, she'd be safe. "Glad to have you along."

"Good, because I need to stop by Grandma's house and pick up some clothes and basic supplies. Also, I want to bring Shua over here to the ranch. I know the neighbors are taking care of her, but I worry she's not getting enough exercise."

He suppressed an urge to warn her about riding all across the countryside by herself. Yesterday, he'd sent her off without being worried. But that was before they'd found Ellen, the second victim of the serial killer.

They drove down Main Street, a wide two-lane road with angled parking on both sides. Like the outlying area, the shops along the sidewalk showed signs of deterioration although most of the storefronts were occupied. At the far end of the street, two churches faced each other. Half a mile beyond was Henley High, home of the Bobcats.

Aiden drove past the gas station with a green neon open sign in the front window. Apparently, Bert Welling wasn't taking off any time to mourn his murdered nephew. Two blocks away at the café, he dropped Tab off.

She waved. "See you in a few."

Circling back, he drove up to the gas pump where the price for regular was a whole lot higher than he liked to pay. Aiden climbed down from the cab as Bert emerged from the office. Dressed in the gray jumpsuit with his name stitched over the breast pocket, Bert looked much too neat and tidy to be a car mechanic, but that was his way.

Ever since he took over the gas station, more than a dozen years ago, he'd adhered to a standard of cleanliness more typical of a tea parlor than a garage. From the spotless windows to the array of tools neatly hung on pegs, Bert's station showed a compulsive attention to order and detail.

Aiden took off his hat and extended his hand. "I'm sorry for your loss."

Bert acknowledged his words with a nod. His clean-shaven face was without expression. Not a single strand of his thinning black hair dared to slip out of place. "Fill 'er up?"

"Yes, sir. And I'm due for an oil change, if you've got the time."

"Drive 'er into the first bay."

Aiden followed Bert's instruction, figuring that while the two of them were inside the garage together, he might be more prone to conversation. Or maybe not. Bert was never the talkative sort.

As Bert moved efficiently through his routine for getting the truck up on the lift, Aiden decided to forego subtlety. "There's been talk that my sister was somehow responsible for David's death. I want you to know it's not true."

"I don't blame Misty," Bert said. "David always spoke highly of her. She was a cut above most of the girls he dated."

"I expect you've heard about Chuck and Woody."

"They're not bad kids. They've worked for me. It takes a lot of effort to keep this place in good repair."

Aiden imagined the teenagers scrubbing the concrete floor in the auto bays with a toothbrush to meet Bert's standards. The image didn't fit into the sheriff's idea of a gang. "You hire a lot of local kids. That's a damn good thing. They need the jobs."

"I'm not a do-gooder," he said as he pulled on a pair of gloves. "I hire people to do a job."

"Have you met this new guy they call Aspen Jim?"

"David brought him. I didn't bother getting to know him. A handsome devil like Jim won't stick around Henley too long. He's a skier. He'll be heading for snow country."

The sheriff had suggested that Aspen Jim was a ringleader. "He's a little older than the high school boys you usually hire."

"Never noticed."

Aspen Jim was an anomaly. A good-looking, mature ski bum didn't fit into the fabric of Henley. This wasn't a glamorous place. The skiing industry in Montana was nothing compared to Jackson Hole in Wyoming or Park City in Utah or any of the Colorado resorts. "Why would a guy like that want to live here? A girlfriend?"

"Don't know. Don't care."

"Yoo-hoo." Tab's voice echoed against the concrete walls of the garage.

"Back here," Bert called out.

She marched up to him and took both his gloved hands in hers. Her blue eyes welled with sympathy. "I'm so sorry about David, Mr. Welling. Can I drop by later with one of Grandma's sweet potato pies?"

Much to Aiden's surprise, Bert cracked a smile. "I'd never say no to one of Maria Spotted Bear's pies."

"Will you be having the funeral here?"

"That's his dad's problem. He lives in Billings." Bert dropped her hands. His thin face became a blank. "My brother, David's dad, did a bad job in raising the boy after his mom left. The least he can do is to arrange for a proper burial."

Tab tilted her head. Her lovely face glowed with kindness, and Aiden knew it wasn't an act. She was able to sincerely look past Bert's natural hostility and see the sadness within. More important, Bert responded to her.

"You spent a lot of time with David," she said. "Showed him the right way to do things."

"But he still ended up dead. David had a weak character, just like his dad. My brother is nothing but a self-pitying, sloppy alcoholic." His gaze lifted, and he frowned as though he'd spotted a spider's web in the corner of the ceiling. "At least David stayed off the booze."

"I'm sure you'll miss him."

"He wasn't good at following instructions. Couldn't remember to clean up after himself. His van was filthy."

Aiden pounced on the possible lead. "What kind of van?"

"Why do you care?"

"I might be in the market to buy a van for Misty to use after she has the baby."

"Go ahead and take a look. The thing looks like crud, but it runs just fine." Bert shrugged. "It's parked in back of the garage. I told David that until he got a paint job, he couldn't park at the house."

As Aiden walked to the front of the garage, Tab patted the sleeve of Bert's clean jumpsuit. "If you need anything, don't hesitate to call. Grandma and I are staying at the Gabriel Ranch."

"I didn't know you were all that close."

"Family friends," Tab said.

"Somebody told me you were there when David got shot. But you didn't see who did it."

"I was too late," she said, "but don't you worry. The sheriff is investigating. He'll find the killer."

She joined him. Together, they circled the whitewashed side of the garage. The back side where the trash cans were kept was slightly less tidy than the front. A beat-up van with a dinged front fender was parked with the nose facing to a light pole.

"I have a change of plans," Tab said. "My client's water broke about a half hour ago, and her husband just got to the café to pick her up. I think she's ready to go into labor, so I need to go back to the ranch, get my stuff and meet her at her house."

He couldn't have been more pleased. Tab was off the case.

"A real shame," he drawled, "you won't be able to do any more investigating today."

"Babies come first."

"Do you need to hurry? Is this an emergency?"

"Not really," she said. "It's a first baby. I'd expect her to be in labor for hours."

Turning back to the van, he squatted to check out the tires and the tire wells. Dried weeds were stuck in the treads and wedged behind the mud flaps. "This van was driven off the road. It might be the vehicle David used yesterday."

"And the shooter drove it back," she said. "He might have left his fingerprints on the car keys."

"Even if he did, the prints can be explained if it's one of David's friends."

"How can we find out who he was with yesterday?"

"We can't go around asking those kinds of questions." Aiden rose to his feet. "I'll suggest to the sheriff that he might want to talk to David's buddies about their whereabouts yesterday. Woody and Chuck are already in custody. Maybe they'll say something useful, instead of being twin jackasses."

She dragged her fingertip through the dust on the back window. "Apparently, David didn't inherit his uncle's obsessive neatness."

He circled around to the front of the van. There was a bike rack mounted on the hood. Two mountain bikes with heavy-duty tires were locked in place. If Misty's mystery shooter hopped onto a bike and rode through the foliage at the river bank, they wouldn't have heard a car engine starting. Hiding a bike would have been far easier than ditching a car or a van.

"Take a look at this," he called to her. "These are really nice bikes. Expensive."

Another voice intruded, "And I've got first dibs."

The man who sauntered toward them had a tanned complexion and sun-streaked hair that flopped casually over his forehead. He wore wraparound sunglasses and a lightweight parka with the hood zipped into the collar. His super-whitened smile flashed as he came even with Tab. This had to be Aspen Jim.

Chapter Eleven

Tab looked at dual reflections of herself in a pair of gleaming sunglasses. The man wearing them took her hand and raised it to his lips. "They call me Aspen Jim."

"I'm Tab Willows." When meeting new people, she tried to keep an open mind, but this guy creeped her out. He reminded her of a lounge lizard without the lounge.

He whipped off his sunglasses, revealing bloodshot brown eyes. "Why haven't I met you before?"

"Just lucky, I guess." She snatched her hand from his grasp. "This is Aiden Gabriel."

"I know who you are. Misty's brother." Aspen Jim replaced his sunglasses on the narrow bridge of his nose. "I'm pleased to meet you, Aiden. How's your sister doing?"

"As well as can be expected," Aiden said, "after watching David die in her arms."

"He liked her a lot, even after she ballooned up."

"That's a nasty thing to say." Tab hated men who made snide comments about pregnant women. "Women are at their most beautiful when they're carrying new life. Artists have always celebrated the pregnant form as a symbol of fertility."

"Not me," Aspen Jim said. "I like my ladies slim and sexy. Kind of like you, darling."

"Have you ever made love to a pregnant woman?"

"No way."

"Then you're missing something spectacular. Several men have told me that it's the most exciting sex they ever had."

"Why would they tell you?"

"I'm a midwife." She looked at her wristwatch. "And I need to get going."

"Hold on a sec." Aiden stepped forward. She noticed that his lips barely moved when he spoke, and she suspected he was gritting his teeth to keep from snarling. "Mind if I ask you a couple of questions, Aspen Jim?"

"No prob." Blinded by arrogance, Aspen Jim didn't realize that he ought to be nervous about Aiden's questions. "I'm glad for the chance to talk to you."

"First, tell me about these bikes."

"They're top of the line." Aspen Jim turned away from her and went to the bikes and lovingly caressed the handle-bars. "Titanium frame, dual suspension and hydraulic disc brakes, these bikes have it all."

"Did they both belong to David?"

"Yeah, and he never really appreciated these super-fine machines, the little dipstick." He winced. "Sorry, I didn't mean to say that. 'Dipstick' was kind of a nickname."

Tab didn't believe that for a minute. Aspen Jim was the kind of guy who used his friends and bad-mouthed them behind their backs. She was beginning to feel sorry for David Welling with his alcoholic father, his cold-as-ice uncle and a friend like Aspen Jim.

"The bikes must have been expensive," Aiden said.

"David got them in trade for doing mechanical work on a Ferrari for some rich dude in Billings. We used to take them out and ride all over. It's important for me to stay in good condition for skiing."

"Were you out riding yesterday?"

"The weather's been great—didn't want to miss it." Aspen Jim hesitated, perhaps realizing that he'd stepped into what might be a stinky alibi situation. "It was early, like ten in the morning."

Smoothly, Aiden asked, "Where did you go? There's a lot of nice, wide open land on the rez."

"I don't know the boundaries. We might have gone there."

"Did anybody see you leaving town or coming back?"

Aspen Jim lowered his chin, and his sun-bleached bangs flopped over the frames of his sunglasses. When he looked up, his glistening smile had vanished. "I wasn't with David when he got killed, if that's what you're trying to figure out."

"Tell me what happened."

Tab was duly impressed with Aiden's questioning. Though he didn't have the credentials to demand information, he showed enough authority in his voice and manner that Aspen Jim was beginning to sweat.

"Me and David took the van with the bikes out in the morning after we had pancakes at the café with Woody and Chuck. We rode the bikes for a while, and then headed back to town. David was kind of mopey."

"Why?" Aiden asked.

"He couldn't decide whether he should stay here in Henley, or go back to Billings and live with his dad. Then he spotted Misty in Clinton's Jeep, and he said it was a sign. He was going to talk to her. If she said he should stay, he would."

"But he didn't have that kind of relationship with my sister. They didn't chat, didn't text each other."

"Only in David's head," Aspen Jim said. "He was always planning to talk to Misty. She was his dream girl."

"So he followed the Jeep," Aiden said.

"That was his plan. I didn't stick around. I took one of the bikes and rode the rest of the way home."

"Did you hook up with Woody and Chuck again?"

Aspen Jim shook his head. "It was my day off. I took a long shower, watched some TV, played a couple of computer games. Then I brought the bike back here and left it with Bert."

"What time was that?"

"Maybe three o'clock, I don't remember. Bert probably can tell you down to the minute. He's precise."

Tab was disappointed to hear that he had an alibi. If Aspen Jim was here at the gas station, he couldn't have committed the crime. Too bad.

"When you dropped off the bike," Aiden said, "was David's van here?"

"No, it wasn't. That's why I handed the bike over to Bert. I didn't hear what happened to David until around seven when I went to the Last Stand Tavern."

"You should have gone to the sheriff right away," Tab said. "Your information might have been useful to him."

"I don't much care for the law. I don't have anything to hide, but I don't want anybody getting into my business."

"But you're willing to talk to me."

"That's correct." He stuck out his chest. "I'm glad for this opportunity to meet you."

"Is that so?"

"I have a business opportunity you might be interested in. I'm looking for investors."

Disgusted, Tab rolled her eyes. Aspen Jim really was a piece of work. His friend hadn't been dead for twenty-four hours, and he was figuring out how to cash in. Brusquely, she said, "We don't have time for this."

"Here's my idea," Aspen Jim said. "I want to provide river rafting expeditions on the Little Big Horn. When the tourists show up for the reenactment of Custer's Last Stand, this gives them something else to do."

"There's white-water rafting on the Yellowstone," Aiden said, "because that river actually has rapids. The Little Big Horn rolls along, slow and lazy."

"So it's perfect for families. Hey, here's a thought. We could hire locals to stand on the banks and act out scenes from the Old West."

Tab groaned.

Aiden asked, "How much do you know about rafting?"

He flashed the super-white smile. "I worked as a guide with a rafting crew on the Arkansas River near Aspen. Think about it, Aiden. With your cash and my expertise, we could have the business up and running by next summer."

Tab had heard enough. She clamped on to Aiden's arm. "We really have to go. Now."

They left Aspen Jim standing by the van, paid for the oil change and climbed into the truck. As soon as they were under way, she let loose. "Do you believe that guy? I think he was lurking around, waiting to pounce the minute he saw you. Rafting on the Little Big Horn? Acting out scenes on the banks? Oh, please, that's the dumbest thing I've ever heard."

"But now we know why a flashy guy like him is hanging around in Henley."

"He wants to con somebody into being his partner. What a jerk! I'll bet he's already screwed up his big money contacts in the ski areas."

"He worked as a guide for a white-water rafting company. That means he knows about nautical knots."

She wasn't sure where Aiden was going with this. "So?"

"When I was talking to the sheriff…" His voice trailed off. "I shouldn't tell you about this, Tab. But you're the only one I can talk to, and I respect your opinions."

Now they were making headway. He wasn't shutting her out of his investigation anymore. "What's important about the knots?"

"Both of the women who were killed were bound with bowlines and figure eights. Nautical knots."

She hadn't expected this twist. "Do you think Aspen Jim is the serial killer?"

"Knowing about knots isn't enough to accuse him," Aiden said. "But he did know Ellen Jessop. They worked together at the feed store."

Staring through the windshield at the dried prairie grasses on rolling hills, she recalibrated her thinking to include the serial murders. Their trip into town to see Bert had been focused on David's death, but they couldn't ignore the possible link. Misty was clearly connected to both since she had argued with Ellen and had witnessed David's murder.

"Next time you talk to the sheriff, you definitely need to mention Aspen Jim as a suspect."

"Sheriff Fielding is already looking at Aspen Jim." He shrugged. "I don't think he seems like the serial killer type. He wouldn't have a problem getting dates. A lot of women might like that sun-bleached hair."

"Not me," she said. "Aspen Jim is a misogynist, the kind of guy who hates women. Didn't you hear what he said about pregnant ladies?"

"I sure as hell heard what you said." He glanced at her and grinned. "Pregnant sex is spectacular?"

"So I've heard." At the time she'd spoken, she'd been trying to make a point that an idiot like Aspen Jack would understand. She hadn't considered how embarrassing her statement would sound. "I'm not an expert."

"You're a surprising lady, Tab. I'm learning that I don't know much about your world and the work you do."

When guys asked about her work, she usually retreated into her shell. They weren't really interested, just being polite. But Aiden was different, and she wanted him to understand her. "How much do you want to know?"

"Everything," he said.

"Starting with the sperm and the egg?"

"Especially about that part."

When it came to flirting, her skills were nonexistent. She preferred saying exactly what she meant, but it was fun to play with Aiden. She keyed her voice to a low, sexy level and said, "I have a feeling that you already know a little something about the fertilization process."

"I like it when you talk dirty."

His jaw twitched as he struggled to keep from laughing out loud. When she punched his arm, he chuckled, and she joined in. A sense of humor wasn't something she associated with the super-responsible Aiden, but here they were... joking around with each other.

It would have been nice to extend this time together. She almost wished she didn't have to go to work, but there was no way to reschedule her client's labor. The truck was already approaching the crossroads that led to Gabriel Ranch, and she'd have to jump into her van and leave immediately.

"We don't have much time," he said. "I wanted to get your impressions of Aspen Jim's account of what happened yesterday."

"It sounded pretty straightforward. And he's got a solid alibi with Bert. The real question is who drove David's van back to the gas station?"

"Chuck and Woody might have known where they were headed. It could have been one of them."

"Could be." Neither Chuck nor Woody seemed dangerous to her. Last night when they were forced to stop the truck, they both surrendered without hesitation. "Why would one of David's friends shoot him?"

"We don't know enough about David to come up with a motive."

Aiden took off his hat and raked his fingers through his hair. When he gazed toward her, his eyes gleamed. For a moment, she forgot about investigating and murders and the baby she was about to deliver. His nearness consumed her, and she couldn't think of anything else.

Until now, she'd done a pretty decent job of acting like an adult instead of a love-struck teenager. But there were these moments when she was with him that she had to pinch herself to make sure she wasn't dreaming.

"What were we talking about?" she asked.

"Motives."

"I've got nothing."

He slapped his hat back onto his head and turned his attention to the road. "What if David was killed because he knew too much? He might have figured out the identity of the serial killer and was threatening to tell the sheriff."

She nodded. "That doesn't tell us who the killer is."

"But it limits the field."

For the first time, she acknowledged to herself that there might be danger. If David knew the killer, so did Misty. And it was likely that Tab had met him. She didn't know his identity, but he knew hers.

Chapter Twelve

The birthing had gone well. A little before eight o'clock, Tab parked her van outside the Gabriel Ranch, hopped out and strode toward the house. When she saw Aiden occupying the rocking chair on the porch where her grandma had been sitting this morning, she couldn't help grinning. He'd been waiting for her. *Sweet.*

As she approached, he stood and sauntered down the stairs. The porch lights shone behind him, silhouetting his long, lean body, wide shoulders and cowboy hat. She had the sense that she was coming home to him, to her perfect man.

"You look happy," he said.

"I love my job. There's nothing as exciting as bringing new life into the world. When I hold the wiggly baby for the first time and hear the first cries, I feel privileged to be part of a miracle. Seven pounds and two ounces, the baby's name is Rosalie."

"Pretty name."

"Pretty little girl." She wanted to hug him and share the thrill but held herself back. The Gabriel Ranch wasn't really her home. Aiden didn't belong to her, and she didn't have the right to grab him whenever she had the urge. "You'll see. When Misty has her baby, you'll see what it feels like."

"I've been around babies before."

"Trust me. A newborn is different."

"Are you tired?"

"I should be after six hours of labor. Not that I did any of the heavy-duty exertion, but the process is a strain."

"How so?"

She tried to think of a metaphor that he'd understand. "You played football, didn't you?"

"Henley High," he said. "Go, Bobcats. And in college."

"Think of a football game, and think of me as the coach. I don't actually run down the field with the ball, but I call the plays and I strategize."

"I don't reckon you choose to punt too often."

"Very funny." The football comparison might have been a bad idea.

"Go on. Tell me what happens after the huddle."

"Mostly, it's about making the mom comfortable, giving her water or tea or sometimes a snack. Some women have pressure on their lower spine, and that means a lot of back rubs. Sometimes, I'll get the mom out of bed and walk around. The last phase of labor, which is called transition, can be intense. That's the dramatic part that you always see in movies."

"When the baby comes out, that's your touchdown."

"But I never spike the baby in the end zone."

"Because that would be a penalty," he said. "Well, Coach, I'm thinking you might need some rest."

"I won't be able to sleep." After a birthing, she was energized. "My endorphins are rushing. I feel good all over."

He reached toward her and placed his hand on her shoulder, setting off a whole different kind of pleasurable reaction. His touch soothed her and aroused her at the same time.

"Let's get you to bed," he said.

She really wanted to say yes, not to the sleeping part but to going to bed with him. Instead, she shook her head.

"I'd rather hop in the chopper and go to Grandma's house."

She'd called earlier to let him know that she still needed to pick up a few things from home. "I won't ride Shua back tonight, but I'd really like to have a change of clothes, my own nightshirt and toothbrush."

"You're sure?"

She cocked her head to one side. "Could it be that you're the one who's too tired?"

"Not me. My day hasn't been action packed." He slid his hand down her arm and linked his hand with hers. "Let's go."

Holding hands, they walked together through the moonlight toward the barn. She rubbed her thumb across the calluses on his palm. Rough hands were an occupational hazard for cowboys who worked with horses and cattle in all kinds of weather. When he squeezed her fingers, electricity jolted up her arm and raced through her entire body. Were they really holding hands?

A pine-scented breeze cooled her cheeks and ruffled the strands of hair that had slipped out of her ponytail. With her free hand, she pushed her hair back. "I must look a mess."

"Not with that beautiful smile lighting up your face. You look great."

His words warmed her but didn't erase her self-consciousness. As her body heated up, she remembered that she hadn't used deodorant after her shower this morning. A change of clothing was definitely needed. Though she'd slipped into comfortable scrubs for the labor and birthing, the shirt she'd worn for the past two days was getting a little ripe.

"After a big game," he said, "I always liked to talk about the plays that worked and the slipups. Give me the rundown on what happened today with—what are their names? Connie and Carlos?"

"I will if you promise not to mention football again. Having a baby isn't really the Wide World of Sports."

"Promise." He ducked his head to look into her eyes. "But

I would like to hear about it. If I'm going to understand what you do, you've got to give me some details."

"When I got to the house, Connie greeted me with a paint-brush in her hand. Apparently, the nursery needed another coat, and she wanted it done before the baby arrived."

"Is that typical?" he asked.

"Different women handle the stress and hormones in different ways. Connie obsessed on cleaning. Even though Carlos promised to take care of the painting, she refused to get into bed. On the internet, she'd read that just because her water broke it didn't mean she was in labor."

"Was she right?"

"Obviously not," Tab said. "I just delivered the baby. I encourage new moms to seek out prenatal information. The more they know, the less scared they are. The downside to that approach is that they think they're experts. Connie felt a little twinge and announced that it was a Braxton Hicks contraction, false labor."

"I'm beginning to feel sorry for Carlos."

"He's a really nice guy, but Connie was driving him crazy. When I finally convinced her to surrender the paintbrush and let me give her an exam, he whispered that I must be an angel sent from Heaven to keep his wife from killing him."

"I've heard that women get mean during labor."

"With good cause," she said. "Having a baby isn't easy."

"What did you do next?"

She decided to skip the clinical description of how she assessed Connie's dilation and effacement. Aiden's interest in her work probably didn't extend to all the gory details. "After I checked her out, I knew she was starting labor. Her pain started getting more intense, and we were off to the races. Six hours later, Rosalie came into the world."

"Giving birth is easier with cows," he said. "They give a

couple of bellows and shoot the baby right out. If the calf is stuck, you just reach inside, grab and pull."

"You might not want to share that comparison with your sister."

They circled the barn, and the helicopter came into view. Last night when she'd been running hard, she hadn't really appreciated the beauty of the machine. With moonlight reflecting off the rotors and long tail, the chopper looked like a giant mechanical dragonfly.

He gave her hand another squeeze before releasing it and digging into his pocket. He took out a sheet of notebook paper that was covered with tight scribbling. Handing it to her, he said, "Your grandma made a list of things she needs."

Tab held the paper close so she could read it in the moonlight. "Half of this is kitchen equipment. Pots and skillets and spices. Why does she need this stuff?"

He opened the cockpit door. "Hop aboard. You know the drill."

She strapped herself into the copilot seat, put on her headphones and prepared for the incredible sensation of swooping into the night sky. Their ascent tonight wasn't as incredible as when she was a chopper virgin, but the thrill was undiminished. She didn't think she'd ever become jaded about flying.

As they soared over the rugged landscape and approached the lights of Henley, she asked, "Did you do any more investigating today?"

"I spent most of the day with the sheriff. He's leaning toward our theory of David being shot by an unknown companion who rode off on a mountain bike. But he still won't dismiss Misty as a suspect."

"What does he think of Aspen Jim?"

"It's a shame Aspen Jim has an alibi. Nobody trusts him except for his teenage buddies, including Woody and Chuck, who think he's a lot of fun. Remember how the Buffalo Man talked about loud parties in the deserted parts of the rez? According to Woody and Chuck, who were both feeling real bad after a night in jail, Aspen Jim provided the booze."

"At least, it wasn't drugs."

"As far as we know." He adjusted the steering to swoop toward the left. "The sheriff agreed with me. Aspen Jim has all the girlfriends he wants. He's a sleazy guy, but he doesn't fit the profile for a serial killer."

Though she respected the psychology that went into profiling, she didn't consider it proof. Serial killers came in all sizes and shapes; they didn't have to look like depraved, drooling monsters. The infamous Ted Bundy had been a handsome, educated, socially adept man who brutally murdered more than twenty women.

When she met Aspen Jim, she'd thought he was mean spirited. The way he looked at her made her skin crawl. His whitened teeth and sun-bleached hair didn't mean he was innocent.

"Anything else?" she asked. "How about the autopsies?"

"The coroner's office in Billings won't get around to a full autopsy for a couple more days, and they're going to start with Ellen Jessop. All the branches of law enforcement—state, local and tribal—are worried about the possibility of a serial killer. There's been talk of calling in the FBI."

She understood why the murder of David Welling wasn't as high priority, but the lack of investigation didn't relieve the stress on Misty. She really wished that she and Aiden could find evidence that would take his sister off the list of suspects. "If David's murder was somehow connected to the others, it would be more important. The sheriff seemed pretty sure that Misty's watch was some kind of evidence."

"Here's the thing," he said. "In a small town, everybody knows everybody else's business. There's just not much population, and it's hard to believe that there's more than one homicidal individual on the loose."

"That points to one killer."

"But David's murder was nothing like the others. He was shot, not strangled. He wasn't held prisoner, wasn't tied up and—most of all—he wasn't a young, blonde woman."

Earlier, Aiden had referred to a murder of opportunity. "What if David knew something about the serial murders? The killer would want him dead."

He turned toward her and gave her a long, hard stare. This scrutiny wasn't like his earlier friendly glances. He seemed to be looking deeper and with more concern. "You're a little too smart for your own good."

"I'm on to something, aren't I?"

"We found evidence of a connection," he said. "One of the deputies and I did a flyover in the Spring Creek area where Ellen Jessop's body was found. We spotted tire tracks not far from the crime scene. The tread matched David's van."

Suddenly uncomfortable, she swallowed hard. Playing at investigation was fun. The idea of finding the truth about these terrible crimes was like turning over a rock and seeing a rattlesnake. "Do you think David was the serial killer?"

"There's a good chance his van was used by the killer. The sheriff took the vehicle to check it out, over the objections of Bert Welling who said the van belonged to him. There were blood traces inside. They'll be checking for a DNA match to Ellen."

As she stared through the windshield at the star-lit skies, a horrible thought occurred. "David might have been following Misty because she was next on his list. But if David was the serial killer, who shot him?"

"Other people used that van," he said. "It was a kind of party bus."

The chopper hovered over her grandma's house, and Aiden

turned on the spotlight in order to locate the best landing spot. She looked toward the lights of the nearby homes of the Martin and Tall Grass families, and Tab regretted the whirring noise of the rotors that would surely waken everybody inside and disturb their livestock.

"Why didn't you tell me about the tire tracks?" she demanded.

"I just told you everything I know."

"But I had to pry it out of you." He couldn't honestly claim that he'd been immediately forthcoming. "Were you trying to protect me again?"

"It didn't seem important." He eased the chopper into a smooth descent, constantly checking the ground below. "We can't pinpoint who used the van. The evidence isn't conclusive."

"And that comment about me being too smart. What did you mean by that?"

"Would you feel better if I said you were dumb?"

It wasn't like she was asking for a badge and a gun with a license to kill. She just wanted to be kept in the loop. He needed to trust her.

"Were you playing me?" she asked. "When you were asking questions about Connie, was that a ruse to keep from telling me about the investigation?"

The chopper touched down, and he turned off the engine before looking at her. "My interest in your work is genuine. I wasn't trying to trick you or divert your attention. I don't play games like that. I say what I mean."

In the light from the instrument panel, she studied the lines of his face, not allowing her thoughts to be diverted by the pleasing symmetry of his features. She knew he was an honest, responsible man, but he was also clever like the coyote in the stories her grandma used to tell when she was growing up. The coyote behaved in all kinds of unexplainable ways, getting the other animals to do his bidding. But there was almost always a moral to the story that showed the coyote was actually helping. Aiden was coyote clever but also good. And she knew he would never intentionally hurt her.

"I trust you," she said.

He reached toward her and lightly stroked her cheek. "That's all I can ask for."

"Let's gather up these things and get out of here."

He nodded toward Grandma's house. "The lights are on. Is that how you left the house?"

"I think so." When she and Grandma set out for the Gabriel ranch, it had been after dark. "Our neighbor, Sam Tall Grass, has been over here taking care of things."

"Does he have a key?"

"Grandma doesn't usually lock up." She swung open the chopper door. "We're so isolated out here that if somebody wants to break a window and get inside, there's not much to stop them."

He didn't have to lecture her about the need for security. Tab had spent most of her life in cities where doors were locked and deadbolts fastened. She climbed out of the chopper and headed toward the sweet little cabin that had been her grandma's home for as long as she could remember.

She liked to think that the house was protected by Grandma's reputation. Nobody wanted to get on the wrong side of Maria Spotted Bear. Still, Tab was reassured when she noticed that Aiden joined her on the porch, and she saw that he'd armed himself. He wore a holster at his hip.

He touched the butt of his gun. "Better safe than sorry."

"Agreed."

Inside the house, she sent Aiden to the kitchen to pick up Grandma's cooking supplies and put them into a cooler. Tab concentrated on the bedrooms, where she packed her clothes and those her grandma requested into two suitcases. Though tempted to take everything, she held back. Tomorrow or the next day, she'd be returning here to pick up Shua.

In a matter of minutes, she had the suitcases ready. As Aiden loaded them into the chopper, she checked the list her grandma had given him.

"Grandma's sneakers," she said with a groan. "I forgot them. I have to go back."

"Not a problem." He fell into step beside her. "I like the way your grandma's house smells."

"I know." The natural fragrance of the many herbs her grandma gathered and also cultivated mingled with years of baking and cooking. "If she could bottle that scent, she'd make a million dollars."

"I never thought your grandma was interested in money."

"That's cute, Aiden. Everybody needs more money." On the porch, she turned to him. "I'll run in and grab the shoes. You go to the horse barn, and I'll meet you there."

She didn't bother turning on lights as she hurried through the house. Tab knew where every chair and table was placed. In her grandma's bedroom, she knew she'd find the sneakers under the bed on the left side. Ducking down, she grabbed them.

When she stood, she looked directly at a window. She saw a shape outside the glass. Moonlight outlined the shoulders and head. Someone was out there. A man stood at the window, staring in at her.

Chapter Thirteen

Aiden had just stepped off the porch when he heard Tab yell his name. There was panic in her voice. She needed him.

He pivoted and ran back to the house, snatched the gun from his holster, dove inside. The lights were off. Turn them on? No, his eyes were already accustomed to the dark.

Tab burst from the hallway that led to the bedrooms. Her grandma's white sneakers were in her hands.

"I saw someone at the window," she said. "He ran off. Toward the barn."

"Did you see his face?"

"No. He had on a hoodie."

The threat was clear. An intruder had been waiting here. Waiting for Tab? Why, damn it, why? Aiden needed to catch this guy. At the same time, he had to protect Tab and couldn't leave her alone. His decision came quickly.

"Follow me," he said. "Stay close. If you hear gunfire, hit the ground."

Gun in hand, he charged out the door and ran toward a couple of scraggly pine trees between the house and barn. Adrenaline surged through him. His senses sharpened. Through the shadows, he saw movement. A man was running parallel to the corral fence, heading toward the horse barn.

"Stop," Aiden called out. "I'll shoot."

The man disappeared around the edge of the barn. From

this distance, Aiden couldn't get any kind of description other than hooded sweatshirt and jeans. He didn't know if the intruder had entered the barn or not.

Likely, he'd gone through the side door. Why else would he have headed in that direction? At the front of the barn, he halted and turned to Tab, who stood close behind him. She wasn't even breathing hard. The woman really could run.

"How many entrances to the barn?" he asked.

"Three. The big double doors on the front and back, and the regular-size side door."

He didn't like the idea of rushing through the side door without knowing what he'd find on the other side. The intruder could be armed. He could be setting up an ambush, aiming his weapon at that door, prepared to shoot as soon as Aiden came though. From inside, he heard Shua give a nervous whinny.

Tab swore. "If he hurts my horse, I'll kill him."

Aiden went to the big double doors at the front and unfastened the latch. "When I open this door, I want you to hide behind it. Stay low."

"I'm coming with you. That's my horse."

"No time to argue. I won't let him hurt Shua."

She stamped her foot once. Frustration was evident on her face. "Okay, I'll stay out here. But let me open the door. That leaves your hands free. Aiden, you've got to hurry."

The double doors were wide enough for a truck full of hay to pull inside. And they were heavy. As Tab grabbed the bar and pulled, he rushed inside and went to the left, ducking behind the edge of the first stall. A few bare bulbs cast a dim glow. Moonlight from the open door spilled onto the packed dirt floor. The side of the horse barn opposite the stalls was two stories tall with a hay loft above. The area below held rough work benches and racks for storing tack and other tools.

Aiden scanned the hay loft in the high part of the barn and listened for the sound of footsteps creaking in the rafters. He heard nothing, saw no sign of movement. If the intruder had climbed the ladder to the loft, he had the best vantage point. But it also meant that he was trapped; there was only one ladder.

Still keeping an eye on the loft, he peeked around the edge of his hiding place. Aiden counted four stalls with closed half doors. The farthest was occupied by Shua. The black horse poked his head through the half door and nickered. Nobody could have been hiding in the stall with the horse. Shua would have been more agitated.

A groan came from the stall beside him. Had the intruder injured himself? A rusty voice called out, "Help me."

Moving carefully but quickly, Aiden came around the edge of the stall and peered over the half door. Curled on the floor was a man with an arm outstretched. "Help me."

As soon as Aiden opened the half door and entered the stall, he was aware of movement at the far wall. The side door whipped open and cracked against the wall. The intruder was getting away, and there was nothing Aiden could do about it.

He wanted to give chase, but he couldn't abandon the person in distress. "Are you injured?"

The answer was a groan.

Aiden dropped to a squat and pulled aside the heavy buffalo robe. On his side with his shoulders hunched, Wally clutched the front of his blood-soaked shirt.

His wound looked more serious than anything Aiden could handle. Lucky for Wally, he had a nurse with him. "Tab," he called to her. "I need you."

In seconds, she appeared at the door of the stall. "I saw the guy in the sweatshirt. He's running downhill, toward the road."

Even if Aiden could sprout wings and fly in pursuit, he

wouldn't be able to catch the intruder and help Wally at the same time. "We're going to have to let him go."

She sank down beside him. Efficiently, she adjusted Wally's position so he was on his back.

The old man let out a groan. "It hurts."

Tab murmured words of assurance as she unbuttoned his shirt and pulled the fabric aside to get a better look at the wound on his upper chest. Breathing in frantic gasps, Wally clawed helplessly at her hands. His pale, scrawny chest heaved. His ribs stood out like a skeleton.

"He's been shot," Tab said. "I need a compress, something to hold against the wound to stop the bleeding."

"Do you have first-aid supplies in the house?"

"No time for that. We need to get him to a hospital. Give me your shirt."

Aiden stood and stripped down to his undershirt, which he whipped off and handed to her. As he put his shirt and jacket back on, he stared regretfully at the open door on the side of the barn where the intruder had escaped. Why had he lured them to the horse barn? He must have known they'd find Wally and help him. It didn't make sense unless he thought Wally was already dead.

Kneeling beside Tab, he grasped Wally's hand and leaned close to his face. The stink from the old man was beyond disgusting. "Wally, can you hear me?"

His eyes wavered wildly. "Am I going to die?"

"You're going to be all right," Tab said. "We're going to take you to the hospital in the chopper."

To her, he said, "You told me I could visit Maria Spotted Bear. You said I could come here. Anytime."

"It's okay. I'm not angry."

"Anytime, you said so."

Tab placed Aiden's white undershirt against the still-bleeding wound. "This will hurt. I'm going to apply pressure to stop the bleeding. Do you have any other injuries?"

"On my noggin. I think he hit me."

"Who hit you?" Aiden asked. "Did you get a look at him?"

"He was a two-face."

"What?"

Tab grabbed his hand and placed it over his now-ruined undershirt. "I want you to keep applying pressure."

"What's a 'two-face'?"

Ignoring him, she spoke to Wally. "Can you sit up? I want to look at your head."

"A two-face," Wally repeated. "Never look him in the eye. He'll freeze your bones down to the marrow."

Though Aiden had no idea what he was babbling about, Aiden played along. "Did the two-face say anything?"

"Said I saw too much. Talked too much."

"Enough," Tab said. "Wally, try to sit up."

With her help, Wally dragged himself off the floor and immediately slumped forward. Dark blood matted the hair on the back of his head. His shoulders heaved. He began to wheeze.

"He might have a punctured lung," Tab said. "Do you have a gurney or spine board in the chopper?"

"Both." Wally's cough convulsed his entire body. He didn't look good. "But it's going to take a while for me to get them unpacked. Is there time?"

"He's lost a lot of blood. I don't see an exit wound, which means the bullet is still in him. The sooner we can get him to the hospital, the better."

"I'll carry him."

"It's not the best procedure. The blow to his head might have caused spinal or neck injury."

He understood her concerns and her medical professionalism, but if they didn't get Wally to immediate care, he might not make it. This was an emergency situation. Proper procedure didn't apply.

"I'm taking him." Aiden slapped his gun into her hand. "If somebody comes after us, don't hesitate to open fire."

He wrapped the buffalo robe around the old man and lifted him like a child into his arms. He didn't weigh much, but carrying him was clumsy. His old hands folded in against his chest. When his eyes closed, he looked half dead.

"Careful," Tab said. "Don't trip."

"Trying not to."

They left the horse barn and went past the house. Balancing Wally in his arms, Aiden got into a regular rhythm. As he strode toward the chopper, he heard that old song in his head. *He ain't heavy, he's my brother.* The Buffalo Man wasn't family or even a close friend, but Aiden cared about what happened to the old guy. *He ain't heavy. He ain't heavy.*

At the chopper, Tab opened the rear door and jumped inside. She pulled a padded gurney down from the wall where it had been stowed. Aiden stretched Wally out on the padding. As he released his hold, the old man reached up and grabbed his arm.

Wheezing and gasping, he managed to choke out one word. "Goodbye."

"You're not leaving," Aiden said. "We're in this together. You and me and Tab."

In minutes, the helicopter was airborne. Using the emergency frequency, he contacted St. John's Hospital in Billings to let the E.R. know that he was bringing in a gunshot victim. There was a closer facility in Henley, but they weren't as well equipped and didn't have a helipad. The extra ten minutes to get to Billings was worth the risk for better surgeons and better possibility for transfusion.

Looking over his shoulder, he watched Tab administer

first aid with bandages and supplies from a well-stocked rescue kit. "Hey," he called back to her. "How's he doing?"

"Resting." She spoke loudly over the sound of the rotors. "Having trouble breathing."

He held the headset toward her. "I've got the E.R. at St. John's on the line. Tell them what you need."

As soon as she had the headset in place, Tab started rattling off medical jargon that sounded like a foreign language to him. Though triage wasn't her specialty, Tab knew what she was doing. Her competence impressed him. Her cool courage amazed him.

Under pressure, she had performed like a champ. Nobody could have done better. He might have to rethink his objections to having her on his team. She was decisive and efficient. When he'd told her to stay hidden, she'd agreed without too much hesitation. When he'd needed her help, she was there.

After she finished talking to the docs, she left Wally and came forward to stand behind him in the cockpit. "How much longer?"

"Fifteen or twenty minutes."

She gripped his shoulder and squeezed. "I think he's going to make it."

He looked up into her beautiful eyes. There was so much he wanted to tell her, but now wasn't the time. "I'm glad we got to him in time."

"He's a tough old guy. The bullet wound and the blow to the head would have killed most people."

"That has to be what the intruder was thinking. He wouldn't want us to find Wally alive."

"That ugly old buffalo robe might have saved his life by keeping him warm so he didn't go into shock."

Wally's survival was the most important thing, but Aiden had to wonder about what the old man had witnessed. He knew something that made him a threat. "Do you know what he meant by a 'two-face'?"

"It's a monster used to scare kids. You know how it goes, clean your room or two-face will eat you."

"Somehow, I can't imagine your grandma using that kind of threat."

"She never had to. She's got an angry glare that always made me toe the line."

"Tell me more about two-face."

"He's a huge ogre with one face in front and another in back so you can never sneak away from him. And he has claws like a grizzly, I think. If you're naughty, he'll come after you. First, he freezes you with an evil eye. Then, he eats you, starting with your toes."

That was all they needed—a flesh-eating ogre. "When Wally comes around, he might be able to give us a better identification. What do you think he really saw?"

"Somebody wearing a ski mask?"

Good guess. He'd seen ski masks designed with monster faces or skull heads. If somebody came at Wally wearing one of those, he might think he'd seen a monster.

Tab leaned closer and brushed her lips against his cheek. Her kiss was so soft and so quick that he wasn't even sure it happened. But he felt her nearness.

"I'm so proud of you," she said.

"Why? I let the bad guy escape."

"The way you picked Wally up and carried him was so terrific. You saw what had to be done, and you did it."

"Anybody else would have done the same. Carrying him wasn't hard." He grinned up at her. "He ain't heavy. He's my brother."

"And you're my hero."

After another squeeze to his shoulder, she returned to the rear of the chopper to tend to her patient while Aiden basked in the glow of her praise. He'd done plenty of emergency rescues and evacuations, but nothing felt as satisfying as this moment. Her appreciation meant the world to him.

As soon as they touched down, he needed to contact Sheriff Fielding and arrange for Wally to be guarded against another attack while he was in the hospital. The old man knew something or had witnessed an event that he didn't realize was important. And the killer had come after him to make sure he didn't talk. That was the only explanation that made sense. If Wally could remember what he had witnessed, he might be key to breaking open the investigation.

It worried Aiden that the attack had taken place at Maria Spotted Bear's house. A coincidence? In his babbling, Wally seemed to be telling Tab that he'd come to the house because of her invitation. Had the killer been following Wally and tracked him to the house? Or was he already there, waiting and watching?

Tab was also a witness. She'd seen the face at the window. Had he been coming for her?

It was a damn good thing that she and her grandma were staying at the ranch. Tab needed protection. From this moment forward, Aiden wouldn't leave her alone and unguarded. Not for a moment.

Chapter Fourteen

The next day, Tab didn't wake until sunlight was streaking through the window blinds in her upstairs bedroom at the ranch. Something was wrong with her foot. She kicked and pried her eyelids all the way open. Misty was sitting on the edge of the bed by Tab's bare feet.

"Brought you coffee, toast and a banana," Misty said.

"What time is it?"

"After ten o'clock."

"Were you pinching my toes?"

"A little bit." Misty pushed herself upright and waddled to the bedside table where she'd placed a tray with the breakfast. "I thought you'd want to be up. You were always an early riser."

If anybody else had been bugging her to rise and shine after the super-strenuous day she'd had yesterday, Tab would have growled for them to go away and snuggled deeper into the warm covers. But she had a soft spot for Misty. Ten years ago, in this very bedroom, they'd giggled and whispered and tried on lipstick. Rearranging the pillows so she could lean against them, Tab reached for the mug of hot black coffee.

After a sip, she studied Misty and decided that this toe-pinching wake-up call didn't really have anything to do with her. Misty had something to say, and she'd chosen Tab as her confidante.

Cautiously, Tab asked, "How are you feeling this morning?"

"I'm okay." She giggled. "The baby is even better, doing jumping jacks inside my belly."

"Aiden said you wanted me to deliver your baby. Is that true?"

"Will you? Please say yes. I want to have my baby here at the ranch."

Tab would check with her doctor to make sure there were no complications that might require hospitalization, but she didn't expect problems. "I'd be happy to deliver the next generation of the Gabriel family."

"All right."

Misty did a double fist pump that reminded Tab of yesterday's unfortunate football metaphor. "You were a cheerleader, weren't you?"

"Head cheerleader."

Tab figured that Misty had sailed through high school as one of the popular kids. She was pretty and smart and her family had money. "Prom queen?"

"Junior prom and senior homecoming queen." Her giggle fell flat. "By senior prom, everybody knew I was pregnant. I wasn't showing or anything, but they knew. They treated me different, like my life was over or something."

Living a charmed existence and then having it taken away had to be difficult. Was that what Misty wanted to talk about? Her prospects for the future?

Tab picked up the plate with heavily buttered toast smeared with homemade chokecherry jelly. Taking a bite, she considered what to say next. She wanted to encourage Misty without sounding pushy or preachy. "Your life isn't over. It's just beginning."

"Yeah, yeah, I know. That's what Aiden says, too." She

sat on the edge of the bed again. "He says that even with a baby, I can still go to college or law school or whatever."

Her eye-rolling attitude showed an almost total indifference to this topic. What was Misty after? Tab didn't have the patience for a guessing game. "You woke me up because you want to talk about something. What is it?"

"It's Clinton," she said. "We had a really big fight yesterday and it was kind of your fault. Because you talked to him and told him he made a smart deduction."

"Don't you think he's smart?"

"Sure, I do. When we're alone and he's not showing off, he's got a lot to say. And he's creative. He writes songs for me and the baby."

"That's sweet." The more Tab found out about Clinton, the more she liked him.

"But now he thinks he can figure out who the killer is, and that's stupid. Look what happened when he went and talked to Ellen about my wristwatch. Clinton ended up being a suspect."

Though Tab had been pushing Aiden to let her participate in his investigative process, she had to agree with Misty. Clinton could say the wrong thing to the wrong person and end up in serious trouble. "What was he planning to do?"

"For starters, he was going to talk to Chuck and Woody. He thinks they know something." She gave an unladylike snort. "Those two toads are lucky to remember their own names."

Still, the toads would be more willing to talk to Clinton than the sheriff. "Did he do it?"

"I don't know." Her concern was evident in the lack of giggling, smirking and eye rolling. "I haven't seen Clinton today, and we usually meet up the minute he comes to work."

"You've had no contact at all?"

"A text message at seven o'clock this morning. It said 'Luv U.' I called, and he won't answer his phone."

"Try sending him a text."

While Misty wrote her message, Tab finished off the toast and the coffee. Misty was right to worry about Clinton, especially after the assault on Wally. Playing games with a serial killer was like yanking a tiger's tail. The beast could turn and bite.

"Done," Misty said.

"I think we should tell Aiden."

"Not yet. I don't want to give him another reason to hate my boyfriend. Speaking of boyfriends…" Her giggle returned. "What's going on with you and my brother?"

"What makes you think there's something? Are you in on this matchmaking thing with your mom and my grandma?"

"I see how he looks at you. He likes you, Tab."

It took all her self-control not to join in the giggles and start gushing. "We're friends. That's all."

"We'll just see about that." Misty tapped a contact number on her phone. "He told me to call as soon as you were awake."

"Now? You're calling him now?"

"The perfect time."

"Give me that phone." Tab made a grab, but pregnant Misty was surprisingly quick.

She hopped off the bed and spoke into her phone. "Tab wants to see you. She's still in bed."

Tab panicked. Her long hair hung around her face in witchy strands. Her blue, cotton nightshirt was only as long as her knees, and the fabric was too thin and clingy. Looking down, she noticed a huge black-and-blue bruise on her forearm, which she must have gotten when struggling to treat Wally. And her teeth weren't brushed. And she had to pee. And the bathroom was down the hall. She didn't want Aiden to see her like this.

But he was already knocking at the door. "Can I come in?"

"No!" Tab yelled.

Misty opened the door and ushered her brother inside. Sweetly, she said, "I'll leave you two alone." And she closed the door behind her.

Tab pulled the covers up to her chin. "I'm not awake."

"I can leave, but I thought you might want an update on Wally."

"Well, yes." And she was acting like a dope. There was no reason for her to be embarrassed. They were only friends, right? She cleared her throat, lifted her chin and said, "Tell me about Wally."

He dragged a chair from the matching pine desk, placed it by the bed and straddled it. "Since last night, his condition has been upgraded to critical but stable. The doctors sound confident about his recovery."

"That's a relief."

She wasn't surprised. Last night, they'd waited until the surgery was complete and the doctors gave them a positive prognosis. Wally's organ damage was limited to a collapsed lung, which was serious but not life-threatening. He had no broken bones. His concussion would bear watching, but there was no bleeding in the brain. The worst problem was a heavy loss of blood from the wounds.

"The docs also said that your first-aid compress to slow the bleeding probably saved his life."

"I can't take all the credit," she said. "There were a couple of bloody rags in the stall with Wally. He must have tried a compress of his own."

"Does that mean I sacrificed my undershirt in vain?"

"Not at all." She'd gotten a very nice view of his bare chest. "It means Wally started his own first aid before we came on the scene. Has he been awake?"

"A couple of times," Aiden said. "The police in Billings have a man posted at his bed to make sure he stays safe."

"Have they been able to ask any questions?"

"They've tried but haven't gotten any coherent answers. According to Wally, a two-face monster attacked him."

To avoid looking at him, she burrowed more deeply under the navy-blue comforter. When she spoke, her voice was muffled. "I wish we knew what happened to him."

"The doctor had a theory. Want to hear it?"

"Yes."

"Would you come out from under the covers? I feel like I'm talking to a navy blue lump."

"I told you I was still asleep." She slanted a glance toward him. His hands rested on the back of the chair and his chin rested on his hands. His eyes were trained on her, and she didn't want to face him. "If you don't like it, you can—"

"Fine," he said. "According to the doc, Wally was shot twice in the back at close range. One of the bullets lodged inside, and the other went all the way through."

"The injury on his chest was from an exit wound," she said. "That's why it bled so much."

"It also explains why Wally isn't dead. The shots were aimed at his heart, but the angle of his body meant the bullets went high. The doctor thought Wally might have been on the ground, crawling to get away."

"The killer must have hit him in the back of the head. Then Wally went down. While he was attempting to crawl away, the shots were fired."

She hated to imagine the old man in his buffalo robe fleeing from a stone-cold killer. Wally must have been terrified and confused. No wonder he couldn't remember anything.

Her grip on the covers loosened. Her embarrassment about her messy hair and lack of hygiene were petty problems when compared to the attack on Wally. It was time for her to grow up. "If we hadn't found him when we did…"

"He wouldn't have survived."

"It almost seems like the killer led us directly to him."

"That's been bothering me," he said. "He must have thought Wally was already dead. Leading us to the barn was a bit of misdirection because his car was parked the other way."

Turning her head, she looked directly at Aiden. He was shaved and showered, neatly dressed in a plaid shirt and jeans. His combed brown hair made her acutely aware of the tangled mess on her head. She reached up to shove a chunk of hair off her forehead.

"Your arm," he said, "what happened?"

"I don't remember when I bruised it. It must have been when I was struggling with Wally."

Gently, he took her arm and studied the ugly mark above her wrist. His hands were cold from being outside. "Does it hurt?"

"Not really."

Her gaze met his, and she sank into the depths of his cool gray eyes. In the facets, she saw flecks of forest green and pure silver, a mesmerizing combination of dark and light. She couldn't stop staring.

Their position should have felt more intimate. She was in bed, after all. If she encouraged him, he might be tempted to lie beside her. But there was no way she'd cuddle when she had to go to the bathroom. Kissing with her unbrushed teeth was absolutely out of the question.

She snatched her arm from his grasp. "What else have you been doing this morning?"

"Talking to the law." He resettled himself in the chair. "Early this morning, Joseph Lefthand went to your grandma's house to investigate. He didn't see any sign of a break-in, but he found a blood trail in the barn that seemed to indicate Wally was shot there and then crawled into the horse stall. And he pulled some fingerprints that he's sending to the sheriff for identification."

"Good for Joseph Lefthand. What about Sheriff Fielding?"

"His new favorite theory, based on the tire tracks from David's van near the dump site for Ellen's body, is that David was the serial killer but wasn't working alone."

"He's not still considering a gang, is he?"

"Now, he thinks there were just two of them. David had a partner, and this partner killed him and attacked Wally."

"That's good news for Misty. It means the sheriff doesn't suspect her anymore."

"I'm just not sure that it's the truth," Aiden said. "I've heard of dual serial killers before. Usually, one is dominant and the other does his bidding."

From the little they knew about David, she doubted he'd be the boss. As a child, David had been shuttled back and forth between his alcoholic father and his strict uncle Bert. His unrequited crush on Misty seemed immature. Aiden called it stalking, but she thought David was one of those guys who drove past his supposed girlfriend's house and sent her unwanted gifts.

She remembered the story Misty had told about her encounter with David. He seemed easily manipulated. A con man like Aspen Jim would be quick to take advantage of someone like David.

But it wasn't really fair for her to draw these kinds of conclusions. Tab had never spoken to David. Though she'd probably seen him around town, she'd never noticed him.

"It's hard to know what's true," she said.

"And there's not much in the way of evidence." He swung his leg off the chair and stood. "What are your plans for the day?"

"I want to check up on Connie and Carlos and baby Rosalie. Other than that, I'm free."

"Tell me when you want to go. I'll drive."

Keeping herself covered, she sat up on the bed. "I don't remember inviting you along."

"I'm going to stick close to you, Tab. Until we're 100 percent sure that the killer wasn't lurking around at your grandma's house, waiting to attack you, I'm your bodyguard."

"Why me?"

"You were a witness to David's murder."

Before she could object, he left the bedroom. When he went out the door, the sunlight dimmed and the room felt empty. Her friendship with Aiden was on the verge of becoming something more, and she was anxious to see what came next.

Chapter Fifteen

After lunch, Aiden, Tab and Misty were on their way to the little house on the outskirts of Henley where Connie and Carlos lived. Aiden rode shotgun in Tab's van, an appropriate seating arrangement given his claim to be her bodyguard.

Earlier, when he announced that plan, he'd expected her to launch into one of her tirades about being able to take care of herself. Instead, she'd ducked under the covers and hadn't complained a bit. Damn, she was complicated—shy but confident, funny and serious at the same time, kind-hearted with others but demanding when it came to herself. She'd picked up street smarts from living in cities, but he knew she would always be rooted in the traditions of her people. Figuring out Tab Willows might be a lifetime project.

His agenda for now was to make sure she was safe. And he'd taken precautions. After explaining the potential danger to Blake, they cut back the daily chores to the bare minimum and put the men on high alert. Every ranch hand was armed, and they rotated in shifts doing guard duty, patrolling near the main house and barns on horseback with rifles. Protecting the herd that was spread out over several acres a couple of miles from here would have been impossible without an army, but the cattle weren't under threat. Danger from the serial killer was aimed at Tab and maybe Misty. And Aiden had it covered.

Being a passenger in her van gave him the opportunity to sit back in his seat and study her as she drove. This afternoon, she looked fresh scrubbed and neat with her raven hair pulled back in a glossy braid. Her blue wool jacket brought out the color of her eyes. His gaze measured the angle of her cheekbones, the stubborn thrust of her jaw and her long, graceful neck. Was it possible for a throat to be beautiful? He was fascinated by the hollow at the base of her throat. She was wearing a necklace with a four-leaf clover pendant, which he recognized right away.

He'd given her that pendant ten years ago, a silly little gift to let her know he was grateful for the way she was handling Misty. She'd kept it all these years. That must mean something.

She shot him a questioning look. "You're staring."

"Am I?"

"Oh, yeah," said Misty from the backseat. "You've been totally checked out, haven't been listening to a word I said."

"Did I miss anything important?"

"You're such a jerk, Aiden." His little sister huffed and giggled at the same time. "Tab, are you sure it's okay for us to visit?"

"When I called Connie, she said the more the merrier. And there was background noise so I think she has other visitors. How could she not want to see us? We're bringing two of Grandma's pies and your baby gift."

"The cutest baby snowsuit, pink with fake fur. I got it in Billings."

Aiden asked, "Weren't you saving that for your baby?"

"I'd rather let Connie have it," Misty said. "I'm really happy for her. Do you think she'll let me hold little Rosalie?"

"That's up to her," Tab said. "But I think she will."

"Since we both will have babies the same age, I know

we're going to be really good friends. We can do play dates together and share babysitting."

"Glad you see it that way," Tab said. "It takes a village, you know."

She parallel parked on the street outside a small frame house with flower beds that would be colorful in the spring and a small crab apple tree to the left of the sidewalk. Carlos worked at the tree nursery, and Aiden had always thought he had talent in landscaping.

In addition to two cars in the concrete driveway, three other vehicles were parked on the street behind them. He wasn't surprised that Connie had plenty of visitors. She was a popular waitress at the local café, and she knew everybody. The whole town had been watching Connie's belly grow and taking bets on when she'd pop. But he hadn't expected to see Bert Welling. The gas station owner, still dressed in his spot-less gray jumpsuit, came out the door as they approached.

Aiden gave him a nod. "Hi, Bert. I didn't know you were interested in babies."

"I'm not." His stern mouth pulled into a frown. "But Connie takes good care of me at the café. Every morning for breakfast, she serves me two eggs sunny-side up, four slices of bacon and wheat toast, buttered light. I'm good to people who are good to me."

"And those who aren't?"

The frown deepened. "See you around, Aiden."

As he went down the sidewalk, he acknowledged Tab and Misty with a slight nod of his head, but he didn't say a word to them. Aiden had to wonder if Bert was aware of his nephew's attraction to Misty. Did he ever talk to David? Did he know anything of that young man's hopes and dreams? It was hard to tell if Bert thought of his nephew as someone who was good to him or as a problem he had to deal with.

Following Tab and Misty into the house, Aiden watched

for reaction from the other townspeople. If Chuck and Woody could be used as an example, lots of folks would be blaming his sister for David's murder. In addition to Connie and Carlos, there were four other people who greeted them. They all seemed friendly. One bland, middle-aged lady who worked as a teacher at the high school gave Misty a giant hug and remarked about how awful it must have been to see David killed.

"It was terrible," Misty said.

He didn't trust his sister to keep quiet about the murder. "She's not at liberty to talk about what happened. That's Sheriff Fielding's order. We're here to celebrate this pretty new baby."

Standing beside the rocking chair where Connie was sitting, he leaned down to get a better look at the tiny bundle in her arms. Sound asleep, Rosalie held one perfect little hand beside her Cupid's bow mouth. Aiden felt a tug at his heart. "She's the prettiest baby I've ever seen."

Connie beamed. "She has black hair, like her daddy."

"But Carlos isn't this cute." He glanced toward the proud papa. "No offense, man."

"None taken. I want my baby girl to look just like her mama."

Tab stood on the opposite side of the rocking chair. "How has she been with the breastfeeding?"

"It's just like you told me," Connie said. "Every three hours or so, she's hungry. And my boobs have turned into milking machines."

"Too much information," Aiden said.

"Get used to it," Tab warned. "You're going to have one of these at your house very soon."

He liked the idea, but he was a little bit scared, as well. "Every three hours?"

"Not your problem," Tab said. "I know you're the most

responsible person in the world, but breast feeding is Misty's job."

He stepped aside to let Misty take his place. Though she cooed and giggled over the baby, he saw a subtle transformation in his sister. She seemed calmer and less focused on herself. An immediate bond formed between her and Connie as they talked about babies and childbirth.

While Tab took Connie and Carlos into a bedroom to talk about other things, he and Misty milled around with the other people. Their interactions stayed upbeat and pleasant, appropriate for celebrating a new birth. Still, there were occasional references to the terrible serial killings and the murder of Ellen Jessop. A hint of fear whispered below the surface of their conversations. A terrible danger threatened their community.

The serene atmosphere changed when Woody and Chuck appeared at the door. Before Carlos showed them inside, Aiden intervened. "If you don't mind, I'd like to talk to these two outside for a moment."

Carlos looked from one to the other. "You all play nice. I don't want fighting around my daughter."

Outside on the sidewalk, Aiden squared his shoulders. "Like Carlos said, I don't want any trouble."

"We get it." Chuck spoke through pinched lips. His tone was hostile. "And if we don't behave, you'll chase us down with your chopper and have us thrown in jail."

After shooting off guns near his house, they deserved to be arrested. Aiden wouldn't apologize for the role he played. "If that's what it takes, then so be it."

Inhaling a deep breath, Chuck pushed out his chest. "My mom told me I had to say I was sorry."

"Not necessary," Aiden responded. "Just don't do it again."

Woody hadn't said a word. He stared down at his boots. In his hands, he held a couple of pieces of loose twine that he kept fiddling with. Instead of his Bronco jersey, he wore a neat blue windbreaker shirt and jeans that made Aiden think he'd also had a talk with his mother. These two young men were out of high school, but their parents were still an influence in their lives.

Woody looked up. "Is Misty here?"

She stepped outside and closed the door behind her. "I'm right here. If there's something you want to say, tell me to my face."

Aiden had never been so proud of his sister. Even pregnant, she was showing more guts than these two guys who accused her in a nasty note and ran away.

"We were wrong," Woody said.

"You were," she said. "What made you do it?"

"We were mad about David getting himself killed."

"I don't buy it." There were no giggles from Misty. "You guys weren't that close to David. You worked with him at the gas station, but you didn't hang out with him much. You thought you were better than him because you were jocks."

"We're sorry," Chuck said. "Okay? Can that be an end to it?"

"Why did you come after me? Who were you talking to?"

Woody opened his mouth but Chuck spoke first. "Nobody, we weren't talking to nobody."

She took a step toward them with her belly protruding aggressively. "It was Jim, wasn't it? That lame-brain ski bum who thinks he's all that." She snapped her fingers in Chuck's face. "Aspen Jim is nothing but a phony."

"You're not going to say that when he opens Little Big Horn Rafting Company. We're going to be the first guys he hires."

"That's right." Woody held up the piece of rope he'd been playing with. "I'm learning knots so I know how to handle the rafts."

Or tie up helpless victims? Aiden had to wonder what other actions Aspen Jim had demanded from them. He didn't see Chuck and Woody as killers; they were basically decent and still respected their parents...if that was any kind of alibi.

He was amazed by how much information his sister had gotten in a short, angry confrontation. In jail, the sheriff had questioned Chuck and Woody extensively and hadn't learned that they were acting on something Aspen Jim had told them. Apparently, the only way to break the teenage code of silence was through another teenager.

Misty braced her hands on her hips. "Here's what I want you to tell Jim. If he's got a problem with me, he can bring it to me himself. Just bring it."

"Whoa." Woody held up his hands to fend off her rage. "The Gabriel family is real kickass."

"You better believe it," Misty said.

"Is it okay if we go in and see the baby now?" Chuck asked. "My mom told me I had to say hi to Connie. After being in jail, I've got to prove I'm not some kind of criminal."

"One more question," Aiden said. "Aspen Jim convinced you that Misty had something to do with David's murder. Who changed your mind?"

"Clinton," they said in unison. "He was there. He ought to know what really went down."

"When did you see him?" Misty asked.

"Yesterday afternoon. He's a good guy, Misty. You're lucky to be with him."

"I know."

For once, Aiden agreed with her about Clinton. He'd taken on the task of convincing people that Misty was innocent. Aiden had to respect him for that.

ALL DAY LONG AIDEN HAD kept to his promise to watch over Tab. They'd done everything together, from a trip into Billings to check up on the Buffalo Man to helping out in the kitchen with dinner. But the day was winding to an end, and he'd have to leave her alone to sleep. Or not…

The best way for him to protect her would be to have her lying beside him in his bed. All day long, they had been touching, occasionally holding hands and exchanging long, lingering gazes. Their closeness sent his imagination into overdrive. When he leaned close and caught a whiff of her shampoo, he'd fantasize about kissing the nape of her neck, drowning in the delicate scent from her hair. Every gesture she made seemed like a caress. The sound of her laughter was sexy. Her sighs penetrated his soul.

Too bad their lovemaking was only in his head. He wanted to separate her from the rest of his family and get her alone in his cabin, but that didn't seem to be happening. After dinner, he and Tab sat in the living room with his mom and Blake and Misty. Maria Spotted Bear had already gone upstairs to bed, but the rest of the crew seemed as if they could spend the whole damn night talking.

"We saw my dad in Billings," Tab said. "He says hello to everyone."

"I've always liked your father," Sylvia said. "When Aiden built his cabin a couple of years ago, he tried to hire your dad to do it. But he was too busy."

"Not many building contractors have been as successful as my dad. He doesn't do much in the way of new construction, but he has four different crews working on renovations and repairs."

Sylvia nudged Blake in the ribs. "We could use some renovating around here."

"I want to fix up the old bunkhouse," Misty said.

Aiden slouched lower in his chair. This was an old argument from Misty. A couple of years back, at the same time Aiden was building his cabin, they'd constructed a new bunkhouse for the crew that lived full time at the ranch. Instead of tearing down the old barracks, they used it for storage. Misty had a different plan. She wanted to turn the old bunkhouse into her own little home for herself and the baby.

She giggled and chattered away about how easy it would be to make the renovations. This afternoon, when she saw how happy Connie and Carlos were, she must have started rethinking her plan to raise her baby alone because she spent the entire drive back to the ranch talking about Clinton.

"I'd like to see it," Tab said.

He hadn't been following the conversation. "See what?"

"Your cabin." Her blue eyes confronted him. "I've seen it from the outside, but I'd like to check out the interior."

He didn't need further invitation. Aiden jumped to his feet. "I'd be happy to show you around."

As they left the main house, he clasped her hand. *This might turn out to be a good night, after all.*

Chapter Sixteen

Once again, Tab was holding hands with Aiden and walking the familiar route from the main house toward the barn. But this time was different. They weren't racing toward the chopper to pursue a bad guy or to visit the hospital. She was on her way to the special place he'd built to give himself privacy—on her way to his house with his living room, his dining room, his kitchen and his bedroom.

She still couldn't believe that she'd invited herself. Asking if she could see his home? That little ruse hadn't fooled anybody. Tab had seen the knowing look that passed between Sylvia and Blake. Misty had been smiling so hard that Tab thought for a moment that the perky little blonde would whip out her cheerleader pom-poms, pregnant or not.

Everybody seemed to want a relationship to work out between her and Aiden. This afternoon, her dad had come right out and asked if they were dating, and he'd looked disappointed when she told him they were just friends.

Maybe that was the truth. Maybe they weren't meant to be anything more than pals. Or maybe she needed to take a risk and let him get close. Her hand, held firmly in his grasp, began to sweat.

"I wish we'd had more time with your dad," Aiden said. "During that summer when you were babysitting, I talked to him a lot, and he had good advice."

Her dad was a quiet man who usually kept his thoughts to himself. When he spoke, he was worth listening to. "What did he tell you?"

"That summer when my dad died was hell. Mom could barely get out of bed. Misty kept a smile on her little face, but I could see she was hurting."

"So were you."

"Mostly, I was overwhelmed. The business of running the ranch kept piling up, and I didn't know what the hell I was doing. Outside contractors tried to take advantage of me because I wasn't as savvy as my dad. Half the ranch hands were fixing to quit. I didn't know who I should trust and who I should fire."

She'd been aware of those pressures, but mostly she'd been consumed by how handsome he was. "You did a good job of hiding how you felt."

"I couldn't let anybody know that I was in over my head and drowning. But your dad saw the truth, and he gave me two pieces of advice. The first thing he said was that it was natural for me to be mad at my father for leaving me with this mess. I had to let that anger out. And you know what? He was right. I remember going for long walks with my dog, and when I was far away and alone, I'd just stand and yell, cursing so loud I could have raised the dead."

On the night she'd decided he was the perfect man, he must have been returning from one of those sessions. "I knew you took night walks with Reilly."

"Don't get me wrong. I don't blame my father for dying. He loved life, loved his life on the ranch. But I was so damn mad at what his death did to me." He gave her hand a squeeze. "Can you guess the second piece of advice from your dad?"

"He told you that there's no shame in asking for help," she said. "That's kind of his mantra."

"It's what you said to me when you were talking about

helping me investigate. And you were right. I don't know what I would have done with Wally if you hadn't been there."

"We're good together."

"I reckon we are."

Her comment wasn't meant to be suggestive, but it sounded like it was. Good together? As in good in bed together? Her tension was rising. Though the night was cool, she was on fire. More sweat gathered at her hairline, and a drop trickled between her breasts. Her hands were practically dripping.

As they rounded the barn, she faked a stumble and pulled her hand away from him. She rubbed her palm on her jeans. "Clumsy me."

"Are you all right?"

Admitting that she was nervous wouldn't be smart—he'd want to know why. And she didn't want to tell him that she was expecting more than a tour of his living space. "Sure, I'm fine."

As long as they continued to talk about the past, she could maintain her self-control, and she desperately wanted to keep that distance. "Do you remember my mom?"

"The beautiful Emma Willows, you bet I remember. I was only ten or eleven when she died, and it was one of the saddest days of my life. She and my mom were good friends. And I remember you were an annoying little pest."

"Me?" She might have gone back too far in time.

"You were a lot younger than me, and you were female. At that time, I didn't want anything to do with girls. No tea parties. No dressing up. No fancy-pants games."

They walked past the gleaming-white helicopter. His house was close enough to see clearly in the moonlight and the glow of a porch light that must have been on a timer. Though his house had wood siding like most of the other buildings on the ranch, the architecture was more modern with an A-frame center section and many more windows. She stumbled again, this time for real. She wasn't ready to go inside.

"Tell me about my mom," she said.

"She had black hair like you, only she didn't wear it as long. And she smiled a lot more than you do. I remember that she loved dancing. She and my mom played the radio while they were in the kitchen, and they always ended up dancing around. So did you, twirling in circles."

"I danced?"

"Don't you remember?"

"My memories of my mom aren't clear. Mostly, I look at photos and make up stories to go along with the picture."

"You were young," he said.

They had reached the steps leading to a large deck that ran across the front and north side. The picnic table and the monster-size gas grill suggested that this was a great place for parties. Easily, she imagined a group of people drinking beer, cooking steaks and sitting around the kitchen table. She hadn't really met his friends. Everybody knew Aiden, but she didn't know who he hung out with.

She followed him up the stairs to the deck and caught hold of his arm. "It's such a pretty night. Can we stay out here? I'd like to hear more about your memories of my mother."

"Have a seat." He gestured to the picnic table. "I'll just step inside and grab a beer. Want one?"

"Sure." She wasn't much of a drinker. The studies linking Native Americans and alcoholism acted as an effective deterrent, but she liked the taste of beer.

When he opened a sliding glass door and turned on a light, she had a view of the interior kitchen with granite counters and stainless-steel appliances. She actually was curious to see his furnishings, but that wasn't the real reason she was here. By staying outside, she postponed the inevitable moment when they would either make love or decide to be friends only. She wasn't sure which alternative scared her more. Though she'd dated plenty of men, her relationships never went deep.

She sat on the picnic table with her feet resting on the bench and took the beer when he returned. He climbed onto the table beside her. "What do you want to know about your mom?"

"I know she and your mom went to the ballet when your mom visited us in Billings. What else did they do together?"

"Watched chick flicks. Back then, it was VCR tapes from the video store in Henley." He tilted his beer to his mouth. "They baked cakes and breads, and tried out new recipes that made me gag. When they decorated for holidays, they always made sure you and me were involved. Since your mom was an artist, the decorating was always a treat. My mom still has some Easter eggs that your mom painted."

It pleased her to know that the Gabriel family had such fond remembrances of her mom. Those good feelings seeped into her consciousness and relaxed her. She inhaled a deep breath and exhaled. The night was still. From a faraway meadow, she heard the lowing of cattle.

Her life would have been different if her mom hadn't died when she was so young. Her dad and grandma had done a good job raising her, always supporting her and making her feel loved, but she missed the advice of a mother, especially when it came to men. Her father taught her to be suspicious of the guys she dated, and he'd never talked to her about sex. Though Grandma was more open-minded, she nursed the hope that someday Tab might marry into the tribe. What did it mean that Grandma was matchmaking with Aiden? Had she decided that Tab better marry soon before she became a dried-up old maid?

Turning her head, she met Aiden's gaze. The vibrant sensations coursing through her were far from withered. She took a long pull from her beer. She had to act or explode.

"I'm ready to go inside."

His touch as he helped her down from her perch sent a jolt of electricity across the surface of her skin. The same voltage shocked her when he rested his hand on the small of her back and directed her through the sliding glass doors. The hairs on her arms trembled as he helped her off with her jacket and hung it on a peg by the door.

As he strolled through the kitchen, he pointed out the major features and appliances. The narrative continued into the adjoining dining room, but she was too preoccupied to listen. Vaguely, she registered that this was a modern design with a spacious living room that rose two stories to the peak of the A-frame.

"It's a prefab cedar home," he said. "Once I had the foundation in, it took only ten days with a full crew to put the…"

The house was tidy, except for islands of masculine clutter. Surrounding the reclining chair in front of the television were cups, slippers and some half-opened mail. She looked toward the staircase leading to the upper level. "Is your bedroom up there?"

"Let me show you."

Her anticipation grew. *This is it.* They were going to the bedroom.

At the top of the staircase, he pointed to an open door. Heart racing, she entered his office. *What?* Her gaze scanned the huge room with a wall of windows. He pointed out that the view from the window allowed him to look at his chopper, the barn and to see all the way to one of the near meadows where cattle were grazing.

Though she was interested in his livelihood, she hadn't come to his home for a lecture about rescue helicopters and ranching. Striding purposefully, she circled his desk to stand in front of him. *It's now or never.*

She reached up and glided her right hand around his neck. Before she could change her mind, she pressed her mouth against his. For a moment, her pulse stopped. Her lungs ceased to breathe. She existed in limbo, waiting and waiting for his response.

When he pulled her into his arms, excitement gushed through her. She'd never felt so intensely alive. As he deepened the kiss, he pressed hard against her, leaning her back against the desk. She thought he might sweep his arm across the cluttered surface of his desk, shove all his papers onto the floor and make love to her right here. A sexy, dramatic idea, but she wanted to go slower, to savor every caress.

His hand was on her breast, kneading the soft flesh and claiming her as his own. He had taken control of their lovemaking, and she was happy to follow his lead.

Staring down into her eyes, he unbuttoned her muslin blouse. His rough hands pulled the fabric aside. Her breasts pushed against her lacy white bra. Her chest was heaving as she gasped for air.

He stepped back a pace. "My bedroom is down the hall."

"Okay."

Holding her against his chest, he moved toward the door. Though she was walking, her feet seemed six inches off the floor. He nuzzled her ear and whispered, "When you said you wanted to see my house, I was hoping this was what you meant."

"I wasn't exactly being subtle."

On the landing outside the office, he kissed the top of her head. "There's something I've wanted to do from the first minute I saw you."

"What's that?"

He took both of her hands and pulled her into his bedroom. "I want to unfasten your braid."

Still holding his hands, she swung in a circle and sat on his king-size bed. "You have my permission."

He sat behind her and leaned forward to give her a small kiss on the nape of her neck. She arched her back as he tugged at the plaits in her hair.

The quiet made her nervous. She had to say something. "I like your house. Did you decorate yourself?"

"I had help from a girlfriend."

Well, that wasn't what she wanted to hear. She didn't want to think of his house as the cattle-ranch version of a bachelor pad. "Was that the long-distance relationship that went wrong?"

"Nope. It was the lady before her. She kept telling me that I needed my own place, and she was right. Having a separate house helped me have a life that wasn't all about the ranch. Unfortunately, that life didn't include her."

A chunk of her unbound hair fell over her shoulder. "You've had a lot of girlfriends."

"Not really," he said. "What about you? Have there been other men in your life?"

"Of course." She could be vague and push the truth away, but she wanted to explain herself. He needed to know what he was getting into before their lovemaking went any further. He might back off, might be freaked out by her lack of experience. But she had to stick to the truth, even if it meant losing the man she had dreamed about for so many years. "Here's the deal, Aiden. I've never been in love."

With slow strokes, he combed his fingers through her hair. "I'm going to need more explanation."

"That's fair." She wanted to lie back and let nature take its course. "You should know the truth."

From behind, he slipped his arms around her waist, rested

his chin on her shoulder and whispered, "You can tell me anything, Tabitha."

The use of her full name seemed special and intimate. Few people even knew that name. "I've never, you know…"

"Tell me."

"I'm still a virgin."

She felt the muscles in his arms clench. Afraid that he was going to pull away from her, she held herself very still.

"A virgin midwife," he said. "Ironic."

"Yes."

"Is this your way of telling me to back off?"

"No."

"How did this situation come about?"

"A long time ago, I imagined the ideal man. Strong. Handsome. Brave. He was everything I wanted, and no other man could ever measure up to him. I'd be kissing a boyfriend, and the image of my ideal man would come into my head, and I'd know that the boyfriend was nothing but a pale reflection."

"And you wouldn't compromise."

"I can't give myself in halfway portions." She turned around in his arms so that she was facing him. "It's you, Aiden. My ideal man has always been you."

He brushed a light kiss on her lips. "No pressure, huh?"

"Are you up for the challenge, cowboy?"

"You bet."

He stretched her out on his bed and slowly undressed her. As her clothing fell away, so did her inhibitions. She wanted to see his body, wanted to feel him. She peeled off his shirt and frankly stared at the breadth of his chest and the intriguing pattern of chest hair that arrowed down to his belt buckle. He was handsome and virile and everything she imagined.

In a matter of moments, they were wrapped in a naked embrace. Moonlight through the window shone on their legs as they intertwined. His hard arousal pressed against her, and she was amazed by how natural their lovemaking felt—natural and perfect, almost ideal.

Gently but firmly, he caressed her waist and her hips and her inner thighs, until she opened herself to him. She wanted him inside her, had never wanted anything more in her whole life. Their kisses went from sweet to fiery hot. *A virgin midwife.* As he had pointed out, it was ironic.

She was an expert when it came to the female reproductive system, including what happened during sex. In detail, she could have identified her physical reactions complete with hormonal references and a detailed explanation of the interconnected limbic system. But her mind went blank.

She felt good, oh so good, and that was the only information she needed. She reveled in her heightened sensations. Fireworks popped behind her eyelids. Goose bumps marched up and down her naked skin. With every touch, every kiss, every thrust, the intensity accelerated. She didn't think she could go any higher, and then came the explosion of relief. There were no words to describe it.

Completely satisfied, she lay on the bed beside him. Had this really happened? She was aware that at some point he'd gotten a condom from the drawer in the bedside table. For that, she was grateful.

Snuggled against his chest, she exhaled a sigh. For everything, she was grateful. "Can we do it again?"

"Was it ideal?"

"I wouldn't change a thing."

He twirled a lock of her hair between his fingers. "I never knew you had a thing for me, even though I should have figured it out. You gave me a clue."

"I did?"

He reached over and touched the shamrock pendant she was wearing, the gift he'd given her long ago. "You weren't saving this necklace because it's valuable. Your attachment has to be sentimental."

"A lucky four-leaf clover," she said. From now on, the necklace would represent this—the luckiest night of her life.

Chapter Seventeen

The next morning, Aiden slipped out of bed early. Before leaving the bedroom, he made sure Tab was cozy under the covers. It gave him immense satisfaction to tuck the dark brown comforter around her naked body while she slept soundly, breathing steadily through slightly parted lips. When he kissed her forehead, she wriggled and made a soft murmur that reminded him of a purring kitten. He was tempted to wake her and start the day off right by making love again.

But he could wait. He wanted their first morning together to be special, with fresh coffee and a civilized breakfast with normal conversation. For a while, they could forget about investigating. This would be their time.

He pulled on his jeans, left the bedroom and went downstairs to the kitchen. Ideally, he'd put together a tray of food with a napkin and a single red rose in a vase. Ideally?

She'd called him her ideal man, and he wasn't sure he liked the title. He'd spent much of his life trying to be perfect, taking care of the ranch and making sure everybody else was happy. *Nobody's perfect.* Sooner or later, he'd disappoint her, and he didn't want to see the look in her bright blue eyes when she realized he wasn't ideal, after all.

Barefoot, he padded across the tile floor in the kitchen. He ground the beans and set the coffeemaker to brew. Food supplies in his refrigerator were scant, but he could make do with a couple of eggs, bread and chunk of cheese that hadn't turned green.

A glance at the digital clock told him it was twelve minutes after eight o'clock. Chores on the ranch would be well under way. Breakfast in the main house would be already prepared, which meant he had the option of running over there and grabbing a couple of plates. But he didn't want to see anyone else, didn't want to share this private time with Tab.

His cell phone on the polished granite countertop rang, and he glared at it. When caller ID showed it was the sheriff, Aiden really didn't want to pick up. An early-morning call was sure to be bad news. He answered anyway. "Good morning, Sheriff."

"I shouldn't be making this call," the sheriff said, "but I owe you for your efforts on the investigation. And I'm hoping you can help me with what I have to do this morning."

His sunny vision of a nice breakfast with Tab disappeared behind a cloud of new responsibilities. Things were about to get nasty again. "Tell me."

"We identified the fingerprints that Joseph Lefthand found at Maria Spotted Bear's house. There were a set of prints on the window and on the door leading into the barn."

Those positions fit with the route for the person Aiden had been chasing. "You got those prints yesterday. Why did it take so long to find the match?"

"We weren't looking in the right place. The prints weren't in the criminal database. They matched a set we had taken recently and hadn't fed into the system." He cleared his throat. "They belong to Clinton Brown, Misty's boyfriend."

"Damn." Aiden hadn't seen this coming.

"I'm on my way to your ranch to arrest him. I already stopped at his parents' house, and they said he didn't come home last night. They weren't worried about him being gone because he stays at the bunkhouse at the ranch sometimes."

"I haven't seen him," Aiden said.

"I'm concerned about taking him into custody. He tried to kill Wally. I have to treat Clinton as a dangerous suspect."

"Give me twenty minutes. If he's here, I'll have him ready to go quietly with you."

"I shouldn't do this." The sheriff paused. "But I trust you. Twenty minutes."

Aiden disconnected the call and set the phone down. When he looked up, he saw Tab standing in the doorway. She wore one of his T-shirts that hung almost to her knees. Her long hair—God, he loved that beautiful hair—fell around her shoulders. Her eyes regarded him steadily.

"All I heard was 'fingerprints,'" she said.

"The prints found at your grandma's house belong to Clinton."

She gaped. "I can't believe it. Clinton shot Wally?"

"It seems like that." He glanced longingly at the coffee-maker. "I have twenty minutes to find Clinton and get him ready to turn over to the sheriff."

"I'm coming with you. Don't even think about arguing with me. I'll be ready before you have your boots on."

Regretfully, he watched her pivot and run back through the house toward the staircase. His hope for a sweet, peaceful morning was gone.

AFTER A PHONE CALL to Blake, Aiden learned that Clinton hadn't spent last night in the bunkhouse. He hadn't showed up for work yesterday. His Jeep was nowhere at the ranch. He'd run away, which was absolutely the worst thing he could do. Fleeing was considered the desperate act of a guilty man.

The best way to find Clinton was through Misty. As Aiden hurried toward the main house with Tab at his side, he checked his watch. "I've got eight minutes."

"I still can't believe that Clinton is a killer."

"Look at the facts," he said. "Clinton had access to the gun when David was shot. It's only his word that he was unconscious. Then, he had a fight with Ellen Jessop. Now, his fingerprints are at your grandma's house."

"That's what you call 'circumstantial evidence,' right? Clinton has a knack for being in the wrong place at the wrong time, but that doesn't make him a serial killer."

He sure as hell hoped not. It bothered him that the father of Misty's baby might be capable of such heinous violence. Approaching the front porch, he said, "I'm going to talk to Misty alone. This isn't a time for worrying about her stress level. I need answers about Clinton, and I need them now."

"Should I explain to the others what's going on?"

"That would be wise."

He charged through the front door and went to the kitchen where his mom sat with Maria Spotted Bear. "Where's Misty?"

"Still in bed," his mom said as she rose to her feet. "What's the matter?"

"Tab will explain."

He pivoted and rushed to the staircase. In less than five minutes, the sheriff would be here. Without knocking, Aiden opened the door to Misty's room.

She sat in a pink upholstered chair by the window, fully dressed with her hands resting on her belly. Her eyes were red as though she'd been crying, and her expression was uncharacteristically grave.

"Where's Clinton?"

"I don't know."

"He didn't come to work yesterday. Did he contact you?"

Hesitantly, she said, "I've talked to him. And he sent me text messages."

"If you really want to protect him, you'll tell me where

he is. Running away like this makes him look like he's got something to hide."

"He knew what it would look like," she said. "That's why he took off."

"The sheriff is going to be here in a couple of minutes. If you're hiding Clinton, you'll be arrested as an accessory. Misty, you could go to jail. I know you care about Clinton. But he's not worth it."

"You don't understand."

"Fine," he said. "You've got thirty seconds to explain what Clinton was doing at Maria Spotted Bear's house."

"He was playing detective. He thought Wally the Buffalo Man might know something and went looking for him. But Clinton wasn't the only person who was searching for the old man. He saw somebody else."

"Who?"

"A guy in a ski mask. Clinton thought it was Aspen Jim, but he wasn't sure."

"And then?"

"He followed them to Maria Spotted Bear's house. He saw the guy shoot Wally and run away. Clinton tried to use his phone to call 911, but he couldn't get a signal from inside the barn. If you don't believe me, you can ask Tab about that. She's told me that it's hard to get a signal. She said—"

"Stay on track, Misty."

"Okay." She nodded. "I don't want to go to jail."

"I don't want that, either." He leaned over her and patted her hand. "You have to cooperate and tell the truth. Then, it'll all work out okay."

"The truth hasn't worked out for Clinton. He knew it wouldn't."

"He must have seen us arrive in the chopper."

"Right," she said.

"Why didn't he approach us?"

"He was afraid you'd think that he shot Wally. Everything is working against him. He looks guilty. So, he made sure that Tab saw him at the window, and then he ran and led you to the barn where you could help Wally."

The story she told was too stupid to be made up. "I believe you."

"Do you, really?" She looked up at him with wide eyes.

From the moment they found Wally, Aiden had been bothered by the fact that the supposed intruder at Maria Spotted Bear's house had directed them toward the injured man. And Tab had mentioned that someone else used compression on the gunshot wounds. She'd thought it was Wally himself, but Clinton might have applied first aid.

He stared hard at his sister. "If you know where Clinton is, you've got to tell."

"I don't know," she said miserably.

"The sheriff is going to start a manhunt. If what Clinton told you is true, the sheriff isn't the only person who wants to find him. The killer will be looking, too."

"You can check the text messages he sent to me. He never says where he is."

Red and blue lights flashed through her window as the sheriff's vehicle pulled up to the house. The sheriff wouldn't want to leave without taking someone into custody. Aiden would have to do some fast talking to keep his sister out of jail.

THE TEXT MESSAGES SAVED Misty…for now. With the sheriff looking over his shoulder, Aiden read the messages on his sister's phone—touching little notes from Clinton, talking about how much he loved her and their baby and apologizing for making mistakes. He never mentioned anything about a location.

Though the sheriff was unconvinced when Misty explained how Clinton happened to be at Maria Spotted Bear's house, he was glad to have another reason to look at Aspen Jim as a suspect. Nobody, except for Woody and Chuck, liked that con man. Maybe this time, Aspen Jim wouldn't have an alibi.

After the sheriff left, Aiden knew they needed to investigate further. Not only did he have to keep Misty out of jail, but he had to clear suspicion from her idiot boyfriend, as well. If Clinton was arrested for these crimes, Misty would be next. She was the Bonnie to his Clyde.

Aiden and Tab were back in the chopper, headed to the hospital in Billings. The only person who could say definitively that Clinton hadn't shot him was Wally, and the old man was close to regaining full consciousness.

As the helicopter swooped through a clear blue sky, Aiden looked over at her. Tab always seemed happy when they were flying. The lady liked to be in the air. He spoke into his headset. "Maybe we can catch dinner at a nice restaurant, someplace with candlelight."

"Don't get your hopes up. If we get any useful information from Wally, we need to act right away."

He agreed. They hadn't told the sheriff that they were going to the hospital, and Aiden was pretty sure that he and Tab were no longer welcome in the police investigation. "We're too close to Clinton. If the sheriff finds out what we're doing, he's not going to be happy."

"Unless the evidence we find makes things worse for him."

"What the hell was Clinton thinking? Running around by himself? Trying to track down clues from Wally?"

"Come on, Aiden." She punched his arm. "Isn't that exactly what we're doing right now?"

"It's different."

"I'm not saying that you have to like Clinton or welcome

him into your family with open arms, but he's not a bad guy. He's trying to find the killer."

"And putting himself in danger."

"Again," she said, "isn't that like you?"

Aiden didn't want to admit that he and Misty's boyfriend were similar in any way, shape or form. Still, he knew that Clinton had been trying to do the right thing and marry his sister. And, according to Blake, Clinton was turning out to be a decent ranch hand. And he loved Misty. "Okay. Maybe the kid isn't so bad, after all."

"Probably not a serial killer." She leaned forward for a better look through the windshield and her long ponytail fanned out across her shoulders. "Of all the people we've talked to, there's only one that makes me think he's disturbed enough to be a psycho killer."

"Aspen Jim?" he guessed.

"I could see him committing murder for money, like a hit man. And I wouldn't be surprised if he was a rapist. But I don't think he's the type to abduct women, tie them up and dispose of the bodies on the rez. That takes a certain kind of horrible obsession. It reminds me of Bert Welling and his spotless jumpsuits."

"But Bert has lived in Henley for at least ten years. Why would he start killing now?"

"This might not be the beginning. He might have a tidy stack of rotting corpses buried in his backyard." She cocked her head to one side. Even while talking about dead bodies, she was beautiful. "There's something dark in Bert Welling. My grandma would call it a curse."

"And a profiler would call it obsessive compulsive."

"Different words for the same thing."

They flew over the chiseled rimrock formation toward the skyline of Billings. They couldn't land at the hospital helipad because it needed to be kept clear for emergencies.

Instead, he'd leave the helicopter at a local hangar and take one of the rental cars.

Aiden didn't much care for trips into the city, but today the hive of activity beckoned to him. He wanted to share experiences with Tab, to see new places and taste new foods.

"I didn't want to spend the day talking about serial killers," he said. "Not after last night."

"It would have been nice to spend some time alone, just being together." Her eyes flashed. "Maybe making love."

"Definitely making love." He glided his hand down her arm. "This is kind of different for me. I like to take my time when I'm getting to know a lady. Things between us have been moving like lightning."

"Not really. We've known each other for most of our lives. We played together when we were kids. And I spent that summer when I was sixteen with a major crush on you."

"But I haven't known you as a woman."

She leaned forward so she could look him directly in the eye. "I think you like to go slow so you can keep everything under control. Neither of us expected to fall into bed together so quickly. It's a little bit wild."

"More than a little," he agreed.

"It's kind of exciting, isn't it? I'm a practical, responsible person and so are you. I don't get swept away by passion."

"Any regrets?"

"None," she said.

That was good enough for him. Starting today, he'd push his plans and concerns aside. Instead of responsible, he'd be spontaneous, letting life take him to places he'd never been before.

But first, they had to catch a killer.

Chapter Eighteen

Because Wally was under police protection, he had a private room at the end of the hallway on the third floor. Tab was glad to see that the old man was being treated well. As the only witness in a potential serial killer case, the local police ought to be taking real good care of him. The uniformed officer on guard duty outside his room knew her and Aiden from yesterday, and he was obviously happy to see them. The poor guy must be bored to death after sitting for hours in a sterile hospital corridor.

He pumped Aiden's hand. "We've got some new information on the case. The autopsies."

"Great," Aiden said. "What did they show?"

Before speaking, he glanced up and down the hall. The Billings police were being careful not to alert the public to the possibility of a serial killer. They didn't want a panic.

In a low voice, the officer said, "The girl's injuries were consistent with the other victim. We're assuming that they were both killed by the same person."

"Was there any indication that there might have been two killers?"

"Not that I heard about." The officer raised an eyebrow. "Is that one of the theories? Two killers?"

"It's been suggested." Aiden shrugged. "What about David Welling?"

"Shot by a .30 caliber hunting rifle, but you already know that. We've got the murder weapon. Cause of death was internal bleeding. The bullet nicked his heart."

"Anything else?"

"Let me see if I can remember." The officer looked up and to the left. "Three cracked ribs, broken wrist, two broken fingers. Scars on his back and buttocks."

Tab was surprised. "Was he beaten before he was shot?"

"These were all old injuries. Some from childhood. Others when he was a teenager."

"He was abused." Nothing enraged her more than the harming of an innocent child. Bert told them that David's father was an alcoholic, but he hadn't mentioned the abuse. "Are there criminal reports or records about David's injuries?"

The officer shook his head. "None that we could find. David wasn't taken to a hospital for treatment. The poor kid had to heal on his own."

Bert Welling dropped a few notches lower in her estimation. He should have recognized that his nephew was being abused. He should have stopped it. Poor David had led such a terrible, unhappy life. No wonder Misty's casual flirting became so important to him. He must have cherished any hint of love, no matter how small.

Aiden nodded toward the hospital room. "Has Wally been able to answer any questions?"

"He's got answers, but they don't make sense," the officer said. "He just babbles about the moon and monsters with two faces."

"The moon," she said, "that's new. What's he been saying about the moon?"

"I don't know. I just heard moon or moonlight."

"Is it okay for us to talk to him?"

The officer stepped aside. "Knock yourself out."

In the private room, a blonde nurse in blue scrubs checked Wally's vitals. Most people look worse in the hospital, but Wally's appearance was much improved in spite of the IV line, the monitor, the nasal cannula, the dressing that covered his chest wound and the bandage wrapped around his head. The ugly hospital gown was cleaner than anything she'd seen the Buffalo Man wear. His patchy beard was shaved clean.

With his eyes closed, he seemed to be having a pleasant nap. A blanket covered him up to his chest. Though it was only eleven o'clock in the morning, a tray with a half-eaten lunch was on the bedside table.

Aiden stood beside his bed. "Are you awake, Wally?"

The old man twitched his nose but said nothing. Tab was pretty sure that he'd heard Aiden but didn't want to respond.

"I need to talk to you," Aiden said. "I want to ask you some important questions."

Wally pried one eyelid open and made a weak murmur that had Aiden leaning close so he could hear.

Tab turned to the nurse. Quietly, she said, "That looks like a lunch tray. Did he have a special order?"

"He wasn't interested in breakfast. He wanted an egg salad sandwich and ice cream, so that's what I got him."

"That was nice of you. Out in the real world, Wally doesn't have anybody to take care of him. I imagine he's enjoying all this attention."

The nurse cocked a cynical eyebrow. "Some people like being in a hospital."

"How's he doing?"

"Would you like to talk to his doctor?"

"Not necessary." Tab knew that waiting for the doc could take quite a while. "I'm more interested in his comfort level. Is he on pain meds?"

"He's pretty well doped up and not coherent."

"The officer said he mentioned the moon."

"Half-moon," she said. "He makes a sweeping gesture with his hand and says 'half-moon' as if we ought to understand what he means."

"I have a pretty good idea." "Half-moon" had to be a reference to the cave. "Thanks."

She took a position next to Aiden at the side of Wally's bed. It was better to let him do the talking because Wally knew him and trusted him. If the old man was going to say anything useful, he'd confide in Aiden.

Straining to hear Wally's mumbling, she pressed against Aiden. He moved his arm, grazing the side of her breast, and she had to stifle a gasp. When she was close to him, all her senses sharpened. He didn't wear cologne but there was a lingering scent of aftershave and another smell that reminded her of leather and wind across the prairie.

Making love last night had changed her in ways she couldn't describe, except to say that she liked the feeling. She had a new confidence and strength, an awareness of herself as a woman. And she couldn't wait until they made love again.

If that didn't happen, if he didn't want to be with her, she knew the rejection would hurt. She'd survive, but the pain of that loss would be so deep that she couldn't stay in this area where she might run into him. She'd run away, go back to Missoula, find another home, another lifestyle, another life.

Aiden glanced at her and spoke quietly. "I'm not getting much from him. The same stuff about monsters in the night."

"Ask him about Half-Moon Cave," she said. "The nurse mentioned it."

"That's a start." He looked toward the hallway. "We ought to get the officer in here. If Wally says anything significant, we need a witness."

She went into the hall and motioned to the officer. "Aiden thinks he's ready to talk."

The officer pulled out a notepad and pen, followed her into the room and stood on the opposite side of the bed. Aiden gave him a nod as he touched Wally's scrawny, pale arm. "What did you see at Half-Moon Cave?"

"It's a bad place. Evil lives there. I heard screaming. Not like when the kids were having parties."

"Did you go closer?"

"The screaming stopped. I figured I was wrong. It was just those kids, those damn kids and their beer parties."

"Did you see them?"

"Two men. They were loud and angry. None of my business. No, sir, I don't go looking for fights."

She imagined Wally in his buffalo robe, hiding behind clumps of sage brush and watching everything. In his way, he'd become a guardian of the reservation land. Nothing happened that he didn't know about.

Aiden asked, "When was this?"

"A week, maybe."

"Is that when you saw the blonde girl? The girl named Ellen?"

"She was loud when she laughed. She made an echo." He opened his eyes wider and blinked. "At Half-Moon Cave, that's when the two-face must have seen me. I ran away, but he sees everything. And he's fast. You can't escape him—no, sir. You can't escape."

His words faded into a mumble, and he closed his eyes. This might be all they got from him, and it wasn't going to help clear Clinton from suspicion.

Aiden switched positions with her. "Talk to him about your grandma's house."

She smiled down at the old man. "Maria Spotted Bear sends her best wishes for your recovery. She's sorry she wasn't home when you came calling."

Without opening his eyes, Wally said, "Kind woman."

"And she makes yummy pies." Appealing to his senses might get him to wake up. "And she grows herbs, fragrant herbs like rosemary and lavender."

His nose twitched and he smiled.

"When you came to visit," Tab said, "the house was dark. Did you go inside?"

He shook his head. "I knew something bad was following me. An evil spirit. Didn't want to bring it inside."

"And you had to hide."

"I went to the barn." His lower lip quivered. "That's where he got me. Two-face attacked me. I told the sheriff. I already told him."

"It's okay," she said in the same soothing voice she used with women in labor. "You don't have to talk about it. I want you to breathe and relax. Let yourself go quiet."

When his agitation had passed, she asked, "After the two-face left you to die, did someone else come to you?"

"A man."

Beside her, she heard Aiden murmur, "Good job, Wally. Tell us about the man."

"I was cold. He covered me with my robe. He tried to help." Wally opened his eyes and looked at her. "Then I saw an angel. That was you."

"What about the man who helped you? Did you know him?"

"He was young. Used his cell phone. Strong hands. I might know him. Don't remember."

She looked across the bed at the officer who was scribbling in his notebook. Wally's information matched the story Misty told them. This might be a break for Clinton.

Leaving Wally to sleep, they went into the hallway. The officer had his cell in hand. "I need to get this information to the chief. Where's this Half-Moon Cave?"

"Not far from where David was shot," Aiden said. "Thanks for letting us see him."

"I should be thanking you. This is a good lead."

Aiden took her elbow and directed her down the hall. He was moving too fast for conversation, and she knew he had a purpose. As soon as they were on the sidewalk outside, he pulled out his cell phone. "I need to make a couple of phone calls."

"Are we going to Half-Moon Cave?" she guessed.

"And taking Sheriff Fielding with us," he said. "I want to get this cleared up as soon as possible."

"I'm kind of surprised that the cave wasn't searched before," she said. "When everyone was looking for Misty's mystery shooter, it seems like the cave would be a good hiding place."

"We checked it out but didn't search thoroughly. The cave is on the other side of the river from where David was killed."

She understood the logic. The Little Big Horn River formed a natural barrier that ran through the rez with very few bridges crossing from one side to the other. Though the current usually rolled lazily along, it was too deep and wide for a vehicle to cross.

While Aiden made his call to the sheriff, she sat on a stone bench under a honey locust tree in a landscaped area outside the hospital. Casting back in her memory, she visualized the place where she'd seen Clinton's Jeep stuck in the almost dried creek bed. The brush at the edge of the river had obscured the view of the water's edge.

On the opposite side, about a hundred yards beyond the riverside cottonwoods and rugged shrubs, a wall of rugged, sandstone cliffs stretched for nearly two miles. Half-Moon Cave looked like a giant hand had reached down and torn a chunk from the wall, leaving a shape that resembled a moon coming halfway over the horizon.

When Tab had been at the Jeep and with Misty, she hadn't been looking toward the cave. The shooter could have fired the rifle, fled into the brush and crossed the river. From there, he could have run or taken a mountain bike to get to the cave or beyond that where David's van must have been parked. When Aiden had searched from the sky, he hadn't gone toward the cave. He'd stayed on the west side of the river.

It was such a simple solution. The shooter had escaped because they were all looking in the wrong direction. The story Misty had told them wasn't a lie. Nor was her unlikely tale of why Clinton's fingerprints were found at Maria Spotted Bear's house.

When Aiden finished his calls, he didn't look happy. He sat on the bench beside her. His shoulders slumped.

"Misty took off," he said.

Chapter Nineteen

After returning to the ranch house, Tab stood at the porch railing and watched as the helicopter rose from behind the barn and swooped toward Henley. Aiden wasn't leaving her behind; they had decided on a divide-and-conquer strategy. While he flew with the sheriff and a couple of deputies to Half-Moon Cave, she would talk to his mother and try to figure out where Misty had gone.

Sylvia stood beside her. In her trembling hand, she held the note that Misty had left behind.

"If I'd known what she was planning," Sylvia said, "I would have lassoed and hog-tied the girl. She told me she was going to the supermarket. Then, I found this."

Tab took the note. Written in purple ink with Misty's flamboyant scrawl, it said: "Don't worry. I'm going to be gone for most of today. Please, Mom, don't worry. I love you."

"When did she leave?" Tab asked.

"A couple of hours ago. She took off a little after ten o'clock. You and Aiden had just left for Billings. Why would she do this? Is it Clinton? Do you think she's meeting up with Clinton?"

"I don't know what to think."

Tab found it hard to believe that Misty had been planning this escape earlier today. Her attitude had been subdued without a single giggle. She'd looked them straight in the eye and said that she didn't know where Clinton had gone. Getting ready to run away with him? Tab didn't think so. Misty wasn't that good a liar.

Sylvia raised both hands to cover her face. "I feel terrible."

"It's not your fault." Tab wrapped her arm around the other woman's shoulders and led her inside. "Let's put our heads together. We can find her."

"Why doesn't Aiden want to tell the sheriff about Misty?"

"Don't worry." Tab inadvertently echoed the note. "If there's any reason to think she's in danger, we'll organize search parties. But for right now, let's keep the sheriff in the dark. He might think Misty has gone on the run."

"That doesn't make sense. Why would she run?" Sylvia's voice cracked. "She's not guilty."

"Sometimes, innocence isn't enough."

It would kill Sylvia to see her pregnant daughter behind bars. The Gabriels were a proud family. Suspicion of murder wasn't supposed to happen to people like them.

In the kitchen, her grandma directed them to seats at the table and placed steaming mugs of tea before them. "Chamomile and valerian with a pinch of mint," she said. "This will settle your nerves."

"No offense," Sylvia said, "but it's going to take more than tea to make me feel better."

"We start with a calm spirit—" Maria Spotted Bear offered her wisdom "—then we will reach a good conclusion."

Tab lifted the mug to her nose and took a sniff of the fragrant potion. She used this same formula to help pregnant women who couldn't get to sleep. "Before Misty left, did she do anything unusual?"

"She was on the phone. She's always on the phone."

"Could she have been talking to Clinton?"

"I don't know," Sylvia said miserably. "I don't want to blame him. If anything, Clinton has been a good influence on Misty. He wants to settle down with her, wants to take care of their baby."

Tab had an idea. "When Misty and Clinton wanted to be alone, where did they go?"

"I wish I knew. Misty used to confide in me. We used to have that kind of relationship. I was so proud of her. She got good grades in school, she was a cheerleader and she had friends. She had ambitions. Everybody liked her."

"And then?"

"It started when she got her driver's license. She was never home. She didn't talk to me anymore."

Tab had heard this story many times before. Young women—even more than young men—were given to bouts of foolishness when they reached the age of independence. Misty had taken a leap into Clinton's arms. She'd fallen in love. They'd made a baby.

"Did she mention any special place?" Tab asked. They were both teenagers living with their parents. Making love in their family homes wouldn't have been feasible. "I hate to say this, but there might have been a motel."

"That's real doubtful," Sylvia said. "Everybody in Henley and this area knows our family. Misty wouldn't have taken a chance on getting caught."

Talking to Misty's friends might lead to useful answers, but there wasn't time to break through the teenager code of silence. And Tab didn't want to start the rumor that Misty was gone.

She tried a different tactic. "During the summer I lived here, Misty and I wrote every day in our diaries. Did she keep that up?"

"She did for a long time, but I don't know where she'd keep a diary. I respected her privacy and never had cause to search my daughter's room. She doesn't do drugs or drink too much." Sylvia winced. "At least, I don't think she does."

Tab rose to her feet. "I'm going upstairs to her room to look around."

"Before you leave," her grandma said, "the BIA agent has been trying to reach you."

"Laura Westerfall?"

"She said it was important."

"I'll talk to her later."

"Tabitha," her grandma snapped, "listen to me. Agent Westerfall offered you an opportunity. You must answer her."

Tab had enough on her plate without worrying about setting up a health center that would serve the pregnant women on the rez and in Henley. Initially, the idea appealed to her. That was before she'd made love to Aiden.

If Tab said yes to the project, she'd be committed to staying in the area for an extended period of time, and she wasn't ready to make that decision. The newly formed relationship with Aiden was tentative. If it blew up in her face, she didn't want to be near him.

"I'll talk to Agent Westerfall soon," she promised as she dashed from the kitchen to the staircase.

Standing in the threshold of Misty's room, Tab took a moment to settle her thoughts. Her intense focus on the investigation left little time to consider what was happening in her personal life. She had given her virginity to the man she'd always thought she was meant to be with. Long ago, she'd cast Aiden in the role of soul mate, unbeknownst to him. Making love to him should have meant that her dreams had come true.

But she was young when those dreams were born. She was older now and ought to be wiser. She shouldn't make too much of one night together.

As her gaze circled Misty's room, Tab identified with the odd juxtaposition of a girlish pink velvet chair and a high-tech computer station. On the bedside table, a fluffy stuffed bunny sat beside a book on the stages of pregnancy. The fantasies of a teenager mingled with adult responsibilities and concerns. *Do we ever really grow up?*

She crossed the room and knelt beside the dresser. Misty used to hide her diary in this secret cache under a loose floorboard. When Tab pried it open, she found a small stack of spiral notebooks with years written on them. The last date was four years ago on Misty's thirteenth birthday.

Combing through these pages would have given useful insights into Misty's life, but Tab didn't have hours to pore over these pages, many of which were scribbled pictures of hearts, flowers and whorls. Misty no longer used the notebooks to record her thoughts. Why would she when she had a computer?

Feeling like a voyeur, Tab turned on the laptop. Misty hadn't used password protection, and her documents were readily available. Scanning the labels, Tab smiled in recognition when she read one labeled "D-Abby." When they first started their journals, they joked about writing to Dear Abby with their problems. She clicked on the document and opened the file.

The first entry, the most recent, was dated on the day of the murder. It said: "Nobody believes me. I didn't shoot David. I would never do that. He's been hurt enough."

Tab recalled the autopsy information. The wounds on David Welling's body indicated that he had been abused for a long time. Did Misty know? Or was she referring to a different kind of pain? Either way, her journal hinted that she knew more about David than she'd admitted.

Tab scanned through the entries. Some were only half sentences about a mood or a random thought. Others rambled on and on, especially those about having a baby and how that was scary and happy at the same time.

Tab needed a reference to a place—somewhere Misty

might have gone to meet with Clinton. When Tab first got the phone call from Misty, she and Clinton said they were driving around, going off road in his Jeep. At the time, their activity seemed odd. Why would a pregnant woman want to bounce all over the countryside? It seemed more likely that they had simply wanted to be alone. Maybe they'd been on their way to a private hideaway where they could lie in each other's arms and forget about the rest of the world.

Tab did a word search on *Half-Moon* and found a reference from several months ago. Misty had written about an abandoned cabin with a corrugated tin roof that was on the opposite side of the Little Big Horn River and wasn't far from the cave. Not exactly a GPS description, but Tab had something to go on. If she could get Aiden to search with the chopper, they might spot the roof.

With a silent apology to Misty for peeking into her inmost thoughts, Tab closed the Dear Abby journal. In the hallway, she put through a call to Aiden that went straight to voice mail. Cell phone reception—as she well knew—was unreliable on the rez. She'd have a better chance of reaching Aiden if she drove to the cave.

THOUGH AIDEN WASN'T AN authorized lawman, the sheriff hadn't objected when he entered Half-Moon Cave two hours ago with the other searchers. They hadn't known exactly what they were looking for, but evidence hidden in the cave might have been important enough to motivate the nearly fatal attack on the Buffalo Man.

In a dark recess at the back of the cave, one of the deputies had noticed scrapes against the wall and had signaled to the others. A flat piece of wood was held in place by three rocks that leaned at an unusual angle.

"Looks like a door," the sheriff said. "See if you can move those rocks."

"I'll do it." The deputy passed his flashlight to Aiden. "There's not much room here."

Single-handed, he shoved the rocks out of the way, creating other scrapes against the wall. He pried away the board and stepped back. None of them were prepared for what they saw.

The beams from all the searchers' high-power flashlights illuminated a grisly pile of bone and desiccated flesh. Tangles of blond hair clung to a dried skull with the jaw wide open in a silent scream. Another skeleton had knees drawn up to the chin. Rotting ropes fastened wrist bones and ankles, but there were no shreds of clothing or buttons or zippers. The victims had been naked when their remains were discarded in this dark, narrow chamber.

The sheriff squatted down and shone his light on a piece of rope. "This knot is different from the ones used on Ellen Jessop."

"He could have changed his method," a deputy said. "These bodies have been here for a good, long while."

"How many do you think there are?"

"Six or seven, at the least."

"How long?" Aiden asked. "How long have they been buried?"

"I'm no expert on decomposition," the sheriff said, "but this isn't a recent grave. They've been dead for years."

The recent disappearances of young women had opened the door to an extended history of killing. These bones offered mute testimony to a horror that had been too long hidden.

"We need to end this," Aiden said quietly.

"We will." The sheriff rose and took a step back. "Let's go outside. I'll contact the state police and Joseph Lefthand. Identification needs to be done properly."

"Doesn't seem right to leave them here," said the deputy

who had discovered the cache of bones in the back wall of the cave when he rolled three heavy rocks out of the way. "I'll stand guard."

"Suit yourself," the sheriff said. "Don't touch anything."

The hiding place was simple but effective. The back wall of the cave was marked by several small openings that led deeper into the earth. Unless you were searching, you'd never notice the rocks that hide the alcove.

Aiden wondered how many people had passed close to this terrible secret and never suspected a thing. People explored this cave all the time. They built campfires near the wide opening at the front. When he was a teenager, he'd come to parties here. As a kid, he and his buddies played in the cave, using it as a clubhouse. They'd never known. If Wally hadn't remembered screams from this place, the burial chamber might never have been uncovered.

Aiden stepped onto the lip outside the cave and looked downhill to the spot where David Welling was killed. His theory that the shooter had escaped across the river seemed plausible. David's van could have been parked up here. A road came within fifty yards of the cave.

The sheriff joined him. "Finding these bones lets Clinton off the hook for suspicion as a serial killer. He's too young."

"And Wally said he tried to help."

"But I still want to talk to Clinton." The sheriff frowned. "I want to know why he took off running. That's the act of a guilty man."

Aiden kept his mouth shut. No way would he implicate his sister who also appeared to be making a hasty escape. He was anxious to get back to the ranch and see if Tab had made headway on the search for Misty. "Do you need me to fly you back to town?"

"I'll wait for the state police," the sheriff said.

His mood was somber, and Aiden understood his regret

and his sorrow. The sheriff and his men had failed to protect these women in life. Now, they felt like they owed these victims. They wouldn't abandon these remains.

"I'm taking off," Aiden said. "If there's any way I can help, let me know."

"I'll be in touch."

He hiked away from the cave. Though the afternoon sun beamed overhead, the sight of those bones cast a dark, angry haze over his vision. Nothing seemed clear. In a world where such senseless, depraved wrongs could be committed, how could anything be right? How the hell could a human being commit those crimes?

The killer had been operating for years. That meant he lived in the area. He was a person they all knew. Aiden might have sat beside him in the diner, might have spoken to him or hired him for seasonal work. He might have shaken the hand that had killed those women.

As he neared the road and the place where he'd left the chopper, he saw another vehicle approaching. It was Tab's van, moving fast enough to kick up a tail of dust.

She parked and hopped out. "Don't you ever check your cell phone for messages?"

"I've been busy."

Coming closer, her expression changed. "What's wrong?"

He didn't want to tell her, didn't want to poison her mind. He only wanted good things for Tab. Their relationship should be about hope and light and everything that was positive. But he couldn't hide his feelings from her.

She looked at him, and she knew.

Without saying a word, she slipped her arms around him and rested her head on his shoulder. He didn't need comforting, but he welcomed her embrace and held her tightly against him. Her heart echoed his. They were in sync, connected.

"You found a body," she guessed, "hidden in the cave."

"More than one." He inhaled the fresh, sweet fragrance of her hair. "There's not much left of them but bones, old bones."

She shuddered against him. "These killings have been going on for a long time."

A brisk wind swirled around them. Tonight would be colder. He and Tab could sit together in front of the fireplace and find ways to keep each other warm.

"Did Misty come back?" he asked.

"Not yet, but I think I know where she is. We need to take the chopper."

As far as Aiden was concerned, his part in the investigation was over. There should be enough forensic evidence from the remains in the cave to identify the killer. After that, it was the sheriff's problem to track down and arrest this monster.

Aiden's only concern was to gather his family close and make sure they were all safe.

Chapter Twenty

In the chopper, Aiden and Tab hovered in the skies over the Little Big Horn and Half-Moon Cave. During the past few days, his six-passenger Bell Long Ranger had been getting a lot of use, and he was glad he'd taken the opportunity while they were in Billings to refuel. "What happened when you tried calling Misty?"

"I called, texted and sent mental messages," Tab said. "I've gotten no answer. The same is true for Clinton. I sent him a text telling him that he was in the clear and it was safe for him to come back."

"And he didn't reply."

"Not yet." She glared at the cell phone in her hand as though willing it to ring.

"You seem sure that Misty took off to join Clinton."

"It's possible that she heard about a really great shoe sale in Billings and took off," Tab said with a smirk. "Of course, she's running off to see Clinton."

"Not that I could ever understand the way my sister's mind works, I still have to ask. Why?"

"It's a woman thing," she explained. "No matter how many dumb things our men do, we keep thinking we can fix them."

He exhaled a sigh. "Let's find Romeo and Juliet before they get into any more trouble."

"We should go east," she said, "away from the river and

the cave. When Misty and Clinton got stuck on the other side of the river, I think they were headed to their hideout."

"First, we scan in the west."

He wasn't going to make the mistake of not covering the whole area. Not again. If he'd circled back around the cave when he first responded to Tab's call, he might have spotted David's van.

"You're the expert," she said.

Aerial surveillance wasn't as accurate as many people assumed. The view of the earth below was expansive, but picking out details was hit or miss unless the searchers were gifted with the vision of a hawk or an eagle.

"We should be able to see a house," he said. "With a corrugated tin roof?"

"According to Misty's description, the roof is rusty, the walls weathered and the windows broken out. The metal cistern beside the house is still operable, but I wouldn't drink any of that water."

"And she wrote about this place in her journal?"

"In great detail," Tab said. "I feel terrible about prying. When I was looking for clues, I tried not to read her private thoughts, but I couldn't help seeing a few things. She's truly excited about having the baby, and she loves Clinton."

"Even though she won't marry him?"

"Love doesn't always end in a commitment."

The steady tone of her voice made him think that she might be talking about herself as well as Misty. The idea of marrying Tab hadn't become part of his thinking, not yet anyway. They'd just taken their friendship to the next natural level, and he wanted a chance to enjoy getting to know her.

"My sister," he said, "has never been big on responsibility."

"Not like you."

She shot him a grin. As always, when they were airborne,

her mood seemed brighter and less guarded. He could barely take his eyes off her, even though he was supposed to be staring down at the ground.

"You're no slouch when it comes to being responsible," he said.

"When I make a commitment, I carry through." Her blue eyes gleamed as she looked toward him. "I had a call from the BIA agent who thinks she can get funding for a women's clinic."

"I like the idea." If Tab was running a clinic, she'd stay in the area. "There's a need for something like that in this area."

"Pregnant women in cities have more options," she agreed. "There are a lot of obstacles on the rez and in Henley. Not only do these women have to travel great distances to seek medical care, but they often can't afford to deliver their babies in hospitals. And they don't think about prenatal vitamins, postnatal care for themselves or breast feeding. There's most definitely a need, but—" she turned her head and looked out the window again "—I don't know if I'm the right person to do this."

He slowed the chopper to hover. "I want you to stay."

She pointed to the ground. "Over there."

Beside a rocky area with a couple of trees was a tumbled-down shack. He lowered their altitude for a better look. Abandoned dwellings weren't unusual in this area, especially not on the rez where property ownership was more clearly defined by who was taking care of the land than by a deed or contract.

Tab peered through the windshield. "It's not that one. Half the roof is caved in."

She hadn't answered his comment about wanting her to stay, and he decided not to push. Later, there would be time for him to show her how much he wanted her in his life.

In a roughly defined grid, he searched a ten-square-mile

area. The packed earth roads on this side of the river were more clearly defined though not well maintained. Nobody was supposed to be living here, and nobody bothered to keep the access clear. After they passed another disintegrating house where only the rock chimney was standing, he returned to the cave. A vehicle belonging to the tribal police was parked beside Tab's van. Joseph Lefthand stood outside the cave, talking to the sheriff.

"I hope they've got enough to catch this killer," he muttered. "God only knows how many lives he's destroyed."

In addition to the women he'd killed, he'd ruined the lives of their families and friends. Aiden couldn't imagine the emotional pain if Misty had been abducted and brutally murdered. When he'd heard that the killer preferred blonde women, he'd been afraid for his sister.

On the west side of the river, he once again laid out a mental grid, starting at a rise in the prairie where jagged cliffs blended into forest. From this distance, Half-Moon Cave was barely visible. A graded gravel road made a zigzag through the pines and evergreens. They quickly noticed four or five cabins that were occupied with wisps of smoke rising from the chimneys.

"They could be staying with someone else," he said.

"Misty never mentioned anyone else in her journal. This was her special place to be with Clinton—their private hideaway."

Adjusting the chopper's altitude, they ascended for a more panoramic view. The landscape lay below them like a relief map. "Look for other smoke trails," he said. "It's plenty cold enough for a fire."

"That way." She pointed. "I don't see smoke, but there's something shiny. Maybe the tin roof."

In less than a minute, the chopper hovered above a stand of trees that surrounded a very small cabin. It couldn't have been more than two rooms. A metal cistern clung to one side. Parked in the back and covered with branches was Misty's SUV.

"We're here," he said.

"I'm getting a text message." Tab held up her phone. "It says for us to come on in."

"If I wasn't so relieved, I'd kick my sister's tail. She puts us through all this worry, and then acts like she's inviting us for a tea party."

As soon as they landed and the rotors stilled, he heard a sharp cry followed by a moan. He reached into the back of the chopper for his rifle.

"You probably won't be needing your gun," Tab said.

"Didn't you hear the scream?"

"I'm guessing it's Misty. And she's in labor."

He froze with the rifle in his hand. His mind became a static wall of sheer panic. It was time. His baby sister was having a baby.

WISHING THAT SHE'D BROUGHT her midwife gear from the van, Tab dashed toward the small cabin and yanked open the door. She saw Misty lying on a ramshackle bed covered by a surprisingly clean quilt that she must have brought with her. Her face was red, and she was breathing hard at the end of a contraction.

As soon as Misty saw her, she struggled to sit up. "Don't come in here."

"It's okay," Tab said as she went toward the bed. "You're going to be all right."

Aiden charged into the small room. Tripping over his own boots, he lurched toward the bed and leaned across Tab to touch his sister's arm, nearly smothering them both in the process. "Misty, tell me you're okay."

"Oh God, Aiden. I'm sorry. I'm so sorry."

The door slammed behind them. A cold voice said, "She'll be just fine as long as you do what I say."

Tab looked over her shoulder. She was staring down the barrel of an automatic pistol. In the dim light from two windows that had been covered with plastic, she saw the gleam of sun-bleached hair. Aspen Jim moved away from the door where he'd been hiding and carefully put distance between himself and Aiden.

"Drop the rifle," Jim said. "Do it now or I'll shoot out your sister's knee. She's been bugging the hell out of me with her moans and groans."

Aiden set the rifle on the floor by his feet.

"Kick it over here," Jim ordered.

"There's no reason to hurt anybody," Aiden said as he pushed the rifle with his boot. "I need to take my sister to the hospital. You can have her SUV."

"Then what? I'd get about two miles away before you called in the law. No deal." He squatted, picked up the rifle and stood it in a corner of the room. "Don't try anything cute. Even if I'm not a marksman, I can't miss at this range."

Tab sat on the bed beside Misty and held her. Sobbing loudly, Misty leaned against her. "I thought I was helping Clinton."

"Get her to shut up," Aspen Jim growled. "I can't stand the noise."

"Misty, look at me." Tab spoke quietly and held Misty so she had to look into her face. "You're going to be all right. Now, I want you to take a deep breath."

Misty shook her head. Her cheeks were wet with tears. "I never should have come here, should have known better. He sent me a text. Said I could help Clinton. He lied."

Luring Misty to this place had been as simple as getting a puppy to fetch a tennis ball. But now wasn't the time for recriminations.

"Deep breath," Tab said. "Come on, now. Do it. Breathe."

Her shoulders trembled violently as she inhaled.

"Good. Do it again."

After another breath, Misty was beginning to calm down. At least, she wasn't hyperventilating.

Standing beside her, Aiden straightened his shoulders and spoke to Jim. "What do you want?"

"You're going to take me for a ride in that shiny chopper of yours, and I'm going to get as far away from this godforsaken country as I can."

"You can't run far enough," Aiden said. "You'd be smart to cooperate, turn yourself in and—"

"Shut up," he yelled. Agitated, he paced forward and back. "A guy like me can always start over. I'm a cat. I land on my feet."

"Don't run. I'll help you with the cops."

"I said shut up." He leveled his gun at the center of Aiden's chest. "I'm not taking the rap for this. I know what they found in that cave. He showed me."

Though concentrating on Misty, Tab couldn't help listening. Aspen Jim was saying that he didn't kill the women they found in the cave. Right now, she couldn't think of a single reason why he'd lie about his guilt or innocence.

"You're not the serial killer," Aiden said. "Those were old bones, and you've only lived in this area for a couple of months. The sheriff doesn't suspect you."

"Why should I believe you?"

"The state police and forensic teams are on their way right now. They'll prove that those remains are from years ago." Aiden's voice sounded completely rational. "Why don't you tell me who showed you those bodies? The sheriff will arrest him, and you'll be free and clear."

Tab felt Misty's body beginning to tense. Another contraction was coming. She wished that she'd checked the time between this one and the last. It was ten minutes, maybe more. Misty was still in the early phase of labor.

"Here we go," Tab said. "This time, I want you to concentrate on your breathing. You said you went to a pregnancy class, right? They talked about breathing."

"I don't remember." Misty grasped her hand and gripped hard. "I can't think."

"Not again." Aspen Jim started his pacing again. "I don't want to hear the moaning. Make her stop."

"That's not going to happen," Tab said. "This baby is coming whether you like it or not."

"I don't like it," he snapped.

"And I hate you," Misty yelled at him. "You're never going to get away free and clear. You're going to jail because you're a murderer. You killed David."

Tab had been focused on the serial killer; she hadn't expected this new revelation. Without thinking, she asked, "Did you see him? Did you see Jim fire the rifle?"

Glaring at him, Misty said, "Damn right, I did."

"You didn't," Aspen Jim said. "I got away too fast. You couldn't have seen me."

"Gotcha," Misty said.

Jim winced and shook his head. "Damn."

"Good job," Aiden said to his sister. "That sounded like a confession to me."

"Cut me some slack," Jim said. "I had to do it. If I hadn't shot David, my partner would have killed me."

"Why did he want David dead?" Aiden asked.

"The little dipstick got scared. He wasn't totally innocent, you know. He had a damn good idea what my partner was doing, and it didn't bother him much until he thought Misty might be in danger. David followed the Jeep out of town to warn her. He was going to betray my partner and me."

"And you couldn't let that happen."

"I didn't kill those girls." Aspen Jim was trembling. "I'm not going to jail for something I didn't do."

"What about the Buffalo Man?" Aiden asked. "Were you the two-face monster that went after him?"

"That crazy old coot deserved to be put out of his misery."

"But Clinton saved him."

Misty reacted to her boyfriend's name. "Clinton? Did you hurt him, too?"

"He came looking for me, but I got away. Hitched a ride out of town and rode the mountain bike here."

Misty let out a fierce groan, and Tab coached her through the pain. This was going to be a difficult labor.

Chapter Twenty-One

Strapped into the pilot's seat, there was nothing Aiden could do about what was happening in the rear of the chopper where Aspen Jim held his gun on Misty and Tab. The women had constructed a sort of nest for Misty using the quilt from the cabin and emergency supplies on board. Given that Misty was in labor, she seemed to be fairly comfortable. Her contractions were coming more frequently.

But Aiden really couldn't see what was going on behind his back. Nor could he hear over the *thwap-thwap* of the rotors and the loud hum of the engine. Aspen Jim refused to let them use the headset intercom that made normal conversation possible and blanked out the noise.

By taking away the headsets, Jim figured he'd eliminate any possibility of calling for help; they wouldn't be able to communicate with Air Traffic Control. He'd also destroyed their cell phones. Aiden's only chance for an SOS was to open the line on the communication panel and broadcast the ambient noise in the chopper. A long shot, at best.

The direction they were headed—south toward the Big Horn Mountains—was sparsely populated and regular ATC surveillance was limited to the few regional airports. Aiden's only hope for summoning help was that somebody at an airstrip happened to be randomly monitoring communications and got the message.

When Misty let out another wail, Aiden craned his neck to look over his shoulder. He hated that his sister was in pain. Again, there was nothing he could do. The baby was coming. Thank God Tab was here.

Thus far, she'd been rock steady. Only once had her fear surfaced. When they were boarding the helicopter, she'd gotten close enough to grasp his hand. He'd felt the tremble in her touch, and it made him angry. He needed all his self-restraint to keep himself from lashing out at Aspen Jim. He couldn't risk a fight. Not while Jim had the gun.

He had tried to reassure her. "I'll get us out of this."

"We'll do it together. You and me."

"That's what I meant."

"But not what you said."

Damn, she was stubborn. Even now, when he could see the panic shimmering in her blue eyes, she wouldn't let him shoulder all the responsibility. This was *their* problem. Together, they would fight it.

Being together, it sounded right. He wanted to be with her in every way. Not just making love, although he treasured those sweet, intimate moments with her above all else. He wanted to go riding with her, to wake up beside her in the morning, to watch the sunset from the porch of his cabin.

They'd get through this. They had to. No weak-willed murderer like Aspen Jim was going to destroy his chance at true happiness with Tab.

Through the front window of the chopper, the snowy peaks of the Big Horn Mountains came clearly into view. There wasn't much time for Aiden to make his move. Though Jim hadn't stated a specific destination, Aiden was pretty sure he wouldn't like what he found when they were on the ground. He wanted to gain control of the situation before they landed.

Jim still hadn't given up the name of his partner—the serial killer who had been operating in Henley and on the rez area for years. It was clear that Aspen Jim feared this man and was desperate to do his bidding—so desperate that he'd betrayed his natural con man leanings and become a killer. Murder didn't come easily to Aspen Jim. His planning was overcomplicated with a bizarre element of showmanship, similar to his idea of a river rafting company that included actors on the banks of the river.

He'd admitted that luring Misty to the hideaway had been the first step in his escape. Getting access to the chopper had been his real goal, and he'd known Aiden would respond to a hostage situation involving his sister.

At Maria Spotted Bear's house, Jim could have shot poor old Wally and left the body to be found. Instead, he'd chased the old man and pretended to be a two-face monster.

When Aspen Jim shot David, he'd managed to pull off a mysterious escape by swimming the river, riding a mountain bike and fleeing back toward town. One complication had led to another and another. He should have gotten away with it.

But Jim had made a mistake. That error told Aiden the identity of Jim's so-called partner. He'd used Bert Welling as his alibi, and Bert had backed him up.

Bert had lied. Why? Bert had to keep his own secrets, to hide a lifetime of cruelty. Aiden remembered the autopsy report that indicated signs of abuse on David's body. They'd assumed his father had hurt the boy, but it was more likely his uncle. Bert Welling enjoyed inflicting pain on others, especially young women.

As soon as Aiden had sorted out the logic, he thought it was obvious that two killers had been involved. The handsome, sun-bleached blond Jim had attracted the women. Bert had killed them. Their problem came when Bert escalated his timetable and grabbed too many victims. The disappearances attracted attention. His reign of cruelty would soon be over.

Aspen Jim lurched forward and grabbed onto the copilot's seat. "I have instructions." He had to yell over the whirr of the rotors. "Go to Jackrabbit Lake. To the campground."

Though Aiden knew the location, he didn't admit it. "I don't know where it is. I need to turn on the GPS for directions."

"So you can call your cop buddies? No way. You'll figure it out."

They were already over the foothills. The landscape transformed from rolling hills to jagged granite formations and forests of lodgepole pine, fir and aspen. A light dusting of snow covered the ground. At this time of year, there were no rangers posted in the National Forest. Officially, the campgrounds were closed.

Hoping to buy time, Aiden said, "I'm running low on fuel. I might have to land before we get to the lake."

"Show me the gauge."

Aspen Jim leaned forward to see the instrument panel. If he moved a little closer, just six inches closer, Aiden could reach back and grab the gun. He subtly unfastened his seat belt as he pointed to the fuel gauge. "It's right here."

"You've got a quarter of a tank."

"This isn't like a car. I'm running low." A blatant lie—the chopper could cover another seventy-five to a hundred miles on the fuel he had left.

"You'll make it. You don't want anything to happen to the precious cargo you're carrying in the back of this chopper. Your sister and your girlfriend? You'd better fly right."

Adrenaline rushed through Aiden's veins, urging him to take action. He had to be careful, couldn't lose control. "Are we meeting up with your partner?"

"That's right."

Bad news. The way Aiden figured, Aspen Jim might be

convinced not to kill them all. The same wasn't true for Bert Welling. He'd take pleasure in watching them die.

"Hey," Jim pointed with the barrel of his gun. "What's that red light?"

"Nothing important."

"The panel says intercom. That's a communication device." His shout got louder. "You're calling for help."

"I can't talk to anybody without the headset."

"We'll see about that."

He pointed the nose of his gun at the control panel as though preparing to shoot. What the hell? Was he crazy enough to fire a bullet into the instruments? There wasn't time to argue with Aspen Jim. He had to be stopped.

Bolting from the pilot's seat, Aiden flung out his arm, making a frantic grab for the weapon. He almost had it. The gun was mere inches from his grasp.

Jim reacted with a yelp. He yanked his arm backwards and fired a bullet straight up, through the ceiling. The gunshot reverberated inside the plane.

Though Jim pointed the gun at his chest, Aiden couldn't stop now. He had only seconds to take control. It was now or never. He lunged.

In a panic, Jim pulled the trigger. The bullet missed Aiden and went into the cockpit. A burst of sparks exploded from the instrument panel. The chopper swerved wildly.

If Aiden didn't get back to the controls, they would surely crash. He wheeled around on his opponent. He couldn't balance, couldn't get his feet under him. Finally, Aiden landed a heavy blow to Jim's chin. His head snapped back. His knees folded under him.

Tab scrambled from the back, picked up the gun and aimed it at Jim. "The controls," she yelled. "Aiden, get us down."

In an instant, he was back in the pilot's seat. He knew the procedure for emergency landing, but he'd never had to do anything like this before. Juggling the directional stick, regaining equilibrium and decelerating simultaneously, he scanned the ground below, looking for a safe place to put down amid rock formations and forest. He'd lost control of the rudder. The rotors sputtered. They were coming down fast.

With a heavy thud, the chopper hit the ground.

A spark danced across the panel and ignited into a flame.

If the chopper had been carrying a full tank of fuel, they might have already exploded. Disaster was imminent. Aiden had to get Tab and Misty to safety.

He scooped his sister into his arms and carried her uphill. His feet slipped in the thin coating of snow. Tab came behind him. Her arms were full of blankets and supplies. She still held the gun in her hand.

A safe distance away from the chopper, he ducked behind a rock formation and lowered Misty to the ground. She clung to his neck and gave him a weak smile. "You're a superhero."

"About time you realized that."

"I've always known. My big brother can do anything."

Tab dropped her load of supplies and knelt beside them. "You scared me, Aiden. For a minute there, I didn't think we were going to make it."

"I'd never let anything happen to you."

He touched her shoulder and squeezed lightly. Her face was the most beautiful sight he'd ever seen. Her eyes glowed like blue stars. Her lips were soft and full. He leaned forward to give her a quick peck on the cheek. Instead, he kissed her mouth, and he didn't want to stop.

"Hey," his sister interrupted. "I'm having a baby here."

Pushing himself to his feet, Aiden turned toward the chopper. "I'll be right back."

Before he'd gone five paces, Tab was in front of him, blocking his way. "What are you doing?" she demanded.

"Going back for Jim." The spark on the instrument panel had grown into a cockpit fire. He could see the orange-red flames through the windows.

"You can't risk your life to save his."

"It's wrong to leave him." Aiden's motives weren't altogether noble. "And he has the only cell phone."

He heard yelling from the chopper. Aspen Jim had recovered enough to take action for himself. He stood in the doorway, weaving unsteadily—a terrible and dramatic pose. He flung curses at them, swore revenge.

He paused as though he knew what was coming.

The chopper exploded in a fireball, throwing the rotors, the plexiglass windows and jagged pieces from the body and tail into the sky. A wave of heat washed over them, pushing them back. Black smoke darkened the sky. A metallic stench poisoned the air.

Tab looked up at him. "That could have been you."

He folded her into his embrace. Her slender body molded against him. Though they had spent only one night together, her curves felt familiar and, at the same time, exciting. They were made to be together.

He nestled her close and whispered in her ear. "I never want to be apart from you again."

"We're lucky there's snow on the ground. The explosion shouldn't turn into a forest fire."

"Yeah, lucky."

She tilted her head to look up at him. "I'm sorry about your helicopter."

"I can always get another. The important thing is that we're safe."

"For how long?"

He knew she was talking about Jim's partner. They were close enough to Jackrabbit Lake that Bert would see the flames from the explosion, and it was entirely possible that he'd come after them. Bert was a tidy man. He wouldn't like to leave loose ends.

Chapter Twenty-Two

Tab's first concern was making Misty comfortable. After a rapid search of the mountain terrain, they decided on a site beside a tall hunk of granite where they could build a fire. Keeping warm would be an issue tonight.

Working together, she and Aiden built a shelter of branches. Her hands were cold. She hadn't needed gloves at a lower elevation, but now she wished she had them. Her only tool was the pocket knife she carried in her purse. Still, the shelter came together quickly.

Watching them, Misty commented, "I'm impressed, Tab. How did you learn how to do this?"

"My grandma showed me how to build my own sweat lodge. If we had more time, I'd make this into a cozy little house where we could live."

"How much time do we have?" Misty asked. Her casual tone didn't completely mask her nervousness. "My contractions are coming every five minutes."

"I'd like to give you a precise arrival time, but I can't. First babies are unpredictable."

"Do you think the baby is all right? It's kind of premature."

Tab left Aiden to handle the building while she went to his sister and held her hand. "You're only a few weeks short of full term. There's nothing to worry about."

Looking up, Misty scanned the skies. The sun had begun

to set, and the clouds were tinted with magenta and gold. "A rescue team ought to be looking for us. That was a giant explosion."

Tab hoped she was right. The flames had already died, but a funnel of black smoke rose in the air. Somebody ought to be searching; there had to be people who lived in this area. If park rangers had been on duty, they would have already responded.

Using the quilt and other blankets she'd grabbed from the chopper, Tab covered the floor inside their makeshift shelter. When Misty was settled inside, another contraction hit. The pain had to be more intense than earlier, but Misty had learned how to breathe and to focus.

"You're doing well," Tab said, "really well."

"I know." Misty licked her lips and forced a smile. "It's because you're a good teacher."

"You're doing all the heavy lifting. Stay strong." Boosting her confidence was important. "I'm going to step outside. There's something I have to do with Aiden."

"More kissing?"

"Maybe."

The kissing was great, but she really wanted to hear Aiden's conclusions about the serial killer. Not an appropriate conversation to have in front of Misty. She needed to concentrate on having her baby without hearing gory details.

Outside the shelter, she saw Aiden leaning against a tree trunk. In the explosion, he'd lost his hat, and he had the collar on his denim jacket turned up. She swung into his arms. "Tell me what you figured out. Make it fast. And make it quiet."

He murmured, "I can think of something else that would be fast and quiet."

Though the low rumble of his voice got her engine revving, she said, "I want to know what you know."

In a whisper, he sketched the broad picture of two killers

with different styles—Aspen Jim and his partner. "Bert," he said, "is the killer."

An image of the gas station owner popped into her mind. His gray jumpsuit looked like it had been laundered by a dry cleaner. His thinning hair was neatly combed. And his hands…his hands were spotless. She shuddered. "I knew there was something suspicious about him."

"Most people wouldn't. He's lived in Henley for years and knows everybody. We saw him at Connie's house with a baby gift."

She thought of all the young men who worked for him and came under his dark influence. They couldn't have known the terrible things that Bert had done. "It took another psychopath like Aspen Jim to finally become his partner."

"We were supposed to meet Bert at Jackrabbit Lake," Aiden said. "He might come after us."

"Could be watching us right now."

Misty called out from the shelter. "Tab, I need you."

She forced herself to step away from Aiden. "Leave the gun here with me. There's a collapsible plastic container for water."

"I know," he said, "it's my container, part of my emergency supplies. It holds two and a half gallons."

"Find a creek and fill it. I only have one bottle of water. We're going to need more."

He pressed Aspen Jim's weapon into her hand. "Be careful."

"Back at you."

Inside their shelter, there was only room for Tab and Misty. After the contraction passed, she figured it was time to prepare for the next phase in delivering this baby. "Let's see how far along you really are. Take off your clothes from the waist down. Leave your socks."

"When you were babysitting me, did you ever think we'd end up like this?"

Delivering a baby while being stalked by a serial killer? Tab could honestly say that scenario had never occurred to her. "I knew we'd always be friends."

"Really?" Misty brightened.

"Not the kind of friends who talk every day or send messages on the internet. We have a bond, you and me. No matter where we are or what we're doing, we'll always be close."

"Is that what you have with my brother?"

"We're bonding, that's for sure." And she had a good feeling about what might come next...if they survived this night.

When Misty was undressed, Tab examined her. Without her instruments, she couldn't state her findings in centimeters, but experience told her that Misty was fully effaced and further along in the birthing process than she'd thought.

She pulled a blanket over Misty's bare legs. "Are you warm enough?"

"Is it possible to be hot and cold at the same time?"

Misty giggled, and Tab was glad to hear the sound. It meant her spirits were good. "You're almost ready to have this baby. Very soon, you're going to have the urge to push."

"How will I know when that is?"

"You'll know," Tab said. "And here's what you do. Try to hold back until I tell you it's time."

She had barely finished talking when the next contraction tensed Misty's muscles. In spite of her focused breathing, Misty gave a loud yelp.

During labor, Tab encouraged the mothers to do whatever felt natural. To get into whatever position felt right and to scream if they felt like it. The sound Misty made would lead Bert to them, but they didn't really have anywhere to hide safely from him.

After twenty minutes, Misty was nearly ready to push.

Where was Aiden? It shouldn't have taken him this long. Tab tried not to think of the terrible things that might happen. The gun lay on the ground beside her. If she saw Bert, she'd shoot first and ask questions later.

Aiden poked his head into the shelter. "Do you want the good news or the bad?"

"Just talk," Misty snapped. "Don't be cute."

"I've heard about this phase of labor," he said. "It sounds homicidal."

"Your news?" Tab prompted.

"I got water." He plopped the container into the shelter.

"That's good."

"There's no way I'm going to be able to build a fire. The wood is too damp. That's bad. But here comes the really good news."

In the dim light of dusk, she could barely see his grin. Drily, she said, "Knock us out."

He flashed a cell phone. "It's Aspen Jim's. I found it near the wreckage, and I put through a call. A rescue team is on the way."

"Great news," Tab said. But she doubted the rescuers would get here before the baby arrived.

The next contraction was powerful. Misty tried to breathe through it but gave up. "I've got to push. Now. I have to."

Operating more by touch than sight, Tab knew the baby was in position. "Next time," she said, "push for all you're worth."

She noticed that Aiden had left the shelter and had taken the gun with him. He was standing guard, and that gave her a huge measure of relief as Misty went into the last phase of labor.

The head crowned. With Tab offering calm encouragement, Misty pushed with every fiber of her strength. The baby was coming. No stopping it now. A miracle was on the way.

The head was out, then the shoulders and the torso. A fully formed baby boy slipped into Tab's waiting hands. He was a good, healthy size, at least six pounds.

Misty gasped. "Is the baby all right?"

The tiny mouth pursed, and the infant let out a yell.

"He's perfect," Tab said. She swabbed away the mucus and placed the baby, with the umbilical cord still attached, on his mother's chest.

Aiden looked in. His head was close to Tab's, and she could see the wonder in his eyes.

"You did it," he said to his sister. "I'm proud of you."

"And your nephew," she said with a giggle. "I'm going to name him after Dad. Matthew Gabriel."

He slipped his arm around Tab's waist. "Thank you."

"Misty did all the work."

"You're brilliant, Tabitha. I admire you."

His praise delighted her, and she would have liked nothing more than to sit back and let him tell her over and over that she was terrific. But there were other things to do before the rescue team arrived.

OUTSIDE THE SHELTER, Aiden took a position higher on the hill to watch over his girls and the new infant. Powerful emotions churned inside him. He was ready for a baby of his own, ready to settle down, ready to start the next part of his life. And he wanted to share that life with his beautiful Tabitha.

He didn't usually make huge decisions so quickly, but he'd never been more certain of anything in his life. She was the right woman for him.

He'd put through another call to the rescue team. They'd seen the plume of smoke and knew the location. They needed a chopper. Since Aiden was out of commission, the closest other rescue service was a good forty minutes away. He checked his wristwatch. Less than fifteen minutes were left. Everything had turned out right.

He heard movement behind him and ducked just in time to avoid the knife that slashed through the air. Pivoting, Aiden faced off with Bert Welling. In one gloved hand, he held a knife. In the other, a pistol.

Aiden couldn't believe he'd let down his guard. His own gun was tucked into the waistband of his jeans, accessible but not in his hand.

"Answer one question for me," Aiden said. "What made you hook up with a fool like Aspen Jim?"

"The ladies liked him. They trotted along with him like lambs to the slaughter."

Hoping to buy time, Aiden kept talking. "Did you ever use a different partner? Maybe David?"

"That boy was worthless. After everything I did for him, he was fixing to betray me. Over what? He thought Misty gave a damn about him. The boy was too dumb to live."

"You know, Bert, if you leave right now, I won't tell anybody you were here."

"How about this, Aiden. First, I'm going to kill you. Next, I'll slice up that pretty Crow girl you've been hanging around with. She'll be my main course. For dessert, I'll kill Misty and her bastard."

In the moonlight, Aiden saw Bert's lip curl into a grin of pure evil. He was enjoying his fantasy. It would be the last thought he ever had.

Diving to the right, Aiden pulled his gun. As soon as he hit the ground, he fired. Not fast enough. Bert had gotten off two shots of his own.

A burning pain paralyzed Aiden's left arm. He aimed with the right and fired three shots into the center of Bert Welling's chest. The old man was dead.

Aiden closed his eyes and touched his upper arm where blood was already seeping through his jacket sleeve. When he looked up, he saw Tabitha leaning over him with the baby in her arms.

"Sorry," he said as he pushed himself up to a sitting position. "I'm going to be okay."

"Damn right, you are." Her voice was determined. "I'm not going to let you go. Not ever."

Epilogue

On Christmas morning, Tab awakened with a jolt. Today would be baby Matthew's first Christmas, and she still hadn't figured out how to wrap his rocking horse. Matter of fact, she hadn't wrapped any presents. Funding for the new women's clinic had been guaranteed, and Tab had been busy—crazy busy. She never could have handled all the paperwork if it hadn't been for Misty pitching in to help.

Rolling onto her side, she reached for Aiden and felt nothing but empty space in the king-size bed that had once been *his* and now was *theirs*. He was already up? She could hardly believe it.

Though nobody would ever call him a slouch, he'd been taking advantage of his broken upper arm to slow down. And she thoroughly approved. Super-responsible Aiden deserved a break after ending the serial killer threat, not to mention losing his beloved Bell Long Ranger helicopter.

She hadn't planned to move in with him, and he hadn't actually invited her. While nursing him back to health from the broken arm and a second bullet that grazed his rib cage, she'd found herself spending a lot of time at his cabin. Without thinking about it, her clothing had taken up residence in his closet. Her music was on his sound system. Her food occupied most of the space in his refrigerator. And here she was, living in his house.

The only thing lacking was a commitment.

Even her grandma was staying at the Gabriel ranch for a few months to help out with the baby. Her property was being taken care of by good old Wally the Buffalo Man, even though Shua was here at the ranch.

Fully dressed in jeans and a black sweater, Aiden came into the bedroom and leaned over her for a long, lingering kiss. "Merry Christmas, Tabitha."

"Same to you."

Though he was no longer wearing a cast, just a brace, the use of his left arm was somewhat restricted. Lucky for her, his injuries hadn't slowed him down in the bedroom. Making love every night was more wonderful than she imagined. She'd taken advantage of his limited mobility to insist she should be on top.

"There are a bunch of presents in the closet downstairs," he said. "I think they need wrapping."

"I'd better get busy." The only gift she didn't need to wrap was the check for two thousand dollars that she and Aiden were contributing to Clinton's college fund. Misty still hadn't agreed to marry him, but he was planning their life together. After missing the birth of his son while he was hiding out near Maria Spotted Bear's cabin hoping to catch Tab when she returned for her horse, Clinton had vowed never to be apart from Misty or his child again. Next year, they would both be in college in Missoula. He would major in veterinary science, and she'd be pre-law.

"I suppose I can help," he said.

"I suppose you will." She tucked her hair behind her ears and gave him a smile. "Do you want your present right now?"

With his right hand, he unfastened the top button on her red satin pajamas—sleepwear that was sexier than anything she'd ever owned before. "I'd like to unwrap you."

"I'm not the gift."

She bounced from the bed and went to the bedroom closet. Tucked into a back corner was a square box. With great care, she'd wrapped it in silver paper with white stars and a delicate silver bow.

In five seconds flat, he demolished her pretty wrapping and tore open the box, revealing a perfect model of his old helicopter. "It's great," he said.

"You taught me how to fly." She kissed him on the forehead. "And how to touch the stars."

"Now it's time for your present." He took her hand and escorted her from the bedroom. "There's a tradition taking root in this family, and I'd like to break the mold."

She had no idea what he was talking about. "Okay."

"First, there was my mom and Blake. Now, it's Misty and Clinton." He went down the staircase before her. "It seems like we're turning into a family of people who are scared to get married."

He seated her in a chair at the dining room table. She noticed his effort to create a mood with a fragrant bouquet of roses and soft music from a classical guitar. Outside the windows, she saw a fresh layer of snow on the ground. It was a white Christmas.

Aiden went down on one knee before her. "I'm not afraid of commitment, Tabitha. I want to spend my life with you. Marry me."

He opened a small black velvet box. A diamond engagement ring winked up at her.

When she looked into his dreamy gray eyes, she didn't see

a bit of hesitation or tension. He was sure of himself. And he should be. He was the only man she had ever loved.

"Yes, Aiden."

They would be together. Forever.

* * * * *